MADNESS OF PEOPLE

MADNESS OF PEOPLE

Shelly Campbell

Megan King

Cursed Dragon Ship
PUBLISHING

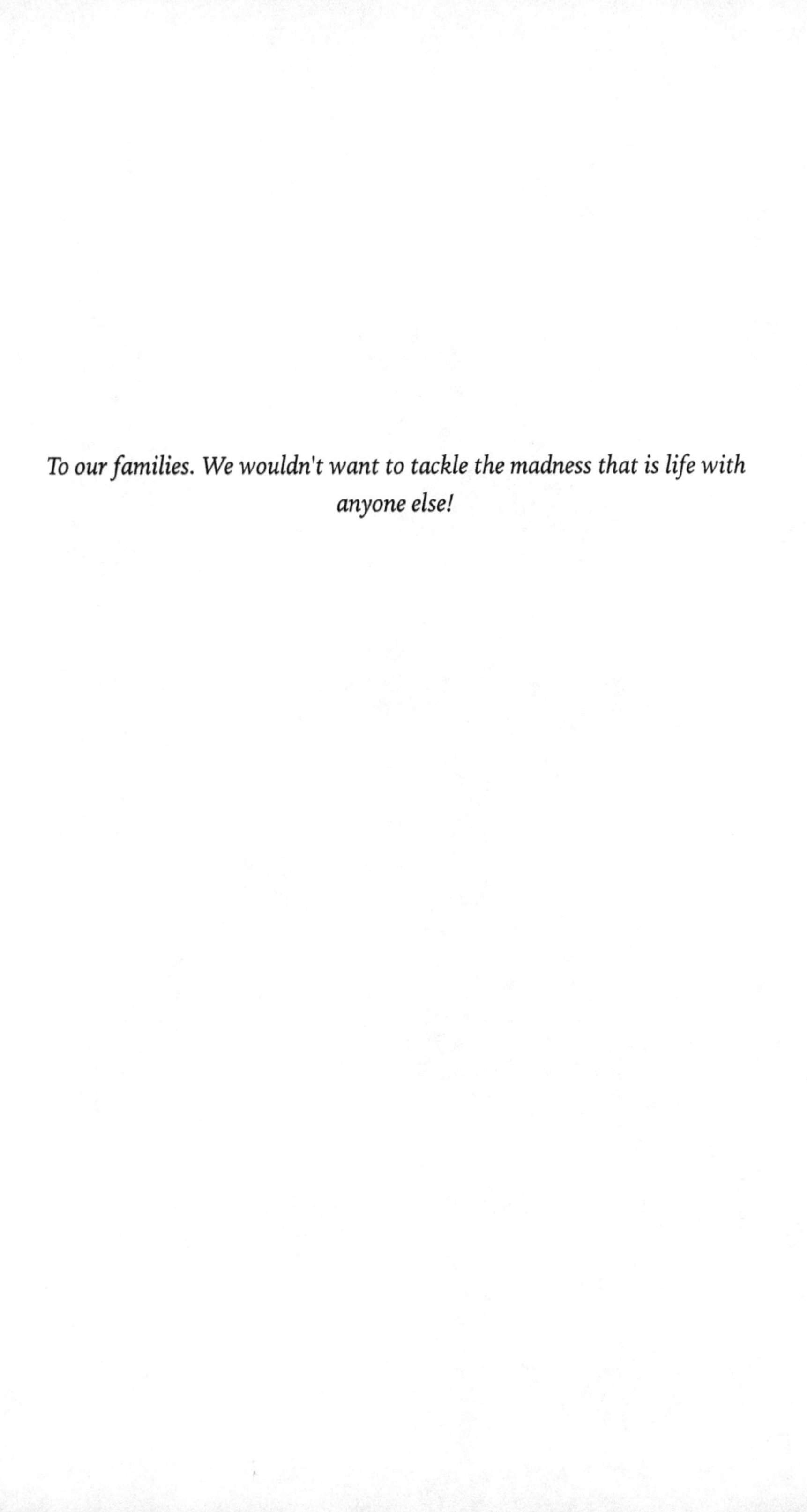

To our families. We wouldn't want to tackle the madness that is life with anyone else!

CHAPTER
ONE

Peeling back the Velcro straps of the ballistic vest, I sighed and eased back until I was lying in the bottom of the rowboat, squinting up at a soft dawn sky. I wasn't supposed to be out here alone, an easy target as a lone fisherwoman on the glassy morning lake, but Sol, I couldn't stand being trapped in that bunker for one more second. It smelled like hundreds of people dying of boredom down there. And old cheese. Apparently, our CEO Kahn had used the shelter as his own personal larder.

It was summer. With the intolerable heat came imposing thunderstorms and seasonal fires. Yesterday, enough smoke had settled in from the west that the desiccated hills surrounding my broken city looked like a Martian landscape. Today, gray swallowed the shoreline completely. The snipers would be blind in this dense smoke. They had already abandoned their posts. I could tell by the tinny sound of bright pop vocals drifting over the still water. For some unknown reason, when the marauders weren't taking potshots at our city, they spent their leisure time listening to Britney Spears at full volume. At first, it was kind of funny. My parents had listened to her as kids. Two weeks in, I recognized it for what it was. Psychological warfare.

Water slapped a gentle tempo against the side of the boat, and the paddles creaked in their oar rests. I kept my gaze on the sun creeping sluggishly over the horizon. It was already hot enough that my shirt stuck to my back and the suffocating vest felt like a boulder on my chest. The Soldamned thing chafed too. Vinton said it was because they never built body armor for all the soft bits women have. "Not everyone's blessed with chiseled abs and biceps that can crack walnuts."

My brother had smirked and flexed, and I had immediately wondered what Robert looked like shirtless. The thought sent tingles down my arms even now. I imagined running my fingers over his bare chest, his stomach, raising goosebumps on his skin. *Reboot, Iris.*

I'd rowed out here to check the minnow traps I'd set last night. In sweltering weather, big fish were too lethargic to be tempted by anything except live bait, so catching supper tonight depended on a lucky haul of minnows now. Fresh fish would do wonders for morale in the bunker. We'd repaired the greenhouses, seeded a new round of crops, and set several more trap lines, but until harvest came in, and we trained some more people on the finer points of trapping, we were scraping by mostly on expired ration packs courtesy of Kahn's secret bunker. If I never smelled freeze-dried cheesy broccoli rice again, it would be too soon.

I knew I should find shelter before the sun rose fully, but living underground felt like slow suffocation. The flat-bottomed boat cradled me gently, and the sun looked distant and harmless peeking past the velvet gray hills. Frogs drowned out the chorus of "Baby One More Time," and these few minutes alone felt like the last moment of stillness the world would ever gift me. I couldn't let go of it.

I should sit up. There were a thousand menial tasks to tackle if my bullet-ridden city was to have any chance of regaining its footing from the edge of civil war. Mouths to be fed. Vultures to scare off. New roles to take on and alliances to forge. But it all felt too big for me to grasp. The heaviness in my chest was more than just the vest. My brain felt like an overheating circuit board, cooling fan seized and squealing between my ears, thoughts blistering like burning plastic. Another meltdown—the third this week—and Sol help me if I was going to let it happen in the middle of a fragging bunker with all of the Shareholders' eyes on me. With Vinton pointedly looking away and Robert hovering.

So, I hyperventilated alone in the bottom of a dented rowboat while Britney belted out the chorus of "Oops! . . . I Did It Again." I told myself I'd move when the song ended. My mind screamed the words *Get up!* But I couldn't. The air had thickened above me, a column of atmosphere paralyzing me. My brain yanked out every cable attached to my will until I lost all sense of time. My mother had always called it laziness. She'd never understood how physical it was. How tangible. A massive web of apathy, and me a twitching fly.

Eventually, I broke free of it, exhausted. I hauled in last night's minnow traps, dumping the swarms of tiny silver fish into the pails between my feet and rowing back toward shore, the skin on my sunburn scarred cheeks tight from dried tears.

When I looked over my shoulder between oar pulls, a man materialized out of the smoke. I froze, certain that the uncle Nate of my childhood had come to fix everything or the older, harder version of him was here for revenge or—and this was the most likely option—a marauder was lining up to blow my brains out, but then the figure started pacing the shoreline and fumbling with their gun like it was too hot to hold.

"Zuse." I swore, turning away and digging the oars deep. *Robert.* How could I possibly mistake him for a vengeful relative, an opportunistic marauder, or anyone else remotely threatening?

Away from air conditioning and sleek offices, Robert clashed with his surroundings. When corporate had still ruled, he'd looked deliciously rugged in tailored suits, but Outside he was a gangly kid playing dress up: blue army helmet perched crookedly on his head, a cloth face mask pinching under his eyes, business shirt crushed beneath a Kevlar vest, cap toe Oxfords scuffed and unpolished. I cringed. Soldamned city shoes didn't belong out here. Vinton had been wearing a similar pair when he'd lost his footing and tumbled into the ravine that broke his legs and back. I swallowed the urge to leap out of the boat, splash through the shallow water, and shove Robert all the way back up the path to the city.

"What are you doing?" he asked in a tone far too like my mother's. The mask he wore didn't do anything to muffle the irritation in his voice.

"Fishing," I snapped, the seemingly judgmental question dialing my anger to an instant 100 percent.

The bow nosed into the shore, metal hull squealing over the rocks. He shook his head but helped me haul the whole rig out of the water. I threaded the anchor chain through the metal mooring post and locked the boat in place. I avoided his stare and took my time unloading brittle plastic pails full of wriggling silver minnows, and my own gun. It was fake. So was Robert's. There weren't enough weapons and ammunition to go around. So, we'd manufactured dozens of replicas over the last week, scavenging the burnt-out shells of the inner core elite houses for water piping and wooden furniture before carefully carving stocks and welding and painting barrels.

Our ruse worked, for the most part. The marauder horde surrounding our city had been a cautious group. As soon as our blue-helmeted enforcers returned to patrolling our streets bristling with guns made mostly of plumbing and old table legs, most of the scavengers had dissipated. The stubborn few remaining were more of a nuisance than a threat. They were smart enough to stay away from Cache and the greenhouses which were guarded throughout the day by Blue Helmets in sun-protective gear. Marauder snipers still fired at us occasionally, but they felt more like shots across our proverbial bow than real threats, aimed far over our heads, taking out streetlights instead of people. They hadn't hit anyone yet, but the Firewalls decreed that citizens weren't allowed Outside without bullet-proof vests and helmets just to be safe. Blue Helmets accompanied us when we checked our traplines too.

"You shouldn't be out here alone." Robert scrubbed his forehead. "Where's your helmet?"

"Like that would stop a bullet. Where's your boots?" My voice raised to match his, overstimulated mind gearing up for a fight I didn't have the bandwidth for. I wanted to skirt around him. I wanted him to grab my wrist and stop me with more than words.

"This isn't about boots. This is about you finding creative ways to get as far from me as possible." He snorted and leveled his gaze at me, shelving the hurt in his blue eyes behind hardness. "I'm allowed to be pissed that you'd pick a pleasure cruise amongst the snipers over talking to me."

I swallowed around the hardness in my throat and tossed my chin toward the disembodied sound of Britney belting out "Toxic." "Sounds like they're on their break. And I'm *working*. Go home, Robert."

"My home burned down, remember? Eat the rich and all that." His voice cracked. The fight drained out of him so quickly it startled me. "And I thought we were done with this, you pushing me away. That night you came home, you let me help you. You let me in, Iris—and it felt good, alright? I'm not gonna lie. But now you're firewalling, like I'm some sort of Soldamned virus."

Virus. I flinched at the word. Robert didn't understand that walls were the only thing keeping me standing. No one in my city knew that my wristband had been the vehicle Nate had used to insert a virus into Kahn's network, crashing his computers and turning his corporate cronies against him. The Shareholders all thought Kahn sabotaged his database himself in a last-ditch effort to stick it to his rebelling middle class. And while I wanted nothing more than to tuck under Robert's arms, squeeze my eyes shut, and block out the world with the firm comfort of his chest, the wolves were still at our doorstep.

I'd helped topple my own city. I'd also left Nate's community crippled, and then I'd run home, leaving an uncle—who everyone thought long dead—licking his wounds and bracing to strike back. I didn't need the tenderness Robert brought out in me. I needed armor. And I didn't have time for boyfriends, not until I fixed the colossal mess I'd made.

Guilt must have leaked onto my face because Robert stepped toward me, pulled his face mask down, and waved at the shattered buildings behind him. "This isn't your fault, Iris. Whatever you're fighting, you don't have to do it alone." He cracked a fragile smile, one that utterly exposed all the softness he hid behind tight collars and smart ties. "You're a badass, I know. But even badasses don't take the world on alone, right? They've got sidekicks. Let me be yours. Please, I'm trying to help. I really am."

I choked on tears. I wanted his help. More than anything, but I was terrified he'd hate me when he found out what I'd done. Besides, Robert's idea of helping was arranging endless board meetings with the department heads that all went the same. Blowhards puffing up their chests, in love with the sound of their own voices, scrabbling for seniority while someone scribbled down minutes. For the entirety of the apocalypse, Kahn had convinced these people they were a corporation, not a cult, and they still clung to what they knew. The meetings were a comfort ritual. They didn't facilitate anything, to my mind.

Here we were, fresh with the knowledge that we'd been sitting on a huge vein of natural copper all this time, and our fledgling democracy hadn't done anything to solidify our next steps—other than vote for a new name for our settlement.

Painted Bluff.

It was the title of a mineral core sample map of our location. Kahn had stashed it in the bunker, tucked in a stack of critical documents from Cache.

So, we were Painted Bluff now.

Staggering progress.

How easily we'd fallen right back into our old, familiar grooves, Robert and me. People looked to him as an eager go-getter who was going places. They saw me as a frazzled wreck who mucked out the goat pens. And why wouldn't they? I kept falling apart in front of everyone. They had no idea I'd been the catalyst who drove them to war, or the escapee who'd saved them all from slavery. They didn't even know that Nate was alive. I needed to focus, but whenever Robert was around, all I could think of was lying next to him in his backyard watching falling stars, his hand on my back, and the soft urgency of his kisses.

"Robert," I breathed, buying time to formulate the perfect combination of sharp words to drive him away before I started crying or kissing him. Or both. "I'm not some lost girl in the wilds you need to protect."

His face dropped. "You know I don't see you like that."

"Then stop being so damned clingy." *Bull's-eye*. Those words hit the mark, and I immediately wished I could take them back. Robert stiffened. Robert, whose mom had killed herself, whose dad had lost his mind and left the upkeep of an obscenely expensive house on his son's shoulders. Robert, whose whole life had burned down around him because of me.

We stood there frozen as music blared down the hillside above us, brash, cheery, and mocking.

The scars on my cheeks burned as my face reddened.

Robert's eyes iced over. He coughed and pulled his mask back up over his mouth and nose. Then he turned and walked stiffly up the pathway. He was already around the bend when an explosion rocked the hillside, shuddering through all my organs.

"Robert?" I meant to yell it, but his name came out dry and dusty. Something cold wriggled between my bare ankle and my boot cuff, and I looked down in a daze to see my wet feet covered in dozens of tiny silver flopping bodies. I'd dropped the minnow pails. Shale skittered down the hillside, and a belch of black smoke mushroomed in the haze above the city. *Run, Stupid,* my mind blared. Snatching up my phony rifle, I scrambled up the trail. "Robert!"

Cracks and thuds of gunfire filled the sky in harried clusters, like the bullets were birds flushed by the explosion. I couldn't tell where the shots were coming from. Everything echoed off the hills. Ducking low, I charged around the bend and nearly collided with the person barreling toward me. Not Robert.

A girl. She wore a hockey helmet with plastic gems glued all over it and when she saw me, she yelped, skidded to a stop, and hoisted a semi-automatic weapon that looked too heavy for her scrawny arms. Her eyes were startlingly white and hard against the black charcoal smeared over the top half of her face.

"Don't!" I barked, bracing my own weapon and glaring down the barrel. *Frag,* I was going to die. A Soldamned little girl.

We froze, panting and sizing each other up; me with my Kevlar vest and moderately convincing toy soldier gun and her with the real deal, a mean-looking piece with a hefty magazine and a rainbow macrame strap with white beads studding its length.

Not beads. I realized, nausea flooding the back of my throat. *Human teeth.* I shook my head and willed my voice to sound calm and authoritative. "Don't be stupid. Here." I lowered my gun and eased a freeze-dried packet of apples out of my back pocket. I'd been using them to bait the minnow traps. "Truce, okay?"

Her eyes widened. She was skinnier than I'd first thought, swimming in her faded hoodie. Charcoal painted cheeks sunken.

I knelt slowly and set the dried apples between us, before backing up. "They're sweet. Like candy."

"Iris!" My name floated over her shoulder, and the young marauder flinched and spat out a pile of words. I couldn't understand them, but they were spoken with enough vitriol that I gathered most of them were swears.

"Walk away before you're surrounded," I said. "Last chance."

Her face twisted.

Robert's footsteps pounded toward us from further up the bend.

The girl hunched her shoulders. Tendons stood out on her neck, and her weapon swayed in her hands. Then she lunged for the packet between us, dodged around me, and sprinted toward the lake. Unraveled bits of duct tape flapped from her wrapped boots.

"Zuse, what are you looking at? Let's go!" Robert's muffled voice yelled.

I jumped and gaped as he grabbed my elbow, and I let him pull me up the path while pops of gunfire slowed around us.

CHAPTER
TWO

The explosion had been caused by a grenade the marauders had launched at Cache. Other than the noise and the belch of smoke, no major harm had been done save a few holes peppering the building's walls—easily patched—and a Firewall with a piece of shrapnel in their butt cheek—not so easily patched.

"Why Cache? They had to have seen us moving all the valuable documents out of there last week." Robert pinched the bridge of his nose and slumped in his chair. He was sitting in for his dad. Paul was too sick to coordinate a board meeting as a Shareholder today—he often was. Crowded at the table around Robert sat the heads of all the departments. Business jackets and gardening aprons mingling with camouflage fatigues, mechanics coveralls and riding leathers, all of us stuffed in a bunker storage room around a table made from several old doors propped up by rain barrels. *I shouldn't even be here.* I squirmed as I sat as close to the wall as I could, wedged in between Johan and a pallet of empty water jugs. I wasn't a department head, but lately, Johan insisted I accompany him to every meeting he attended.

This was ridiculous. A literal explosion and we were still sitting down to hash it out by talking in circles. And I thought I was bad at making big decisions.

Claude's dad—Mom had told me his name was Reynold—spoke for the Firewalls. "It was a diversion. They knew we'd come running if it was Cache." He scrubbed the back of his neck, eyes not meeting anyone else's and, suddenly, I felt for the man. I knew that weight of shame and self-loathing that came with screwing up. It settled bone deep sometimes.

"What were they after then?" my mom asked. She was head of the Search Engine's now. The vacancy had opened up when her predecessor fled at the start of our civil war.

Reynold cleared his throat. "Goats."

Mom stopped tapping her pen on the table. "Excuse me?"

"They took all the goats."

"All that firepower for farm animals?" Robert asked.

"They're starving," I blurted, recalling the marauder girl's hollow face and bony arms, how she'd snagged the dried apples like they were the first meal she'd seen in days. "I saw a kid who looked like a scarecrow. I don't think they care about stealing high ticket items. They're probably as desperate as we are if their larger group left them behind."

"Well." My mother smoothed her hair. "Now we're the ones starving. Reynold, your people were supposed to be guarding those animals while they grazed."

The man bristled. "When explosions happen, shepherding critters isn't my people's first priority, ma'am."

Mom turned from him dismissively, pinning Elaine from Food Bank in her sights. "How many ration packs do we have left?"

"Levels are already low. I've moved the chicken crates into Greenhouse Five. Easier to guard than the coop, so we'll still have eggs for now."

"Thank you. And the gardens, Johan?"

The old gardener shook his head. "I can't make plants mature faster, Anne. We're growing trays of sunflower shoots. Corn, beans, squash, and potatoes, but we're weeks away from a useable harvest—and that's assuming we aren't raided again."

"What's to stop them?" Reynold spat. "They're getting braver. We saw that today. Won't be long until they figure out we're marching around up there with mostly toy guns and not enough ammo to win a fire fight. We need to shake these vermin off our doorstep *now*. My people need more guns. *Real* guns. We show these stragglers that there are no easy meals left here, and they'll move on just like the rest of their pack did. We sit here and do nothing, and they'll strip us—"

"This doesn't need to be another fire fight," I interrupted, and everyone around the table paused to look at me like my head was on backwards. I couldn't get the picture of the marauder girl's face out of my mind, her dark eyes wide and scared. "How many of them are left? Twenty? Thirty? We could help each other. They need food. We need well-armed allies to the west to keep the URLs off our back once they regroup. Let's aim their guns outward instead of in. Get them interested in this place thriving instead of falling."

"A scavenger's *always* more interested in something falling. It's in their nature. Mark my words, you hold your hand to a marauder, they'll bite it sooner than shake it," Reynold said, jamming a thumb toward the Power Supply Unit head. "Your people need to get the spare generator ready to move. And yours"—he pointed to my mother— "need to find us a big-ticket buyer who pays in arms and ammunition. Fast. We wanna head-hunt us some folks knowledgeable on copper mining? They ain't coming unless this place is secure."

Vinton's riding partner, Mark jumped in. "Security means nothing if we're cut off and starving. What we need is supplemental food to get back on our feet, a fuel supplier to keep the lights on and the bikes running. Rail runners charge more than we can afford right now. So, we can only reach as far as we can ride. If the URLs have cut us off from the west coast supply train, we need to start reaching east with a purpose. We can trade the rest of the critical documents from Cache to build some alliances, gain some trust. Stuff like gasket manufacturing and oil recycling. People will value us as partners if we teach them some of those processes. But we can't announce that we're sitting on a shitload of copper until we've built the network to produce it, else some mining conglomerate's just gonna come steamroll us and take everything."

I couldn't help but stare at Mark as he spoke. This was the most I'd ever heard come out of his mouth in one sitting. Heat rose to my cheeks as I realized I'd always thought of him as an accessory to Vinton, like his bike or wheelchair. I didn't even know the man my brother loved.

Everyone devolved into heated arguments after that. Nothing productive happened. I couldn't even remember what action items we left with. Robert tried to catch my gaze as we filed dejectedly out of the meeting room, but I squeezed through the door before him and headed straight for the bunkroom down the hall. I didn't turn around when he called me. Sol knows I wanted to, but I just couldn't. *Everyone ignored you in there. You're flustered. You're shutting down, and you need to sleep before you say something else hurtful to him.*

I crashed for most of the day, surrounded by the snores of the family we shared a storage room with, suffocating in the exhalations of too many people packed like sardines. Later, when I filed to the communal dining room, I didn't eat because absolutely nothing about freeze-dried strawberry Cream of Wheat sounded appealing. But I did pocket an unopened packet. Dad saw me and followed me to the bunker's front vestibule where all the spare bulletproof gear hung.

"Hey kiddo. Need a topside partner?"

"Okay." Dad was easier to deal with than Mom. Besides,

after the explosion this morning, the Blue Helmets were likely not as amenable to letting solo trips outdoors slide in exchange for extra meal packets. I grabbed the canvas bag that Oupa kept well stocked with hand-tied flies, hooks, and spoon lures, and I shoved the ration pack inside. "I'm going fishing. You got time?"

"Not on cleanup crew until after sunset. You've got two rods?"

I nodded. We shrugged into bulletproof vests. My chest tightened when Dad grabbed two blue helmets off the shelf and handed one to me. Blue helmets reminded me instantly of every run-in I'd ever had with Vannevar. I had no urge to wear one, but I'd already been hassled once today for breaking protocol.

At the bunker's clamshell doors, a Firewall signed us onto the muster board and handed us replica rifles before letting us through.

David Kahn's burnt-out shell of a house yawned around us: peeling, corrugated-metal walls, a monolithic stone hearth with the melted remains of a fissured flat screen clinging above the mantle, a couch that was nothing more than a mounded skeleton of coiled springs with gobbets of upholstery foam as yellow as subcutaneous fat. Our boots crunched through fallen plaster as we aimed for the front door.

Outside, empty brass shells winked red in the hazy setting sun. Sheets of paper and plastic shards of plant pots peppered the street and gathered in corners like fall leaves. Stacks of over-turned desks sagged into each other in bloated rows of barricades.

Dad remained prudently silent as we navigated the steep path to the lake. He was worried about me, but he always waited for quiet moments to broach serious subjects. He said nothing when I stooped on the dusty path where I'd dropped my buckets of minnows. He brushed mosquitos away from his face while I picked several handfuls of bloated, white fish out of the dirt to use as bait. I expected he wouldn't ask me how I was doing until we'd cast our lines into a quiet lake.

What I did not expect was company.

As we stepped onto the shoreline, movement near the beached rowboat caught my eye, and my spine iced over. "Dad," I whispered over my shoulder, holding up my hand to stop him.

The marauder girl from earlier today crouched in front of the metal mooring post, her gun slung over her back and a hack saw in her hands. She had the chain slung over a rock and was sawing back and forth, ineffectually, her frustrated words sharper than her tool.

I dropped the slimy minnows in my hands, slid my rifle off my shoulder, and handed it back to Dad.

"Iris . . ." His low voice shook.

Swallowing, I held my palms out. "Hey."

The girl whipped around, the whites of her eyes and her teeth bright in the dusk light. She clawed her gun off her back and aimed it at me as I crouched. "Hey, don't shoot. We have a truce, remember? Truce."

"Truce," she barked the word like an order. Mosquitos stuck to her arms, but she didn't swat at them.

"Yeah, truce." I opened the canvas bag slowly and pulled out the freeze-dried Cream of Wheat. It crinkled in my hand as I held it up, and the girl's gaze hooked on it. "That means I give you food and you don't blow my brains out."

"Mîciwin. Food." She jabbed her gun barrel at the scrap of beach between us.

"Put your gun down first."

Her face scrunched into a confused scowl.

"Your rifle." I pointed delicately. "Put it down. Dad, put down our guns."

I heard him sigh behind me, the crunch of gravel beneath his shoes and then the clack of metal on rocks. "Gun down, then food, Okay?" I repeated.

The girl scuffed her worn boots before letting her arms go slack. She was so short, her weapon's tip nearly grazed the ground as she backed up, chin raised and eyes fierce.

Something about her reminded me of a rooster, all scrappy attitude, and sharp spurs. Without taking her gaze off me, she squatted, lifted her macrame strap over her hockey helmet, and laid her gun where I couldn't reach it. "Food. Mîciwin."

I set the ration pack on the gravel beach and backed away.

When the girl judged we were far enough, she sprinted, snagged the food, and retreated. Shouldering her gun, she tore into the package with her teeth and shoved a fistful of dried flakes into her mouth.

"No, not like that," I said as she coughed, sending white powder spraying past her lips.

"Wîhcêkan." She gagged, scraping her tongue.

"You're supposed to mix it." I cupped one hand like it was a bowl and drew a circle in my palm, like my finger was a spoon. "Mix it, understand? With hot water."

Her nose wrinkled with disgust, and she said something I didn't understand that sounded derogatory.

Dad cleared his throat "Uh, tanisi?"

The girl's head shot up. "Kipaskwâwinîmon?"

"Um, okay. Only a little." Dad rubbed his palms down his legs. "Uh . . . nipaskwâwinîmon." He pointed at the half-crushed ration pack in her hand. "You need to add . . . nipiy."

"Nipiy?" The girl squinted at him and then pointed to the lake.

"Âha. Kisâkamitêwâpoy," Dad said.

"What the hell is going on?" I whispered.

"This is amazing." Dad licked his lips. "She, uh, speaks Cree."

"Which you understand because . . .?"

"Before I met your mom, I worked for the government in Alberta digitizing and translating historical documents from

Cree to English. I had a whole local team helping me. They taught me the rudimentary stuff. I didn't realize it was a marauder dialect."

"Tell her not to steal my boat—our boat."

"Hang on." Dad slapped a mosquito on his forehead. "Ôsi. Kaya kêt niyanân."

The girl straightened and rattled off something rapid fire.

"What did she say?"

"I missed it. Something about the water belonging to everyone."

"Tell her I want to be friends. Friends don't steal."

"Otôtêmimâwak." Dad pointed at his chest, then me, then the girl. "Otôtêmimâwak êkâ kimotamâkêwin"

"Mîciwin?"

"Yes. Âha. Mîciwin. Mâka êkâ kimotamâkêwin ohci niyanân."

The girl nodded once. "Tapwehta." Then she turned, grabbed her hacksaw, and marched down the beach away from us, crumpled ration pack pressed against her chest.

"What did she say?" I asked.

Dad smiled faintly. "She said yes. Agreed. This is incredible. We have to tell your mother."

I swallowed, remembering how Reynold shot down my suggestion of an alliance in this morning's meeting. Mom hadn't jumped to my defense. Neither had Robert or Johan. "You tell her. She listens to you."

CHAPTER
THREE

Over the next few weeks, the forest fire smoke cleared and Painted Bluff found our footing. With Dad as a translator, we brokered a fragile peace with the residual marauder group. They were a couple dozen strong, mostly families, and they'd fallen out with their larger group who'd grown too violent for their taste.

"Kiyânaw nôhtê tipinawahikan," they'd said. "We just want shelter."

They agreed to act as lookouts in the western hills in exchange for food and clothing. If Nate's URL group came looking for revenge, we'd have an early warning system at least, but the arrangement left us scrambling for supplies enough for all of us.

I was relegated to hunting and fishing full time while Johan and Olivia juggled gardening duties with training fresh recruits to our traplines and teaching people how to fire a crossbow. It was good for me. I relaxed enough that I let my walls down.

I didn't avoid Robert in the hallways. The world felt safe enough for small comforts like holding his hand under the dining room table and snorting at his cheesy jokes. Every day that Nate didn't retaliate, it felt less likely that he would. So, I let my guard down and let Robert in.

Then one morning, I returned from hunting with three prairie grouse over my shoulder and spotted Robert's familiar form exiting a Seacan behind the generator building.

My neck prickled and my insides liquified, like a wax candle melting from the inside out. I knew the interior of those shipping containers intimately. Claude's dad, Reynold, had stuffed me into one before my trial for breaking the solar panels. I'd avoided the prison cells ever since, not just because of the harrowing memories of my confinement, but because of who inhabited those cells now.

A sick heat rolled over me, lukewarm acid licking all my muscles as Robert turned and recognized me.

His face dropped. "Iris?" he called from across the street.

My face pinched into a tight smile as I turned from him and quick-walked in the opposite direction, the dead birds flopping against my back.

"Iris. Don't," he puffed, jogging to catch up to me.

"Don't what?" I squeaked. *Get yourself under control.*

"Judge me before I get a chance to explain." His hand closed on my elbow, and I swatted it away, drowning in the crest of messy emotion flooding me.

"Don't touch me! What in Sol's name . . . What are you doing?"

"Gathering information." He ran a hand through his hair. "That's what a Search Engine does, right?"

"Talking to *them?*" Nausea clawed up my throat. "Why?"

"We can't keep Vannevar and him caged forever."

At first, the words sounded so alien, they didn't make sense. I took several seconds to absorb them, breath ratcheting faster. "H-He sabotaged us, let us all starve. She held a gun to my head. And you want them free?"

"I'm not saying that." He shook his head, face souring with

irritation. "I'm saying they're a resource. And they're human, Soldamnit. Everyone's conveniently forgetting they exist because it feels better that way. When's the last time you thought of them, Iris, huh?"

That was unfair. It was one of the ways my mind sabotaged me—and Robert knew it. I'd told him. If someone wasn't front and center in my proverbial line of sight, they just didn't trip my attention switch. My brain set them aside until something external reminded me they existed. *No, I don't remember the last time I thought about Vannevar and Kahn. I don't want to.*

"She tried to shoot me." My voice came out too loud.

"It was a *fake* gun, Iris." Robert barked.

"Not the first time, it wasn't!"

"What?"

Zuse, why did I say that? I had no urge to reboot the moment when Vannevar brought me to my knees in the muddy side yard of Robert's house, so I deflected. "I thought you two were never an item."

"What the hell is that supposed to mean? This isn't about her. Kahn has connections that I don't." Robert raised his voice. "He's not stupid. He wouldn't sit on a mound of copper all these years without setting himself up with proper contacts. Buyers. Experts on copper mining. I'm using him, Iris. That's all."

His voice matted in my head, clumping my thoughts and muting my senses. *He's been talking to Vannevar and Kahn behind my back. Advocating for their release.* My mouth dried at the memory of Vannevar's hand snarled up in my hair and Kahn's cold eyes.

I walked away. I don't even know if Robert kept talking or if he followed me; I just shut down and walked away.

Everything went wrong after that.

WE WERE SLEEPING TOPSIDE AGAIN. Salvageable Seacan homes had been repaired and reset on their foundations. My family had reclaimed the small unit we'd shared before I'd fled Painted Bluff, and it suited me fine. It was easier to avoid Robert when we weren't crammed together inside a bunker. He spent most of his free time at the prison cells anyway.

See, a cruel voice in my mind needled. *He's chosen who he wants to spend his time with.*

One day, around noon, I woke to the sound of gunfire.

Marauders. I was ashamed that my mind went there first, but there it was. *Nate* was my immediate second thought.

"Don't open the door," Vinton hissed as I rolled out of my bunk. He was blocking the doorway with his chair.

I glanced at our parent's empty bunk. "Mom and Dad?"

"Greenhouses, I think. Shut up." My brother cocked his head and listened through the door. Somebody outside bawled like a wild thing. There was shouting and scuffing feet down the street. A wordless shriek cut off at the shot of a rifle.

"Clear?" A Firewall shouted.

"All Clear." Someone reported back.

"Casualties?"

"Just one. Fatality."

Vinton exhaled and sagged in his chair.

"Move," I hissed, diving past him and cranking open the door latch.

The midday sun blinded me.

The Firewalls on the boardwalk looked like blurry silhouettes, their rifles still tucked against their shoulders. When my aching eyes finally adjusted, I spotted a body near the end of the boulevard, face down, sun so harsh it made her gobs of blonde hair look white against the widening puddle of bright blood beneath her.

Vannevar.

"Where's Kahn?" Reynold bellowed as he sprinted up the street.

"North. We've got men on him. He won't get far."

"Vinton, get your Browsers moving!" Reynold shouted, hard gaze latching onto my brother as he wheeled onto the street behind me.

"No roads to the north. Bikes will be slow." Vinton shouted back, but he was already pushing toward the garage.

"They'll be faster than a prisoner on foot. How the hell did they get out?" Reynold grilled a Blue Helmet I could only assume had been on guard duty. His helmet's sunshield was flipped up, and he clutched a hand over his bloodied nose.

"Someone didn't close the door latch properly. Bitch jumped me. Let Kahn out and ran. I didn't mean to kill her, sir. I thought I could just wing her." His voice quavered, face growing paler by the moment.

Vannevar's parents streamed onto the street. Their screams snagged in my chest like fishhooks. Elaine rushed over and covered the girl's body with a blanket before wrapping Vannevar's mom in her stout arms.

"Where's Peter?" Reynold lowered his voice. Vannevar's brother was a Firewall too.

The man with the bloody nose answered, "Went after Kahn. Him and Claude together."

"They see this?" The old Firewall nodded toward Vannevar's body.

"No, sir."

"Thank Sol for that, at least," he huffed.

Motorcycles growled to life and the garage overhead door squealed open. Mark and two other Browsers rolled their machines out and mounted. Vinton wasn't among them, likely because his modified bike wasn't suited to heavy offroad conditions. Neither was he. Reynold climbed onto the back of one of the motorcycles, and the group grabbed gears as they sped toward our northern border.

More people wandered onto the lane, pouring out of their patched homes and the greenhouses. At some point, Dad wrapped his arms around me, and Mom started drilling me with questions I didn't have the bandwidth to answer.

I couldn't stop staring at the lumpy blanket on the road. Vannevar's parents' harrowing wails were inhuman and unending. Far beyond them, at the opposite end of the street, someone stood alone. Fists clenched. Eyes wide. Scuffed Oxford shoes rooted in place.

Robert.

I wanted to go to him, but my bones were calcified in place and my mind was snagging on every detail. He wore a helmet with a sun shield just like the Firewall's. Long sleeves. A layer of sunscreen so thick I could see it from here. Which meant he had planned to be outside for a while today. He'd been visiting Kahn and Vannevar again.

Someone didn't close the door latch properly.

I felt sick.

WE WERE CRAMMED into the bunker meeting room again. Robert, my mother and all the other department heads, Johan, and me. There wasn't a proper boardroom set up elsewhere, so we kept meeting down here.

"Run me through it one more time." Mom massaged her temples.

Reynold took a deep inhale through his nose before speaking. "We tracked him as best we could. He doubled back and met someone on the rails east of here. A runner with a fast ride.

Kahn must have paid through the nose to rendezvous with them."

"Paid with what?" The Power Supply rep snorted. "How in the hell was he communicating from inside a prison cell?"

"My Firewalls were under strict orders not to talk to the prisoners," the old Blue Helmet said. "But we've got someone right here in this room that cozied up to them, don't we, Mr. Lycos?"

I swallowed the immediate instinct to leap to Robert's defense. *You're not his guard dog, Iris.* Besides, I wanted an explanation too. One that didn't point toward an attraction to Vannevar.

Robert straightened. All the softness went out of his eyes as he met Reynold's accusing gaze. "What are you implying, exactly?"

"Only the obvious. Someone left that girl's cell door unlatched. She's been batting her eyes at you since you were both kids. And then we have Kahn miraculously procuring himself resources and a get-away vehicle from the outside world, conveniently after all these tête-à-têtes with you."

"I convinced him we were going to let him go free and he spilled the information I needed. Simple as that. Are you accusing me of abetting an escape?" Robert's voice was dangerously low.

Reynold looked like a bull ready to topple the table and charge. "Not formally. Not yet. Look, I know—"

"*Your* son and Vannevar's Soldamned *brother* were on duty when they escaped. Sounds like you're doing your best to divert blame as far from your department as possible!"

"Stop this." Johan didn't yell—he rarely did—but something about the head gardener's voice leveled the room, silenced his peers, and made me wonder just how many people knew that he was a co-founder of our city. "We will not seed another civil war here. Vannevar is dead. Kahn has escaped. As much as we wish to, we can't change either of those dreadful facts. We need to move forward rationally and rapidly, because David has a wide web of resources outside of this settlement. He's never been one to put all his eggs in one basket. He built influential connections before the collapse, and he's cultivated them ever since. He'll pull together allies quickly. He'll tell them about the copper deposits here, and he *will* lead the first company greedy enough to bulldoze us, just to see us fall. David has effectively forced our hand. If we intend to keep this place, we need to move faster than him. Liquify assets. Secure allies and copper miners now. Mark, how are the Browsers faring on that front?"

My brother's riding partner unfolded a roadmap that was dog-eared and velvety with age. He smoothed it onto the table. "We've been scouting further east along the old highway. The rail runners and merchant convoys so far have all been independent operators, no URL group overseeing them. Seems disorganized as hell, but once they realize we're not marauders on motorcycles, and we tell them the extent of the trade routes we're looking to set up, their eyes all light up brighter than the sun. They've been trading intel with us just for the promise of getting a piece of the distribution pie. We have a hub town here, with a confirmed hospital." He jabbed at a circled dot nestled in the midst of the Rocky Mountains. "First building we've run into with electric lights, and that town's got a vested interest in keeping their hospital powered up. Word is their generator windings are short-circuiting. Their machine's days are numbered, and they're in the market for a new unit. Now, they'll pool together resources to buy one, but it'll take them some time, and they're still negotiating shipping costs with the rail runners. I don't know if they've got access to anyone with mining expertise. They *do* have a deal with a biodiesel refinery on a hydro dam in Alberta, west of Calgary. That's where they get all their fuel from. Maybe they could give us a contact there? Or the refinery itself might need another generator?"

The Power Supply rep shook his head. "If that plant's

saddling a hydro dam, I imagine they have all the power they need."

I gulped, wondering if it was the same refinery Nate had covertly crippled years ago when they became a little too competitive for his tastes.

"Vinton and I know the routes," Mark continued. "We can take Radia and John with us. Press the hospital committee to make a quicker offer on the generator, maybe insinuate that we've got other buyers interested? Radia's a hell of a negotiator. If we send her and John on to the refinery, even if they aren't interested in the generator, she can present us as a reliable bulk fuel customer. Lock down a shipment deal direct from the source. That'd give us a couple of options to offload the generator for arms or equipment and set us up with the fuel to power whatever we need to set up mining operations."

"And if the plant doesn't want a generator, how will we pay for those first fuel shipments?" Mom asked.

"We could leave a motorcycle. Radia and John could double back on one machine. There can't be too many operable Sommer 462s out there. Bike like that is probably worth its weight in—"

"No." Mom interrupted. "They're antiques, Mark. Running far past their time. Half of the reason Browsers are mandated to ride in pairs is so you have spare parts. It's too risky for Radia and John to make such a long trip home relying on one machine. If it breaks down, they'd be stranded." Her voice cracked and betrayed her.

Everyone in the room knew that Radia and John weren't the real source of my mother's anxiety. They could walk to the nearest set of rails, if all else failed. Rail runners charged prohibitive rates, but Browsers could barter their handguns along with the more valuable motorcycle parts for passage home. Vinton, however, relied on his modified ride entirely for mobility and it was one of a kind. A breakdown or an accident meant his partner leaving him behind to go for help.

"You know what's riskier? Kahn coming back here with reinforcements while we sit on our hands," Mark answered her quietly.

"We still have no idea where to look for copper mining crews. And neither the hospital nor the refinery is a firm generator sale," Mom said.

Robert cleared his throat. "I think I can kill two birds with one stone there. What do you all know about Coaltana?"

"The coal company down in Fernie?" Someone piped up.

A tingling heat swarmed my stomach and swelled up to crowd out my lungs. *Coaltana.* Shit. I didn't realize I'd bent over on my stool until Johan edged closer and put a hand on my back.

"Iris?" he whispered.

"They're slavers." I choked out far too loudly, and everyone at the table turned to me with raised eyebrows. Zuse, how could I tell them this was the company Nate had p-mailed? He'd sent pigeons to Fernie, where Coaltana was based, inquiring how much he could make if he sold us all into slavery after sacking our city.

"Honey." Mom leaned toward me and pasted on an uncertain smile. "That's not uncommon away from our borders. Many large corporations own slaves." Turning back to Robert, she asked, "Who is your contact? I wasn't aware you had connections in the energy industry."

"Are you fragging kidding me?" I barked. "Slavers? You're all just going to let that roll off your backs?"

"Iris." The cold warning in my mother's voice signaled that Anne had already burned through her motherly condolence quota for the day. "We understand if you're too emotional to contribute, but the rest of us don't have that luxury. We need to consider every solution available." I flinched as she turned away from me again, neatly ignoring her tablemates squirming in their seats. "Your contact, Robert?"

He drew a deep breath and leaned back. "Not my contact. Kahn's. I *have* been talking to him, trying to root out information we could use. He's smart, but anyone talks if they're tired and hungry enough."

"Go on."

"Kahn said he supervised some mine site construction projects, before starting his own company. He was chummy in business school with the guy who became Coaltana's CEO, and they've kept in contact over the years." Robert licked his lips and shot an apologetic glance at Johan. "He kept a few private birds operating outside of your aviary, told me where their roost was, and let me send a message to put out feelers with Coaltana. Long story short, they want the generator, and they'll sell us a small crew of miners, equipment, and foremen in exchange for it. Their CEO doesn't just deal with coal in Fernie. He's got copper mines down south too, and a workforce experienced in both industries." Robert pulled several neatly folded p-mails from his jacket pocket, laid them out in a row, and tapped them one by one. "They have their own train and are willing to ship the miners and equipment here first, and take the generator back on their return trip, so long as we send them a goodwill delegate before the trip to seal the deal."

"A delegate?" Mom stared at Robert with an intensity that I couldn't understand.

He nodded slowly, face pale.

Johan sagged in his seat and sighed deeply.

I couldn't grasp the threads of what was going on. "What's a goodwill delegate?" I whispered.

"It's a delicate way of saying we'll give them a high-ranking hostage to guarantee the safe arrival of their purchase."

"Which one of your dad's cronies did you hang out to dry then, boy?" Reynold sneered.

A brief, humorless smile touched Robert's lips before he met the Firewall's gaze across the table. "Me."

"Zuse," Johan swore quietly.

"No." I gagged and stood even though dizziness fizzed through my head.

"I told them I was Paul Lycos's son and they accepted. It's all here. They've signed a pre-sale contract." Robert's hand shook as he pointed at the neat strips of paper he'd set out. "It's a done deal as soon as we respond."

"All in favor?" My mom's voice cut through the ringing in my head, and the majority of the department heads in the room raised their hands. *Oh Sol, no.*

"Passed." She jotted the results in the meeting minutes.

How could she? I balled my fists against the scream building in my chest. The buzzing in my head grew so loud I could barely hear who spoke next.

Robert was the first to leave when the meeting adjourned.

I was the second.

"TRUST YOU?" Words spilled out of me burning and sticky with bile as I ricocheted down the hallway after him. "I'm supposed to trust you? What the frag was that heartfelt speech about that day at the lake if you're pulling this shit behind my back?"

Robert didn't turn, just straightened his tailored jacket, and quickened his pace, the clack of his shoes echoing off the cement walls.

I couldn't hold the question in any longer. It was burning me. "Did you let her go?"

"What? Let who go?"

"Vannevar."

"Zuse, Iris." He sighed. "The fact that you even have to ask shows how much *you* trust me."

"That wasn't an answer."

"I'm not dignifying *that* with an answer. I'm trying to save us." He kept walking.

Rage balled up in my stomach and I spit words like fire. "No, you're trying to suck up to everyone who still owns a business suit. You could have sent *anyone* else. You could have sent your dad."

Robert spun so fast that I collided with him. Before I could back away, he gripped my arms hard. My stomach dropped at the abruptness of it all, the closeness, the comforting smell of him, his breath hot on my cheek. "My dad can barely dress himself most mornings." His gaze raked over me, scalding and desperate. "And he drinks himself unconscious most nights. He's not going anywhere. Who would want him?"

"I-I didn't know. I'm sorry." Paul Lycos and I had no love for each other, but I'd had no idea he'd degraded so much.

"No, you're not, Iris. You're not even *here* most days. You avoid me any time I try to talk. I tried to tell you. I would have . . ." His voice cracked.

"Don't do this—this deal with Coaltana. They're slavers. People are property to them, and you've hardly even travelled away from here. You don't have proper shoes." I swallowed. A frantic thought gripped me. If I leaned in right now, if I kissed him, I could make him stop. Make him forgive me for what just happened. I could talk him out of this. Softening in his grip, I reached up to stroke his jaw and pull him closer, but Robert stiffened before our lips touched.

"It's done, Iris," he whispered. "Stop being so damned clingy, that's what you wanted, right? You got it."

Then he turned and left me standing there in the harsh echo of his departure.

CHAPTER
FOUR

couldn't breathe underground. Reynold was already back on shift at the bunker entry, faded blue helmet pulled down low, chin strap dangling. He turned as I heaved open the clamshell doors but didn't move to assist me.

I half expected the old Blue Helmet to bar my way, but instead, he snorted, shouldered his weapon, and offered me a joyless smile.

I shouldered past him out onto the boardwalk with my gaze pinned to the hillside at the end of Main Street, detouring only to step around a dark brown stain. The three Firewalls posted before the roll-up door of the Browser's garage scowled at me but didn't move to stop me. I yanked open the entry door and retreated from the suffocating heat into cool dimness that smelled perpetually of new rubber and old oil.

"Don't come in here with that face." My brother spoke from behind the disassembled hulk of his motorcycle. Everything ahead of the gas tank was stripped off and laid out on a low table in tidy rows, like a parts diagram in a technical manual.

"It's the only face I have," I snapped. My older sibling had always excelled at teasing irrational anger out of me, and I welcomed it now, because anger felt more actionable than the fear curling in my belly. I scanned the mechanic's bay for other Browsers. A row of meticulously clean motorcycles rested like horses sleeping in their stalls. Stained wooden tables held metal trays of parts bathing in solvent. Faded red toolboxes lined a pegboard back wall bristling with gaskets, seals, and stacked bins of bolts, nuts, and washers. One corner of the shop had been cleared to make room for a weight bench and barbell set where Mark was heaving through a set of bench presses with no spotter. He and Vinton were the only ones here.

"No pouting in the shop. We should really get a sign." Vinton waggled a socket wrench at me. "What's wrong now?"

"Did you know about this?" I hissed. "This deal Robert made with Coaltana?"

He snugged something cylindrical into a vice, wheelchair squeaking as he shifted. I caught his glance toward Mark before he answered. "No one tells me anything. I fix bikes. I drive them. I bring back looted computer parts. I don't lounge in fancy boardrooms sipping ice water and kissing office ass."

Mark slammed the barbell into its rack, sat up, and shook his head.

"You knew about it then?" I asked Mark.

"Not until he brought it up in the meeting."

I strode toward Vinton, gripping the upholstered seat between us. "You can't take him."

"Who? Your boyfriend? Don't worry, I won't. I'll be carrying a chair and fuel. He'll ride with Mark, or Radia or John. Probably for the best. I'd flatten his pretty little nose if I got within hitting distance—Soldamn it, I can't break this bolt loose." He frowned at the part in the vice.

"Warm it up with a torch and use the Allan key I modified." Mark offered without looking.

"He can't go. *Zuse,* he's hardly ever been out of an office. They'll eat him alive out there."

Vinton raised his eyebrows and ignited a handheld torch. It bathed his face in pale blue. "So says the expert hunter who trekked through the wilds for what, a whole week? You did alright and he will too. You know what? He held his own when the fighting started here. Surprised me. All he has to do now is ride bitch to Fernie surrounded by armed riders. Maybe he'll surprise you and actually survive this without you sticking your nose where it doesn't belong."

"Could you stop being an asshole for one second? I'm being serious." I clenched my jaw.

My brother ignored me, while heating up the disassembled shock, slotting a wrench into the end of it, and grunting with satisfaction when the bolt let go. "I'm being serious too. It's a milk run, Iris. We've talked to the rail runners. Coaltana keeps tight control of the access roads all the way down to Fernie. They've kept their territory remarkably clear of marauders for years now. He'll probably be safer with them than he is with us."

No, my mind blared. He wouldn't be safer as hostage with a company who entertained offers of child labor, who were willing to negotiate the wholesale roundup of our city into forced bondage, who coldly calculated exactly how many lives lost was an acceptable margin while shipping human cargo via rail during the bitter winter months. I couldn't let slip that I knew these things because our dear uncle had arranged to sell us, and I'd seen his correspondences with Coaltana. My brother might be a jerk, but he was smart, and he knew all my tells. If I started talking, I'd slip up and reveal that Nate wasn't dead. And I'd already mourned the loss of my uncle twice. No need for my family to do the same. "I'm coming," I announced.

"Shit, no." Vinton coughed and turned to Mark. "We're out of fork oil. Can I use motor oil in its place?"

"Ten weight will work." He grunted in between bicep curls.

"I said I'm coming."

"Iris." My brother avoided my gaze, pulling a spring out of the shock and laying it precisely on the table with the other parts. "No, offence, but you've been sketchy ever since you got back. I don't think the road is the best place for you right now."

"Sketchy?" My voice cracked. "I'm fine!"

"Yeah, you sound golden." Vinton drawled.

"This isn't fragging funny!" I snarled, slamming my hands against my brother's disassembled bike hard enough that its landing gear creaked and diesel sloshed in its tank.

Mark froze mid-curl. Vinton wiped his hands meticulously on a rag before setting it down and wheeling to face me, his face sober and his eyes hard. "Exactly what I'm talking about. Sketchy. Look, I don't know what the hell happened to you out there, but I need to be able to predict what my team is going to do on the road. I need to count on them. And I can't count on you right now, Iris. Nobody fragging can. You want to keep your pretty boy safe? Do us a favor? Stay. Home."

ON THE WALK back from the garage, my head felt like a squirrel's nest, every thought stuffed against the next, drowsy and pink and helpless, but my body felt like a coiled snare or like lightning building up in a storm, eager to discharge and impossible to contain.

I hated it, feeling like a chicken with its head cut off. Brain gone but muscles still screaming to run, soaking in the hopelessness of trying to get the two to merge back together. I carried that dichotomy with me back past Reynold, down into the bunker, past the closet we had slept in during our stay, to the end of the hall where the gardeners who had yet to repair a home topside still shared what used to be a large storage room. Johan and Olivia had spearheaded restoring the greenhouses.

They hadn't rebuilt yet. The concrete room was cordoned off into sections with blankets and tarps hanging off rearranged shelving units. Stuffed with stackable cots, clothes hanging on makeshift lines, and trays of wilting plants from the greenhouse, there was barely enough room to navigate to the back corner Olivia and Johan had claimed.

I stopped and blinked at the pinned-up rug busy with a checkerboard of vibrant chevrons and geometric patterns on a dark brown background. It had once been the centerpiece of Oupa's living room. I'd played on it with Olivia as a child. Now it served as the makeshift doorway in a concrete prison. I cleared my throat. "You home? Can I come in?"

Olivia swatted a corner of the rug aside and stepped out onto my side, red cloud of hair soft around her face, the only soft thing about her. Dark eyes appraised mine as she blocked the entry. "What in the hell happened in that meeting? What did you do?"

"What did *I* do? Zuse."

"Don't bullshit me." She leaned closer, words barely a whisper, but they stung nonetheless. "Something big happened and he won't even talk. He's like a zombie. Spill, Iris."

"He's here?" I peered over her shoulder.

"Of course." Olivia raised her hands and let them fall to her sides with a slap. "Of course, you want to talk to him and not me. You're all holing yourself up in that meeting room like snakes down a hole, and I'm the only one talking sense around here, trying to get people to do the reasonable thing, pack up, and leave. Listen." She jabbed at my chest, dirt still fresh under her fingernails. "He may answer to those fossils in Corporate, but you answer to me. If we're friends at all, if you want to see him, you answer to me. So, spill. Are we leaving, or just waiting for Kahn to come back with reinforcements?"

"Neither." Heat pooled behind my eyes as I picked at the ragged skin around my thumbnail.

Olivia, ever observant, softened all her hard edges and put a hand on my shoulder. "What is it?"

"Robert volunteered to be taken hostage by a mining company. They're slavers."

"What? Why?"

"Insurance. They're buying our generator and prepaying with a mining crew and equipment. Enough to get us started."

"Holy shit. His dad is never going to let that fly."

"His dad doesn't know. He lined up the whole deal without telling anyone. Just dropped it in the meeting today. It went to vote and passed."

"He let you know in a Soldamned board meeting? What an asshole."

I was the asshole. I'd avoided Robert and walled him off and now I was paying for it. "Can I see Oupa, please?"

She snorted. "You won't be able to talk any sense into him. I've tried."

"Please, Olivia." My stomach twisted tighter. I wasn't here to talk sense. Furthest thing from it.

My childhood friend tensed but stepped aside from the hanging rug. "Go easy on him, yeah? Everyone keeps forgetting he's an old man."

"Yeah. Okay." I croaked and pressed past her.

The co-founder of our community lay on a cot facing the concrete wall. His back was to me, and the blankets around him were rumpled and thin. I fought the urge to smooth them out.

"Hey, Oupa." I shuffled down the narrow alley between his and Olivia's cots and sat at the edge of her bed across from the strongest man I knew.

He looked small, like the cot was quicksand sucking him in and he didn't have any fight left in him to struggle against it. Instead of answering me, Johan raised a hand to trace the seam in the concrete wall he was facing. "David wanted to use cinderblocks for all our bunker jobs. He argued it was more cost-effective, and we wouldn't have to pay off cement truck drivers to keep our locations secret. I said that cinderblock walls didn't have the lateral strength to hold up to the weight of the soil and would require extra waterproofing."

My neck prickled at the listlessness in his voice. I couldn't parse the direction of this conversation, or how I was supposed to participate, so I scuffed my boot on the floor and stayed silent.

"Of all the pieces of my advice he could have taken to heart, David chose foundations. I helped build the *foundation* of this place and didn't even know it. He kept me occupied on another project until the greenhouse packages arrived later, long after the bunker was buried, and the entrance concealed. I should have known it was here though." Johan rolled to face me and sat up with a soft groan. "Did I ever tell you that Vannevar's father was a cement truck driver before the collapse?"

"No," I answered. Zuse, where the hell was this going?

"Second job. He was a security guard at a mall on night shifts, and he drove for a concrete company. I met him on one of our other builds. He settled here because I convinced Kahn to use concrete on a bunker I didn't even know about. Vannevar's father would never have known the place existed if I hadn't argued against cinderblocks. His family would have never settled here. And now his daughter is dead. If I hadn't argued against cinderblocks, this place"—he waved his hand around us —"would have likely flooded or collapsed by now. Vannevar's family would be living somewhere safe, and Kahn would have fled from a civil war instead of hunkering down. It seemed like such a small decision at the time though."

"Oupa, this isn't on you. They made a million choices that brought them to this point."

"So did I." He offered me a frail smile. "And it's a point I never wanted to be at. War, Iris. We fought each other. Killed each other. A Firewall killed an unarmed girl on the street today.

And I brought us here. I let David rule for far too long. I didn't leave; I didn't take all these families away when we had the chance because I got attached to buildings and greenhouses and the idea of proving myself to him. I never changed. And yet, I expected David to. My Sol, what I naïve old man I am."

"We all held onto ideas we didn't want to let go of." My mind circled back to Nate, bright-eyed with a laugh big enough to break anyone's defenses. I traced my finger over a patch on Olivia's sleeping bag, waiting for Johan's breathing to even out. I hadn't even thought about Vannevar as somebody's daughter before today. Zuse, I wished I had something other than awkward silences to offer my mentor.

After a while, he cleared his throat. "You aren't here to talk about David or Vannevar, are you?"

I pinched my lips and ran through every debate point I'd rehearsed on the way here one last time. "I want to go with Robert to Fernie, to Coaltana, and I want to stay there while they're holding him. I can make up for the cargo space I take up on a motorcycle by hunting as we go. We're practically out of ammunition, and a crossbow would be a good visual deterrent while we're on the road. And I can take some seed stock. If we get an opportunity to trade, I'd make sure it was a fair deal. The Browsers have no idea which species are valuable. Robert has never travelled cross-country. He's a lone hostage. He needs someone who can watch his back once the Browsers drop us off. And Coaltana gets an extra goodwill delegate if I stay."

"And you care for him," Oupa said.

"What?"

"You want to go with Robert because you care for him." A small smile twitched on Oupa's lips. "You forgot that part."

"That's irrelevant." My cheeks flushed.

"I disagree."

"Don't try to change the subject. I'm going."

Johan grabbed my hand gently. His skin felt like sandpaper. "You don't need my permission. I'm not stopping you, Iris."

"Vinton is." I pinned him with a hard stare. "Mark too."

"Ah, I see." Johan sat back and let my hand slip out of his. "This isn't you asking for Oupa's blessing. This is requesting a co-founder's clout against the Browser's department head."

"I can't let him go alone, Johan."

A long sigh bled from the old man's lips. "I'll see what I can do."

CHAPTER
FIVE

W hat is this?" I gaped at the monstrosity bolted onto Mark's sleek motorcycle, and he snorted but didn't answer.

Vinton did. His movements were short and full of tension as he wheeled toward me in his riding leathers and thrust a helmet into my stomach hard enough to make me *oof*. "Sidecar. We brought it out of storage just for you. You think I'm gonna waste an extra vehicle, Browser, and fuel ferrying your boot-licking ass around? You wanna be a third wheel? You ride third wheel."

He didn't speak to me after that. Neither did Robert when he arrived. Birds warbled and the crisp smell of the lake wafted up to us in the pre-dawn. The skies were heavily overcast so Mark and Vinton had decided to take advantage of the sunless conditions to start our trip early. Otherwise, we'd be travelling mostly at night.

We said quiet goodbyes to our families.

Dad pulled Vinton and I both into a rough hug and spoke into our hair. "Look after each other."

"We'll be back in a few nights. It's no big deal." Vinton deflected.

Mom had tears in her eyes, but kept her expression tempered. She'd argued with me most of the night before giving up. She didn't like losing, but she smoothed my hair and pulled me into an awkward embrace. "Listen to your brother." Her kiss smeared lipstick on my scarred cheek.

Radia and John checked over each of their machines, tire pressure, brake pads, and drive belts with the quiet choreography of a couple who'd practiced this dance a thousand times before. Mark and Vinton did the same.

Radia passed around a jar of sunscreen, and we slathered the stuff onto the only exposed skin we had left, the backs of our necks. Our riding gear covered everything else. The helmet pinched my ears as I jammed it on. It smelled like someone else's sour sweat. I climbed into the utilitarian sidecar, all checkerboard aluminum and frayed fiberglass. A cracked leather seat revealed glimpses of yellowed foam, most of it already pulverized by countless other butts enduring hundreds of kilometers of bumpy trails. Stowing my gear between my feet, I sat, shifted the crossbow onto my lap, and clutched the worn grab bar with my free hand. This thing didn't feel secure at all. It felt like an afterthought.

"I've never seen any of you use a sidecar before," I said to Mark.

"It's been in storage. No one's ever volunteered to ride in it before. Here. You'll need 'em." Mark tossed a pair of riding gloves onto my lap.

"Th-thank you." I tried for a smile, but he'd already turned from me, donning his helmet and mounting the bike. Robert climbed on behind Radia. He looked out of place in work boots, frayed jeans, and a faded puffer jacket. As I watched him cinch up his pack straps, he didn't spare me a glance.

We left the city without incident.

At first, the wind cooling my face and the white noise of the engine muffled by my helmet eased the tension in my legs, but it didn't last.

By the time the ruins of Kamloops came into view, my mind felt like a scrambled egg and my jaw hurt from clenching it. As the western shore of the glassy lake narrowed into a meandering river, it materialized out of the cloud cover, the ghost of a civilization, less than two decades dead. Vinton had told me of this place on the opposite end of the lake from us. It may as well have been on the opposite side of the world. It started with a smattering of industrial buildings, large metal-clad, faded to mint green. Then a warehouse, bigger than any building I'd ever seen, windowless and monumental, flanked by an immense, empty parking lot. Our whole city—greenhouses and all—could have fit under its roof with room to spare. I squinted to read the name emblazoned on the building, but the letters were peeling and all I could make out was *STCO*.

"What is that?" I bellowed at Mark.

"Their food bank," he yelled back.

"Mother of Sol," I murmured. What kind of a population had warranted a food supplier this huge? And how on Earth had they kept it stocked? It looked like it could swallow entire trains into its depths.

Further on, houses dotted the hills, seemingly at random. Skeletal steel arches spanned across the wide ribbon of divided highway brandishing rows of crooked metal signs peppered with shot but still indicating exit points and street names. Low slung commercial buildings and gas stations with lonely pumps standing at attention scrolled by.

My teeth clacked as Mark bounced over a heave in the crumbling pavement while navigating around the burnt-up husk of a semitrailer with no tires. And then the valley opened up around us. As far as I could see, streets branded the brown-tufted terrain in linear grids, like a massive circuit board etched into the landscape. Every flat spot was clogged with orderly rows of houses, crammed with cars, prickling with streetlamps. The trees grew in straight lines. I'd seen pictures like this of course, but in person it was staggering. I couldn't grasp how this place must have looked, what it might have sounded like when it was alive.

"How many people lived here do you think?" I asked Mark as we dismounted to detour around an underpass clogged with cars, tattered tarps, and metal drums. Radia and John had already coaxed their bikes up the steep bank of the crumbled off-ramp and were stabilizing Vinton's bike while he made the climb still strapped in. Robert had walked back down the hill to help us.

"Before?" Mark grunted, giving his machine just enough throttle to walk it up the steep incline. "Somewhere around 100,000."

Zuse. 100,000. That was more people than I'd ever see in one place in my entire life. I glanced over at Robert. He'd stripped off his jacket and was sweating through his T-shirt. The road dust must have been bothering him, because he'd put on a dust mask like the one he'd worn during the smoky conditions weeks ago. He looked as shell-shocked as I felt. I'd seen a town before this, at least—on my way to Nate's. But this was Robert's first foray past the confines of the commune we'd been taught was the center of the world, and he was making the pilgrimage as a high-stakes hostage. I wished I could talk to him, tell him I was sorry about Vannevar, take his hand, but he avoided my gaze and kept the motorcycle between us as he climbed the hill, flushed and coughing.

We remounted and drove through several kilometers of city before the terrain reverted to dusky green flats, dotted with grazing big horn sheep, edged with clay plateaus that looked like yellowed rows of molars from some colossal half-buried jawbone. Behind them, a backdrop of soft mountains carpeted with stunted pines hemmed us in. Before Johan had taught me to hunt, a space this wide open would have made me hyperventilate. Now, it was the distance that did it. The sheer number of kilometers where the road smoothed out and the motorcycles travelled fast enough that my hair whipped my neck and insects pinged off my helmet. The yawning expanses away from the train tracks where we saw no sign of people at all, not even a hint, just swathes of undulating forests, rocks, and mountains that looked like they didn't miss the absence of humans at all. Kilometer after kilometer. Hour after hour. How elating and horrifying at the same time to imagine stepping off this road and never being found again, simply because I was an irrelevant speck in a vast, indifferent world.

We passed several more towns, some of them nearly swallowed by wilderness, others nursing tiny populations, none of them as massive as Kamloops. Once, we passed a caravan on horseback, and Vinton paid their navigator a few copper tokens to update route conditions on our map. I recognized the coins as rail runner toll fare. Apparently, it passed for currency off the rails too. I had no idea where Vinton had acquired them or what he'd traded to do so. *If this all works out, we'll never have to worry about having enough copper again.*

Even with the cloud cover, the day grew hot and muggy. When the highway broke apart so that we had to slow the motorcycles to a crawl to navigate tectonic plates of asphalt amidst creeping shrubbery, Vinton called for a stop. We nudged the bikes far off the road, into a copse of trees hugging the river.

"Lunch?" Robert guessed.

"Something like that," Mark answered, dismounting, and stretching until his back cracked.

"We clear, Boss?" Radia peeled her helmet off and looked to Vinton, not Mark, for an answer.

So, Mark was department head in the office and Vinton led in the field. Nice to know I'd pissed off not only my crotchety brother, but our team captain as well.

Vinton squinted at the glacial blue river like he was mapping out its meandering current. "Good a place as any." He yanked off the Velcro straps securing his legs. "Knock yourself out."

Radia and John whooped in unison and peeled off their shirts.

I gaped at the woman in her bright blue bra kicking off her boots before shimmying out of her riding leathers.

Robert coughed and turned away.

"Uh. What's happening exactly?" I turned to ask Mark, but he was undressing too and Mother of Sol, his back looked like a marble sculpture of some Greek god.

"Tradition," he said over his shoulder, grinning and lobbing his sweaty shirt at Vinton. "Like a christening, but for us instead of the bikes. We do it at the start of every big tour. Start out clean. Wash away all the bugs from the last ride."

The Browsers kept their machines immaculately clean, so Mark was tossing something metaphorical my way with the washing off bugs bit—I hoped.

Radia retied her dreadlock ponytail and squealed as she trotted toward the water in her underwear.

John scrambled behind her in close pursuit, his briefs a shade of neon green I'd never seen before. "Ow. Shit. Careful. The rocks are sharp." When his partner slowed at the edge of the water, he scooped her into a bear hug and the two of them flailed into the water with all the grace of a pair of moose embroiled in battle. They went under and popped up sputtering, mouths agape.

Radia spat water and gasped. "It's not that bad."

"Says every person ever dunked in icy water." Vinton smirked as Mark handed over his holstered gun and belt.

"Ah, he smiles!" John bellowed. "We should have christened sooner. Get in here!"

Mark dropped his pants, revealing a pair of tiger print boxers that made John and Radia guffaw and cheer. "Part of the tradition." He shrugged sheepishly at me. "Wear something colorful."

"Didn't get that memo," Robert mumbled, cheeks impossibly red.

I couldn't reconcile the image of Mark in business casual yesterday with the sight of him now with only a swatch of orange and black protecting his dignity.

"Where did you get those?" Vinton snorted.

"Been saving them. Last time we were at the coast, one of the Seacans at the docks had a whole crate full. Can't imagine why no one cleaned them out before now." He cocked an eyebrow.

"Can't imagine." Vinton repeated and took a long, appreciative look at his partner's rear end. His face sobered when he saw me gawking.

"You too." He waved an arm at Robert and me.

I choked.

"I'll pass," Robert blurted. "Didn't bring my tiger prints."

"Brought enough for everyone." Mark grinned.

"Go on," Vinton said.

"No thanks," I answered.

"Wasn't asking. It's tradition. You insisted on coming. You wanted to be a part of this. Be a part of it, Iris." My brother's eyes were steely, but his voice was soft, and I couldn't tell if he was taking another stab at me or extending an olive branch. He was weird like that sometimes. Prickly with a soft underbelly. Always ready to fight, or roll over, whichever he gauged would be most effective in the moment.

"*You're* not swimming." I winced because it only occurred to me after I spoke that I didn't even know if he still could. "Neither is Mark," I added to soften my words. His partner was still standing casually beside him clad in nothing but his underwear.

My brother scanned the bank opposite us. "Not many people travel during the day, but someone's still got to stand guard. Be a real shame if an opportunistic traveler relieved us of everything we owned while we were splashing around half naked. We'll go in when Radia and John are done. Cool down now. We won't get another opportunity. It's hot and the road dust builds up pretty quick."

"Don't make me come back there and carry you both!" John flexed his biceps and Radia pretended to faint.

"When in Rome," Robert murmured and untucked his shirt.

"Oh Sol." I didn't realize I'd said it out loud until Vinton grinned. *Everyone will see the sunburn scars on my shoulders.*

"There's an oversized T-shirt in my bag. Mark made me pack it. You can change in the trees if you like."

I did.

By the time I picked my way to the water's edge, Robert was already in up to his waist. He wasn't muscled like Mark was—few people were—but he was lean and broad-shouldered with a chest that looked perfect for laying one's head on. *Zuse, Iris.* I diverted my attention to the dragonflies ricocheting off the water around us.

He waded cautiously over to me, and now that I wasn't looking him in the eye, all I could focus on was the spot where his stomach muscles tapered at his hips. And it was all too much: Radia and John's playful screams, unfamiliar fabric clinging to my ribs, Robert with his hair slicked back and goosebumps on his arms.

"Iris, I—" he started, but I didn't hear the rest because I held my breath and let my knees buckle. Cold water rushed in and numbed my skin. My braids floated around my head like snakes. The sharp world contracted to blurry limbs, a gentle current, and the rush of water in my ears. I stayed submerged until all my air bubbled past my lips and my lungs felt hot and hungry. I stayed until my skin stopped crawling, and my heart crowded out every other feeling in my chest and, when I couldn't stay under any longer, I pushed off from the cold silt and bobbed into a back float.

I had drifted downstream of everyone else by the time I stood up, far from shirtless Robert. My limbs felt like cement, but my thoughts felt combed out and cooler.

"Better than a board room meeting?" Mark shouted from the shore.

I nodded.

I didn't know what I expected the Browsers to be like, but this wasn't it.

After we dried off and dressed, we settled under the trees and ate honey oat bars. I showed everyone where to look for wild strawberries, and we gathered handfuls of the tiny, sweet fruit until our palms were stained red. Mark didn't join us. Instead, he handed Vinton's gun to John and carried my brother to the river's edge.

Everyone pretended to be fully immersed in foraging while he helped Vinton undress, then eased him into the water.

My brother only tolerated his partner hovering at his shoulders for a few steps before waving him away and settling into a strong backstroke. He looked like he belonged there, a merman in tie-dyed shorts, his legs curling in soft repose as he glided through the blue. There was something comforting about the two of them chuckling and trading quiet words while they splashed. For a few minutes, Vinton and Mark weren't leaders or Browsers, they were just a couple out for a swim.

I'd never seen my brother with all his armor off, exposed and unapologetically at ease. And I'd never felt so much like I was part of a group as I did right then. I knew it wouldn't last. But I also knew these were exactly the type of moments you held onto, because they were fleeting.

CHAPTER
SIX

The rest of the day was hot, dusty, and grueling. By late afternoon, the sour smell of smoke permeated the air—heralding an all-too-common summer fire nearby. Often the highway collapsed entirely, and we'd have to bypass it, picking through trails so narrow, branches clawed at sides of the motorcycles. Many of the paths bottlenecked until they were impassable, and every time we were forced to wrestle the bikes around to retrace our route, heat rooted through my guts.

The rest of the machines could fit. It was the sidecar stopping us, and from the choice words the Browsers muttered under their breath as we heaved on hot motorcycles and fought off swarms of ravenous, clinging mosquitoes, I sensed that part of the group had argued with Vinton about bringing an extra bike and Browser instead of hobbling Mark's machine.

Any goodwill I'd harbored toward my brother evaporated. He'd known the sidecar wouldn't be ideal, and he'd done it anyway. I'd gone over his head to secure a spot on this trip, and he'd projected his anger in a way that guaranteed his team would resent me for coming. And it wasn't like backtracking on these wretched trails benefitted him. His modified bike wasn't built for off-road conditions. He couldn't lower the stabilizers on rough terrain without risking them bending or cracking, and without them, Vinton couldn't ride. That meant every time we slowed to a crawl, my brother was forced to find a level spot to lower his landing gear, and Radia or John had to double back to scramble his bike over the choppy bits while Mark piggybacked my brother in a harness they'd made for occasions such as this.

As the hours chugged by, my travelling companions settled into sullen determination and ignored me completely.

Robert didn't fare much better. At one point, we dismounted to turn the bike around, and he stepped in to try and help Mark haul the back end of the machine around. He lost his footing and burned his forearm on the motorcycle's exhaust.

"Zuse!" Mark snapped. "Just stay the hell out of the way and let me handle it, would you?"

Radia unpacked the first aid kit and told Robert, "Keep that bandage moist and hold it on there for a bit, yeah?" But under her breath, she mumbled, "Who doesn't know to stay away from the exhaust? Damned desk jockeys."

Humiliation flashed in Robert's eyes, and I suddenly wanted to slap Radia, to square up with her and force her to apologize. *Simmer down. They all hate you right now. Don't make it worse.*

No one else spoke after that, except for curt orders and frustrated cursing.

The sun had already set behind the clouds by the time we pulled into Golden for the night, three hours later than expected and running on our reserve diesel. A fuel station at the intersection of Highway 95 boasted a half-shattered plexiglass Petro-Canada sign with a maple leaf background backlit by a snarl of LED string lights stuffed into the hole in the front. We pulled the bikes up to faded pumps and two men with shotguns exited the low garage adjacent.

"Easy, all of you. Turn off the headlights." Vinton spoke quietly to us before straightening in his seat and holding his palms up toward the approaching men. "Amos! That you? It's me, Vinton."

"Thought your kind only travelled in pairs." One man paused to spit on the oil-stained tarmac. "Hell of a crowd."

"Making a split run and transporting some of our folk this time around." Vinton thumbed at Robert and me. "You wouldn't shoot a man who's paralyzed, would you?"

Amos slapped his comrade's shoulder and guffawed. "That depends. You bring me them glow plugs you promised?"

"I did. And I believe you mentioned an interest in a roll of high temp gasket material and some oregano oil?"

"Bless you, boy, you've got a memory on you!"

"Mark, why don't you go in and arrange payment while we fill up. We'll be needing around 90 liters, if you can spare it?"

"Course we can." Amos sounded insulted. "I told you, we've got reliable suppliers."

"Much appreciated." Vinton nodded. Mark went inside. Once we were squared up, Amos's coworker came out—this time sans shotgun—and removed the locks from the pumps so Radia and John could start filling.

I felt insubstantial, like there was nothing holding me together but caked sunscreen, road dust, and dried sweat. My sit bones felt like someone had taken a sledgehammer to my pelvis. I wanted nothing more than to drink my weight in water, lie down, and sleep. I needed to reset my mind. When Mark remounted the bike, I swayed in the sidecar.

"Hold on, you two. Almost there."

I glanced at Robert on Radia's bike. He was rigid and cradling his burned arm.

Shit.

The short cruise through town was a blur of candlelit windows, rows of tied horses and wagons, and the odd bicycle. Other than a solar buggy, we were the only motorized vehicles on the streets. Mark said this place had a building where you could rent rooms to sleep in by the day, but that was out of our price range. And besides, we weren't staying the night, only resting our eyes for a bit. We needed to keep out of the sun as much as possible and that meant taking advantage of as many nighttime hours as possible. We'd stay with the bikes while we napped. They were too valuable to leave unguarded.

We chose a park a few blocks off the highway sporting a playground with rust-streaked equipment on an island of curled up rubber matting. Radia and John made quick work of setting up a tarp over one of the swing sets, and we parked underneath and spread out foam mats and sleeping bags.

"Ladies room to the right. Guys to the left." Vinton announced before wheeling toward the trees adjacent to the playground. Mark followed him.

When they returned and my brother settled on his sleeping mat, propped up against the base of the swings, he beckoned Radia and John over. "Amos mentioned that the doc keeps late hours. Hospital is just south of here. You'll see it." He pressed a stack of copper tokens into Radia's hand. "Take him with you." He nodded toward Robert.

"I don't need a hospital," Robert hissed.

"Doesn't matter." Vinton leaned back and put his hands behind his head. "These two are heading that way anyway, and I'm not delivering damaged goods to Coaltana. They want their security deposit in top condition, I expect. Get that arm looked at."

The fact that Robert didn't argue further made my stomach drop. He looked like a ghost.

Radia thanked Vinton before they left. Her voice cracked, and I might have been deliriously exhausted, but I swear I saw tears in her eyes.

As the Sommer's taillight receded into the night, I doused a handkerchief with water from my bottle and scrubbed sunscreen and dust from my face and neck. Mark laid out his mat beside

Vinton's but then left us to do chin-ups at the monkey bars. I did my best to hold in my questions and sip water slowly, but I had no control when I was tired. "Why is Radia going to the hospital?"

"She's pregnant," Vinton answered.

I choked and sputtered "Without permission?"

Vinton smiled faintly, eyes still closed as he reached into his jacket and withdrew a small flask. "Kahn's gone. Nobody needs permission to live their lives anymore." He took a sip.

I shimmied into my sleeping bag and stared at my brother. His legs jerked as he sat. Sometimes he got muscle spasms after long days.

"Want some?" He offered and I shook my head.

"Where did you get all that fare?" I changed the subject. "That much copper would cost you your teeth."

"We told the other department heads awhile back that the engine seized on one of the motorcycles and we'd have to break it down for parts. It wasn't completely a lie, the head gasket was going, and we had no replacement, but there was still some life left in the motor. We stripped the bike down and kept everything but traded the engine to the rail runners. Even leaky, it was valuable enough to fetch some copper."

My stomach twisted. "Civil war. All of us starving, and you've got booze and a secret stash of copper?"

My brother took another long slug and winced. "Glad you think so highly of me. Corporate used to send us out on survey runs with nothing, and it hasn't gotten better since they fell. Everyone with a suit thinks we can just breeze on out into the big world and bring home treasure without greasing some palms along the way. It costs copper to survive out here, Iris. You saw that on your ride back from Nate's camp, surely? And how the hell are John and Radia supposed to convince that refinery that we're big-ticket fuel buyers if they don't flash a bit of copper, huh?"

A thought struck me out of nowhere. I glanced over at Mark grunting through a second set. "You knew that Radia was pregnant. Both of you. That's why Mark recommended her for this run, isn't it, because you scouted here and knew there was a doctor and a hospital."

He shrugged. "We lucked out finding out about the doctor. He's got a reputation for helping moms-to-be. Makes these powdered liver supplements, chocked full of folic acid. Pricey." He wrinkled his nose. "I bet it tastes like shit too. Anyway, it's a good thing, because your boy's liable to get his hands on some ice and aloe for that arm. Only way he'll get any sleep tonight." He raised the flask like he was toasting something. "See, it all worked out."

My Sol, sometimes he reminded me of Nate so much it made my chest ache.

Mark dropped from the monkey bars and started doing burpees.

"What the hell is he doing?" I muttered. "He's obsessive."

My brother snorted and rubbed his palms down his jittering thighs before answering me in a fettered voice. "Yeah, he is." He spun the flask's cap between his finger and thumb before taking another sip. "Wanna know why?"

I froze. He was doing it again, exposing a soft side he'd never let me see before. He really *was* tired. Tired enough that he didn't even wait for my answer.

Gazing at Mark, smile fading on his face, Vinton said, "You saw how it is today. The good and bad of it. It's not always easy. I-I'm not an easy partner to travel with."

I swallowed at the shame in his voice.

"Back when we were rookies on our fifth run together, we were on the Coquihalla just south of Merritt. It floods real bad down that way. Most of the highway's gone, but there are a few sections where you can get up to speed. We were on one of them near dawn when this guy jumped out of the ravine and threw a spike belt across the road. There wasn't any time to stop. We both went over it, laid our bikes down. Mark was still sliding down the road when he came up with his pistol and fired a shot toward the guy. I don't know what kind of idiot he was if he'd been casing out Browsers and didn't know we carried. We keep our holsters visible enough. Anyway, it scared the shit out of him—I guess he wasn't armed. Not a ton of people were before Nate's URLs' failed shipment armed every marauder for miles."

I winced at that.

"I was still on my side when this guy tore off down the hill, jumped on a waiting horse, and took off. Strangest thing was, he was alone. Wasn't a marauder. Best we can figure, he was just a lone vulture, looking to disable the bikes so he could make us walk. Planning to come back to steal the machines while we were gone. We had a tire repair kit but there was only enough material to patch my bike. Mark wheeled his machine down an incline and covered it in brush and we doubled up. About ten kilometers out of Merritt, the front tire went flat again, so we had to stash my ride too. That's when Mark started carrying me."

Vinton paused, jaw tight. He took another sip from his flask.

"I, uh, I was so damned worried about leaving my machine behind. We'd hidden it better than Mark's but the electric actuators for the stabilizers are irreplaceable. I'd never ride again if someone nicked it. It was all I could think about. I didn't even notice Mark was hurt until he started limping about a kilometer in. His ride didn't have crash bars and he'd scraped up the side of his leg pretty bad. It was hot out. We were draped in emergency solar blankets, but he'd left almost everything else behind to carry me and we didn't have a lot of water. I kept hassling him to stop and refill, but he got it into his head that we were going to make it into town and convince someone to ferry us back to the bikes before the sun got too high. Even back then he pushed himself too damned hard.

"Got to the point where he couldn't carry me anymore. I must have argued with him for half an hour to leave me behind. He looked ready to pass out. I said some awful shit to him to make him go. Sometimes you've gotta be an asshole to get things done and I was that day. In the end, he left me wedged in a little ravine out of sight of the road, sweating under a solar blanket. He looked like a puppy someone had just laid a beating on when he went. Told me later he was scared shitless that he'd come back, and I'd be gone, or dead. Said he swore over and over again on that long walk that he'd get strong enough to *never* leave me behind again. And that's what he did." My brother glanced at Mark doing sit ups. "That's what he's doing. Figures he's got to be strong enough for the both of us." His voice cracked.

"Shit," I breathed.

"It was nightfall by the time he came back. By then I didn't give a damn if I ever rode again. I just remember thanking Sol that Mark was alive." A gentle laugh puffed past his lips. "He had a flashlight duct-taped to his helmet. He was slathered in zinc sunscreen and riding the shittiest looking bicycle I ever saw. A kid's one with a wagon tied to it. He looked like a clown. I laughed so hard I thought I would puke. My bike was where we left it; Mark's wasn't." My brother sighed. "He redlined after that."

"Oh my Sol. I never knew."

"Because we did our best to keep it quiet. Mark's family and all the Browsers took a cred cut to chip in, but it still took us a year and a half to pay for the loss of that machine and none of the other department heads would budge on their budget to help us. They said it was Mark's responsibility and that was what hazard pay was for. So, excuse me if I choose to part off some machinery to take care of my own, because sure as hell, no one else is going to."

"Sometimes you have to be an asshole," I murmured. We sat in silence for a bit with only the sound of Mark's heavy breathing and some lonely dog baying in the distance. "That why you brought the sidecar instead of another Browser and bike?"

Vinton dropped his gaze to me. Moonlight through the tarp took on a blue cast and made him look wrung out and older than his years. "I can't risk losing another machine. Besides, our people back home need every drop of diesel they can get until we make this deal. No diesel, no generators. No power, no mining equipment. Filling an extra tank felt like taking food out of mouths and I wasn't willing to do that. You put me in a hard spot, Iris. I'd rather piss off my crew and convince them I'm motivated by petty revenge than have them thinking any deeper about it. There are worries enough on the road."

He pocketed his flask, leaned back, and smiled crookedly. "Plus, it was satisfying as hell rattling the shit out of you today."

"Asshole."

"Damn straight. Take a nap. We roll in two hours."

I WAS SLEEPING by the time Robert, Radia, and John returned, but woke later when my arm went numb from propping it under my head. Rolling onto my back, I cradled my tingling hand. Cold night air stung my nostrils, mosquitoes darted around my ears, and the blue tarp rustled gently above.

Suddenly, I felt claustrophobic. My sleeping bag clung to me like a dog-pile of wet blankets. The air was too humid with the exhalations of other sleepers. Clawing at the zipper, I squirmed out of my bedding and sat up in the dark.

Behind me, someone coughed, stifling it the way people do when they're trying not to disturb others. I turned toward the source and barely made out Robert lying on his back. Indentations lined his nose from where the dust mask he'd been wearing had pinched. I couldn't tell for sure, but I swore I saw the flash of his eyes. His breaths came in short, shallow gulps.

Drops of rain pattered the tarp above us before I gathered enough courage to whisper, "Robert . . . Are you okay?"

He shifted and let out a thready sigh that ended in another choking cough. "Go to sleep, Iris." Then he rolled away from me.

But I couldn't. His coughing kept me up, needling me any time I dozed until, even in the silent moments, I waited for the next round to start.

CHAPTER
SEVEN

We rose just past midnight, folded the tarp, and packed. John stoked a tiny camp stove with pinecones and made us mint tea. He insisted Robert keep some extra sachets to help with his cough. We ate vacuum-packed protein rations from the bunker that were likely older than all of us. They tasted like chalky plastic with a hint of cookie dough and were only marginally more palatable when warmed over the fire.

Vinton took Radia aside doling out quiet instructions and another stack of copper toll coins and she pulled him into a long hug. Radia seemed the type that embraced people like she did life—wholeheartedly.

"I expect to be regaled with tales of how you dazzled those refinery boys into giving us a steal of a deal on fuel." Mark grinned and pulled her into a hug.

"Sure thing, Boss," Radia said. She hugged the rest of us in turn before she and John got on their motorcycles and left, filling the air with diesel exhaust and an uncomfortable vacuum —the kind you felt when a full house vacated after a gathering, and you were the last one there. I'd never felt that feeling until

Nate's house. Our Seacan had never been large enough to entertain guests.

We'd only been travelling together for a day, but somehow it seemed wrong to be carrying on without John and Radia's ebullience. Vinton and Mark watched until their teammates' taillights disappeared over an eastern hill.

Robert didn't watch at all.

He packed his bag with one hand, his bandaged arm tucked close to his chest. All of his movements were careful and contained, like he'd aged a hundred years today. When I asked if I could help, he answered shortly. "I'm fine."

Part of me ached for him. Even in the bike's headlights, I saw that the back of his neck was sunburned despite his religious applications of sunscreen and the cloud cover yesterday. He looked uncomfortable in jeans and boots that were too big for him, and he hadn't spoken more than a few words to any of us. But another uglier side of me was disappointed by how fragile Robert seemed away from an office. If one day on the road had been enough to break him, how in Sol's name did he expect to survive being held hostage? Did he have it in him to adjust to a world without mahogany desks and air conditioning, or had he been too coddled, and I'd only seen strength in him because I'd wanted to?

Vinton had said Robert surprised him while I was gone, that he'd handled himself well during the fighting, and my brother wasn't one for idle compliments. But as I plunked into the sidecar and Robert swung tiredly onto the broad seat behind Mark, he looked phased out and withdrawn, more like a child up past naptime than a high-stakes corporate player.

Quit being so damned cold, Iris. He's out here isn't he? Trying to fix things for everyone back home. Who are you to judge what his best should look like? I clamped a hand over the crossbow in my lap as Mark eased the Sommer over ruts and bumps in the grass to start the second leg of our journey.

"Only six more hours. We'll get there just after sunrise." Vinton shouted to us with a cocky grin.

Out of the corner of my eye, I thought I saw Robert shudder before pushing his facemask up over his nose.

WE RODE south on a highway tucked between a jagged mountain range and the gentle flats of a flood plain cradling a massive river. It looked like liquid slate in the moonlight. Waterwheels studded its banks wherever there were inhabited homesteads. We passed the occasional well-lit canoe, barge or fishing boat, the occupants aboard waving casually at our bouncing headlights as we went by. There was more traffic on the river than the road—which was slowly crumbling away into wilderness. More than once, I found myself imagining that I was gliding down that glassy water with fireflies bobbing around me, instead of clinging onto a noisy bike in a sweaty, dust-coated helmet getting my teeth rattled out of my head.

We met a northbound caravan of horses and merchants, their long line of lanterns snaking into the night. One of them specialized in shoe repair, another stocked cases of old prescription lenses and colorful frames. Mark was nearly sold on a pair of sunglasses with a small sticker boasting 100 percent UV ray protection but couldn't barter the seller down to an affordable price. Vinton paid for information again, reviewing his map with one of the older women who penciled in some updates, and let us know that there were fires to the west.

We stopped to eat where the river widened to a sprawling, shallow lake with shores choked with verdant water lilies boasting delicate white blooms. They were all tucked in for the night and looked more like onions bobbing on the water than flowers. Dark mountains nestled along the water's length under a starry sky growing murky with windborne smoke.

We gagged down the rest of the protein bars, filled our water bottles, and got back on the bikes.

But we didn't outrun the smoke.

As we picked our way south, it blew in from the west, swallowing the night sky.

Vinton pressed us at a punishing pace, and Mark, who'd been offering the odd jovial comment as we went, clammed up and concentrated fully on navigating the increasingly rough patches of road. At least we had plenty of open ground for detouring and weren't manhandling our machines on tree-choked trails. *It could be worse.*

And then, five-and-a-half hours out of Golden, it got worse.

The smoke blocked out the sunrise. Ash floated down like dirty gobs of snow, caking the bikes. Blackened pine needles settled on our clothes. Startled deer darted across the road with white-rimmed eyes and open mouths. After one particularly close call, Vinton stopped his bike, and Mark rolled up beside him and pulled his handkerchief down.

"Visibility's too bad."

My brother clenched his jaw and shook his head. "We can punch through this. The map puts us at half an hour away from Fernie."

"It's right on top of us, Vinton. Animals are running from it. We can't outrace a wildfire."

"There's no other route this side of the pass. If we backtrack, it's a six-hour ride—in the blazing sun—back to Golden. And then a whole damned night to loop back down from the Alberta side. The rail runners said the highway south of Longview is nothing but abandoned ranches. No rails. No towns. No aid if we break down. Plenty of marauders though, waiting to pick our bones clean. I'm not risking that." He tightened his grip on his handlebars. "We can push through."

"I can't," Robert wheezed.

We all turned at the unexpected desperation in his voice.

"What?" Vinton squinted.

"I can't do this anymore."

My brother snorted and shook his helmeted head. "Sure you can, Pretty Boy. Just hang on and let Mark do all the thinking like you have all ride, yeah? You can even close your eyes if you want."

"Enough," I bristled.

Mark pinned Vinton with a cold warning glare while Robert let out a short, frantic laugh. "It's not like that."

"What's the problem then? You want to get to Fernie, don't you?" My brother jabbed a finger to the east. "It's right over there."

Robert hunched his shoulders, sucked in a whistling inhale, and mumbled something that his mask muffled.

"Speak up!" Vinton peeled off his helmet and leaned closer.

"I have asthma," he barked.

Only the chattering idle of the motorcycles broke the silence that followed. As the three of us gaped at Robert, numbness thrummed through my ribcage.

His gulping, shallow breaths punctuated the smoky air.

Vinton clamped his mouth closed. He opened it for several false starts before blurting, "Bullshit. Asthma is fatal."

It had been since the collapse. Our school files had pointed out that one of the leading causes of childhood death—along with severe allergies—was asthma. When the power grids failed, medication production and distribution came to a crashing halt alongside every other power-hungry supply chain. For a while, rescue inhalers and epinephrine auto injectors fetched top price on the caravan markets. Then they expired. How horribly ironic would it have been to survive the end of the world, only to succumb to a bee sting, peanut butter, or pollen later on?

Everyone knew somebody who'd died from an asthma attack

or anaphylactic shock. Most people with these conditions didn't make it to adulthood.

"It's mild." Robert puffed. "Smoke triggers it. I thought the mask would be . . ." His words faded out and he curled in on himself, face gray, tendons standing out on his neck.

I grabbed his hand without thinking. "We need to get him back to fresh air." And when my brother didn't respond fast enough, I barked. "Now!"

All of the vitriol drained from Vinton's face. He nodded, jammed his helmet back on, and U-turned his bike. Mark followed.

"Hang on." I shouted up to Robert, still clutching his clammy hand. "We'll get out of this."

TWENTY MINUTES LATER, with the sun rising higher above us, Robert's hand went slack in mine. He tipped away from me. I yanked on his arm and yelled at Mark. The motorcycle skidded to a stop, and I stood and clutched at Robert's shirt.

"Hey! Hey, look at me." I patted his cheek and his gaze rolled toward me listlessly. *Shit.* "Robert, come on. Stay with us."

I didn't realize Mark had dismounted until he gripped Robert under the armpits and hoisted him up. "Switch seats with him. We can belt him into the sidecar, and you can hold onto him."

"He bad?" Vinton bellowed from ahead of us.

I nodded dumbly. *Oh Sol.*

"There's a house up ahead. Come on." Vinton didn't wait for us to respond, just peeled away toward a compact two-story farmhouse with a broad wraparound porch and meticulously clipped yard.

I bit back on the panic solidifying in my lungs and helped Mark maneuver Robert into the sidecar. As I bent to click the seatbelt over his hips, he grasped my hand clumsily and spoke in between whistling inhales. His lips were blue. "I'm late. For work. You have. To dress him."

"Yeah, for sure." I forced my lips into a casual smile. *Oh Sol, he was delusional.* "Don't worry about it. We're going to get you inside, and we can talk then, yeah?"

"Let's go!" Mark leaped onto the bike and patted the seat behind him.

I gripped Robert's T-shirt and clung onto Mark, tears stinging my eyes and blood thundering between my ears. We bumped up the dirt drive and set several dogs to barking.

Please, let him be okay.

CHAPTER
EIGHT

"H ello?" Vinton yelled from his bike. "We need help!"

The covered porch was completely enclosed with chain link fencing panels. Three dogs snarled at us as they paced within, tan with black faces, curled tails and raised hackles.

"Please, we're not marauders!" Mark shouted, jumped off his bike, and approached the front steps with his hands raised.

The dogs lost it, ricocheting off the fencing, tossing their heads back and baying wildly.

Mark cupped his hands over his mouth and hollered, "We're travelers on our way to Fernie. The fire stopped us. Our friend has asthma. He needs shelter from the smoke."

The front door creaked opened and a lanky older man with a comfortable belly eased out with a sigh. He held a rifle but didn't aim it at us. When he let out a sharp whistle, the trio of dogs stopped barking and swiveled their heads to him. "Good boys," he said, fishing in his pocket and doling out a treat to each one in turn before raising his gaze to squint at us.

"You're lucky I put the dogs away or they'd be chewing on you right now. Asthma *and* a guy with a wheelchair. You're really going all out. All you're missing is a hunchbacked old crone with a cane. Was that supposed to be your job?" He tossed his chin toward me.

"Please." I yanked off my helmet. "My friend. He can't breathe."

"They were chasing coyotes earlier. That's why I put them away." He continued as if he hadn't heard. "Some nights, a whole pack of the mangy buggers will lie in the ditch at the end of the drive." He pointed behind us. "You can see their ears poking up. They send the smallest, sickliest one limping up to the house, trying to bait my dogs so they can ambush them. Killed one of my pups last year."

"We're not baiting you, sir," Vinton said. "Just honest folk who need a hand. We'll go back up to the end of the drive if you let us leave him here. We can leave fair payment behind with him. I've got copper. Just take him inside until the smoke clears and he catches his breath. That's all we're asking."

"You expect me to believe that a bunch of *honest* folks just decided to take their friend—with asthma—on a pleasure cruise during wildfire season to a slave town. Probably stole them bikes too. Look here—"

"Jesus, Marty." A round woman emerged from inside and shouldered past the man toward the padlocked chain link gate. "Shut up and look at the kid's face, would ya?"

"Arlene, don't you open that gate." Marty warned.

"He's as gray as the grim reaper. Kennel the dogs." She dug into her ample cleavage and withdrew a key before nodding at us. "One of you can come in the house with him. Leave your weapons. The rest of you stay out here, understood? There's a sunshade out by the garden you can get under. Marty, I said *kennel* the dogs!"

The dogs and Marty both tucked their tails and rounded the corner of the caged-in porch.

Arlene popped the lock, unthreaded the chain, and swung open the gate. "Come on then."

"Yes, ma'am." I shrugged my crossbow off my back and tucked under Robert's arm to boost him up.

"If they try anything funny, you yell." Vinton spoke under his breath. "We'll be right here."

"How about we all quit moaning about whether we're gonna stab each other's backs and concentrate on saving this boy, eh?" Arlene tutted and wrapped a strong arm around Robert's waist as he stumbled up the stairs.

We squeezed through the front door directly into a sitting room with floral upholstered couches and floor-to-ceiling shelving displaying hundreds of boxed figurines with exaggerated huge heads and wide-spaced black button eyes gazing out of cellophane windows.

"Sit him down." Arlene steered us toward one of the couches, batting aside a pile of decorative cushions. "I'll go boil some water. Something hot will loosen up those lungs, I wager." She dropped one of the pillows at my feet and, when she straightened, whispered in my ear, "Calm down if you want him to calm down, Hon." She smelled like hand lotion did when it got old and soured.

I hadn't realized that my own breaths were coming in gasps. Shaking out my hands, I plopped down beside Robert on the couch. He folded forward, fingers digging into the fabric of his jeans and unblinking eyes staring between his feet. Every inhalation sounded like someone was garroting him.

"I don't know what to do," I whimpered. "Tell me what you need." *Nice, Iris. Really damned helpful. Snap out of it.* "Breathe with me, Robert. Okay. Big slow breaths." I slipped my hand over his, and he gripped my fingers hard enough to make me wince.

I don't know how long we sat like that, him clutching at his chest and me willing air into his lungs with every fiber of my being. It felt like hours, even though I knew it couldn't be. At one point, Robert's eyes met mine and he wheezed a single word.

"Caffeine."

At first it didn't click. The word seemed so random; I thought I misheard him. "C-caffeine?"

He nodded, blue gaze pinned to mine.

"Zuse. Caffeine will help?"

Another nod.

"I have black tea. In my bag." I shot off the couch and grabbed my backpack where I'd left it slumped on the floor. "I have black tea!" I shouted loudly enough that Arlene heard me from the kitchen.

"Halleluiah, girl. Now we're talking."

ROBERT HAD CHOKED on the first few sips of bitterly strong brew but managed to down two mugs in between hanging his head over the porcelain basin of steaming water and eucalyptus leaves that Arlene had set on the coffee table. His breathing evened out, his coloring came back, and he thanked our host profusely as she dabbed aloe on his burned arm before wrapping it with a fresh bandage.

"Get some on that sunburn too." She handed Robert a cut chunk of aloe leaf and he squeezed the gelatinous innards onto his palm and then applied it to the back of his neck. He fell asleep not long after that.

The sight of him laying there in a rumpled T-shirt, drawing deep even breaths, toppled the careful wall of composure I'd been battling to hold up. I unthreaded my cramped fingers from his and drew a breath that snagged on the way in. My vision washed out and I wiped heat from my eyes.

Arlene patted my thigh like we were family and pointed

toward the hall. "Bathroom's on the right. Go have yourself a good cry. Scream into a pillow, whatever you need. I'll have something ready to eat when you get back, how's that sound?"

"Okay." The word came out squeaky as I jerked to my feet. I didn't need to cry. I needed to crash. Bile boiled over in my throat, and I barely made it to the washroom in time. Closing myself in, I slapped up the toilet seat and retched into the bowl. *If there hadn't been a farmhouse. If Arlene hadn't let us in. Oh, Sol. I nearly lost him.* Another deep heave rolled through me along with a choking heat. *He didn't even tell me. He let us ride right into the smoke and didn't say a damned thing until it was almost too late.*

A string of saliva wobbled on my bottom lip. *You should have seen the signs, Iris. He wore a mask outside even when no one else did. He coughed all night.* I sagged back, leaning my cheek on the cold edge of the bathtub and picking at the mosquito bites on my arms as my mind delaminated from the present. Gummed-up tension stretched and snapped like an old label peeling away. My hands and legs twitched as my whole body short-circuited. I latched onto mundane details: the guttering beeswax candle on the toilet tank, how the tiny hexagon floor tiles felt like reptile scales, and the cobweb between the frosted glass sconces in the light fixture looked like the letter 'Y.' It felt like if I didn't fixate on something, I might not be able to find my way back from this shutdown. There'd be no reboot. Just a crusted shell left behind, a carapace of Iris. Why in Sol's name did my body think coming apart at the seams was the solution to every crisis? I couldn't do this right now, in a stranger's bathroom.

Yet here I was, standing in the path of a meltdown the size of a mudslide.

When I came back to myself, the candle was shorter, my arms were bleeding from the scabs I'd picked, and the stuffy air still smelled faintly of bile. I stood carefully and used the bucket of water beside the toilet to flush it. Then I washed my hands and arms at the basin with a block of goat milk soap that smelled like peppermint, dabbing my arms dry with my shirt so that I wouldn't get blood on Arlene's lacy hand towels.

When I exited the bathroom, the hallway was dark. Lamplight and conversation flickered from the sitting room, and I edged toward it despite my skin crawling at the idea of polite small talk.

Blinds had been pulled over the windows to keep out the heat of the sun. Robert and Mark sat on the couch across from Arlene's husband, Marty. Vinton slouched in his wheelchair petting one of the dogs, which had wedged its big head onto his lap. The other two were sprawled on the scratched hardwood floor. Everyone except the canines looked painfully awkward, like actors on a stage who'd forgotten their lines.

"Iris!" Vinton welcomed me too loudly.

"We came in," Mark stated.

"Sun's getting high, and Arlene's a big softie," Marty muttered.

The dogs glanced at me with perked ears and droopy eyes before deciding I wasn't worth getting up for.

Robert said nothing, but his eyes were clear and full of concern as he took me in. He saw it. I could tell by the frown line creasing his forehead. He knew that I'd broken and pasted myself back together again. All I could think of was how, when he'd been confused, he'd said *I'm late for work. You have to dress him.* Even though he'd been fighting to breathe, Robert was more concerned for someone else's welfare. I wondered who was dressing Paul each morning, wrestling him into a presentable version of himself while his son was away. Did he even know he'd left? I hadn't considered how much that must be weighing on Robert until just now.

"Feeling better?" I whispered.

"Much better." He patted the couch beside him. "Thank you."

I took a seat, overly aware of his thigh brushing against mine.

"Marty!" Arlene's voice yelled from the kitchen. "Can you go get some rosemary?"

The man slapped his knees and stood with a bright look on his face, like he'd been drowning in here and his wife had just thrown him a lifeline. The dogs scrambled to their feet too. "Rosemary!" he repeated like it was a farewell and took his leave, stomping out the front door with an umbrella to shield him from the sun, the dogs bounding out behind him.

Vinton puffed out his cheeks and sagged in his chair. "Thank Sol, I thought he'd never leave."

Mark stood rapidly, crossing the room to squint at the collection of boxed figurines. "It's been killing me not asking about these. They've all got eyes like sharks. What are they? Voodoo dolls?"

"Don't touch them," Vinton said.

"Don't worry."

"I dunno. I think they're kinda cute," Robert offered, tilting his head to one side.

"'Til they kill you in your sleep. All the boxes say 'Pop'. Hey look, Iris! This one's you: Katniss Everdeen. She's got a bow and everything."

Vinton wheeled closer to inspect the shelves. "And there's you." He pointed at a green, muscled figure on a lower shelf. "Hulk."

Mark scoffed. "I wouldn't be caught dead in purple pants."

"Only tiger print boxers."

"There's a line. And purple crosses it, okay?"

While the pair bantered, Robert leaned closer and said, "Arlene insisted we shelter in place while the sun is high. Says it will rain later today—that she can feel it in her ankles." He smiled softly.

I tried for a smile but could feel it wavering on my lips. *You just about died. And everyone's just dancing around it, pretending it didn't happen. Zuse.*

"Are you okay? Do you need to go somewhere quieter? I could ask if there's somewhere you could lie down?"

I couldn't catch half of his words. I was too caught up by the stubble on his cheeks and how his bottom lip had cracked. He smelled like home and safety, and it was so damned incongruent with how I felt right now, I couldn't reconnect. "I'm fine."

"Look, I'm sorry." His head was tucked so close to mine now, his breath teased my hair against my cheek. "I haven't had an attack like that since I was a kid. I-I didn't think it would be a problem."

"Okay," I answered robotically. *Shit. That wasn't the right answer, was it?*

"Food's ready," Arlene called.

I only remembered snippets after that. A tender grouse served with fresh greens and fried mushrooms. No one talked while they ate. Arlene offered us rhubarb crumble, but we declined, bellies full and heads heavy.

"You all look fit to fall asleep on your plates," she said. "Marty's made up the spare room, but there's not enough space for all four of you up there." She glanced at Vinton's chair, "And it's a narrow set of stairs."

"No worries, ma'am." Mark smiled. "My partner and I are partial to napping where we can see our bikes, I'm sure you understand. We'll be fine out on the front porch, so long as there's shade."

"Men and their shiny machines." Arlene wiped her hands on her apron and nodded at Robert and me. "Well, this one needs to stay out of the smoke until the rain tamps it down, so you two are upstairs then. Marty, string out the hammocks for these boys. There's a basin in the bathroom and another in the bedroom if you all want to freshen up before you sleep. Water pump is on the back porch."

Vinton cleared his throat. "Ma'am, we've already intruded enough and we're on a time sensitive journey—"

"One your friend will never see the end of if you take him back out there right now. I didn't patch him up just to see my work go to waste or have you all crash your fancy motorcycles down a ravine because you were too stubborn to stop and sleep. You asked for our help, boy. Have the grace to take it."

Even my stubborn brother was smart enough—and tired enough—not to argue with that.

Robert let me go up to the spare room first. The smell of cedar greeted me as I opened the door. It was hot, but not stifling. The room had low plaster walls, open rafter ceilings and a large bed with a white patchwork quilt. Dust motes swam in slats of light creeping through the shuttered dormer window. A bedside table held a hurricane lamp and a box of matches. Tucked into the corner, a triple panel divider cordoned off a dresser with a basin and folded towels. A cotton night gown and a men's plaid bathrobe hung off the divider.

I stripped out of my sweaty clothes and washed quickly, scrubbing my hair with peppermint soap before rinsing and drying off. The oversized night gown smelled line-dried when I shrugged it on. I was sitting on the edge of the bed, re-braiding my damp hair when a soft knock sounded on the door.

"All clear?" Robert's voice was muffled, but recognizable.

"All clear," I croaked.

He slipped inside and closed the door carefully.

I wanted to stand, but my knees felt wobbly, and my hands gripped the blanket like I was perched on the edge of the world, instead of the edge of a mattress.

"You okay?" he asked and I fully meant to say *Yeah. Fine. Fantastic, actually.* But instead, tears started burning my eyes.

"Ah, Zuse. Iris, I'm sorry." He crossed the room in three strides and grabbed both of my hands.

I gulped air, shocked by the sudden connection.

"I should have told you. About the deal. About my asthma. I just wanted to fix things and instead, I keep fragging it all up."

"I don't think you're clingy," I blurted.

"I know." He pulled me against his chest. Wisps of my hair snagged on the stubble of his chin as he hugged me hard.

"You scared the shit out of me." Tears rolled down my cheeks.

"I know. I'm sorry."

"I don't want to lose you."

He stroked my hair and kissed the top of my head.

I kept my ear pressed to his chest and let the rumble of his reverberating voice drown out everything else.

"I don't want to lose you either. Sidekick forever. Promise."

"Don't," I choked.

"Don't what?"

"Don't promise." On my last night in our city, the evening Robert had invited me into his house and broken down, confessing that he felt absolutely alone, I'd said he could hold onto me. I'd *promised* him I wasn't going anywhere, and Soldamnit if that promise didn't turn into a curse. The next morning, everything fell apart, and I became a fugitive.

Robert tucked me under his chin, slipped one of his hands into mine, and hooked my little finger with his. "Pinky swear, then."

We held each other until my arms grew sore and my legs restless. Letting go of Robert felt ominously symbolic, like he'd be lost to me as soon as I loosened my grip, but my betraying body could only stay still for so long, and when I fidgeted in his embrace, he cleared his throat and said, "Zuse, I'm sorry. I stink. I should get cleaned up."

I wanted to tell him that he didn't stink, that I could lose myself in the smell of him forever, but that seemed like an incredibly stupid thing to say out loud to someone, so instead I mumbled, "I used most of the water."

"I don't need much." He grinned.

As soon as he started undressing behind the divider, I stood and flapped my hands. My feet tingled as I walked. *Reboot, Iris.* But I couldn't stop thinking about him shirtless at the river, how lean he'd looked compared to Mark's bulked-up physique, not skinny but spartan. His skin naturally darker than mine despite never being in the sun. His ribs flexing as he breathed. The sparse line of hair below his navel.

Stop it. I flapped my hands harder. *You saw him for what? A second? Quit fixating.*

"I don't think I've ever worn a bathrobe in my life. You?" Only the top of his head was visible over the divider. A bare arm reached over to drape his jeans over his shirt.

"Uh, no." I paced, losing myself in the slap of my feet on the floor, settling for tapping my fingernails against my teeth because it was inappropriate to run in here. Thoughts licked through my mind like hummingbird tongues, quick, darting, and slippery.

You should tell him about Nate. While you're both alone. When will you be again? If you're taking down walls, that should be the first one. He needs to know why your city fell, and that Coaltana isn't the only danger we're facing. He'll understand.

"It looks like something a grandpa would wear." Robert continued casually even though only the barest of barriers shielded his nudity from me. Water trickled. "I don't get why people were so into them. Just towel off and get dressed. Why do you need in-between clothes."

I must have lost time again, because the next thing I knew, I was back sitting on the bed and Robert knelt before me, plaid bathrobe haphazardly tied at his waist. I jerked as he slipped his warm hands into mine. "Hey. I didn't mean to talk your ear off."

"I'm just tired." I gulped. His hair was curly when it was wet, boyish despite the seriousness in his eyes. I wanted to run my fingers through it.

The house creaked and clicked as the wind picked up outside.

"Tuck you in?" He offered his hand.

I let him pull me to my feet and turn down the bed. The sheets felt starchy, but the mattress was far softer and cleaner than anything I'd slept on in a while.

"How is it?"

"Mmmm. Like laying on a hundred puppies."

"Oddly specific." His teeth flashed. "Hey, is this supposed to be like one of those romance movies where, if I'm a gentleman, I offer to sleep on the floor, but later you feel so bad about how uncomfortable I look, you cave and let me share?"

"Depends on if you're a gentleman," I murmured, muscles already melting into the bed.

"I'll stay on top of the covers. And the grandpa bathrobe should be enough of a deterrent should you get any ideas."

"Deal." I smiled and patted beside me.

The mattress jiggled as Robert eased down and slipped his hand into mine. We fell asleep like that, like it was routine. Like we'd always been like this.

CHAPTER
NINE

Pulses of lightning flared through my closed eyes, and thunder thrummed through the clouds far overhead like a grinding industrial machine suspended in the sky. It took several moments to place where I was. At first, I thought I was back in Nate's house, the cozy upstairs bedroom with the smell of Christie's cooking wafting up the stairs, and the click of Masie's claws in the hallway.

Not there. This is . . . The room was dark around me. Fat drops of rain smacked the thick panes of a small dormer window. *Arlene's house. Arlene and Marty who saved Robert.* I listened to his even breathing beside me and tried to match it but couldn't.

A sizzle of lightning oversaturated the room. On its heels, a concussive explosion of thunder shivered through me.

Robert jumped beside me. That's when I realized he was awake too.

We rolled toward each other.

"That was close." He leaned in so that I could hear him over the wind. "Hold me?"

I giggled at the melodrama in his voice and slipped my hand into his. "And ruin your tough guy act?"

"Honestly, I think I'm kind of shit at it. It hurts flexing my biceps all the time around Mark."

I reached out in the dark to playfully squeeze his upper arm but misjudged, grabbing his forearm instead.

He hissed and flinched out of my reach.

"Oh Sol, I'm sorry!" I yelped, remembering the burn too late.

"It's okay," he gasped. "I should have re-bandaged it."

"Let me." I sat up fumbling for the matches at the bedside table.

Lightning strobed through the room, flashing off the glass of the hurricane lamp. I lit it despite Robert's assurances that he was fine.

"Do you have anything left from the first aid kit?" I asked.

"Arlene gave me an extra roller gauze. In my pants pocket."

I fished through his jeans until I found it. As the storm drew mournful noises from the gutters outside, we sat cross-legged on the bed, knee to knee. Robert loosened the plaid bathrobe and eased his burned arm out of its sleeve. The wound was ugly and egg shaped, dark, blistered skin rimmed in red. I carefully rewrapped it, and though I pretended to be wholly engrossed in securing the bandage, I couldn't stop taking him in: the raised tendons and soft braided blue veins at his wrist, the hollow above his collarbone, the moment when every hint of humor left his gray-blue eyes, swept away by a soft hunger that I felt echoing deep in my belly.

Reaching up, I brushed a curl of hair away from his forehead.

The brash, boyish Robert from a year ago would have cupped my cheek by now, drawn me into an irresistible kiss with utter confidence that I'd return the gesture. But this Robert didn't.

He's waiting. Giving you space, I realized. *He's scared.* And suddenly, nothing seemed more essential than being as close to him as possible.

I leaned in and kissed him, savoring his dry lips on mine, his strong jaw under my fingers, the little moan he tried and failed to hold back. Shivering, I fell into him, pouring everything I didn't have words for into our deepening kiss.

He cradled my head with both hands, fingers tangling in my hair, curling around the back of my neck.

I didn't give him time to lead. Light-headed with the taste of him, hungry at the sight of him half undressed, I pressed my palms against his chest, kissed the hollow of his neck, and leaned into him. I swam in the cyclone of my own thoughts.

Am I doing this right? How exactly do you advance things from one step to the next without being terribly, horribly awkward? But the way Robert was responding, stroking the small of my back, his breathing eager, and his eyes drinking in every detail of me told me I was doing something right.

We kicked the blankets aside, stretched out on the big bed, and pressed against each other like it was cold. I couldn't differentiate between the roar of blood in my head and the thunder outside. Robert's chest felt like the kind of shelter that could weather any storm. My ribs pressed against his with only the thin fabric of the ridiculous nightgown between us, and the delirium of that contact, the certainty that if I wrapped myself up in him enough, no one could separate us again, flooded me with warmth. The nightgown twisted and hitched as I hooked a bare leg around him.

He didn't stop me.

There was too much to keep track of. The heat, the choreography of how I'd imagined this should go, swallowing my awkwardness and projecting the confidence of someone who knew what they were doing, swamped by the dizziness of the momentum we were building together, how much I needed him to fill all the holes I couldn't shore up in myself, it all bowled me over.

I didn't even feel like myself when Robert ran his hand up my side and I reached down past his stomach. His breath caught as my fingers hooked on the bathrobe belt.

"Iris," he panted, voice full of pleading.

At first, I couldn't tell if he was asking me to stop or keep going.

But then he grabbed my wrist lightly. "We shouldn't."

"Why not?" I whispered. I wanted to, didn't I? He did too, there was no denying that.

"Because." He shifted back from me slowly, like I was a snake, and he was afraid of moving too fast. "You . . . haven't before. H-have you?"

Suddenly, I didn't feel like a woman Robert craved. I felt like a stupid child playing dress up. "And you have?" I asked quietly.

He didn't say anything for several long breaths. The tension between us warped into something awful. It made my chest ache.

"You have." I repeated.

"Please, don't be mad," he said.

"Zuse, Robert!" I shoved him away. "People only say that when they're about to tell you something guaranteed to piss you off. With who?" I gulped and swallowed twice before I could force the wretched name past my lips. "Vannevar?"

He winced. "It's not like you think."

Sick heat drowned all the life from my limbs. I remembered how devastated he'd looked when he'd seen her laying in the street. "Y-you said. You *said* you and her were never a thing."

"We weren't. I didn't even like her." He reached for my hand, and I snagged it away.

"But she was good enough to dock with, yeah? And I'm not." My voice broke.

"Just let me explain, okay?"

"What needs explaining? I don't think there's any way you can spin this that ends well for you." Rolling away, I sat up and hugged my arms, bare feet dangling over the bed while lightning burned an afterimage of the dormer window into the back of my eyes. *Stop crying. Just stop.*

"I didn't want to, Iris. She is . . ." Breath leaked out of him. "She *was* manipulative."

My face screwed up. I twisted to face him. All the sourness I'd been trying to shove down tasted like gunpowder smoke coming back up. "You let her go, didn't you? You left her cell unlatched."

"I didn't."

"I don't believe you."

He eased his bandaged arm back into the bathrobe, wrapping it tightly across his chest and snugging up the belt. When he looked up again, the hurt in his eyes dried every acidic word on my tongue.

"You don't have to believe me. I'm telling you because I don't want secrets between us, so just listen for one second, okay?"

I clenched my teeth and squeezed my eyes closed.

"You've seen my dad. What alcohol has done to my family. I hate the stuff. I've only been drunk a few times in my life. And one of them was with her," he croaked. "She just showed up uninvited, like always. Dad was pulling an all-nighter at the office. Mom had just had an episode and was sleeping. I wanted Vannevar to leave and she said she would if I mixed us a drink from the bottle of gin my dad kept on the top shelf of his bar. 'One drink,' she said. So, I poured." He took a thready breath. "She didn't leave, of course. She kept mixing us drinks until the bottle was empty. By the time I realized she'd been pouring mine way stronger than hers, we were already kissing. I was wasted, but I could have stopped it, could have pushed her away. I didn't. I just let her." His voice cracked. "It didn't feel real. More like watching a bad movie. I don't even remember most of it. I didn't want her to be my first, but I fragged up and just let it happen. And I regret it."

The bed shifted behind me, and I stiffened.

"Iris, I don't want your first time to be something you regret, okay?" He reached for my hand again and this time, I was too stunned to pull away.

"I like you. I want you. I do. But I want things to be right between us when it happens. And this feels . . . rushed." He offered me a hesitant, sheepish smile. "It feels ungentlemanly."

Something between a laugh and a sob barked out of me.

Robert tugged me toward him until our foreheads touched. "I can sleep on the floor, yeah?"

"Don't be stupid. It's not a romance movie." It felt like the furthest thing from it. *Vannevar.* Soldamnit. I wanted to puke.

"Don't hate me," he said.

I swallowed hard. "You didn't do anything wrong. There's nothing to hate. She used you." I couldn't say anything else, not without crying.

Robert curled against my back, breathing into my hair while I clasped his hand against my chest. We lay utterly still, like we could stall time if we didn't move, but my mind never stopped.

He opened up to you, an earnest voice elbowed its way through the ugly thoughts swelling in my mind. *You should do the same.* He'd laid himself bare, told me something I could have shunned him for. But try as I might, I couldn't bring myself to do the same, couldn't string together the right words to tell him I was the one who'd destroyed our city and turned my uncle and his URLs against us. The sour jealousy in my stomach, aimed at a girl who wasn't even alive anymore, burned everything else away.

THE STORM DIDN'T LET up until evening. We packed up and paid Arlene and Marty for their generous hospitality with several pouches of black tea, an assortment of rare heritage seeds, and the last of Vinton's copper. Arlene stuffed Robert's jacket with wax packets of eucalyptus leaves. The dogs snuffled our feet and leaned into us for back scratches.

"You seem like good kids." Marty tugged at his moustache nervously. "I don't mean to butt into your business, but how about you all head back north? You've had your little adventure—I know young ones need that from time to time. No shame in going back home, though. None at all. Tell your friends you made it all the way to the wall. They won't know any different. Fernie's nothing but a slave town. Nothing but death and coal dust. You don't need to see that."

My throat dried out.

"Thank you, sir." Vinton nodded shortly. "I assure you we'll be heading home just as soon as we can."

I knew it was my ragged nerves, but I felt like crying as we rode up Arlene and Marty's drive, their house shrinking behind us. I'd probably never see them again. *Why in Sol's name does that matter? You don't even know them.*

We headed south. Fortunately, the storm had either snuffed out last night's fire or changed the prevailing wind enough to clear the worst of the smoke from our route. It was still slow going because what was left of the road was greasy with a slurry of rain and ash, and the night was overcast and pitch black.

With nothing visual to distract me, my mind replayed the same images in a loop: Robert beside me on the couch, clutching my hand, his breath coming in gulps. And later, in the bed, his hand stroking my thigh, how he'd held me like he wanted to savor me and devour me at the same time, my name on his lips like a plea. Had he held her like that? Whispered her name into her hair?

Stop it. He could have kept it secret, and he didn't. He's trying to build something honest with you, part of my mind assured, but another insidious voice countered it. *No, he's treating you like a child, someone he has to hold back with, someone too impulsive to make her own choices without regretting them later. We're the same Soldamned age.* Sixteen years old. Legally considered adults by our society. Robert was old enough to barter himself off to a slave company as collateral and no one batted an eye, but I wasn't mature enough to dock with? I couldn't let it go. I couldn't stop thinking about his lips on my neck. The last stretch of road to Fernie seemed never ending.

We stopped often so that Mark could navigate Vinton's bike through the trickier portions. At one point, we lost the road completely and had to stop in the middle of a clearing to consult our hand-drawn map.

"We're close." My brother frowned at the paper smoothed over his gas tank, speaking around the penlight in his mouth. "And we're not stopping after this, so take a piss if you need one."

Mark dismounted, approached Vinton's bike, and unhooked the folding chair from his rear bike rack. "You too."

"Fine." My brother leaned down and jerked the Velcro straps around his calves free. He let Mark help him into his chair.

The motorcycles ticked as their engines cooled. I picked my way through the bushes to relieve myself. When I broke back into the clearing, I saw Vinton, still in his chair, beckoning Robert.

"Come here for a sec, will ya?" My brother was a black silhouette backlit by headlights. "Mark's still taking a shit. You wanna give me a hand here?" He pointed at his wheel. "Is something hung up in the spokes? It keeps jamming."

My stomach twitched. *Vinton doesn't ask for help. Not from anyone but Mark.*

I lunged toward them.

Robert leaned down.

Vinton torqued into a swift uppercut that cracked Robert's head sideways, sending him crashing to his hands and knees.

"Vinton!" I screamed, but he ignored me, bending over Robert and yelling in his ear.

"That was for lying, for neglecting to mention a condition you knew could frag up this entire run, *and* for having the balls to think you could shack up with my sister under my watch and get away with it. You *ever* put my team in danger again, you ever *touch* my sister, I'll leave you dead at the bottom of a ravine for the crows to pick clean. You understand?"

Robert nodded, clutching his cheek and rocking back and forth.

I closed the distance between us as my brother wheeled away. "What the frag?" I bellowed before sagging to my knees. "Are you okay?" I put my hand on his back, but he shrugged it off.

"I'm sorry. He's such an ass." I glared at Vinton's back and projected the next bit loud enough for him to hear. "He thinks he can get away with it because he's in a chair."

Vinton flipped me the bird without turning around.

Mark trotted into the clearing still doing up his pants. "What happened? Ah Zuse, he finally clocked him, didn't he?"

"You knew it was coming?" I yelled.

"You didn't? Come on. You volunteer to share a room with Pretty Boy and don't expect your brother to army crawl up those stairs to defend your honor? I practically had him in a headlock the whole time we were out on that front porch just so you two could have some privacy."

"I'll kill him," I spat.

"Iris," Robert puffed. "Leave it."

CHAPTER
TEN

e didn't see Fernie as we closed in on it because it was late into the night, but we smelled it. An overwhelming stench of rot hung in the air, sending my mind immediately back to the muddy night in Robert's back yard when I'd opened the food bin and was hit by the reek of spoiled food. My stomach twitched at the reflection of far too many sets of green eyes tracking us from the ditches. Coyotes dipped their heads and perked their ears before skulking away from the clamor of the motorcycles.

And then we rolled up to it, a formidable fortress wall slicing across the overgrown road. Snaking far to our left and right, it was a towering mosaic of rusted school buses, old combine tractors, welded panels, and stacked metal drums. Corrugated steel granaries stood at attention like watchtowers in increments.

As moonlight oozed between the inky clouds above, we pulled out flashlights and scanned the barricade for a door. I caught movement to my left, a fox trotting along the base of the fortification not twenty feet from us. When it stopped and nonchalantly glanced back, I saw it was gripping something in its slender jaws.

A hand.

A decomposing hand. Gray with milky fingernails and a gnawed off pinky.

"Robert." I gulped and pointed.

"Mother of Sol." Mark tilted his light up, gaping at the top of the wall far above.

It was ringed with razor wire and stout wooden pikes. Impaled atop almost every one was a human body. Some spikes held multiple corpses sandwiched against each other. The bodies displayed varying states of decay from freshly bloated to bleached ribcages and spines. A great horned owl coasted silently through the watery beam of Mark's light to land on a corpse's white belly.

I had no idea what I'd expected of the mining town, but this wasn't it. Exhaling several bile-tinged breaths, I blurted, "We should go back."

Robert shifted behind Mark, his voice tight. "I don't think these types of people forgive reneging a deal."

"Frag that. Let's go," Mark said.

The clack-clack-clack of chain winches snapped through the night air. A city bus with faded street signs tacked over its windows rolled backwards alongside the wall exposing a narrow passage.

"Too late." Vinton sighed, gripping his revolver across his lap. He cranked his handlebars, and his headlight swept toward the opening. "Here comes the welcome wagon."

I caught a brief glance of trench coats and rifles before a lighthouse lens blazed to life from the wall, swiveling to catch us in its beam.

"Lay down arms!" A man's voice snapped.

My brother tucked his gun into his thigh holster. Mark showed his palms and Robert did the same. I toed my crossbow further into the footwell of the sidecar, out of sight.

"State your names and business."

"I think you know already." Vinton squinted and pushed his helmet up onto his forehead. "Or you wouldn't have opened your doors."

"Names and business."

Robert dismounted and stepped further into the light, shading his face with one hand. "My name's Robert Lycos. I'm the delegate from Painted Bluff. I've been corresponding with Mr. Clowes. He's expecting us."

"He was expecting you a day ago."

"We can raincheck if it's inconvenient." My brother's voice was too sharp. I recognized it as the kind of prickly tired he got before he crashed. *Zuse, not now, Vinton.*

"The delay was my fault." Robert cut in smoothly. "I'd like the opportunity to apologize to Mr. Clowes in person."

One of the wall sentries snorted. "Well, he's already retired for the evening. He restricts business transactions to daylight hours and won't be receiving guests until morning. If you surrender your weapons and vehicles peaceably, you can spend the night in a holding house—"

"Not happening," Vinton snapped. "Not the motorcycles."

"Then I suppose you'll be waiting with the corpses and coyote shit."

"Now, let's be reasonable, Jordan." A new voice cut in. "First off, how 'bout we quit shining the spotlight in their faces."

The blistering light at the top of the wall dimmed as someone partially shuttered its concentrator lens.

A horse clopped through the gap in the wall, trotted past the edgy sentries, and then high stepped in place, mouthing its bit. "Evening!" its rider called in a sunny voice, before dismounting and pulling the reins over the animal's head.

"Frag me, a cowboy," Mark whispered under his breath. "What's next?"

The man strode toward Robert with his hand out and his horse following behind him. "Ben Breyman, Mr. Clowes's liaison. I believe we've communicated via p-mail a few times. Pleasure to meet you face-to-face, sir." A frown creased his brow as he noticed Robert's swollen eye. "Difficulties on your way down?"

"A few bumps in the road. Nothing we couldn't handle." Robert took his hand and shook it firmly. "We're here now, as arranged."

"Happy to have you." The cowboy's bright smile returned.

I gaped at him. He was our age, tall and beautiful. There was no other way to describe it. Clad in a leather jacket, snug jeans, and an honest-to-Sol cowboy hat, this was a person who turned heads. Even in the washed-out glow of the headlights, his eyes were a startling blue, like a mountain bluebird against a grayed-out sky. Tanned skin and dirty blonde hair only accentuated the color. I wasn't the only one who noticed.

Mark stammered through his introduction next and stared awkwardly afterward.

"Ma'am." Ben turned to me.

I found myself unable to speak at all as he grasped my hand and flashed me an effervescent smile. *Soldamnit, this one looks like he stepped off the cover of one of Oupa's romance novels, only not so cheesy.*

"I'm sure you're all exhausted." He held out his hand to my brother last and Vinton shook it stiffly. "Mr. Clowes has set aside rooms in the estate for you. His train is on standby for an early morning departure, and my crew and I will be accompanying your team to help transport and secure the generator."

"The train. Yeah, I've heard about it." Vinton spoke slowly.

Ben Breyman beamed. "A 1925 Baldwin Locomotive Works built Consolidation 2-8-0. Last of its kind 'round these parts."

"Quick question about that. Why exactly did your boss make me beat up my bikes and waste my fuel if he had an easy ride up the rails available?"

The cowboy's eyes lingered on Vinton's motorcycle. "You've

done an impeccable job maintaining your machines. I'm sure you can appreciate how labor intensive it is to preserve a complex rig that's far past its prime. I'll be honest with you, steam locomotives are money pits, so Mr. Clowes limits our engine's use to major cargo hauls, like your industrial generator."

Or slave runs. That was the part he didn't say out loud.

"I'm entirely at your disposal now, though," Ben said. "Whatever you need—"

"Just the train ride, thanks. I don't need Clowes's yes-man holding my dick whenever I want to piss."

"Vinton," I hissed.

Robert coughed.

Ben Breyman smiled wider and tipped his hat at my seething brother. "Good to hear, sir. Dick holding isn't exactly my specialty. Rest assured; I could find someone willing if you change your mind though."

Mark turned red as a beet.

Vinton growled "Don't call me, sir!"

Ben turned back to me. "Hey, is that a Vixen?"

I glanced at the crossbow in the footwell. He must have seen it when we shook hands. *Sharp eyes.* "It is," I said.

"My daddy had one when I was little. Let me shoot it a few times before the string snapped. We never could find a proper replacement. Good bow. Draws like butter, doesn't it?"

Ah shit, he's going to take it.

Sure enough, he said, "Sorry to say that Mr. Clowes does enforce a strict no-weapon policy within his walls, but I promise you, my men will take the utmost care of that bow during your stay. Same goes for all your weapons. If you'd be so good as to let Mr. Jordan here have a look through your bags, we can be on our way."

"The motorcycles stay with us." Vinton demanded.

"Of course. Shall we?" Ben flipped the reins over his horse's ears and grunted as he vaulted back into his saddle and headed toward the wall.

WE IDLED the bikes through Fernie behind Ben on his horse. When Vinton asked him if we could pick up the pace, he apologized and said, "Smokey here would ruin himself if I let him canter on pavement."

"Smokey," Mark mumbled under his breath. "The damned horse is named Smokey. This guy's right out of an old western."

In the hazy dark, the streets on either side of us were colorless, like travelling through a black and white photograph. Water pooled in ruts on the road and the smell of sulfur permeated the air. Coal dust clung to every surface, souring the air with the taste of burning matches, smearing windows until the lamplight within looked grimy and weak.

As we closed on the mine and the railyard, rows of low-slung clapboard tenement housing with tar-patched roofs and deep eaves squatted behind twenty-foot-high fencing. Stout logs and rows of razor wire separated the slave quarter from the rest of the town. Spiderwebs of clotheslines were draped heavily with threadbare pale overalls and jackets. Skinny cats darted under front porches.

Oil lanterns hung on makeshift poles. Women in faded blue dresses swept black dust from doorsteps, scrubbed laundry, and scolded children in patched jumpers. Men grilled food and baked bread over makeshift barrel stoves. Everyone who was awake paused to gape at the motorcycles as we cruised by.

Outside the slave compound, the homes on the other side of the street had been lavishly restored, scrubbed, and painted. The windows were all dark, as if Fernie's paid company men deemed themselves too superior to share waking hours with the slaves their CEO owned.

We rode on, closing in on the center of town. The yards got bigger and the houses cleaner.

A church bell tower with a metal-clad roof glowed in the weak moonlight. When we navigated closer, I noticed that its pinnacle had been fitted with a post and a long crossbar with pivoting arms at its end. Lines of cables ran down from the apparatus. It looked like a cross between a windmill and a marionette. A signaling device?

Across the street, cordoned off from the rows of tidy bungalows around it by a stone parapet wall topped with wrought iron, the manager's estate was a world unto itself.

It occupied an entire city block, surrounded by spans of impeccably manicured green and flanked by rows of towering, ancient trees. Centered by two generous converging drives stood the closest thing to a castle I'd ever seen.

We pulled up to a stately four-story brick facade, ribbed with sandstone and capped by a sharp-pitched pyramid roof—complete with a delicate pointed tower of its own. Numerous chimneys sprouted like tin mushrooms. Below them, narrow dormers with stained glass windows jutted from the slate shingles. Green patina cornice with squares that looked like teeth trimmed the roofline. A massive foyer jutted proudly toward us, topped by a bright cloth awning and a stone crest I didn't recognize. Dozens of lanterns bathed the front entry in warm light. Lacquered oak double doors polished to honey gold greeted us, along with a row of women and men in starched blue dresses and overalls. More slaves.

Ben scanned their faces as if he were looking for someone before clearing his throat and saying, "The staff will take you from here. There's a carriage house 'round back for your machines." He tipped his hat. "I'll be seeing you all in the morning."

I'D NEVER SEEN anything like the interior of the Clowes's estate, but my mind was stretched too thin to appreciate any of it. Details mashed together: stained glass windows with stripes as green as new leaves intersecting delicate circles that looked like telescope lenses, mosaic tiles made up of thousands of tidy squares in contrasting black and white designs, warm brass railings and cool slate stairs worn from thousands of feet. *How old was this place?*

A man in faded blue pointed Mark and Vinton toward an office on the main floor whose double doors were wide enough to allow wheelchair access. "It's not the guest suite, sirs, but every comfort has been provided," he said.

His compatriot, a woman, directed Robert and I toward a stairwell. I numbly moved toward it, but my brother snatched my wrist.

"No. Not a chance. You're coming with us this time," he said flatly.

"Frag off." I wrenched out of his grip and lunged toward the stairs. "It's none of your damned business where I sleep."

I was already halfway up the steps when I heard Robert say, "I'll talk to her."

"You damned well won't!" Vinton barked.

"Leave it." Mark's low voice cut in.

On the first-floor landing, I paced until Robert and the woman in the blue dress caught up. My cheeks burned as we continued up another flight of stairs to a ridiculously huge bedroom. The woman paused at the door, squinted, and surveyed our ash-smudged clothes for several awkward moments before nodding curtly and saying, "Master Clowes will be expecting you at breakfast an hour after sunrise." She closed the door behind us.

CHAPTER
ELEVEN

Robert crossed the room and crumpled against a cherrywood chest of drawers with an oval vanity mirror. He tugged at the collar of his T-shirt and exhaled several shaky breaths.

I couldn't move, couldn't speak without spitting fire. Instead, my gaze raked the room, and I stuffed my overwhelmed head full of its fine points. An ornate cast-iron fireplace with a marble tile surround yawned in the wall opposite me. Beneath my feet, a faded tapestry rug swam with red sunflowers, white daisies, and purple crocuses. Walnut-stained wood paneling with thick baseboards and chair rails anchored the room and complemented the mint paint.

The bed was a floral monster. I'd never seen one so huge. It looked large enough to sleep an entire family, and its ivory coverlet with embroidered roses had been tucked with enough severity that I was sure whoever made it had anger issues. The floor looked more inviting to sleep on.

"You're not staying," Robert said so quietly I almost didn't hear him.

"*I* choose where I sleep," I retorted.

He straightened and looked at me through the mirror, bruised eye slitted and puffy. "I meant you're not staying here in Fernie. You're leaving with your brother in the morning."

"Oh yeah?"

"It's the safest option."

Heat boiled up my stomach, coating my throat and souring my words. "Is it now?"

"Vinton and Mark will back me on this."

"Of course, they will!" I shouted. "You let them believe you fragged me. Vinton'd crawl over glass to keep me from you." My stomach ached. "I'm *not* leaving."

"We're stronger than you. If it comes to it, we can load you onto that train by force." His head dropped. "I don't want it to come to that."

"I'll jump off the damned train," I spat.

He shoved away from the vanity and turned toward me. "Iris, please—"

"Don't *Iris, please* me!" I barked. "I am *not* leaving you here alone with slavers!"

"And I'm not losing you again!" he bellowed, closing the distance between us and pressing his hands on either side of my face.

I snorted and tried to pull away, but he held firm.

When he spoke, his voice was so raw it made my throat close. "Soldamnit. I didn't want you to come. I didn't want you in danger. You have *no* idea what it was like after you disappeared. I thought you were . . ." He looked away, neck muscles cording even as his thumb stroked the old scars on my cheek. "I thought you were dead. Out in the woods. Somewhere alone."

Tears burned my eyes.

"I can't lose you again, okay?" He pressed his forehead to mine, breath ragged. "I don't have anyone else left, Iris. My Dad, he's not . . . I just can't. Please, tell me you'll go home. I'll be back soon. Just a few days. As soon as they get the generator here. This has a happy ending. We just have to wait for it a bit, okay?"

I closed my eyes and took a deep inhale through my nose. "It's not a happy ending if I don't get to choose."

Robert's hands shook as they slid from my cheeks. His head tipped back, and he blinked at the ceiling.

He's shutting down. I swallowed but continued anyway. He needed to hear this. "It's not fair to tell me you can't lose me, but in the same breath tell me to walk away and leave you behind in a place that skewers people they don't like. It's not fair to make my choices for me behind my back." I reached for him, tracing my fingers over the brow of his bruised eye. *Bring him back.*

He shuddered under my touch. "Those people on that wall, left for the scavengers to pick apart. I never should have made this deal. I just want to protect you."

"I know," I whispered and closed the distance between us. I stroked his collarbone and then the back of his neck until his breath hitched and goosebumps rose on his skin. "I don't want your protection, Robert. I just want you."

He leaned into me and kissed me hard, like I was the only air in the room, and he was drowning without me, like he could convince me with his tongue instead of his words. The urgency of it took my breath away. He tasted like sweat and ash and desperation. Everything in me rose to the occasion, anger distilling into desire, fear shifting into compulsion, each scattered thought whipping into alignment.

And then Robert cut the connection, pulling away while we were both still panting. He smoothed my hair back and kissed my forehead. "I want you too, but . . ." His voice broke and he tried again. "I'm scared to death of the mess I've steered us into, and I don't want you in it."

"If our roles were reversed, you wouldn't leave me here."

"And you wouldn't let me stay," he rasped. "So, what do we do?"

"Nothing. Leave tomorrow for tomorrow."

"I don't know how to do that."

"I do." I put my head on his chest, and he wrapped his arms around me cautiously. "Stay here with me." His heartbeat whooshed in my ear. "Tomorrow doesn't exist. Don't think about it. There's just right here and right now. Just us."

"It's not that simple."

"Yes, it is."

"Your brother—"

"Is not my keeper. And there's a lock on the door." I turned from him and twisted the bolt home.

He didn't stop me.

"Is this you trying to coerce me into letting you stay?" His voice was soft, insecure, utterly unlike the front he put on for the rest of the world.

"No, Robert. It's not." Maybe it had started that way, but that wasn't what this was now. I needed him. Despite my anger, I knew he was right about one thing. He, Vinton, and Mark were stronger than me. Johan wasn't here to plea my case or exert his clout as a co-founder. If Robert and my brother chose to force me onto the train home tomorrow morning, I wouldn't be able to stop them. What if it all went wrong after that? What if tonight was the last night we had together? I needed him. Simple as that.

I kissed his bruised eyelid, his cheekbone, the warm hollow where his jawline swept up to his ear. I took in the smell of eucalyptus. Beneath it, Robert smelled like himself, a heady mix of safety and subtle strength that threaded through my nerves and feathered up my spine.

Last night, I'd rushed things, dove headlong into him like our desire was a cliff to leap off, unaware that Vannevar had pushed him the same way. I wasn't her. And I couldn't handle taking this further if it meant Robert rejecting me again, no matter how gently he let me down. "Tell me to stop," I whispered into his ear, "and I will."

"Don't stop." His fingers traced my jaw, thumb brushing across my lower lip.

When I found his mouth, he opened up to me, his tongue slipping past my teeth and his exhalation, a soft growl. I remembered our first kiss, how young we'd been. I'd been worried that I might taste like what I'd eaten for lunch. How achingly awkward and innocent it had all been. This didn't feel innocent. It felt like we were emptying and filling each other at the same time. It felt like a current looping between us, magnetic and crackling.

Robert's fingers brushed past the hollow between my collar bones, tracing a soft line between my breasts. I gasped and we broke apart. "I can stop too, if it's too much," he murmured. "It's okay to change your mind."

"It's not too much." I tugged at his T-shirt until he peeled it off over his head. I lost myself in the contrast between hard muscle, soft skin, and coarse curls of hair. I could do this. I could slow time down until it stopped. I could take a moment that was just mine. Leading him to the bed, I said, "Tell me how we're supposed to be, Robert."

"Like in old romance movies?" His eyes crinkled and a boyish smile lit his face as he sat facing me on the mattress.

Sol, I love that smile.

"We're halfway there. I'm already shirtless and devastatingly muscular," he said.

"Devastatingly, yes." I ran my hand down his uninjured arm and smiled when he flexed his bicep.

"You let your hair down." He frowned with quiet concentration, gently unknotting my hair ties, undoing my braids, and combing his fingers through them.

"You tip my chin up and kiss me softly."

He tilted my head to meet his before brushing his lips against mine. "Like that?"

"Mmm, yes." I leaned back from him. "You watch me undo my shirt. You've always wanted to watch me undress."

He swallowed hard. "Guilty."

I unbuttoned my shirt but didn't take it off. Shifting to my knees, I straddled his legs, pulling his hands to my hips. "You want me on your lap, but you're too gentlemanly to put me there."

"Oh Sol, I want you," he groaned, pulling me against him and kissing me harder. Stubble raked across my lips while his hands slid up the back of my shirt and pressed against the small of my back.

"You need me." I moaned and rocked against him, heat gathering in my core.

"More than anything," he panted.

My shirt slipped off my shoulder and he kissed the scars there.

I guided his hand to my chest, over my thin shelf bra.

His kisses grew desperate, teeth nipping my bottom lip as he pressed against me, guiding me back until I was lying in the big bed with him braced over me. "This is where the old romance movies fade to black."

"Frag the old romance movies." I reached past his stomach and undid the button on his pants.

"Wait." He rested his forehead against mine and took a deep, steadying breath.

"Stop?"

"No, I-I don't have any protection."

"There's more than one way to love." I stroked him and he shivered. "I'm sure we'll figure something out together."

We figured out several ways. We explored each other with tempered eagerness, me wary of Robert's bruised eye and burned arm, him considerate and tender as we navigated my first time experiencing any of this with a partner. It felt strange and deeply familiar at the same time, urgent yet relaxed, awkward but full of moments of quiet grace. Serious and silly in turns. It felt like home. He felt like home.

And for a glorious moment, there was no tomorrow.

CHAPTER
TWELVE

At some time after dawn, a brisk knock sounded on the bedroom door. We tentatively opened it and found several sets of formal clothes hanging on the doorknob. A jug of steaming water and several hygiene items were lined up neatly on a tray on the floor. I found an obscenely huge bathroom at the end of the hallway while Robert cleaned up, shaved, and dressed. When I returned, I had to bite down the urge to stroke his clean-shaven jaw and smooth my hands over the pressed perfection of his dress shirt.

This was the Robert I'd fallen for a year ago, clean-cut and comfortable in expensive clothes. City Robert.

I couldn't reconcile it with the impressions of last night still fresh in my mind: bare skin, rough mouth, strong hands. *Sol,* how I'd prayed morning wouldn't come, but it had.

Neither of us spoke about whether I was leaving or not. It was easier to cling to the intimacy we'd nurtured last night, pretending we were a comfortable couple meandering through our morning routine.

We dabbed fresh toothbrushes into mint powder and brushed our teeth side by side. Robert combed my damp hair, and I re-braided it. I wrinkled my nose at the prim dress that had been left for me, a stiff, high-cut ivory gown with lace trim and a zipper up the back that I wouldn't have a chance of getting into or out of by myself. It came with a selection of stockings and several sizes of shoes and satin gloves. *Who dresses like this for breakfast? And who on earth gauged my dress size last night?* Then, I remembered the woman in the blue dress giving us both the once over before she left.

Ben Breyman escorted us from our room at precisely one hour after dawn, his easy affability at odds with his starched formal surroundings. As he led us to the dining room, I swallowed the stress building in my throat and asked, "What does Clowes want with our generator anyway?" It had been niggling at me. "He'd have to line the pockets of his competitors just to access enough diesel to run it, wouldn't he?"

"No, ma'am. Coal mines leak natural gas, even once they're used up and abandoned. Mr. Clowes is capturing the methane, compressing it into a few pressurized railcars, and piping it up to his house. He's going to convert your generator to run on natural gas. House is still wired for electricity, and he's scooped up antique electrical devices for ages. He's dying to plug in every gadget he's got and show them all off at dinner parties." Ben smiled but there was something hard behind the boyish grin, something forced.

I swallowed thick disgust, remembering the empty air-conditioned boardrooms and the Shareholders lavish houses. Our rich had wasted power too. I shouldn't be surprised.

"Here we are." He stopped at a set of double oak doors and knocked gently. That's when I noticed that Ben Breyman was wearing a shoulder holster and a revolver tucked against his ribs.

"Come." A sharp voice ordered from within.

The cowboy ushered us into a brightly lit dining room. The table had been set with a ridiculous assortment of fresh fruit platters, corn cakes, sliced cheese, boiled eggs, and plump sausage links.

A man and three women in formal wear were seated at one end of the table. Flanking them, a row of slaves in blue uniforms stood at attention. The man, noticeably shorter than his table-mates, wore a waxed moustache and a business shirt done up so tightly, it pinched his neck. His gaze pinned to us as we walked in.

"Mr. Clowes?" Robert stepped toward him, hand outstretched. "Pleasure to meet you, sir. I—"

"Ah, look. What a precious little pet." One of the women in an asymmetrical dress draped in reams of bright green fabric interrupted. "Amelia, I told you the gown would suit."

"It would if she put her hair up properly." Another woman with severe makeup tapped her lacquered nails on the table.

The curly haired woman between them, Amelia, I assumed, answered, "Your girl didn't send any powder up this morning? Those scars need covering. Pity. She's got good skin otherwise."

I felt like a doll on display. One who'd been dragged through the mud. My cheeks reddened and I fought to keep my gaze level.

"Mr. Clowes," Robert said again, voice tighter. "It is Mr. Clowes, isn't it?"

"Darwin Clowes." He undid his pearl cufflink and rolled up his sleeve before clasping Robert's hand brusquely. "And you must be Paul Lycos's boy. We knew each other from college, you know. I beat the pants off of him in golf on several occasions. Sit." He beckoned to the empty end of the table.

"Where's Vinton and Mark?" My voice wobbled.

Ben Breyman stood behind us at the double door with his hands clasped behind his back.

No one answered me.

Robert cleared his throat. "Perhaps we got off on the wrong foot? I'd like to apologize. It's been a long trip."

"It *has* been a long trip." Darwin Clowes bristled. "An entire day too long, by my count. And I don't take kindly to dealing with people who can't meet deadlines, Mr. Lycos." He stabbed two sausages off a platter and scraped them onto his plate. "This is a poor start to our business relations."

Robert clenched his jaw before answering, "Just a few bumps along the way, sir. We're here now."

"Took a few bumps yourself, I see." He tapped his cheek and then pointed at Robert's bandaged arm with his fork. "Tell me, Mr. Lycos, have your *delivery* people treated you amicably? Nothing worse than unruly help."

My hands felt clammy in their dainty gloves. "Where's my brother?" I said, louder this time.

"Ben?" Clowes raised his eyebrows at the cowboy.

"He said he felt under the weather when I visited him this morning, ma'am." Ben flashed a reassuring smile. "He and his partner will join us for lunch, I'm sure. You both must be famished. Please, have a seat."

My neck prickled. Vinton would never admit to being ill— certainly not to a stranger. *They're lying. Why are they lying?*

"Ah, I almost forgot." Darwin Clowes snapped his fingers at one of the slaves. "Tell him they've arrived? He's been *so* eager to reunite." He nodded at Robert before producing a handker- chief and dabbing at his forehead.

The girl Clowes had addressed bustled into the hallway and when the double door opened next, a man stepped into the dining room.

My lungs froze and my mouth dried out when I saw him.

It was David Kahn.

Sweat prickled in my armpits and adrenaline flushed through me. My hands jerked, but my feet anchored in place.

Ben Breyman closed the double doors and the sound of a lock clicked.

"Citizen Robert." Kahn took his glasses off, pulled a neatly folded pocket square from his suit jacket, and started polishing the lenses. "You've been the subject of our dinner conversation for the last two nights running, and, I must say, it has not been a promising performance review thus far."

The three women tittered, bending their heads towards each other.

"S-sir," Robert immediately relapsed into his placating middle manager voice, and I shuddered. "How—"

"How is my gray matter still intact in my skull instead of painting the side of a hill outside *my* compromised city?" Kahn's hands shook as he slid his glasses back into place, but he pinned Robert with the steady gaze of a predator who'd already disabled its prey. "My boy, I've been in business since before the end of the world. I secured a network of connections before you were even born. Did you honestly think you could play me? How delightfully naïve."

"I wasn't playing you."

Kahn squinted. "I believe your words were something along the lines of 'I convince him we're going to let him go free and he spills the information I need.'"

Robert stiffened.

Oh Sol, he'd said that at the meeting, when Reynold was accusing him of abetting Kahn's escape. Thoughts clacked in my mind like switches at a railway junction until everything funneled together into one thundering conclusion.

"You had an informant?" I didn't realize I'd spoken out loud until Kahn's cutting gaze swung my way; the man who'd tried to hunt me down, the only person who knew I was the culprit behind the virus that had crashed our city. Blood rushed between my ears loudly enough that his next words sounded muffled.

"You can buy anything if you have enough wealth. Even people. Thought you could burn it all down so easily?" His lips twitched into a smile. "I've got several heads, Iris. And the one you chopped off with your little stunt was dying anyway. The city was stagnating. I would thank you for burning off the chaff and pushing me toward a much-needed restructure, but I'm not in the habit of commending traitors."

"What stunt? What's he talking about?" Robert's gaze flicked to me, but I couldn't answer him. Words dried in my throat.

"Ah, she hasn't seen fit to inform you then? How interesting. You see, when she abandoned you, she sided with the URL group to the west. Even so, I would have brought her back into the fold, even after she stole from me."

"You're a liar. I didn't steal," I choked.

"I don't think you're in a position to accuse. You led me to believe you'd been kidnapped. You sent your wristband and a ransom note on a thumbnail drive. A lie, impregnated with a virus that wiped out our network and started a needless civil war." Kahn's cold eyes turned back to Robert and his voice lowered. "The whole situation must have been quite distressing for Paul, especially on the heels of your mother's unexpected death. I never got a chance to ask you during our prison visits, how is your father holding up?"

"Do *not* bring them into this." Robert's voice was a stripped wire.

"Why not? They're a part of it. I'm simply highlighting the dangers of siding with someone who cannot perceive the consequences of her actions." Kahn nodded toward me. "This one is *bad business*."

Robert licked his lips. "What's he talking about, Iris?"

My mind short-circuited. My lips trembled, but I couldn't speak.

The woman in green leaned toward Amelia and said, "Darwin was right, this is positively juicy."

"Come now, boy," Kahn admonished. "You've always been a rational thinker, no? And there's no plausible reason why I would have crashed my own network. I was winning. *My* Shareholders were holding the city. Why would I shoot myself in the foot? She was a Trojan horse."

Robert clenched his jaw and shook his head. "You're lying. Iris, tell me he's lying."

"She won't," Kahn said.

"Shut up!" Robert roared.

I flinched.

The women yelped.

Darwin Clowes's chair scraped as he stood and drew himself up to his full, unimpressive height. "Watch your tone, sir."

"Iris," Robert pleaded under his breath. "Just tell me he's lying."

Before I could speak, Kahn set his pocket square onto the table, smoothed it down, and set something on it.

A silicone wristband.

My wristband. The one that had deactivated and blacklisted my name as soon as Kahn sent his men after me for stealing fertilizer, a crime Vannevar had framed me for.

"See for yourself." Kahn motioned to Robert, pressing a thumbnail drive onto the table beside the bracelet. "It's hers. How would it come into my possession if she didn't send it to me? She was still wearing it when she left. Ask her if you doubt me."

Robert picked up the bracelet, flipped it inside out, and ran his thumb over the imprinted name on the interior.

Iris Ecosia

His shoulders dropped.

My vision whitewashed.

"Iris?" he whispered.

"It wasn't supposed to take down the whole network, just the cred programming," I blurted.

"Oh, Sol." He put a hand over his mouth for several breaths before swallowing. "People died. *A lot* of people, Iris."

"I know. I'm sorry."

"You're sorry? That's it?" His voice cracked. "You came home and lied through your teeth for weeks. To me. To your own family. People died. And you're sorry?"

I couldn't handle the hardness in his voice, Kahn's ruthless eyes on me, the whole room full of impassive strangers witnessing my humiliation and fear. Something was fragmenting in my chest, melting my insides to glue.

"You aligned with her, Robert." Kahn's words were gentle, incongruent with his sharp features and tight mouth. "You attempted to exploit me to your advantage and push a backdoor contract on my affiliate. Then you made a run on my assets. I'm a majority stockholder in Coaltana. Did you know that? I allow Mr. Clowes here a certain amount of autonomy to run the place, but he's in this position by my grace, isn't that right, Darwin?"

Clowes coughed and smiled uncertainly. "I've always considered it more of a mutually beneficial partnership."

Kahn's shrewd gaze raked the lavish dining room. "Benefits you've squandered on needless extravagance," he said bitterly before turning back to Robert. "And you were put in the position of Search Engine by my grace as well. I took care of you and your family. You grew up wanting for nothing. Yet, you chose to side with my enemies, foment a civil war, and *still* have the gall to assume afterward that I would point you toward one of my nest eggs so you could raise the wreckage of *my* city against me with *her*?" He raised a long finger toward me.

"Wanted for nothing?" Robert hissed. "You worked my mother to *death*."

"Moira was a feckless woman who never worked an honest day in her life."

Robert lunged, grabbing Kahn's shirtfront.

Ben Breyman was across the room, gun drawn and pressed against Robert's temple, before I could process it.

The trio of women at the table squealed.

Robert yelled, "Don't you say her name. *Never* say her name!"

"Hands off," Ben barked. "I'll ask you once."

"It's quite alright." Kahn's voice was maddeningly unshakable. He shrugged out of Robert's grip with a sharp jerk. "I wanted to confirm his sensibility—or lack of it—and I have. Darwin, tell your man to stand down."

"Ben, enough," Clowes snapped. "You're upsetting the women."

"Yes, sir." The cowboy backed up but didn't holster his weapon. His gaze flicked to the row of unnerved servants and then the women at the table. "Apologies, ma'ams."

Kahn smoothed down his jacket and straightened his glasses. "I sheltered you from the savagery of the world beyond your doors, and I see now what a mistake it was. You're all children. The lot of you. But out here, business is war, Citizen Robert, and I cannot coddle adolescents, or abide backstabbers. Nor can I leave them unpunished. So, listen to me very carefully." Kahn leaned close enough that his lips brushed Robert's ear.

I strained to hear his words over my own heartbeat smashing through my skull.

"Your contract with Mr. Clowes is reneged. He has already sent your deliverers on their way with a contingent of armed men and miners, *not* in exchange for a generator, but because I ordered him to. If my city is to be razed, it'll be done on my terms."

Vinton and Mark. Oh Sol. They're gone. It's just Robert and me.

"And my terms are you are no longer Mr. Clowes's *goodwill delegate.* You're my property. I compensated Darwin handsomely for your purchase. You can buy anything if you have enough wealth. Even people."

Oh, Sol. I tried to breathe, but only a choking noise came out. My mind toppled like a house of cards.

"I'm a fair man, and I'm in need of a personal aide. It's a better position than you deserve, all things considered."

"Eat shit," Robert rasped.

"There are ladies present!" Darwin Clowes snapped. "You will keep a civil tongue in your head, or I'll have it removed."

"I can control my own chattel, thank you very much, Darwin." Kahn straightened and smiled coldly. "You'll do everything I say, Robert. Do you know why?" He glanced at me pointedly. "I've purchased her as well."

"No," Robert wheezed.

A whimpering noise bled past my lips.

"I'm going to stick her in a hole in the ground so deep, she'll never see daylight again. And if you don't obey my orders precisely, I'll have her whipped to death. Do we have an understanding?"

"Robert?" I sobbed.

"Don't, sir, please." Robert clutched at Kahn again. "Just me. Take me. She can go home. I'll do anything you ask."

Ben Breyman moved toward us.

I bolted for the door, and he grabbed my arm.

"No," I wailed.

"Iris!" Robert howled, rooted in place by Ben's gun aimed at him.

"Easy now. Come with me, ma'am. We don't want anyone getting hurt." The cowboy said.

"Ben, get her out of here!" Clowes ordered.

"Darwin, no!" Amelia snapped. "She is *not* leaving this house!"

I latched onto those words, stupidly hopeful that the woman with the curly hair was coming to my defense, but then she added, "Not in that gown. It's worth more than her life."

My guts dropped. *This isn't real. None of this is real.*

"I'll have her change out of it straight away, ma'am." Ben assured.

And then, we were in the hallway. Robert was still yelling my name, but static danced between my ears and my legs were on autopilot.

Ben Breyman gripped my arm hard and yanked me close.

"Your turn to listen. You have a choice now, ma'am. If you want to take your own life, you'll find a way, and I don't rightly blame you, but if you want to live, you'll need this."

He pressed something into my hand, and I blinked down dazedly at a folded piece of paper.

"Give that to the first shift boss you see. If Kahn is serious about putting you in the mines, you need to talk to Miles Flaherty. He'll get you onto the trapper crew, and that's as easy a job as there is underground. Just have to sit in the dark and open and close ventilation doors on command. If he's bluffing about the mines and keeps you on as house staff instead, you'll be shared—they like to lend and borrow us like garden tools. If that's the case, then do everything you can to avoid being Mrs. Clowes's lady servant—Amelia. You saw her in the dining room? Curly hair?"

I nodded dumbly.

"She puts on a civil front, but she's got a nasty habit of cutting her girl's arms up because she likes to see them bleed. Luckily, she's a stickler for good hygiene, so if you scratch at your head, let on that you've got head lice or the like, it should be enough to repel her interest.

"On the occasion that you're publicly whipped, be sure to scream nice and loud on the first strike or the whip man will lay into it on the second one. The crowd likes girls to weep and repent all biblical-like right off the hop. Do that and it'll go better for you."

Ben's words faded into a blur as the shock of what I'd landed myself in set like concrete in my lungs. I was a slave. Mother of Sol, I was a slave.

CHAPTER
THIRTEEN

Once, when I was little, for no particular reason, I smeared crab apple jelly all over the keyboard of Mom's laptop. Then, I closed it so she wouldn't see. Later, I felt guilty and, when she went to the bathroom, I opened the sticky laptop and tried to wash it off.

I'd ruined it, of course. Mom had yelled. Dad had spent that night dismantling the gummy computer and wiping off each delicate part, piece by piece, but it hadn't been fixable.

That day, after Ben marched me to the slave quarters, my brain felt like the innards of that laptop: tacky, waterlogged, and irreparable. Someone needed to dissect me and scrub all the sludge out because I couldn't operate like this. My mind felt cold, and memories of my last moments with Robert snagged like fishhooks in my belly. The betrayal in his eyes, the raw fear in his voice, how he'd screamed my name as Ben pressed me down the hall. His voice cutting off, like someone had struck him. I couldn't stop replaying it all.

I processed moments with clinical numbness, like snapshots.

WE WERE in some sort of store. It looked mostly bare, and the man behind the counter checked my name against a list on his clipboard. "We tell him we need more men, and he sends little flowers instead," he grumbled.

Ben leaned closer to the man. "This one belongs to his higher-up. You'd do well to pass on that she's not to be harmed without his leave."

The man shook his head and pushed a stack of clothes across the counter. "One overcoat. Two pants. Two shirts. Three pairs of socks and underwear. One pair of boots. One lunch tin. One lantern and two candles. Don't waste them. You only get two sticks for the month. You need more, you pay for it."

WE ENTERED one of the tenement houses. A fireplace with blackened bricks dominated one end of the room. The walls were crudely whitewashed, and two were lined with bunks and lumpy straw mattresses. A chair, a small stool, and a spinning wheel were the only other pieces of furniture in the sparse place.

Ben handed me off to a hefty woman in a pale blue shirt and trouser set that matched mine. Her shirt sleeves were rolled up, and she wore a stained apron cinched under her sagging bosom. She rapped a wooden spoon on the cast iron pot hanging from the hearth hook before wiping her hands on her apron. "Lord, where's this one from? Looks soft as spiderwebs. Is she Clowes's new toy?"

"Worse." Ben raised his eyebrows. "His boss's."

"And what exactly am I supposed to do with her?"

"He wants her in the mines. I was hoping Miles needed more trappers."

The woman hardened at this. "As a matter of fact, he does. You tell your master that Nella's boy—eight years old he was— got run over and killed by a coal tub last week! You know him, Ben? Little imp was working seven days a week. Hadn't seen sunlight in months. Fell asleep at his post, he did. Would it kill him to give the children a day off? *One* day a week. You ask him that."

Ben sighed and dropped his voice. "He doesn't give me his ear any more than he does you, May."

"Nonsense. You're in his bloody pocket. Closer to his ear than any of us are. People are getting hot under the collar and there's gonna be an explosion that'll burn up more than coal dust. Mark my words."

Ben left.

I shifted my pile of clothes to hold out the folded paper to the woman named May.

She smiled softly, revealing a gap between her top teeth. "Don't bother, dove. I never learned to read. Wanted to, and then the world ended, and the books all got burned."

"Miles Flaherty," I whispered. I was supposed to remember that name, but my mind was shutting down, like someone was flipping breakers and crashing every critical system I had.

"Plenty of time for that." She nodded toward the bunks with her head "Put your things down, bottom bunk, right-hand side. That's mine, but I don't mind hot-bedding with you if we're on opposite shifts. Now, go lay down before you fall down, girl. You look green as a gooseberry. I'll take you to the colliery at whistle blow. And we'll get you sorted out."

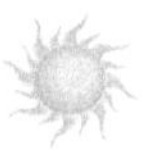

MILES FLAHERTY WAS the day shift boss. He had no teeth, but a reassuring smile. Nevertheless, I was terrified as we crossed the reinforced threshold of the mine's main manway. Lines of workers with lanterns and lunch pails streamed out of the black shaft and into the predawn gray. The children looked like miniature adults, lean, hard, and stone-faced. I couldn't tell the men from the women because everyone was coated in black dust with red-rimmed eyes, sweat-streaked skin, and white teeth. The colliery smelled like matches and damp rocks. It was immediately colder than the night air outside. We walked until we reached the main haulage line where Miles instructed me to climb into one of the empty coal tubs in a trip being hauled back down the slope by a pony and driver. The other carts filled up with oncoming shift workers.

The driver was a girl younger than me. She wrinkled her nose at my clean shirt and pants. "Ah, a green un. Where to, Boss?"

Miles hopped into the coal tub beside me and reclined back to lay slouched in it, his knee bumping mine. "If you sit like a princess on a pony down here, you'll knock your head off before your first day starts. Get your head below the rim. The sky's real low down here." He let out a wheezing cackle as I ducked down, and the workers behind him echoed it. To the driver, he said, "Drop us at Henry's gate, would ya?"

"Sure thing." The girl nodded. "I've been sick of hoofin' it to open that one myself." She clucked at the pony, and the trio of carts jostled and creaked down the rails. Blackness swallowed us.

I couldn't slow my breathing. *I'm in a hole. There's an entire mountain on top of me and nothing's holding it up but toothpicks.*

"Never been downhole before?" Miles spoke over the growl of the cart's wheels.

"No."

"It'll grow on you. Weather is always the same—hotter at the coal face, mind you, but right temperate where you'll be stationed. No snow, no bugs or sunburns, and your job is simple enough a five-year-old can do it."

"I heard it killed an eight-year-old last week." The heat in my voice surprised me. Emotion hadn't crept through the blockade of numbness since Ben Breyman peeled me away from Robert yesterday.

Miles Flaherty shifted beside me and coughed. "He fell asleep on the job. So long as you stay awake, should be right as rain."

We didn't speak anymore. I don't know how far we rolled down the long incline. Kilometers. An hour. Maybe longer. Only the dim light of the driver's oil lantern illuminated the way ahead of us. Timber beams and bolts drilled into the roof scrolled overhead. We passed several large wooden doors held open by squinting children. They closed the doors behind us as soon as the carts cleared.

At some point, our driver barked, "Whoa there, Ruby." She heaved back on the brake lever and pulled on the reins before jumping down and squeezing past her docile animal.

"This is you." Miles slapped my leg lightly. "Hop out. Your side."

My head bumped the ceiling when I rose from my crouch. There was little more than a foot between the top of the coal tub and the stone above. I reached out blindly to the side, and my palm brushed against the hewn wall, only inches from the cart's sidewall. "The wall's right here. Where do I get off?"

"Should be ahead of you. To your right. There's a manhole. Feel it?"

I did. An alcove was carved into the shaft wall.

"Climb on down into that." Miles instructed.

He held my forearm with a steady grip as I dropped feetfirst over the side of the cart into the hole in the wall. My shins knocked into something. I reached down and felt a wooden bench.

"There you are." Miles said from the cart, passing me my lunch pail and lantern. "Like I said, job is dead simple. You've seen it done already. The ventilation door is just ahead of the pony—Ronnie's already opened it for you. All you've got to do is close it behind us nice and quick once we're through. Mind you shut it all the way though, or my workers won't get air pushed down to them like they're supposed to. And keep tucked into the manhole when the carts go by, lest you want to get run over. Got it?" He slapped the front of the coal cart. "Ronnie, let's go."

"That's it?" I blurted.

"Pretty much. We're the last trip down, so just listen for the next one coming back up the line. You'll hear the rumble. Open the door for them and close it once they're gone. Should be about one every hour or so. They won't slow for your door once they know you're posted here—we've got quotas to meet. So best stay alert and open your trap prompt-like if you don't want to cause a wreck or catch a beating. Oh, and there's a hole in the wall further up the shaft to do your business when nature calls. You'll smell it if you take a walk. If—at any time—the roof gets to working, let the next driver you see know."

"Working?" I asked. *Sol,* I didn't understand half of what he was saying.

Miles sighed. "If the roof gets to creaking and groaning, *working,* let a driver know, understand? My miners are busy pounding, blasting, and drilling at the face, and they won't hear it like you can. It means the roof's getting stressed and wanting more reinforcement."

"Stressed?" I repeated, but the carts were already jolting and creeping away down the slope. "Wait." I gulped, holding up my unlit lantern. "My light."

"You only get two candles a month, love, and this isn't a job that needs light." Miles called back to me. "You ain't afraid of the dark now, are ya?" He laughed. So did the other miners riding down with him.

I stumbled out of the alcove and onto the tracks, following the sound of them, running my fingers along the cold, damp wall as my heart clawed at my throat, and a blackness deeper than I'd ever known smothered me.

Don't cry. Don't cry. Find the door. Do your job. A five-year-old can do it.

My hand bumped into a wood ledge. I hissed as a rough plank drove a splinter deep into the pad of one finger. Finding a knotted rope handle on the opposite edge of the panel, I yanked back, surprised at the weight of the door and how it groaned on its hinges when I pulled it. It rattled against its jamb with a clunk, and I stood in front of it, my breath sawing faster as the sound of the cart train faded.

There was *nothing*. No light. No hint that light had ever existed. No sound except for my whimpers echoing off the walls to taunt me. I sucked at the splinter in my finger and homed in on the pain of it, the hot, copper taste of my blood in a world of cold, dead, deep black. I needed it to be an anchor because I was unravelling. All my emotions from yesterday avalanched onto me, my own personal roof caving in. Nothing could reinforce this. I was far past the point of shoring up.

I sobbed in the dark. I would have screamed, but I was horrified that the sound of it would bring tons of rock down on me, so I bit my knuckles. I tripped over a rail tie and crashed to my knees. I pushed myself to my feet and paced in the dark.

Numbness peeled away leaving behind raw and bleeding panic. I couldn't do this. My skin crawled with the lack of stimulation. I couldn't just sit with my thoughts in the dark. With no distraction, they stabbed at me, an endless barrage.

Kahn is going to eat Robert alive and you're never going to see sunlight again. Vinton and Mark are going home with a crew of men they don't know has been sent to take Painted Bluff. Another fight. Another battle. They won't stand. My whole family will die or be driven into the wilds. Vinton can't travel without his motorcycle. My parents can't hunt. Johan is too old and tired to do this. He and Olivia will starve to feed everyone else. You should have stayed. At least you would have been useful there.

You lied to him. He told you about Vannevar and you never told him about Nate, about crashing the network. There was hate in his eyes when he looked at you. Disgust. He'll never hold you again. He'll leave you down here, because this is where you deserve to be. You're going to die in the dark.

"Stop it." I beat my fists against my temples and paced faster, taking deep draughts of air that smelled like sulfur and rotten eggs. "Just take the next step."

My boots scraped in the dark. "Just take the next step," I repeated. It became my mantra. I shuffled back to the alcove. I set my lunch pail and lantern under the little bench. I walked up the rails away from the door and gagged when the smell of urine and feces overpowered everything else. *There's the bathroom then.*

I turned around and paced the other way. "Take the next step," I murmured. *What was my next step?* That was easy. Survive the day. I could do this. I could open doors. Sol knew I was good at closing them. Did that *all* the time.

I waited for my eyes to adjust, but they didn't. The darkness around me remained impenetrable. Time stretched and so did I. I touched my toes. I jogged in place, did lunges, squatted against the wall with the cold stone against my shoulder blades. I did everything I could think of, and it was still *ages* before a faint rumble announced a cart train on the other side of the trap door.

I opened it and dived into the alcove. "Okay." I stuck my head out and squinted into the dark. A current of air blew my sweaty hair back from my face. It was a long time before the trip rolled up the slope enough for me to catch the glow of the driver's lamp. And then it wasn't a glow. It was so blinding I could barely see the silhouette of the pony hauling the train.

"You clear there?" A boy's voice shouted as they approached. *Miles must have informed all his drivers that there was a green trapper at this post.*

"Yes," I shouted back, voice too loud as I pressed back into the alcove. "Clear."

I caught sight of the pony's broad face. Its nostrils were flared, and its ears flicked toward me as it went by. Lather mixed with coal dust and matted the animal's coat. The driver's lantern overwhelmed me, but I made out a flash of white teeth and a waving hand as they went by. Three tubs full of coal rumbled behind them.

I closed the door.

They rolled up the rails, a ring of light worming up the slope and then disappearing until I couldn't hear the thud of the pony's feet or the creak of the cartwheels.

All that was left was a green afterimage burned into the back of my eyes.

That was it. That was the only human contact I was going to get down here.

Miles said about one an hour. At least ten more to go before shift end.

Take the next step.

By the time the fourth trip went by, I was too tired to pace anymore. Without the sound of my boots scuffing, I could only hear the odd drip of water and something that sounded like rustling leaves in the dark—I had no idea what that was. After the fifth trip rolled by, I sat on the bench in the alcove and opened the lunch pail May packed for me. I ran my fingers over the contents in the dark. Pepperoni sticks, a potato bun, and a slice of hard cheese. A small thermos of mint tea.

And that's when I heard scurrying rushing toward me. Before I could process it, something climbed my boot and tiny claws dug into my shin as it scaled my leg. I screamed and shook it off.

It squeaked and immediately latched back on. Cold tail, wet fur. This time I kicked the rat hard enough that it thudded into the opposite wall and stayed there, hissing.

I wheezed in the dark and slammed the lid back onto my lunch pail.

So, there are rats down here. And they're used to being fed.

Sol help me, I can't do this.

CHAPTER
FOURTEEN

The sun had set by the time we stepped out of the mine. I lost my way in the maze of tenement houses and had to awkwardly ask people where May lived. When I found the right rowhouse, she was already spooning out bowls of cream of potato soup with carrots and peas to the rest of my roommates. People sat on the edges of their bunks and slurped noisily.

"Go clean up. You're tracking black everywhere." She nodded at me. "There's a shower around back." The shower was a nozzle below a rainwater cistern on a tall stand. I scrubbed my hands and face until my skin tingled. I changed into my second set of clothes. When I reentered the rowhouse, May had taken her apron off and had dressed in mine clothes. She told me she worked in the tipple. I had no idea what that meant. I wolfed down a bowl of soup and my untouched lunch, heedless of everyone in the room watching me.

"You know your way around a garden?" May asked.

I nodded, mouth full of bread.

"Good. Everyone's got jobs around here. You can make sure the soup pot is restocked for when our shift is done, got it?

"

Plenty of leeks, potatoes, onions, and carrots in the plot at the west end of the street. Don't touch the tomatoes or the grape vines. Those are Mr. Leung's, and he'll flay you if you steal from him, understand?"

I nodded again.

The night shift whistle blew, and May and a couple of others went out the door.

I didn't speak to anyone.

I slept like the dead and didn't wake up until the midnight whistle.

Then, I found the garden, buried my hands in the dirt, and cried at the smell of soil. I missed old Iris, the one who spent her days with dirt under her fingernails surrounded by vibrant green. Iris who breathed fresh air and braved watching the sunrise over the lake. I didn't think I could find my way back to her if I tried.

I wondered for the thousandth time how Robert was doing, if he was safe. I rehearsed what I'd say to him if I saw him again, the perfect combination of words to erase the hurt and disgust I'd seen in his eyes when Kahn had told him of my betrayal. At night, I dreamt of his lips on my skin, his hands on my hips.

MY DAYS WERE DISTILLED into counting coal trips, and my nights divided by shift whistles: one at midnight (the lunch whistle), another an hour before our shift started, and the last to draw us into the mine.

I never saw the sun.

By the fourth shift, it was killing me. It was worse than any desk job I'd ever been tied to. The hours of inactivity, the lack of stimulation, the forced confinement in my own head, every thought biting and tangling with the next one, busier than the rats that raced over my feet at lunch time. I needed something to latch onto. A goal. A task. It didn't have to be a big one. I was a trapper in more ways than one, and I could use that below ground just as well as I could above.

ON MY FIFTH SHIFT, I traded most of my lunch to Ronnie the pony driver in exchange for a spool of wire. By supper time, I'd snared four rats.

When I presented them to Miles at the end of our shift, he looked shocked and then aggrieved. "What'd you do that for? They're our warning signs. A pack of rats get to running, we know a collapse is coming. They can hear it before we do."

"Overseer says he'll pay two credits a piece for them," I countered.

My shift-boss's dirty brow wrinkled. "Two chit a piece? Where'd you hear that?"

"I read it on a poster in front of the store."

"You *read* it." Miles grumbled. "Bastard's bent on taking anything that might save our lives, ain't he? Well don't wave 'em around for the boys to see if you want any of them chits to yourself."

From then on, I tucked the rats I killed under my overcoat, and only presented them at the back door of the company store when there weren't other miners shopping. I accrued enough credit over the next week to buy myself a box of matches.

My next shift downhole, I lit my candle, tucked it into its lantern, and examined the hole I'd been spending my days in for the first time. There wasn't much. Narrow tracks. Alcove and wooden bench. The trap door itself was a medieval looking thing with solid planks and tarnished boltheads. I squinted and walked closer to it.

Someone had drawn on the wood in white chalk and charcoal. The etchings were faded but recognizable up close: line drawings of great horned owls with dramatic feather tufts, sharp, narrow beaks, black bars bracketing their intense eyes, white patches at their throats. Dozens of them had been etched onto the gate, different sizes, but all posed the same, perched sideways with their heads turned so that their severe stares met anyone facing the door.

Everything about them was perfect, the white discs around their eyes, the soft curve of their folded wings, their lethal talons. Whoever had drawn these, they knew birds. They'd spent hours watching owls.

And then someone made them a slave and forced them down this hellhole.

My eyes filled with tears. I traced a cold finger over a half-smudged bird. I'd opened and closed this gate, brushed past these birds how many times now without knowing they were here? This wasn't my cross-shift's work, I was certain of that.

I'd only caught glimpses of the trapper who worked the gate at night during our shift change. He was a nine-year-old boy who suffered severe tremors in his head and hands. He could barely manage opening and closing the trap. I didn't think he could manage the fine motor skills required for artwork this precise.

Then it was the boy before you. The eight-year-old who got run over by a trip because he fell asleep outside the alcove.

Here I'd been, moaning about the ugliness of this place, unaware of the delicate beauty an eight-year-old had left behind. And the colliery was already stealing it away. A layer of coal dust already obscured the flock of owls. Soon they wouldn't be visible at all. When I tried to dust one off with my sleeve, the drawing came off along with the black grime. So, I spent the next hour carefully studying the drawings, smoothing out the dust at my feet, and trying to imitate their lines on the floor with my finger. Then, I set my lantern under the stool, shielded it with my jacket, and drew the same lines blind. My copies looked like cat scratches next to the boy's art. I burned a whole candle trying to reproduce the drawings with any proficiency. A two-week allotment of light gone in what seemed like an instant. After shift, when I went to the tenements, I asked May what the boy's name was.

Henry. His name was Henry.

That night, I scratched the image of an owl into the bed post, and I etched his name beneath it. I thought about his mother, how she'd probably never seen the birds, how she probably never would. I wanted to change that. I wanted the birds to brighten her day like they had mine.

NEXT SHIFT CHANGE, someone crashed into me hard enough that we both dropped our lunch pails.

A boy my height gripped my arm and pulled me up. I blinked into a coal-blackened face, black wisps of hair and hazel eyes. He smelled like rotten teeth.

"Didn't see you," I mumbled, stunned.

He picked up my lunch pail and tossed it into my arms.

Before I'd recovered, he'd melted into the lineup of miners on their way home. Miles Flaherty was waiting at the manway when I got there. Miners crowded around him as he spoke.

"Listen, lads and lasses. The steam engine that runs the fans is down today, but the overseer isn't budging on our quotas. Now, the engineers expect to have the ventilation up and running in the next couple of hours. Until then, keep a sharp eye on each other, you hear? If you see any rats getting lethargic or on the run, if you see lantern flames burning too high or too low, raise the alarm and get yourselves up the slope, understand?"

There were several sullen nods and more than a few grumbles. Miles did his best to rally the miners. "Remember now, Master Clowes has a big generator coming up the rails as we speak, and he promised we'll be running on a reliable electric system soon. Let's show them what we're made of until then, yeah?"

"The generator isn't coming." I don't know why I said it, but I did, and it was loud enough that the gathered crew turned to me. Maybe, it was because I saw how their eyes brightened when their shift boss told them things were going to get better soon, and it was a false bright spot. Not like Henry's owls. Not pure. A lie. One that had rolled easily off their master's tongue to grease his slave's wheels and keep them working hard, just like Kahn had done to us. One that made Miles Flaherty an unwitting liar too, and he didn't deserve that. None of them deserved this.

"What was that, lass?" The toothless man scowled at me.

"I said the generator isn't coming. I'm from the city that made the deal to send it. Clowes's boss was my boss too. He cancelled the generator order. He told me himself, right before he sent me here. And even if it had been coming, Clowes's man told me he planned to use it to power his castle up on the hill. It was never for the mines. Never for us."

"Don't go raising people's hackles on nothing but rumor." Miles snorted. "I won't have a rabblerouser on my shift."

"Naw, she's right." Another man spoke up. "My mate Bill is a gasfitter, and he says they've been laying pipe from mine number four up to the estate for near a month now. What's he running gas up to his house for if not a generator? I haven't seen the boys laying pipe anywhere 'round here. Have any of you?"

Several more people cursed and muttered their protests. One of them called Clowes a greedy bastard.

"Enough!" Miles straightened. "Shut your gobs! I'm not intending on visiting the whipping post today, are you?" He jammed his finger toward me, and I clenched my lunch pail tightly enough that my knuckles whitened. "Are any of you?" He bellowed at the rest of the crew. "Now are we working or are we grousing? We have a quota to meet, and I intend to do it."

He slid into the coal tub beside me, more to ensure I didn't fire anyone else up than anything else, I was sure of it. Once we started rolling, he hissed. "What'd you go and do that for? I set you up with an easy gig. No heavy lifting. No explosives. No crawling on your hands and knees in water that smells like Lucifer himself bathed in it. And this is how you repay me, is it? Wind up my crew when they've got a hard and dangerous day ahead of them?"

"I'm sorry," I said, but I wasn't sure I was. Kahn had underestimated me before and he was doing it again, sticking me into the bowels of the earth, burying me alive, and too high on himself to realize the empire he and Clowes had built was teetering, imbalanced, and full of cracks. Cracks obvious enough that even a green girl could see them. I wasn't anyone special, but I could widen cracks. I wasn't a stampede, but I'd nip at some bloody heels if that's what needed doing. I couldn't seem to build anything meaningful in my life, but Sol knew I was good at tearing the world down around me. I'd done it with Nate, with my city, with Robert. Why not here too? What did I have to lose?

Miles took my lantern and candles for the trouble I'd caused. I mentally prepared to spend another shift in the black, but it was different now that I knew the owl drawings were there. I felt like if I squinted just right, I could see them, hear their deep, soft calls of *hoo-h'hoo-hoo-hoo.*

The ventilation fans didn't come back on. I couldn't feel a

draft any of the times I opened the gate to let the morning trips through. Ronnie, one of the few drivers who spoke with me, mumbled when she went by, "It's hotter than the devil's ass crack down there." Her pony, Ruby, was soaked in sweat, mouth open, and nostrils quivering.

"You got enough water?" I asked. I hardly drank any. My gate wasn't deep enough down the slope to get hot, and driving was harder work than being a trapper. Everything was harder work than being a trapper. I'd gotten into the habit of handing my canteen off to Ronnie so she could fill hers.

"No time to stop today. We're already behind on quota." She passed without slowing. "Them bastards up top expect us to keep pumping out coal the same whether or not they give us air to breathe."

I settled into the alcove to take my lunch. Since I'd started trapping the rats, they'd grown smart enough not to harry me when I ate. So, at noon I skimmed my fingers over the contents of my lunch pail without fear of something crawling up my legs to beg for scraps.

I frowned. It wasn't *my* lunch. The food was parceled in beeswax and May didn't own beeswax wraps, to my knowledge. She folded our food in old linen, plus this thermos was shorter and squatter than mine, with a handle in its metal cap.

The boy from this morning, I realized. *He handed me the wrong lunch pail.* My gut ached as I sifted through the unfamiliar container, expecting it to be empty. The kid had been going off-shift after all.

But then I unwrapped a sandwich that smelled like honey bread with thick sliced corned beef. There were two slices of salted jerky as well, and a firm piece of fruit. I held it up to my nose and took a deep breath of autumn sweetness. An *apple!* Where in Sol's name did the boy get an apple? There weren't any trees in the tenement, and I hadn't seen fresh fruit for sale at the store. And why hadn't he eaten any of it? A paper crinkled as my fingers brushed it. It felt crisp in my hands as I pulled it out. A note?

I wish I had my lantern.

This was something important. I could feel it in my chest, but I couldn't do anything about the darkness except wait for the next trip to come and hopefully bribe the driver to slow for long enough for me to hold the paper up to the light. That didn't happen.

The next trip didn't come. None of them did.

Instead, as I sat in the dark, a sound like rustling leaves swelled on the other side of the gate.

I stuffed the paper in my pocket and the food back into the lunch pail. Then I stood.

My legs tingled and my knees loosened as the scratching and chittering echoed up the shaft. I held my breath and took several hesitant steps toward the gate.

Was that . . .

A wave of rats rammed under the narrow gap between the gate and the rails. They spilled over my boots and darted past, squeaks shrill as nails on slate. My stomach lurched. Woodenly, I turned to listen to their retreat up the slope.

"Shit," I blurted, dropping the lunch pail and sprinting up the tracks blindly. Blood whooshed between my ears.

Something massive whomped behind me like the heart of the mountain had come to life with one single pump. My ears popped. A shockwave tore me off my feet. Chunks of wood hammered my back and head. The world fizzled and the air felt like breathing in wasps. I don't remember anything after that.

CHAPTER
FIFTEEN

My consciousness skipped like a stone in a river. Snatches of awareness caught in the current. Ronnie the driver's voice in my ear. A wet handkerchief tied over my mouth and nose. My arm slung over her shoulder. Dust clotting so thick, her lantern couldn't cut through it. Dust burning my eyes, scratching my throat, filling my lungs.

I WAS facedown on the bunk in May's tenement house. There was a towel over the pillow. I couldn't stop wheezing. Someone held a chunk of ice against the back of my pounding head. Cold water slithered down my neck. May undid my braid and picked splinters of wood out of my hair. They littered the floor.

That was the trap door, I realized. *It blew apart.* My face crumpled. "The owls," I sobbed.

"I'm gonna stitch a cut in your head now, dove." May spoke with a level voice. "Stay still and it'll hurt less."

I felt every prick of the needle, the thread pulling through the holes. I couldn't stop crying.

The owls.

NIGHT SHIFT DIDN'T GO into the mine until the ventilation system came online again, the gas and dust cleared, and the night shift boss cleared it as safe. They pulled thirty bodies out of the rubble that night. Fifteen more they never found. May told me that the trapper who ran the gate one down from mine broke most of his ribs and one of his legs, and the ones further downhole probably died instantly. No one at the coal face survived, including our shift boss, Miles Flaherty.

The colliery shut down for a day for a mass funeral. There wasn't enough ground in the slave quarters for a cemetery. Instead, Mr. Clowes had designated one of the abandoned mines as a crypt. I saw the sunrise for the first time in what felt like forever. And then I followed a line of wailing families into a cramped, abandoned mine and wondered bitterly at the irony of pulling all those bodies out of one hole in the ground just to ferry them back down into another. They'd never escape the mines. Not even in death.

The miners sang a low, harmonized song that sounded deep as the holes they dug into the earth. I couldn't understand the words, but the melancholy in it, the way they sang like it was a song they'd practiced far too many times, pulled at my chest.

It wasn't until after the ceremony, as I sewed up my torn work clothes in preparation for my next shift, that I felt paper crinkling in one of the pockets and remembered the boy who'd collided with me and the switched-out lunch pails.

I snatched up my lantern and went to the outhouse around

the back of the house. It was the only private room I had access to.

My fingers tingled as I pulled out the folded slip of paper and held it up to the candlelight. Breath drained out of me as I read the first words, written in compact and tidy cursive.

I.

I don't have words for how sorry I am. I swear to Sol I'm going to fix this. I'm going get you out of there. What part of the mine do you work in? Who is your supervisor? Contact will keep you updated on plan.

Love
R.

My throat closed. I folded the paper and pressed it against my lips. *Robert.* A half-laugh, half-sigh bubbled past my lips. I missed him so much it carved a hole in me. *He doesn't hate you. He wrote, Love R.* A stupid, girlish thought, but my head still felt scrambled from when I'd hit it, and my thoughts were even more scattered than usual. *I don't have anything to write with. Coal is too hard.*

I put out my candle and rushed to the supply store before the start of shift. The shopkeeper had pencils. I'd seen him use them on the tally sheet. He frowned at me as I walked in.

"Cutting it close to shift, aren't we?" he said.

"Can I buy a pencil from you?"

He flapped his lips. "What's a trapper need a pencil for? They're more expensive than you can afford on your chit, girl."

"Do you have anything else to wr—" I almost said write and then remembered that people here considered it flaunting to say you could write. No one liked a slave who acted above their station. "Do you have anything to draw with? I like to draw." I pasted on my most vacant grin.

"Now, you're in luck." The shopkeeper flashed his teeth in a cruel smile that told me I was about to get ripped off. "Mr. Leung makes charcoal out of his old grape vines. He brought in three packets for me to sell last week. Even got a piece of chalk in with them. How's that for a fancy art set?"

"How much?"

"Twenty rats or three candles. And I won't take credit on neither one."

"Thanks," I swallowed and left, defeated.

As I slogged to the mine for my shift, I looked for the boy with the hazel eyes, the one whose breath smelled of rotten teeth—Robert's contact, I assumed—but I didn't see anyone who looked like him. Half of the night shift had been shifted onto days to compensate for our lost miners. Maybe we were working the same shift now?

Down in the main haulage line, the carpenters had built new trap doors. Mine still smelled like sawdust. Sticky lines of sap smeared on my fingers when I ran them across the planks. It felt foreign, naked, and impersonal.

There were no rats to catch. They'd all fled or died in the explosion.

I couldn't slow down my breathing. No matter what I did, it came in shaking pants, like I was a cornered thing.

THAT NIGHT, I asked May which house Mr. Leung lived in and what shift he worked.

"He's day shift, like you. Why do you ask?"

"I want to help him with his tomatoes." I lied.

"Ah," May grinned. "Figure he'll share if you put in some hard labor?"

"Maybe."

"Best of luck with that."

I shoveled down my portion of pea soup and headed for the house May had described: two rows over from ours, sunflowers lining the front porch. An old man with hooded eyes and a shock of frizzy white hair answered the door when I knocked.

"Mr. Leung?" I asked.

He looked me up and down and spoke with a deep, unruffled voice that contrasted his emaciated form. "The answer's no."

"I haven't even asked you anything yet."

"No, you can't have any tomatoes. I'm canning them at the end of the season, and I count them every day. I'll know if one's missing. You can't have any grapes either. They're not even ripe. Eat them and you'll have the shits for days, so don't even—"

"How did you know Henry?"

"Excuse me?" His hand clamped the door hard.

"Henry, you knew him well?"

"How did *you* know him?" he rasped, words thick with emotion.

"I-I didn't. I'm new." My head hurt and the stitches in my scalp felt tight and hot. *Come on. Use your words, Iris.* "I'm a trapper at his old gate. Did you ever see his birds?"

"His what?" Mr. Leung's brow creased.

"He liked to draw, didn't he?" I swallowed. "He was good at it. And he loved owls."

His lips trembled. "How did you . . ." His gaze met mine, eyes sharp with pain.

"Mr. Leung, he drew the most beautiful owls on his gate in the mine. Great horned owls."

A shaking exhale burst out of the man. "Oh Lord, there used to be a pair of them that called to each other from the rooftops after dark. Henry loved to watch them."

"Sir?" My voice wobbled. "There's been days I thought I couldn't get through down there. Days when it felt like the mountain was coming down on top of me, or my mind was coming undone in the dark, and I'd close my eyes and think of him drawing in the black, creating light where there was none. Black charcoal and white chalk owls, a whole flock of them. The shopkeeper told me you sell him charcoal sets with white chalk. He was going to charge me three candles for one. Now, there's no way any trapper could afford that, but Henry had a set, didn't he? He got them from you direct."

"He did." The words sounded like a sob. "What are you after?"

"I want a set. What did he pay you?"

"What did he pay?" Mr. Leung dragged a hand down his face and took a long shuddering breath. "Henry was my grandson. He didn't pay me anything. I gave him a set. He's the reason I started making them."

I reached into my pocket and held out the second candle in my monthly allotment. "It's almost a full stick. I only lit it tonight for a few minutes."

"Awfully early in the month to be trading off half your light for frivolities, girl."

"I already burned my first candle memorizing those birds. It's *all* my light." I gulped. I'd be spending weeks in the dark if this worked. "And it's not frivolity to me."

He squinted. "You know how to write?"

I was too worked up to lie convincingly, so I just nodded.

"I'll not have my head on the line for slanderous graffiti that does nothing but get backs covered in whiplashes."

"It's not for that."

"What then?"

I could have told him that I wanted to write to my boyfriend on the outside, to let him know I was alive and safe after an accident killed or maimed most of our shift, but this was more than that. More than notes. More than escape. My throat clogged up and unexpected tears filled my eyes. "The explosion . . . t-the owls, they're gone, and I don't know if anyone else but the drivers and I ever saw them. I can't sit down there without them, sir. They were so alive. They-they just belong on that gate, and I want to put them back. I'm not an artist, like he was, but it's *wrong* down there without them."

Mr. Leung gave me a charcoal set, and he let me keep my candle.

R.

I'm a trapper. Main haulage line. Day shift. Not hurt in explosion.

Love

I.

THE CHARCOAL STICKS WERE THICK, so I had to write the letters large and blocky. It was all I could fit onto the back of the note Robert had written me. Exhilaration needled through me as I saw the boy with the hazel eyes in the shift lineup exiting the mine that morning. He met my gaze under the brim of his hat. His thin moustache twitched as he nodded and held his lunch pail away from his body.

I did the same with mine, and we traded as we passed without breaking stride. I kept my eyes forward and tried to take deep breaths as my heart crowded my throat. After the long trip down to my gate, I lit my candle and tore open the lunch pail.

I.

My hands are shaking. Tell me you're okay. We felt the explosion here and they won't tell me anything. I can't breathe. I can't get out of this bloody house. You have to be okay. I'd feel if you weren't, wouldn't I? I can't do this alone. Please.

Love

R.

I read it over again until my eyes blurred, and the paper shook in my hands. "Robert," I said his name out loud, and it echoed down the shaft. "I'm fine. Do you hear me? You're not alone." Then I folded the note carefully and slid it into my shirt pocket. I pulled out the charcoal set, and I started sketching the faint outline of a great horned owl on the trap door. It wasn't nearly as elegant as Henry's had been. It never would be. My bird was awkward and unproportioned. I rubbed it out several times until I recreated something close to what I'd remembered. Then I took a deep breath and traced over it in bold, unapologetic lines.

The next ones came easier.

Ronnie the driver stopped her trip on the next load up. I heard her sharp voice call, "Whoa," and Ruby snorted and crunched to a halt, tack jangling as the pony shook her head.

I leaned out of the alcove frowning. Drivers didn't stop unless their trip went off the rails. "You okay?"

But she wasn't. She'd stopped in front of the open gate. Her gaze was locked on the fresh drawings, and she was crying.

"You do this?" she pointed.

I swallowed. "Yeah."

She sniffed and nodded several times, still looking at the birds. "He was a good boy. I never meant to . . ." Her words faded into a long wheeze and my chest squeezed hard.

Oh Sol, it was her.

"We were way behind on quota that day," she continued. "And he was always daydreaming, forgetting to open his door. I came up with a full load, and his gate wasn't open. I remember squeezing past Ruby, yarding it open. My lantern burned out when the breeze came through and I didn't relight it. I didn't even *think* to relight it. We were so late." Her face crumpled, and her pony flicked her ears and nickered at her driver softly. "It was my fault. Ruby wouldn't walk. I thought she was having a stubborn spell—even though she rarely does—but she knew he was on the tracks, and I whipped her until she screamed. I whipped her until she walked on. He should have woken up from all the noise we made, but he didn't. I asked his Mama after, and she said Henry had these spells sometimes where he fell down and shook. It must have been that. He woke up when we ran him over though." Her next words came out in a low wail. "And he started screaming. I knew right away what I'd done, but it was too late. He was so little and bleeding so bad as I held him." Ronnie took a huge shuddering breath and fell silent.

"Ronnie." I gulped. "He never should have been down here, and they never should have been rushing you. It's not your fault. It's theirs. *They* put us here. They put quotas on your head."

"But I drive," she wailed. "I could have relit the lantern."

"They could have given you enough oil to last the month instead of making us pay for light."

She straightened, shaking herself and drawing up the reins. "I gotta go."

"Ronnie?" I stepped out of the alcove and held my hand out to Ruby. The pony's pale muzzle was warm and prickly with whiskers. I held up the charcoal set Mr. Leung had given me. "Maybe some of the other trappers want to draw birds too? I think Henry would have liked that."

A hoarse laugh burst past her lips. "Half of them can't draw, and none of them can afford to waste their light. He could draw in the dark, you know? When he ran out of candlesticks, he'd just keep going."

I nodded, pulling the letter from my pocket and tearing a strip off it. Hastily, I laid down the lines of a great horned owl, tufted head feathers, stern brow, sleek body, blunt tail. Then, I blew out my candle and eased it out of my lantern. "Here." I handed her the paper, candle stick, and half of the fragile charcoal sticks. "Now they've got a guide and some light, if they want it."

She took them. I heard from another driver that by the end of shift, all the gates in the mine had owls drawn on them.

R.

You are not alone. Sorry I didn't tell you about virus. Wanted to stab at Kahn. URLs promised to get my family to safety. Didn't mean for people to die.

Love
I.

THE NEXT MORNING, on my way to work, the black-haired boy with the rotten teeth and I traded lunch pails again. I saw owls scratched onto the side of the tipple house and on some of the coal tubs too.

Our new shift boss stood at the colliery entrance. He looked like life had wrung him out and dried him into rawhide. He was frowning and beckoning to all the oncoming shift as we arrived. We were half the number we'd been before the explosion.

"Listen up," he said. "Overseer wants us to start greeding it out today."

Several miners swore quietly. Others shook their heads and scuffed their boots. "We don't have enough experience on shift for this," one man spoke for the rest.

I leaned into the miner standing next to me. "What's greeding it out mean?"

"We're room and pillar mining, love. Cutting corridors of coal that all connect like streets and alleys in the seam. Once you reach the end of the seam, like we have, you go backward, start stacking crib blocks and tearing out the coal pillars 'til there's nothing left but timbers holding up the mountain." He shrugged and smiled nervously. "That's greeding it out. Formation caves in as you back your way out of it. If you do it right, if you got men who know what the roof sounds like just before it's ready to give way, they get you out before the whole thing collapses on top of you." He leaned closer. "And we don't have those men no more. Lost 'em all in the explosion."

The shift boss hollered over our heads. "Listen now, we've plenty of cribbing for blocks and we'll take it nice and slow."

"When have we ever taken anything slow?" someone shouted.

Widen cracks, Iris. Widen cracks. I took a few breaths to work up to it. "No coal if you all die down there. Does Clowes understand that?"

"There's always more miners." A woman hissed. "He'll just buy up more slaves to stick down the hole if we don't go, and starve us to death to boot. I've got mouths to feed. I know you all do too."

"No slaves where I'm from." I raised my voice. "Plenty of copper too. My old boss just sent a crew of your people out that way to take it for himself, but it's not his. We took his city from him, and we don't want him back. There's food enough for all of you. Fair wages and enough room to build your own—"

"Shut your gob, girl." The shift boss bellowed. He waded through the miners toward me, and they parted like an oil slick retreating from soap. "Listen really close, 'cause I'm only gonna say this once." He stuck his finger in my face, breath hot and thick with the smell of old alcohol. It oozed from him, sweet and sickly, like overripe fruit. "I'll not go to the whipping post for insurrection on my crew, and nobody cares about how pretty the world is outside these fences. You wanna know what happened to the last crew that went on strike here? The company men came in with guns and shot anyone who wouldn't go underground. Then they starved out *all* our families for weeks, the ones that went on strike and the ones that didn't too. Everybody."

"If you all die in a collapse, your families will starve to death anyway," I countered.

The punch came out of nowhere. I was on the ground with my eyes running before I realized the shift boss had struck me. My cheek felt numb and the stitches on the back of my head burned.

I'd never been hit before. The quickness of it, how it felt more like electrocution and less like a blow, stunned me. I lay on the ground for far too long, more shocked than anything else.

Nobody helped me up. They shuffled into the mine as I scrambled for my lunch pail and lantern.

And I just cupped my cheek and followed them, adrenaline pumping through me hard enough to make my hands shake.

You Idiot. You're not a revolutionary.

But I couldn't swallow the fire in my belly, no matter how hard I tried.

CHAPTER
SIXTEEN

I.

Thank Sol, you're alive. Don't apologize for the virus. You were shell-shocked when you came back. We both were, I think. Kahn wanted a war. He wanted to tear it all down and start over. He started it, not you. He's got Clowes cowed here and is smug as hell about taking over this place too. It's disgusting. They sit and eat and drink and talk about the mines like they're on another planet, and people are nothing more than numbers on paper. I'm going to get you out. Can you get transferred somewhere above ground?

p.s. I've sent you some pencils and paper. Do you need anything else?

Love
R.

R.

I screamed in the mine today. I pretended to lose it, that I was claustrophobic, and I didn't stop until they let me go home early. It wasn't a stretch. It's hard being down here with no sun. It's cold. Too much time to think.

After the explosion, people are getting more and more angry and scared. The workers have been ordered to mine in a way that causes the formation to collapse as they go. It's dangerous and a few people got buried alive yesterday.

So, Kahn is still killing people. He's stupid to think of us as numbers on paper. Numbers on paper aren't dangerous at all. People are wearing arm bands with owls stitched into them. It's become a sign of rebellion here. I think they're going to strike soon. The ventilation system keeps breaking down and there's no new workers. They can't take much more of this. I'll ask May if she can get me into the tipple house. They sort coal there to load onto the train. What do I need? I need you to tell me how we're getting you out. I'm not leaving without you.

Love

I.

I.

The tipple house is good. Keep your head down and be safe. I've checked the load schedules, and the train makes a day long loop to the southwest once every two weeks. A little hub town. They take bulk deliveries from Fernie and distribute them from there. It's not home, but it gets us closer to it. We're getting you out on the next train. It's three days from now. They use mule trains to pull the coal cars from the tipple to the train yard, right? My contact has smuggled people out before in a coal car with a false bottom.

Tomorrow night, look for the rail car with the blue dot painted on the inside of its brake handle. Crawl underneath and you'll find a panel that opens via a recessed button hidden above the axle. Just enough room for one person to lie inside. I'm told it's tight. Someone will let you out at the rail yard and get you into a larger crate and loaded into a box car. I'll meet you there, okay?

If, for some reason, I don't make it there, don't get off the train until after it unloads. I'm told the hub town's yard is too well lit to risk an escape there. So, wait until the train is empty and turning around to head back to Fernie. That should be first thing in the morning and the siding loop has more cover.

Burn this letter, I.
Love
R.

R.

I tried to keep my head down, but things got bad here. Ten people died in a collapse yesterday and the miners that were left walked off the job. Clowes's company men shot people and ordered the bodies left where they fell. This morning, all the vegetable gardens were dug up and destroyed, and they've closed the shop that sells food. They burned down any tenement houses that had owls painted on them. No one's ever seen it this bad here. There's talk of lighting the mine on fire or disabling the locomotive. I don't know if this place will last until tomorrow night. I hope it does. Promise me you'll meet me on the train.

Love
I.

There was no letter the next morning, no hand off. I didn't see the black-haired boy with the hazel eyes. I started my shift at the tipple house, and nearly everyone sported an armband with a stitched owl on it. I didn't even know who was making them and handing them out. The air felt full of static. No idle chatter like there was in days previous. Just pursed lips, quick black fingers, and coal clattering as we tossed it down different chutes.

After my shift, as I passed May walking to hers, she grabbed me by the arm and said in a low voice, "Do us a favor, dove, and stay in the house tonight, yeah? Looks to be a storm coming."

I gaped at her and nodded slowly.

I didn't stay in the house.

As soon as it was dark, I headed to the tipple yard and darted between the already loaded coal cars in the siding. The cart with the blue dot on the handbrake was there. The paint looked black in the moonlight, but it was there. My palms were clammy and my breaths short as I scanned the yard for movement, but the drivers who ran the cars under the tipple chutes were concentrating on the main line, and the siding was quiet. I slipped under the sharp steel wheels, trying not to think of Henry. When I found the recessed wooden button, the hidden panel clunked open, hitting me in the shoulder. It was smaller than a coffin inside, full of coal dust and cobwebs. I had to suck in my exhale all the way to close the panel, and once it clicked, I rested my cheek on the gritty wood, squeezed my eyes closed, and counted my breaths.

You can do this. You're going to see Robert soon. We're going home. This has a happy ending.

My legs fell asleep. I couldn't move them much to compensate. I tried to turn my head, but there wasn't room, and for a few agonizing moments, panic hijacked my nervous system, making my heart spasm and my breaths whistle through my teeth.

You've been in the guts of the earth, Iris. You can handle a rail car.

It took a long time to get a handle on my breathing. I didn't know how much time passed, but it felt like hours until I heard someone releasing the handbrakes on the cars behind mine, then mine, then the one ahead of me. The train jerked, the couplers clacked, and we started rolling out of the slave quarter. Light shone through a small crack in the sidewall, and I sucked in my belly and inched toward it. Seeing a narrow slit of the world passing by eased my claustrophobia.

We passed the razor wire fencing and crept toward the rail yard. Whoever was driving the mule train stopped, cranked the handbrakes on in each car, and ducked under mine to pop the panel open without saying a word.

We were parked by a stack of crates. One of them had a hinged lid that was propped open, and it was half filled with chain hoists and winches.

Before I climbed in, I caught sight of the steam locomotive, a leviathan, black as coal, its long body studded with bolts, pistons, and connecting rods. The engine was idle, but everything about it seemed under tension: the *tick tick tick* of warming metal, the snap of valves deep in its innards, short snorts of steam and constant dribbles of hot water, like it was marking its territory. It felt like standing next to an armed bomb.

People swarmed feverishly around it. Drivers led teams of apathetic mules hauling wagons loaded with glistening mounds of coal. They used a conveyor to feed it into the tender behind the locomotive. A pair of men stood up top, peering into the tank as a six-inch spout blasted water from a squat tower into the train's thirsty belly.

I slipped into the open crate. Cold rolls of cable pinched my skin, hand winches poked my backside, and packing straw scratched my arms. I eased the lid back into place, and made myself take deep, trembling breaths in the dark. It wasn't until one of the men outside secured the crate's latches I'd undone that I panicked again.

The urge to fight my way back out of the crate struck me like a blow to the head. I wanted to claw at the wood until splinters jammed under my fingernails or kick the container to pieces. Adrenaline drowned me, stealing my breath and filling my head with the certainty that I'd suffocate in here and die.

Just breathe, Soldamnit. It's not as bad as the squeeze you were just in. What's wrong with you? I sucked air through my nostrils, holding each breath for as long as I could before exhaling, dialing my body back down because I couldn't fail at this stage. I had to make it onto the train. I had to make it back to Robert. Nothing else mattered.

I bit back a yelp as two men hoisted the crate. On the incline of a ramp, one of the winches shifted and clunked into my elbow. The impact numbed my lower arm, but I didn't dare shake out my hand until the workers set down the cargo box and the rumble of their voices receded.

Freight doors closed with a squeal, and the locomotive outside chuffed and ticked while its boiler breathed back to life.

Now what? Is Robert here too, tucked away in a crate like I am? I wanted to call his name so badly, I had to bite my tongue to stop myself. *Wait until the train is rolling and you're both out of this Solforsaken place.*

Adrenaline fizzled through me like electricity arcing up my nerves. Time warped into something meaningless. It took forever for the train to blow its mournful whistle and for the squeal of its drive wheels and the huff of its pistons to announce our departure.

I waited until it felt like we were going fast and the clack of the wheels on the rails vibrated up my back and then I called Robert's name tentatively.

Nobody answered.

"Robert?" I called louder.

Nothing.

I called for the next hour, as loud as I could, until anxiety clutched my chest like hawk's claws and tears ran down my sweaty face. *Oh Sol, something's wrong. Someone's supposed to come and open this, right? Where is he? He said he'd come.*

He didn't. No one came.

At some point, my muscles spasmed so badly, I couldn't breathe through the pain anymore. In agony, I kicked at the end of the crate. My heel went numb, and the impact shivered up my shin, but I couldn't stop once I started. I felt like a horse, stuck in a stable, kicking my way out, but these boards weren't budging.

Panic spilled over in me, and I wailed and kicked harder. Nails squealed; boards loosened but held fast. My nose ran and my hair stuck to my face as I howled, "Please, Robert? Somebody, let me out! Help me! Oh Sol, please help!"

That's when the crate latches clunked open, and the lid lifted.

Cold air blanketed me, and a lantern blazed to life, blinding me.

"Robert?" I blubbered, sitting up and grabbing one of the chain hoist handles.

"How about you put that down and come out nice and slow."

When I didn't comply immediately, Ben Breyman's voice drawled, "I'll shoot you right now, ma'am. I don't stomach stupid very well, so let's be smart about this."

I put down the chain hoist, slumped back down, and cried. Stupid, lost-girl cries.

Robert wasn't coming. We weren't going home.

"How long were you sitting there?" I croaked between sips of water. Ben had offered me his canteen.

"Since we started rolling." He held his gun slack in his hand, sitting with it propped between his knees, an idle threat. A lantern threw light between us, casting oscillating shadows across his calm face in the neatly packed box car.

"And how'd you know I'd be here?"

"Someone left a letter under your boy's door yesterday. I read it before he could. *I don't think this place is going to last until tomorrow night. Promise you'll meet me on the train. Love I.* That's how you ended it, right? Didn't read like the first you'd sent either. Easy enough to figure out that your boy was planning on smuggling you out. Only one way out of the slave quarter—although I've got to thank you, I've been trying to figure out for ages how these bastards were hiding people. That's a slick set up with the coal car. Someone was a fine carpenter. Shame to destroy such craftsmanship."

"Where's Robert?"

"You been taking some beatings, ma'am?" he frowned and pointed at his cheek.

I'd forgotten my bruised face, the shift boss's punch. It seemed so long ago. "Where's Robert?" I asked coldly.

Ben snorted, straight teeth flashing in the dark, eyes animated. "In his room, where he's supposed to be, I'll wager. He's the sacrificial type and you're the fire starter, aren't you?"

His soft smile infuriated me. "Got me all figured out, yeah?" I snarled.

"No, ma'am. But I've seen plenty of your type before." Ben's face grew serious. He leaned his head back against the wall.

"My type?" I slammed the cap back on the canteen.

"Desperate folk who've been backed into too many corners like dogs who aren't afraid to bite 'cause they've tasted the blood of those who hurt them once before."

"I'm not a fragging dog!"

"We all are, though, aren't we? Fighting over scraps while rich men lap up cream. That's the way the world works. Even an angry sun can't change that so long as there's greedy folk around to hoard wealth. You bite your master once, and they never forget it." He pointed at me. "And you're a dog they already know is a biter. You think they're senseless enough to ever let you near their hand again?"

"Better than the kind of dog you are. One who tucks his tail between his legs, shows his belly, and pisses himself any time he gets attention." I'd wanted those words to burn, but maddeningly, Ben Breyman smiled again and offered me a mocking bow.

"I'm the dog who's never bit anybody. Never growled. Never raised my hackles. I'm the one who sleeps at the foot of their beds, guards their families, protects their interests, licks their bloody boots if I'm asked to." His blue gaze flashed to mine, eyes ice cold and voice unwavering. "They'll never see it coming when I strike, Iris. I'm the dog that doesn't give any warning at all before I kill."

CHAPTER
SEVENTEEN

en Breyman was my own personal warden for the short trip. We hadn't yet reached the central hub that distributed coal and cargo to several buyers, but we'd be heading back toward Fernie in the morning once we'd dropped our load. Occasionally, Ben would confer quietly with one of his men when they opened the hatch in the ceiling and climbed down the welded rebar ladder to beckon to him.

Apparently, that's how the brakemen and anyone else transferred between cars while the train was at speed, out the ceiling hatches and across the couplings. It seemed incredibly dangerous.

My ribs felt like a cable had been wrapped around my chest, each breath tighter than the last.

This wasn't the smooth ride Darrin's electric hand car had provided on the night I'd hijacked my way back home from Nate's. Instead of rolling down the tracks, our box car often felt like it was skidding down a mountainside. The big door rattled in its frame, and vibrations propagated up the ribs of the walls and settled deep into my organs.

At our first water stop, Ben opened the big freight door,

helped me down, and followed me as I stretched my legs. He let me go unaccompanied to the bushes to relieve myself on the condition that I talked to him the entire time his back was turned.

"Nice and loud. If I can't hear you, I turn around and start shooting, understand?"

I said I did and proceeded to hurl every insult imaginable at him for the duration of my pee break.

I'm ashamed to say that I slept when we started rolling again. A smarter person would have plotted their escape, but my brain was tired, and my body hurt almost as much as my heart. Ben was an adversary who dealt with unruly folk all the time, not an uncle who'd severely underestimated his niece. He wouldn't make the same careless mistakes Nate had. I was caught like an animal in a snare. I'd just left Fernie, and now I was going right back there again. Once the resignation of that set in, sleep came easy enough because it was the only escape I had.

When I awoke, Ben was surprisingly conversational and answered most of my questions without reserve.

He let me keep the freight door open while we were at speed, but only while he sat beside me to ensure I wouldn't jump.

"Bailing at this speed will likely kill you, and if it doesn't, I will, understand?" He'd warned me, resting his hand on the gun holstered at his side. His eyes were dead calm and analytical, someone used to holding the upper hand.

"Have you always been such a prick?" I asked.

He grinned, leather coat creaking as he shifted beside me. "Yes, ma'am."

When the rails curved hard enough, I caught glimpses of the stout, black engine towing us, glowing under the moonlight. There was something primal about the heartbeat of its cylinders pumping and the chalky, black banner of smoke it left in its wake. Half of the time, with the brakeman scrambling between the cars to control our descents, it felt more like being tied to a runaway animal than an amenable piece of machinery.

Water towers weren't the only thing dotting the railway in increments. We passed countless other towers with the same pivoting arms and pulleys as what we'd seen installed on the church tower in Fernie. Once, I caught one moving as we went by, the main spar swinging horizontally and the arms on the ends pivoting upward like hands surrendering. I couldn't fathom their purpose, and the next time I saw one of the strange towers easing into juxtaposition against the low-hanging moon, I pointed and asked Ben, "What are those?"

"Semaphore towers," he answered. "Each one's manned twenty-four hours a day. They use telescopes to see the next tower in line, and they can communicate a hundred different encoded signals. It's lightning fast and more reliable than pigeons. We have this line, another running from home almost to Kamloops, and a third one down south. Invented by two French brothers in the eighteenth century, I'm told. What's old is new again, ma'am."

"Stop calling me, ma'am." The wind was blowing the smell of him toward me. Horses and hay, like he'd just lain with someone in a barn. Probably did on the regular with charm oozing off him like that. I swallowed hard. "What's with all the formalities anyway?"

He ducked his head, letting his hair fall into his eyes to mask his expression. "I, uh, was raised that way. We were trained real young to call our masters by their proper titles, ma'am." He laughed nervously at his own slip. "It kind of stuck, even after Mr. Clowes paid off my indentureship. Hard to forget a lesson that's been impressed upon you with a willow switch."

"You're a slave?"

"Was." The train leaned into another bend, and he pointed at the locomotive, its headlight carving a path ahead of us. "Funny story. They used to stuff me into the firebox of that engine right there, once a week, every time they cleaned it. For a long time, I was the only one small enough to fit in and shovel out the soot before they steamed out the tubes."

"You work for Clowes now? He pays you?"

"No, ma'am. I mean, no miss. He pays for my room and board. I won't earn a wage until we're square." He grabbed the toothpick he'd been chewing on and flicked it into the dark.

The night air was cold enough that I started shivering. I hadn't brought my work coat. I hadn't brought anything. Swallowing hard, I asked the question that had been burrowing through my mind since I woke. "Did you tell him about my letter to Robert?" If he had, if Clowes and Kahn knew I'd attempted escape, they'd whip me when I got back, probably to death.

Ben shrugged off his jacket and put it over my shoulders. It should have been a kind gesture, but it felt apologetic instead. His answer was quiet. "I had to, Iris. Couldn't drop everything to get on this train and catch you otherwise. You never should have run."

That's it then. Kahn will kill me. Kill Robert. I should have felt frightened, but instead, I felt numb, paralyzed. "Why don't you run?" I heard myself ask.

"Nowhere safe to run to." Ben Breyman stood and hauled the freight door closed. We didn't talk after that.

ELEVEN HOURS after my attempted escape, we unloaded our cargo at the hub town and the empty train looped back toward home. Twenty-three hours after that, we rolled back into Fernie, like I'd never even left.

I sensed something was wrong as soon as the train bore down into its long, squealing deceleration, and two of Ben's men came barreling down the ladder and spoke to him in choked, agitated tones. He swept past me and thumbed toward the crate. "Get back in there, quick."

"W-what?"

He leaned over me like I was thickheaded and enunciated each word. "Ma'am, if you want to live, get back into the crate and do not make a noise until you hear my voice calling you, understand?"

He unlatched the crate and heaved the lid open. I climbed in and flinched as it slammed closed, barely missing my head. "What's happening?" I squeaked, but if Ben heard me as he secured the latches, he didn't answer.

Feet stomped up the ladder at the rear of the freight car, the roof hatch clanged closed, and I was alone in the dark again. *Get out!* my mind howled over the rush of blood in my head. *This is your only chance to escape, while the train is slowing down. If you wait until it's stopped in the yard, you're dead.*

Bracing my back against the far wall, I tucked both knees against my chest and kicked hard. My boots struck wood with a clunk that hammered up my heels. The planks didn't budge, but this time I didn't panic and collapse. I clamped my teeth and pounded on the same board over and over again until it finally gave way. Rough wood scraped my ankle as I cleared the board and worked on the one beside it. Bent nails snagged my pants and clawed at my ribcage as I wormed my way out. I raked straw out of my hair and felt my way along the wall to the hatch at the front of the car, heading the opposite direction of Ben and his cohorts.

Brakes squealed and the train decelerated further.

Hauling myself up the welded rebar ladder, I shoved the overhead hatch until it squealed open. The wind tore it out of my grasp and mashed it against the roof with a bone-grating clang. Damp air sour with acrid smoke rushed in, whipping my hair back. My palms slid on wet metal as I clambered onto the top of the car. Rain pelted my back and neck. Scanning the cars behind me, I couldn't see anyone else up top. *Hurry,* my mind blared, but terror solidified in my limbs and with my hair plastered to my face, I could barely see the drop between cars ahead. I groped for a handhold, clung to it, and maneuvered my legs over the edge. The soles of my boots squeaked and skittered off the wall. Metal bit into my stomach. My hands cramped and my wet shirt flapped against my back. For a heart-stopping moment, I was certain I was about to fall. My frantic brain pictured it in high resolution, my body cracking into the couplings and rag-dolling onto the tracks before dozens of metal wheels sliced me into something unrecognizable. *Just like Henry.* Then my toe hooked on a ladder rung. I sobbed an exhalation and eased myself down.

Between the cars, chains clinked and chattered. I braced against the pull of deceleration as the train slowed even more. And then I heard a voice to my right.

"Shouldn't be out here. Idiot."

I spun and took in the silhouette of a slight man clinging to the brake wheel. *Shit.*

"You ain't one of his." He hissed and reached for me.

I jumped. There wasn't time to consider it. I just bunched my legs and launched myself off the ladder as far as I could. I barely had time to get my feet under me before I hit the steep bank. Air pounded out of me. My ankles screamed at the impact. I crashed to my knees and somersaulted, limbs flailing, unable to stop my inertia. Adrenalin pumped through me as I skidded to a stop, and before my body could inventory its injuries, I scrambled to my feet and tottered into a copse of scraggly trees.

I collapsed there, blinking into the soft purple of a dusk sky while raindrops tapped my cheeks and the train receded toward the weak lights of the railyard. Hot pain flared in one knee. A horrible ache bit into my shoulder and pierced my neck. My mind flashed back to Vinton as I remembered him after the fall, a wreck at the dusty bottom of a ravine, his legs shattered and his eyes wide with shock. *You deserve this,* a wretched voice in my head insisted. *You deserve more than sunburn scars from that day. You should be hurt like you hurt him.*

That's when I heard the first gunshots.

Pops and cracks interspersed with sharp yells from the yard.

Oh Sol, they're coming for me. I tucked further into the undergrowth.

The locomotive let out a long, piercing whistle as it shuddered to a stop. And then another. It kept bawling into the night like some great animal brought to its knees by a pack of predators.

I froze, but the gunshots and yells didn't get any closer, and it took a moment before I realized what was happening. Ben wasn't shooting at me. Someone was attacking him and his men. That's why he'd told me to hide in the crate. Why would the town strike their own transport as it returned home? A high inhuman screech boiled up before cutting off abruptly. Oh Sol, this wasn't some half-hearted scuffle. *People only scream like that when they're being killed.*

Panting, I blinked down at my torn pants and bloodied knee. My heart kept cramming up my throat. I felt like running and vomiting at the same time. Rolling my shoulder and flexing my ankles, I tested if I'd broken anything, and the pain didn't get worse. *So, run. You're not hurt, and this is your one chance to get to Robert.* If Clowes's town was in an uproar, its manager might be distracted enough for me to reach his hostage undetected. We could escape together in the chaos. I could still make this right.

I heaved to my feet and scrambled up the incline, over the rails and away from the clamor of the train yard.

The wind changed and I gagged at the acidic taste of it. It burned my eyes and throat. Blinking at the horizon, I saw a faint glow flickering from the direction of the slave quarters and the mines. I trotted in the opposite direction, toward the semaphore tower on top of the church and Clowes's estate. But as I dodged through dark alleys, the sound of fighting grew closer.

Company houses with neat yards and fresh coats of paint hulked in the dark, blinds snugly shut and inhabitants still and hushed within. There were no open windows. No one sat on stoops or smoked on porches. The whole town felt like a held breath.

I barely managed to tuck into a side yard before two men in ragged light blue coveralls sprinted down the street toward the Clowes's estate, lanterns bouncing. I was close enough to see the grim set of their faces and hear the fuel sloshing in the jugs they hauled. They rounded a corner, and I almost worked up the courage to ease out of my hiding spot when I heard the pound of hooves on pavement.

Three riders on horses clattered by at a full gallop, leaning low over their saddles, guns drawn and ready. "There!" One of them skidded to a stop and pointed down the road the first two men had taken. The other two yanked their mounts around and spurred them onward. Moments later, gunshots and startled shrieks filled the acrid air.

"Stop right there. Unless you want the next one through your ear!" someone bellowed.

Slipping across the street, I threaded through side yards, painfully aware of my weaponless status.

I was three blocks away from Darwin Clowes's mansion when a single runner in light blue overalls bolted out of an alley ahead of me. I jolted to a stop at the sight of him and he did the same.

He was tall, built like a spider, all limbs and odd angles in the dark. He didn't carry a lantern. Instead, he gripped a meat hook in one fist and a butcher knife in the other. The blade was already black with blood. He straightened and spat on the road. "Dressed awfully nice to be one of us."

I glanced down and realized I was still wearing Ben Breyman's leather jacket zipped over my own work clothes. "I took a jacket." Unzipping it, I held it open so he could see the coal stains and the worn light blue. "Look, I'm from the mines."

"Don't recognize you. Don't see no armband neither, darling. That means you're one of them." He prodded the meat hook toward Clowes's house. "Talk like one of them," he purred and bolted toward me.

"No," I yelped, spinning and sprinting. Heat surged through me, and I poured all of my energy into the flex and release of my legs eating up ground, the smack of my heels on asphalt. Perhaps I could have shaken my pursuer had I veered off the road, but I was far past the point of rational thought. I ran like a flushed animal, too stupid to evade, darting straight down the open street. Over the thunder of blood in my head, the thud of his boots and the puff of his breathing closed in behind me. He was catching me, eating up ground with long-legged strides I couldn't hope to match.

Fire licked through my lungs and breath rasped out of me. I imagined the meat hook plunging deep into my shoulder and the butcher knife's keen edge parting my throat at any second. The man was nearly on top of me when a rider with a cowboy hat on a gray horse charged onto the road ahead.

I banked into a front yard, skidding on the wet grass.

The rider raised a weapon, and something whistled past my shoulder.

My pursuer grunted and toppled to the ground.

I looked back in time to see the fletching of a crossbow arrow protruding from his shoulder as he dropped the meat hook and rolled.

One blue fletching. Two red. *My crossbow arrow.*

"Don't!" Ben barked, driving his horse to block my path as I tried to lunge around him. He drew his handgun and levelled it at the man on the ground. "Drop the knife, Yanish, or the next shot won't be a crossbow bolt and it won't miss."

"Turncoat." The knife clattered to the ground, and the man named Yanish bared his teeth and spat. "Grace would slice your throat herself if she could."

Scowling, Ben leaned down and extended a hand to me. "Get on the horse."

"You took my crossbow." I blurted.

"Get on the goddamned horse, Iris!"

I did. I rode in stunned silence with Ben Breyman's arm clamped around my waist all the way to Darwin Clowes's estate.

CHAPTER
EIGHTEEN

en took his jacket back. We stood outside the closed varnished doors of the Clowes's dining room for several long breaths without knocking. I ignored the itch of blood running down my shin and the stitches pulling at my scalp and gaped at Ben's face as he blinked rapidly at the wood paneling. His fingers remained clamped on my arm, just above the elbow.

He took a handkerchief out of his pocket and wiped the sweat from his upper lip. Then, he raked his fingers through his hair, squeezed his eyes shut and rolled his shoulders. Stress melted from Ben's face, replaced by that maddeningly affable smile, but his grip on my arm didn't change.

"I saved your life tonight," he whispered. "So do us both a favor and keep your mouth shut."

No you didn't, I thought. *You stole my crossbow and brought me to my death.*

He knocked on the door, two restrained raps. It reminded me of the way I used to knock on Mom's office door when I really didn't want to go in.

"Come." It wasn't Darwin Clowes's nasal voice that answered from within. It was Kahn's.

I froze.

Ben took one last exhale, smiled wider, and pulled open the dining room doors.

The room within blazed with candlelight. I was hit immediately with the smell of candied ham, brussel sprouts, and cigar smoke.

Six people dressed in starched formal wear sat at the lavishly set table. Amelia Clowes and her two friends sat on the near side of the table. Kahn, Clowes, and Robert sat on the far side, facing us. Behind them, a row of servants in light blue stood at attention.

"Iris?" Robert's voice cracked and his face fell as he saw me. "Oh Sol, no."

My eyes blurred and my breath snagged. I opened my mouth, but Ben pinched my arm hard and pulled me to a stop.

Kahn's smile was tight, but he purred with satisfaction when he spoke. "There she is. Your slave is a reliable retriever." His eyes flicked to Ben.

"You doubted it?" Mr. Clowes huffed. "This has turned out to be a sour evening indeed." To Ben, he snapped, "Could you not have cleaned up somewhat before bringing her? Look how you've upset the ladies."

They'd all swiveled in their chairs to face us. Mrs. Clowes covered her lips with a lace kerchief. The plunge of her evening gown showed all the tension in her neck. She stared at my bloodied knee a little too long before glancing away. "My appetite is quite ruined," she murmured.

Her friend, the one who'd worn the severe make up on our first visit, arched a manicured brow and lazily wafted an ornate feathered fan.

The third woman, the one closest to Robert, listed in her chair and giggled loudly. "She looks like a wet rat. He does too.

Is this how you keep your help, Darwin?" She took several gulps of red wine.

Robert sagged in his seat, face an unhealthy color, food untouched, but glass goblet drained.

Is he drunk? I wondered, breath burning my nostrils. *I've been worried for his life, and he's been sitting here drinking with spoiled rich girls?*

"Tell us you've cleared the rabble at the yard, at least?" Kahn glared at Ben.

"Yes, sir. It was a more aggressive effort than last time, but my men have contained it and I've doubled the guard around the estate tonight."

"Are they still playing at an uprising?" Amelia Clowes asked. "I heard they've adopted a little bird as their flag. Hardly threatening, is it?"

"We'll squash it, my dear. We always do." Mr. Clowes waved one of the servants over to refill his wine glass, a girl, younger than me with black hair and hazel eyes.

Ben's fingers spasmed. He stared hard at the girl as she poured. "They lit mine number two on fire, sir."

"It was almost done producing anyway. I'm not worried about the loss. It's them who'll have to live with the fumes, stupid creatures," Clowes said.

Kahn's cold eyes fixed on me with something I'd never seen in them before. Possessiveness. "Take it from someone who's weathered a rebellion, Darwin, and don't underestimate how willingly stupid people rise against their betters."

Clowes waved him off. "Shall we have dessert?"

Kahn replied with his gaze still locked on mine. "I'm not sure Robert's up to another course."

There wasn't enough air in here with the cigar smoke swirling overhead. I was losing the conversation, backsliding into panic.

"I'll eat his portion." The tipsy woman stood, walked behind Robert, and playfully slapped his back.

His reaction was immediate and incongruent. He sat bolt upright and screamed.

"Sibyl, you oaf! His back." The woman with the fan hissed.

"I forgot!" she snapped. "Really, Darwin. Talk to your whipping man. He's ruined the poor boy. Look he's bled through another shirt." She plopped back into her chair.

I couldn't process the words because Robert was clutching the edge of the table, saliva bubbling between his teeth. His hands were bound at the wrists. *Why is he tied?* "Robert?" I croaked and he flinched.

Whipping man. "What did you do?" I snarled at Kahn and his lips curled into another sneer.

"Slaves get corporal punishment for their crimes, Iris. And you weren't here to pay for yours."

"What did you do?" I roared again despite Ben twisting my arm hard.

Darwin Clowes snapped his fingers at Ben. "I'll not have this getting out of hand at my table."

"Yes, sir." He drew his weapon and pressed it against my temple.

"Again? Is this really necessary?" Amelia Clowes wrinkled her nose.

"Some semblance of control? Yes, it is," Kahn snapped at her. "How easily they forget their place if you don't keep them on a short leash."

"I'm sorry, Iris." Robert sobbed.

I'd never seen him cry before. The devastation in his bloodshot eyes broke me. "Please." I gulped, tears blurring my vision. I wanted to say something else, something to fix this, but all I could get out was the same word, over and over. "Please. *Please.*"

Kahn shook his head, disgust stamped on his face. "Control yourselves."

The drunk woman patted Robert's arm and passed over her sloshing glass. "Have some wine, dear. Or I have something stronger if you'd rather?"

Kahn pulled his napkin off his lap, placing it beside his plate before standing and rounding the table to stop before me. I found myself blinking at his chest. I couldn't look further up. I'd claw his eyes out or collapse in a heap if I did. Breath boiled out of me, too loud and too fast.

"Apologize for raising your voice," he said.

"Someone help him, please," I whimpered.

"Apologize, or I'll send him back to the whipping post right now and you'll watch."

Ben's gun nudged my temple. "I'm sorry." I gulped, gaze pinned on Robert.

"Look at me when you say it." Kahn grabbed my chin and I cringed. He wrenched my head up.

His face looked dead, like no emotion had ever lived there, but his eyes betrayed him, sharp and hungry behind his severe glasses.

"I'm sorry."

"I'm sorry," Robert's wail echoed mine. "It was all my idea. Please don't hurt her." Everyone at the table neatly ignored him.

"Go and stand with the others." Kahn waved me toward the servants standing rigidly along the back wall.

"Help him, please." I tried to turn my head to plead with Ben, but he kept his weapon pinned to my head and marched me over to the other slaves. His gaze kept slipping to the girl with the black hair.

"Keep your mouth closed. Last warning." Kahn sat with a sigh. "Every word out of you will be a lash for him, tomorrow. Am I understood?"

I clenched my teeth and nodded.

"Ah look, dessert's come." Amelia Clowes spoke brightly

over Robert's moaning. Two more servants bustled in balancing delicate plates with thick wedges of cheesecake.

"Raspberry," the woman with the fan whined. "Amelia, I told you I despise raspberries."

The servers set a plate in front of everyone seated, including Robert. They cleared his untouched dinner plate as he slumped over it. A large splotch of blood bloomed on the back of his shirt.

Nausea gripped me as I blinked at it.

"Let's get back to business, shall we?" Clowes scooped up his fork and shoveled in a mouthful of cake, speaking around it. "Ben, you can stand down. She looks to be controllable now."

"Yes, sir." He lowered the gun and let go of my arm but remained standing nearby.

Clowes continued, "You were saying, David, before we were so rudely interrupted?"

Kahn didn't touch his dessert. "I fear Fernie has become unstable. I don't trust you have your people under control here and I've had my fill of insurrections. I'm taking the managerial position in Mullan. The man I posted there has a wife who can't tolerate the cold winters so I'm sending him further south. I'd like to oversee an operable copper mining operation myself and send a bigger workforce to my city. You'll lend me your coach."

Clowes's shoulders tensed. His tone was hard, but still reverential. "I'd be delighted to. It's currently being repaired but should be operable in a few days. Will that suit?"

"Can you keep your slave quarter under control until then?"

"Certainly. I have more reinforcements from our clients en route as we speak. Ben and his men have made the Mullan run several times. They'll ensure you have a safe journey down."

"Thank you, but I don't need your spies along for the ride." Kahn glanced at Ben. "What's to stop him from putting that gun to my head as soon as he's out of your sight?"

"Obedience." Clowes spat crumbs. "I don't need a fence

around this one." He jabbed his dirty fork at Robert and me. "Just as you're using him to control her right now, I hold leverage over Ben—not that I require it. I picked him up when he was a child and he's proven to be quite loyal." He put down his cutlery and wiped his mouth. "Would you like a demonstration?"

The girl with the black hair made a small sound in her throat.

Ben's gaze iced over, and he shook his head at her almost imperceptibly.

And then, I recognized her, realized why I knew her face. She had a rash on her upper lip, the same spot where the boy with the hazel eyes had worn his moustache. Same height. Same build. Her breath smelled like rotten teeth. This was Robert's contact. The boy with the lunch pail wasn't a boy. *Ben knows her? Why on earth would she help orchestrate my escape, just for him to bring me back?*

"I'd like to ensure my head remains on my shoulders," Kahn said. "I don't need to see him perform party tricks, thank you."

The drunk woman clapped her hands and bounced in her chair. "Oh, I love party tricks. Show us, Darwin!" Something was wrong with her, I realized. The pupils of her eyes were dilated unnaturally, like two black holes.

Robert kept his head down, breaths coming in wheezes.

Oh Sol. My gaze drifted to the smoldering cigar in the ash tray in front of Mr. Clowes. *His asthma.*

"Ben, sit." Clowes pointed to the empty seat to Robert's left.

"Yes, sir." He strode away from me and took a seat at the table, carefully setting his weapon in front of him.

Clowes snapped his fingers at the black-haired girl. "Give me Robert's dessert."

She did, throat working.

Darwin Clowes held the plate under his chin, snorted loudly, and spat a thick wad of phlegm onto the raspberry puree. Then he handed it to the woman with the fan. She pursed her red painted lips and daintily spat an addition onto the plate before passing it to Kahn.

"This is ludicrous," he said, pressing the plate toward Mrs. Clowes.

"Come now, David. Feel free to be creative about it." She reached into her elaborately styled hair and plucked out several strands, laying them across the defiled dessert.

"Amelia, I didn't get a turn!" the intoxicated woman cried. Stumbling to her feet again, she hiked up her skirts and swept past Robert and Ben, dilated eyes as wide as buttons. "Wait!" she slapped at the wrist of a servant who was clearing away the platter of ham. Grabbing a fatty chunk of meat, she stuffed it into her mouth, chewed several times, and expelled the masticated mess onto the cake.

"Heaven's, Sibyl." Amelia sniffed.

The smile had dropped from Ben's face. He stared straight ahead, Adam's apple bobbing.

The room went silent except for the whistle of Robert's breathing.

The girl beside me exhaled hard.

The stench of rotten teeth and cigar smoke coated my throat.

"Pick up the cake, Ben," Clowes ordered.

"Yes, sir," he said hoarsely. His chair squealed as he stood. He pushed the gun aside with a trembling hand and set the plate down before him.

"Eat it."

Ben winced and cleared his throat. He turned to look at Amelia, blue eyes pleading, but his voice was even when he spoke. "Ma'am, could I trouble you for a fork?"

"This is repulsive and entirely unnecessary." Kahn clipped his words as Mrs. Clowes ran her tongue over a clean fork before holding it out to Ben.

"You questioned me, David. You've accused me of losing

control of my slaves and I'd like to prove a point, if I may?" Clowes said. "Go on, Ben."

Robert's head turned to me, just enough for his eyes to meet mine. The terror in them rooted me to the spot. I'd seen it before in animals I'd downed with my bow but hadn't yet killed. That unmistakable mixture of panic and pleading at the same time. I clapped both hands over my mouth to curb the sob swelling up in me.

Ben Breyman stabbed the fork into the cheesecake and shoved a chunk littered with glistening bits of ham into his mouth.

Sibyl gagged.

"Good boy," Clowes said.

We all watched in horror as Ben choked on the mouthful. It took him three tries to swallow. When he moved to put the fork down Clowes held up his hand.

"No. Eat it all."

"Enough." Kahn pushed away from the table.

"But it isn't." Clowes barked. "Respectfully, David, you've never travelled south. It's a long trip through dreadfully dangerous country. You'll need an armed escort who knows the way, and he does. You questioned how well I control my property, and I am showing you."

Ben gripped the fork hard, knuckles white.

"Hurry, my boy. I think your tablemate requires medical attention." Clowes raised his eyebrows at Robert. His lips were turning blue.

Bile scalded my throat and blood reverberated between my ears. This wasn't happening. It couldn't be. This was something out of a deranged horror movie. I clamped my teeth hard enough to send pain firing up my jaw while Ben shoveled forkful after forkful of congealing cake into his mouth.

At one point he retched loudly, and Mrs. Clowes clucked her tongue like she was scolding a small child.

Sibyl made a guttural barking noise and lurched toward the door.

"Let her go, Darwin. Belladonna and wine do not mix well. She's embarrassing herself," Amelia said.

"Fine, Sibyl, you're excused."

The rest of us watched until Ben finished the last bite and set down the fork. By the time he was done, the servant with the black hair was flushed and staring hard at her scuffed shoes.

"He does what I tell him, David." Clowes crushed his half-smoked cigar into the ash tray before him. "*Whatever*, I tell him."

"Bravo. Point taken." Kahn arched an eyebrow. "I'm having my slave seen to before he drops."

"Of course. The medic is staying in the loft above the carriage house. Ben, if you'd be good enough to show David and Robert the way?"

"Yes, sir." Ben wiped his mouth and picked up his weapon. "Right this way, Mr. Kahn." He grabbed Robert's elbow and eased him to his feet.

I trotted numbly out the door after them.

In the hallway, Robert stumbled, and Kahn nodded at me, unruffled. "Make yourself useful."

I tucked under Robert's free arm, careful to avoid touching his back. "I'm here," I whispered. "I'm right here, okay?"

"Oh Sol," he rasped as we crashed out the back door into a cold night filled with the smell of burning. "I'm sorry. I wanted to . . ." He didn't have enough breath to finish.

We crossed the yard in abject silence, Kahn following at a distance behind us. Ben remained outside as we tromped up the carriage house stairs. I heard loud vomiting as the door closed behind us.

Kahn refused to let me stay. He steered me back down the stairs as soon as I deposited Robert on the medic's couch. "I assume you have a secure place to keep her?" he asked Ben when we got to the door.

"Yes, sir," the cowboy answered.

Ben took me to the cellar flanking the kitchen and I slept on the floor of the narrow, locked room with all the other kitchen staff.

I worked in the kitchen for the next three days. I was given a scratchy woven blue dress to replace my coal-stained work clothes. One of the girls I worked with was the one with black hair and hazel eyes. She didn't speak, but she responded to the name Grace. She spent most of her time at the pot scouring station, staring out the small window above the sink. Occasionally, she'd drop what she was doing, pull out a pad of paper and a stub of a pencil from her dress pocket, and jot something down. I caught sight of a sketch of an owl on one of the pages before she saw me and pocketed the notepad hastily.

She didn't leave the kitchens at all. Her days delivering letters in disguise were apparently over.

I didn't see Kahn or Ben or Robert until we left the Clowes's estate and started our journey south.

CHAPTER
NINETEEN

hat in Sol's name is that?" I blurted as Ben led me roughly from the kitchen to the carriage house. Two men were rolling a vehicle through the large overhead doorway that looked like nothing I'd ever seen.

It had a wide alloy base with metal spoked wheels as thin as a motorcycle's but far taller. All four tires had gouges deep enough to deflate an air-filled tire, indicating that these ones were solid rubber no-flats. Anchored onto the chassis was a sleek gray metal pod with dark tinted windows, an oval door, and a luggage rack topped with solar panel roofing. I couldn't see any motor or batteries.

"That is Stagecoach One. Some fancy car company produced a limited run of them soon as they saw the end of the world coming. Figured they could still make a buck off the rich if they focused on modernizing horse-drawn vehicles. I'm told this one comes with regenerative braking, hill assist, and lithium-ion batteries."

"I don't know what half of that is," I huffed.

"Neither do I. All I know is the Prime Minister had one—back when there was still a government—and that made Mr.

Clowes want one as well. He gets what he wants." Ben's words were edged in anger, his hallmark smile absent. He marched me up to his gray horse, clucked his tongue, and patted my head while the inquisitive animal watched. "Smokey, hold 'em," he said to the horse and then to me, "Stay right by him. You move too fast or run, he'll take you down and he'll use his teeth to do it."

I froze and swallowed hard. Smokey nickered softly and blew warm breath down the back of my neck.

Ben went to help the two men hook up the carriage tongue while four matching horses in harnesses waited to be led into their positions. There were seven other horses with single riders, one of them was towing a cargo wagon that looked ancient compared to the stagecoach. I recognized members of Ben's crew from the train.

Gazing back at the massive house softening in the evening light, I willed Robert to walk through those doors healthy. I'd thought of little else these past days. The abject misery on his face when he'd recognized me, the ache in his voice as he'd repeated the words *I'm sorry,* and the tormented realization that I'd assumed the worst of him as soon as I'd set foot in that dining room—as soon as I'd seen his empty wine glass, it all undid me.

I had scrubbed silver platters and cast-iron pots with raw, chapped hands, dissecting every moment of that horrible night, laying it bare and replaying what I could have done differently. I'd dreamed about blood splotches soaking through white dress shirts. The need to know that Robert was alright shredded my nerves and stole air from my lungs. I couldn't consider the alternative.

So, when he stepped off the back door stoop behind David Kahn, dressed in business casual and keeping pace with the man who was now his master, my heart vaulted into my throat and my head filled with error codes. I didn't even realize I was lurching toward him until something snagged the fabric of my shirt's shoulder and yanked me backward.

Yelping, I slapped at the hand that held me, but it wasn't a hand.

Smokey squealed and flared his huge nostrils.

The horse bit your shirt.

"I told you not to move!" Ben barked. "You're lucky he didn't take your arm off."

Huge, yellowed teeth flashed to my right as the horse let go. I swayed, rooted to the spot, breath sawing out of me as Kahn swept by with a smug sneer and Robert passed without even looking at me, face flushed and eyes expressionless.

"Robert?" I squeaked.

Kahn nodded to Ben. "This one's still healing. He'll be riding inside with me."

"Yes, sir." Ben nodded. "We'll secure your things."

"Put her with the rest of the baggage. I want no trouble."

"Yes, sir."

Something in my stomach went nuclear, a heat I couldn't stop, a meltdown of emotions radiating through my ribcage. The horse must have sensed it because he glared at me with white-rimmed eyes, his head and tail held high.

As soon as Kahn and Robert climbed into the sleek carriage and closed the door behind them, Ben dropped the harness lines he'd been untangling and strode toward me with his hand on his gun. "Don't," he hissed. He didn't stop until we were standing face to face, and I couldn't look anywhere other than into his hard, blue eyes.

"Don't what?" I growled.

"Don't make trouble." His jaw muscle twitched. "Can you not keep your head down for one damned second?"

I raised my eyebrows. "You going to shoot another man's property, Ben?"

"If it comes to that. If I'm ordered to." He leaned closer, wearing that incongruent bright smile like a mask.

Don't lean away. Don't let him intimidate you. "I don't believe you. You're not a killer. You're a coward."

Ben's smile didn't waver, but his eyes deadened, and his grip tightened on his holstered gun. His leather jacket creaked as he straightened and stared me down until I finally looked away. "Roll over and show my belly, right? They feed me table scraps and everything," he whispered. Then, he turned on his heel and strode away, tossing his next words over his shoulder loud enough for everyone else to hear. "Make yourself useful. Start packing bags. Anyone slacks off and I'll have Smokey here take a piece out of you."

THE BAGGAGE TRUNK was little more than a ledge on the back of the stagecoach capsule with a retractable awning to protect cargo from inclement weather. I balanced precariously on two suitcases looking back the way we'd come at four of Ben's men bringing up the rear. The other four were posted at the head of the caravan, and they'd all donned ballistic vests under their jackets before we left the Clowes's estate and headed south. I was the only unprotected person outside. I felt naked in my threadbare dress.

I shivered violently before Ben offered me a gray blanket from his horse's saddlebag and I was almost certain he'd waited purposely, ensuring that the cold ate away at my resistance before he offered the barest of comfort. My leg muscles were seizing so badly, I couldn't have run if I tried. Soldamnit, was every move he made a calculated manipulation?

We travelled under a blustery evening sky that threatened rain but never delivered. As we made our jarring way south and merged onto a larger thoroughfare, Ben stopped periodically at the semaphore towers lining the road, passing handwritten notes to the operators within, checking in with Clowes, I assumed. Other travelers gathered around us. People riding bicycles, or astride mules, or riding wagons pulled by goats, they all carried lanterns and adjusted their pace to match ours.

"What's the deal?" I asked when Ben pulled alongside the coach.

"Security." He stretched in his saddle. "Less likelihood of getting robbed blind by marauders if you attach yourself to an armed caravan. We'll clear them off when we stop for the morning."

Four hours into our journey, we pulled into a rest stop and the coach door opened. Working by lamplight, the crew folded down the panels of the cargo trailer revealing a portable kitchen. One of the men started preparing sandwiches and another set up a pop-up lavatory for Mr. Kahn that the rest of us weren't allowed to use. We took turns following the dirt trail into the bush that smelled overwhelmingly of human waste. I gathered up my skirt, breathed through my mouth, and resolutely followed Robert, well aware that Ben was holding up his lantern to watch us from horseback.

Robert was zipping up his fly when I intercepted him. He startled at the sight of me and then shook his head. *What the hell?*

"We need to talk." I gulped.

"I don't think that's a good idea," he said slowly.

The words struck me square in the chest and threw me back to the moment at Robert's doorway years ago, the first time I'd ruined his life with a single typo. "How dare you." My voice wobbled.

He held out his palms and swallowed hard. "Didn't mean it like that. H-he's using me against you. Knows the best way to hurt you is through me and I don't . . . I don't want to be that tool."

"Bullshit. You never meant to escape with me. You intended to be his tool for a good long time." I'd meant to do this rationally, but Robert's eyes were already filling with tears and so were mine.

"I was *protecting* you. He would have killed you." The short laugh that burst out of him was a garbled, broken sound. "Would have found my way out, eventually. Just needed you safe first."

"Eventually? Sol Almighty." I couldn't stop the heat warping my words and twisting my face.

"You're angry because I took your whipping?" An answering heat ignited in Robert's eyes. "I'd do it again."

"I didn't ask for a martyr," I sputtered.

"I'd do it again." His voice slurred even as tears spilled down his cheeks. "You weren't there. Y-you didn't hear the things he said he'd do to you."

"Do not twist this!" I yelled. "You told me we were both going home in those letters. That we'd meet at the train. You *lied* to get me to leave."

Ben urged Smokey through the brush toward us, his lantern bathing us in light.

Robert's eyes met mine. They looked strange. "I-I can't do this, Iris. Can't be close to you without him using it against us. I keep f-fragging it all up."

There was something wrong with him, I realized. At first, I'd thought it was pain causing Robert's words to run together, but his pupils were too big, like Amelia Clowes's friend's had been at that horrible dinner.

"Are you taking something?" I leaned toward him, squinting.

"Sybil felt sorry for me. Gave me something to help . . . with the pain. Don't tell anyone."

Before I could say anything else, Ben reached us, and Robert stumbled past me. I didn't see him for the rest of the night.

BY DAWN, I felt like a gutted fish, like something essential had been ripped out of me and air wasn't sustaining enough to breathe. The cook on Ben's crew stoked his stove and made us pan-fried potatoes and bacon. He plated two portions, carefully garnishing them with a side of thin sliced strawberries before delivering them to Stagecoach One. The rest of us ate our meals out of tin cups with wooden spoons.

I didn't think I was hungry, but the potatoes were delicately spiced with pepper and lemon, and the bacon was crisp and salty. It warmed my belly and left me staring forlornly at the empty bottom of my cup.

Kahn and Robert stood outside while Ben converted the benches in the stagecoach into beds. Robert kept his back to me, but the sight of him still reddened my cheeks and wound my chest up tight. He looked unsteady and stiff on his feet like someone learning to walk on ice. The awkward way he held his arms away from his sides sent an uncomfortable tingle up my back. I couldn't imagine how badly his wounds must have been hurting him to make him resort to heavy drugs. He'd told me how much he hated alcohol, how it had ruined his family. I wanted to slip my hand into his. I wanted to corner him and scream at him. Mostly, I wanted someone to grip me by the arms, shake me awake, and assure me that none of this was real.

All my emotions balled up in my throat as Kahn helped Robert gingerly ascend the steps of the coach and Ben closed the door behind them.

One of the men doled out reflective solar blankets and I shrugged under mine gratefully. I spent the rest of the day huddled in its folds. The smell of pine needles and strong-brewed tea filled my nostrils. My eyes ached from the bright sunlight and the cookstove smoke, but I couldn't sleep. I yearned for music in my ears to drown out my thoughts. I missed sleeping in a real bed. I couldn't remember the last time I'd slept soundly.

The majority of the crew settled under their solar sleeping bags wordlessly while Ben and the cook kept their ballistic vests on and their guns visible as they took the first watch, tucked under pop-up sunshades. Shadows moved behind the tinted windows of the stagecoach. In the still heat of the day, I heard the murmur of conversing from within, and it turned my stomach. So, I concentrated on other sounds outside, the cook splashing dirty dishwater against a tree, the soft scrape of bristles as Ben brushed his horse. I drowned in the unending, chaotic current of my thoughts.

At some point, clouds darkened the sky, and the temperature dropped. Ben and his watch partner navigated around their sleeping cohorts to crowd closer to the cook fire. They poured cups of tea from the kettle bubbling over the coals and offered me one when they saw I was awake.

"You should sleep." Fire danced in Ben's eyes as he passed me a chipped mug. "We've got ten more nights of this to get you to your new home."

"Don't call it that," I whispered.

"Sooner you accept your new station, the easier it'll be."

"More slave-to-slave advice for me? I think I've had my fill, Ben."

"You know what he's doing, right?" He tossed his chin toward the stagecoach. "Making your boy a favorite, making sure everyone hates him. Isolating him and keeping him off-center so he's got no one else to turn to. And here you are just fanning the flames, confronting him, stirring up emotions, doing Kahn's job for him. Rich people don't know how to deal with us any other way except as tools. For someone unwilling, you're making a mighty willing tool right now."

"As opposed to you? You're the most willing tool of all, aren't you?" I gulped a mouthful of scalding tea that burned all the way down. Blinking up at the churning clouds, I asked, "Do you even feel like a person anymore?"

"Not for a long time," he answered immediately, smile quick on his lips.

The cook squirmed uncomfortably beside him.

Silence folded around us, interrupted only by the bubbling hiss of sap, the percolating kettle, and the tinny crackle of coals.

The heat of my mug stung my chapped hands. I squeezed it tight and forced myself to take three deep breaths. Then I said, "I worked with Grace in the kitchen."

Ben flinched visibly, the smile falling from his face.

"Who is she to you?"

"She's none of your business, ma'am." His voice was low with warning.

"The man you shot on the street, the one who called you a turncoat, he said Grace would cut your throat if she could."

"She would," he rasped. "I'd do the same for her. We'd put each out of our misery if we could, but Clowes keeps her too close for that."

"She's his leverage against you. A hostage?"

A slow sneer twisted his face. He took a long swallow of tea before answering. "Nah, ma'am. We all just follow Darwin Clowes's orders 'cause we love his good and righteous ways."

I gulped at the venom in his words, realization clicking into place. "He's holding someone you love, every one of you. Every man on your crew, using them against you."

Ben didn't answer. He looked like a demon through the heat-waves, eyes too bright, face wrestling through emotions so quickly I couldn't track them.

The cook cleared his throat. "That's how he grooms us. Picks the poor bastards who only have one person left they love and snatches them away."

"Shut up, Lawrence," Ben snapped, but the man continued undeterred.

"Makes it look like a pretty little favor too. 'I'll get your wife out of the mines and into the tipple house,' he told me. 'Keep her safe, feed her three square meals, give her a job with a chance of earning out her indentureship.'" A shaky sigh bled from the man. "By the time he's got his claws in them, it's too late." He pointed to the young man gently snoring beside him. "His father." He kept indicating other sleepers around the fire. "Mum. Wife. Cousin. Brother. Brother there too. Girlfriend."

The circle ended at Ben. He looked less like a demon and more like a broken boy now, clutching his cup like it'd fall to pieces if he didn't.

"Who's Grace?" I asked quietly.

"My sister," he whispered.

My mind immediately went to Vinton, Mom, and Dad. I couldn't imagine what I would turn into if someone used them against me. *Don't have to worry about that. You've dug yourself a big enough hole that you're never going to see your family again.* Swallowing against the intrusive thought, I said, "What if she was safe? What if they all were?" My mind scrolled outward, thoughts jumping synapses like they were bright, burning stars.

Ben snorted. "Never going to happen."

"Not before. None of you had anywhere to go, but our city's a stronghold. We could make it even stronger together."

"Doesn't matter." Lawrence the cook frowned. "If we run, Mr. Clowes tortures our families. He's expecting a message sent up the tower line every few hours. We don't check in, they're good as dead."

"We could save them. Split up your crew. Keep sending messages up the line. Tell him we're heading south, but some of us go back north. Distract Clowes. Your town is like a tinder box. It wouldn't take much to cause another riot. A bigger one."

"And who do you think the miners would come for first?" Ben hissed. "We're Clowes's right-hand men. They consider us turncoats, all of us. They'd tear us up before we could save anyone or make a run for it."

"You saw our motorcycles. We have more. Our Browsers would help. You all have horses. We could be fast. In and out before Clowes knew what hit him."

"Enough. Stop talking nonsense around my fire." Ben tossed the dregs of his tea into the flames sending steam billowing.

I leaned closer. "If it's nonsense then why are you afraid to answer? What if she was safe, Ben? Theoretically. Humor me."

He studied me through the smoke like something wild and unafraid of the dark. "Well then we'd be a pack of dogs with no leashes, wouldn't we, ma'am?"

CHAPTER
TWENTY

The clouds cleared, and sunset ripened the sky into apricot tones. Mountains receded, and the landscape yawned into a vast grassland. Tawny fields of desiccated crops looked like fire in the orange glow. Slack barbwire fences bordered the road, and crows with nacreous eyes and dull beaks cocked their heads as we rolled by. Clouds of gnats swarmed us, setting the horses' skin to crawling and their tails whipping as they bit the big animals' backs and bellies. My legs twitched and my stomach cramped. I ached from sitting wedged amongst the luggage in the baggage trunk. Restlessness crackled through me, threaded under my skin, and tugged at my muscles.

Ben had been avoiding me all evening. My jaw clenched at the idea of asking him for favors, but I needed to move. I hadn't walked, run, or worked since I left the kitchen at the Clowes's estate. Every second I stayed still balled up like static in my bones.

The next time he slowed his horse to check on his rear guard, I called to him, my voice embarrassingly thin. "Hey, could I walk for a bit?"

He picked a bur out of Smokey's mane. "Do you think I'm stupid?"

"Where would I go?" My voice cracked. "It's endless grass out here. You're all on horseback. You'd run me down in a heartbeat. I just need to stretch. It's not a big ask."

"You'd fall behind. Marauders like to pick off the stragglers. You've got no protection." He thumbed at his own ballistic vest. "And my job is to get you and your master to Mullan alive and whole."

"Stay with me, then. I'll walk beside Smokey. You can see marauders coming for miles on terrain like this and I could ride behind you to catch up to everyone else if we needed to. Fifteen minutes, Ben. Please." Zuse, I sounded pathetic.

Smokey squealed and threw his head up, sidestepping away from the stagecoach, but Ben controlled him. "You can pace when we stop for a break."

"I can't . . ." The rest of my words stuck to my tongue like feathers. I scrubbed at my eyes with the heels of my hands to hide how my face was crumpling. How could I explain that I felt like I'd scratch my own skin off if I didn't burn this nervous energy? It wasn't normal, was it? Just another Iris anomaly.

"Fifteen minutes." Ben wrenched his hat down over his brow. "No talking. No nonsense. Understand?"

"Thank you," I blurted.

He didn't bother asking the stagecoach driver to stop, just eased his jittery horse alongside and then held out his hand.

I awkwardly pulled myself out of the baggage trunk and swung my leg over Smokey's broad back, gripping Ben's shoulders hard as the horse flinched and snorted.

"Smokey, easy!" he barked, reining in until the rear riders and cook's wagon swept past us. "We're going to stretch our legs a bit. Be right behind you," he told Lawrence.

Then he stopped in the middle of the gravel road, dismounted, and helped me down. I expected him to vault back into his saddle. Instead, he rummaged through his saddle bag, shook out an oiled-leather hat with a wide, floppy brim and a built-in bug net. He handed it to me, grumbling. "Better than a solar blanket during the day and keeps some of the bugs off at night. Doesn't do a thing against these damned no-see-ums though, unfortunately." He waved a gnat away from his face.

"Thank you," I answered, wincing at the stiffness in my knees.

Smokey tossed his head and pinned his ears, but Ben controlled him with a sharp, "Whoa." He led the animal forward with a yank, setting a grueling pace. "I told the house staff to wash your things and get them back to you. Did they?"

I jammed the hat on and lengthened my stride to keep up. "They didn't."

We fell into silence. The hat smelled like horses and leather from old books. *It smells like Ben.* I cut off the uncomfortable thought and focused on the road ahead. My ears filled with the sound of our boots crunching on gravel. The even percussion of it tamped down my anxiety and soothed the ball of tension pulling on my insides. We settled into silence.

For ten minutes, we walked at a pace brisk enough to loosen my limbs and quicken my heart. The scratchy dress clung and chaffed under my armpits. Sweat dampened the band of my bra and between my thighs. It wasn't until I felt a rush of warmth soaking my underwear and trickling down my leg that I realized I had bigger problems than sweat. My stride faltered as my mind scrambled to count the days since my last period. *Oh, Sol. Not now.*

Smokey danced nervously and squealed. Ben swore under his breath and held his reins fast. "What is with him toda—" Stopping, he looked back at me shuffling to a stop in the middle of the road, my legs pressed tight together, holding my skirt away from me.

He glanced at his agitated horse before his piercing gaze

settled back on me, understanding dawning on his face. Clearing his throat, Ben asked quietly, "Your time of month?"

I couldn't meet his gaze. Humiliation swamped me as I nodded.

"He smells it on people. Makes him jumpy. Always has." Ben's cheeks reddened. "You, uh, don't have any supplies?"

"I told you, I don't have anything except what I'm already wearing," I choked.

"Don't worry. There's a roadside market ahead, about an hour away. They stock most things a traveler could need." He dug a med pack and a canteen out of his saddlebag and motioned to the open field flanking us. "Go take care of yourself as best you can, and we'll get you back to the coach. I'll buy whatever you need when we stop."

I tromped through the long grass and kept my back to Ben, hot tears burning my scarred cheeks as I washed and wrung out my underwear in a dusty, dark field. I cleaned myself and made a pad out of several layers of bandages. Then I splashed water on my face and cranked the hat down over my eyes as far as it would go before returning to Ben and Smokey.

We caught up with the crew and I crawled back into the baggage trunk fiercely wishing I could crawl underground instead.

BY THE TIME we reached the roadside market, my mouth was dry and my limbs lax with exhaustion.

The market was nearly a mile long. Covered stalls scabbed together with corrugated metal and plywood jostled for space. Cannibalized billboards boasted fresh neon spraypainted letters and blinking lights directing us to shoemakers, bicycle repairmen, clothiers, ointments and tinctures, and ice-cold raspberry mint tea. The air smelled like beeswax, oranges, and freshly baked bread.

Our caravan halted on an apron midway down the line and was immediately swamped by barkers plying their wares. My pounding head reeled at the noise, and I pressed my back against the wall behind me.

The stagecoach wobbled on its shocks, and feet plunked down the extendable steps. I heard Kahn's voice but not Robert's. "Another stop? I didn't order this."

"Restocking, sir. It's the last market for some time," Ben answered.

"Tell me, is your master physically incapable of travelling without an unwieldy entourage?"

"It keeps the ambushes down to a minimum, sir. Could I offer you a refreshment while you wait?"

"Save your coddling, boy. I don't need a babysitter." Kahn brushed past Ben and neatly ignored the buskers. I knocked on the fiberglass shell of the coach and called Robert's name, twice, but I couldn't hear any movement inside and he didn't answer.

Once the mob of sellers thinned, Ben fetched me and led me to a stall packed with stacks of folded clothes in bright colors. "You have a dressing tent?" he asked the gray-haired woman behind the counter.

She put down her knitting needles. "For three hundred grams, I do."

Ben reached for a pouch under his ballistic vest and doled out a few chunks of natural copper and a small roll of wire. The woman dutifully weighed them on her scale, snipped a length off the spool of wire, and handed the rest back to Ben.

"Price is going up, I hear." He nodded at the half-completed sweater on her lap. "Wool pool out east sprung a leak in their storage facility and a whole season's worth of fleece got mildewy."

What an odd thing to say. Ben didn't seem like the type to strike up meaningless conversation and how would he know anything about a wool pool out east?

"Shame," the woman raised her eyebrows.

To me, Ben said, "I'll wait and pay for what you choose when you're done. Throw out the dress."

"Thank you." I mumbled.

I selected two pairs of canvas pants with drawstring waists and roomy pockets, two cotton shirts, a wool sweater, six pairs of handsewn linen underwear, and the same number of terry cloth pads. Ben paid for them all and waited while I changed and led me back toward the coach.

"Was that your money or Clowes's?" I asked as we went.

"I don't have money. I have an allowance." Ben's sharp eyes scanned the crowd around us as we walked.

"Which you just spent on me." I swallowed.

"You're welcome." He smiled in that empty unnerving way that I was starting to understand was a sign of him shutting down.

"I'm not her."

"What?" He leaned closer.

"I'm not her and helping me—pretending you're helping her instead—it changes nothing, Ben. Grace needs you to make a real move."

"Shut your mouth, ma'am." He gripped my right arm and pushed me through the crowd.

I had nine more nights to turn Ben Breyman against his master.

CHAPTER
TWENTY-ONE

That morning when we stopped, Kahn called me over to the stagecoach. "Come, earn your keep for once. His bandages need changing."

A sick heat glued my insides together. I'd been wrapped up in my own discomfort all night while Robert nursed terrible wounds in Kahn's apathetic company. When we'd been at the market, I'd been so focused on getting through to Ben, I hadn't even thought to ask for bandages or pain medication for Robert. What kind of person did that make me?

"L-let me get a med kit," I stammered as Kahn strode down the steps, leaving the coach door flung wide open behind him. Ben's was the only kit I'd seen, so I asked him for it, cursing myself for the bandages I'd used up this morning. Then I climbed the stagecoach steps.

The interior was brightly lit, upholstered in gray leather and molded plastic with chrome accents. Accordion blinds had been pulled to cover all the windows. Warm, stale air wafted through recessed vents, and two plates with half-eaten ham sandwiches balanced on a fold-out table. A jug of water sat between them.

Robert sat sideways on one of the benches, his back to me, undoing the buttons on his dress shirt.

I tried to bottle up my breathing as my nerves snagged into high gear. My mind scrambled to catalog every detail of him, like there'd be a test later where I'd have to reconstruct him from memory: the swirl of hair at his neck, the determined set of his shoulders, the tension in his back as he curled away from me.

"Close the door." His words were cold and clipped. Stone cold sober. They hit me like a slap.

"You sound like Kahn," I snapped back, slamming the door behind me. "Been chumming with the enemy a bit much, yeah?"

He snorted, shrugging out of his shirt, every movement guarded. "You should talk. Every time I look out the window, you're making eyes at the Lone Ranger out there, taking leisurely strolls, letting him buy you clothes. What the hell are you playing at, Iris?"

"What am I . . .?" I gripped the med pack tight enough that its metal lid creaked before answering him in a barely reined-in voice. "I'm saving us. That's what I'm doing. Ben and his men are trapped just like we are and they're ready for change. I'm talking them into it."

"Bullshit." He turned to face me and winced when the bandages taped to his back puckered and creased. His eyes looked normal today. No unnatural dilation. "The guy's a con artist and he's playing you. He says whatever he thinks you want to hear. He's been hand-fed by Clowes since he was in diapers. He's not going to turn."

The awful image of Ben eating the fouled cheesecake flared in my mind. "Maybe he's sick of being hand fed."

"Are you serious right now?" Robert's cheeks mottled red. "He held a gun to your head at dinner, but all he's got to do is bat those blue eyes, flash that stupid grin, and say, 'Yes, ma'am,' and you're falling over yourself to save him. He's the *enemy*, Iris. They all are."

I slammed the med kit down on the upholstered bench between us and wrenched it open. "Oh, I'm sorry. I'm not in here doing the good work, getting all my meals delivered, taking belladonna until I can't see straight, and lapping up every word that comes out of Kahn's mouth." I snatched up the scissors, fingers trembling.

Robert grabbed my hand and held on tightly enough that I couldn't pull away. Metal pinched my fingers. His hand felt unnaturally hot. "I only took it twice. Nothing else was working for the pain, and you have no idea what it's like in here," he said hoarsely.

"You have no idea what it's like out there. Don't patronize me." My gaze was drawn to his chest, the tense rise and fall of it. I wanted to lay my hand there and steady his breathing. Instead, I swallowed and said, "You're hurting me. Do you want your bandages changed or not?"

He let go immediately, snatching his shirt and rubbing at the rough seam in the sleeve's cuff. "I'm sorry." He gulped.

"Turn around."

He did.

I reached for a loose corner of tape near his shoulder and Robert flinched.

"Sorry," he repeated.

I eased the bandage back as delicately as I could, but his skin was red and blistered beneath. Some of it sloughed off with the tape. "I think you're allergic to the adhesive. How long has this been on?"

"I don't know." He sounded tired. "Day before yesterday, I think?"

When I peeled back the corner of a thick dressing, it was yellowed underneath. "Zuse, Robert. These should be changed daily." My voice cracked, and his breath ratcheted higher as a sickly sweet odor filled the air.

"I know that. I can't reach them, and even if I could, he hasn't given me clean bandages to replace them."

Inch by inch, I worked the dressings free as tenderly as I could, but my hands were shaking and there were scabs enmeshed in the gauze. By the time I'd peeled the soiled bandage away, Robert was sweating, and his wounds oozed fresh blood.

"How's it look?"

It was the ghastliest thing I'd ever seen. Long, gaping slashes ribboned over his spine, ribs, and up one shoulder like pale alien mouths. None of them had been stitched. Raw flesh glazed in pus peeked out between slabs of puffy, white skin. Angry red blazed around the borders. It was infected. Badly. I must have been silent for far too long because Robert's next words were soft and determined.

"I love you. You know that, right?"

"Don't!" I barked, tossing the soiled bandage to the floor. *Now! Now is when he says it out loud? And only because he's afraid.* "Don't you dare drop that now. For all the wrong reasons. It's fine. It's infected, but you'll be fine."

"When would you rather I say it? I don't think we'll have too many other chances, Iris." He sniffed and rubbed his fingers over his shirt sleeve cuff harder. "The things he says he's going to do to you . . . I can't . . . If I were stronger, I'd strangle him, I swear. I've never wanted to kill a man before, not even during the fighting. Now, I'd shoot him myself if I could."

"Shhhh. He's all talk." I dug through the med kit and found a small vial of iodine, but there wasn't nearly enough to apply to a wound this large. "He doesn't have it in him to torture anyone himself. Kahn has always delegated."

A harsh bark coughed out of him. "He delegated my whipping. He watched the whole time. I underestimated him, Iris. He's sick. He can't be reasoned with, and he wants to hurt you in all sorts of ways, do you understand me? It's all he talks about. You need to run."

"Can you stand? We need to go outside and irrigate this." My pulse pounded between my ears.

"Take one of those horses and run while they're all sleeping."

"No. I'm not going anywhere without you. We're leaving together. We're going home, Robert. You promised me a happy ending, Soldamnit, and I am holding you to it." *Hold it together for him. Don't cry.*

"We're down to two choices, Iris, and that's not one of them." His voice broke and he stood unsteadily. "You run. Get your cowboy to help you if you have to. Or you stay, and I kill Kahn before he gets to you. You know what they do to slaves that kill their masters, right? We get whipped to death."

"We're going outside." I choked, turned, and opened the door. "Quit talking." Grabbing the jug of water, I dumped the vial of iodine into it and sloshed it around. This was the fever talking. Had to be. Robert wasn't a killer.

I went down the stairs, and he followed me gripping the handle on the side of the stagecoach with white knuckles as he eased down the steps.

Kahn stood consulting a map with Ben. The rest of the crew tactfully ignored us.

I grabbed a towel from Lawrence the cook and rolled it up on my way back to Robert. "Can you lean forward?" I asked. "I don't want to get blood on your pants." It seemed like the stupidest thing in the world to be worried about right now.

He braced himself against the wheel well of the stagecoach.

I soaked a dressing in the iodine solution and wrung it out over Robert's back doing my best to catch the pink run off with the towel. By the time I'd emptied the jug, he was breathing hard, and his face was gray.

I helped him back up the steps and closed the door behind

us before draping a fresh dressing over his shoulder and back and securing it with tape. The smell of the old bandages filled the confined space. It made me want to gag.

"Iris, leave, please." He spoke quietly. "Please?" Then he turned, cupped my cheek, and kissed me softly. His lips were hot and dry as they brushed mine.

The coach door swung open. "That'll be quite enough," Kahn snapped.

I sprang back from Robert. As I did, I saw him pocket the surgical scissors from the med kit. I couldn't stop him without giving him away, but I held his gaze and mouthed the word, *No*.

"Clean up this mess and get out."

Nodding, I bent to pick up the sterile paper wrappers and the old, wadded bandage.

"Not you. Him," Kahn said, eagle eyes pinned to mine hungrily. "I need a word alone with Iris if you would be so good, Robert?"

"No." He pressed me behind him, and his hand twitched towards the concealed scissors in his pocket.

Raw fear paralyzed me as Kahn reached up with uncharacteristic speed and gripped Robert's bandaged shoulder hard.

Robert screamed and crumpled to his knees.

"You forget your place, slave." Kahn twisted his grip and the cry turned into a bubbling shriek.

"Stop it!" I howled, but no one heard me.

Kahn grabbed Robert's elbow and hauled him to his feet shoving him out the door and slamming it behind him as he stumbled down the steps.

My hip caught on the folding table and one of the tin plates crashed to the floor spilling its sandwich.

Kahn flipped a latch on the door that was likely a lock and turned to face me. "Hand me a napkin and clean that up," he ordered.

"Yes, sir." I passed him a folded cloth napkin and he stood

over me wiping his hands as I raked the sandwich back onto the plate and shoved the discarded bandages into my pocket. I couldn't slow my breathing down. It kept coming out in short little pants, like a dog's.

"Now clear the bench and take a seat."

I did. I put the extra bandages away, did up the clasps on the med kit, and hung Robert's wrinkled shirt on a hook alongside a business jacket. It felt like someone else's hands doing the work, like my body was just ticking away while my mind screamed to escape.

He wants to hurt you in all sorts of ways.

Robert howled outside. The stagecoach jiggled on its shocks and a fist slammed against the door.

I jumped and yelped.

And then all the sound outside stopped.

Kahn set the napkin on the table and took off his vest, reaching over me to hang it beside Robert's shirt.

"I'm on my period." I blurted.

His long nose wrinkled. He reached up to take off his glasses and adjust their frame. "Good. He's spoken to you about what I intend to do. If you leave here bleeding, he'll assume it was my doing."

A messy sob stole all my breath. My hands fisted in my lap, and I wondered if I was fast enough to get behind his back and choke him. No, I decided. He was stronger than me. He'd peel out of my grip as easily as he'd disabled Robert. Sol, I'd never seen the man be physical before. He'd always had Firewalls to do it for him.

"We haven't had opportunity to get reacquainted since your little rebellion, Iris, and I want to remedy that. It seems you've misjudged the esteem I hold for you, so let's make that clear right now, shall we?" He put his glasses back on and leaned ahead, a whisper of a cold smile touching his lips as I recoiled.

"You are a stupid, impulsive girl who thinks too highly of

herself. Do not presume that because I spent a tidy sum of money procuring you that you have any worth at all to me. You do not. Neither does Robert, although he's got a good head on his shoulders and will make a fine personal valet once I break his spirit, but the point is, I can easily find a replacement who will do the job equally well. Neither of you are special. So, I don't particularly care whether you live long miserable lives as my slaves or die quick, terrible deaths. I'd consider either outcome money well spent, understand? He is a pawn. He has his uses, but he's not a valuable piece, and he's easily sacrificed to advance the game for more important players." He spread his long-fingered hands, palms up. "I am a man who uses the tools he's given, whatever they may be. *You've* crashed my city. You've attempted to escape. Do you know what I'm going to do to you right now?" he asked in a tone as gentle as a schoolteacher's.

Another sob rocked me, and I shook my head, unable to speak.

"I'm going to do nothing. I'm not going to hurt you at all."

Breath whistled out of me, and dizzy heat washed through my limbs.

"You think I'm lying. I'm not, and I'll tell you why." He set his hands on his lap, his voice matter of fact. "You're not even a pawn, Iris. You're less than that. If I want to bed a girl, have someone pleasure me, clean up my messes, or bring me dinners, I can think of a thousand other people who could do it better than you. You are incompetent. Worthless. A pebble in my shoe. Nothing more, nothing less. Your torture is that you are so broken, you are useless to me, but you are worth quite a lot to him, aren't you?" Kahn nodded toward the door. "I wonder if we can't break his spirit a bit right now?"

I clenched my teeth. "I won't hurt him."

"You already have. He took a whipping that was meant to be yours." Kahn stood and I shrank from him again, but he was only reaching for his vest pocket. "Do you know what these are?" He extracted a small pill bottle with dozens of capsules in it. "Antibiotics. I bought them from an enterprising gentleman at the roadside market today. Remarkably expensive. Do you have any idea how difficult it is to distill penicillin effectively nowadays? I chatted with the fellow for quite some time about the process." He turned the bottle in his hands. "Anyway, I do believe infection is a common occurrence with lash wounds. How are Robert's doing? He seemed poorly today."

"You know they're infected," I choked. "You practically guaranteed it."

"What a happy coincidence we have a cure right here then, isn't it?"

I swallowed hard and flexed my fingers. *Just get out of here alive.* "What do you want me to do?" I croaked.

"I want you to scream, Iris," Kahn said. "I want you to scream like I'm hurting you in all the ways I've told him I would. And I want you to make it convincing. He doesn't get a single dose until every person outside this door believes you've been violated. Do we have an understanding?"

I screamed. As soon as I started, Robert bellowed outside. Feet scuffled. Ben's men barked orders.

Kahn shook his head and gestured impatiently for me to carry on.

I shrieked louder.

"Tear your shirt," he ordered, pulling out his pocket watch.

I did.

"Come on, now. Beg like you're *actually* here against your will. If I have to coach you all the way through this, we're done."

I screamed until my throat was raw and my eyes throbbed and I couldn't hear anything outside of the ringing in my own head. I wailed until my voice went hoarse.

Kahn sat across from me, indifferent, his gaze pinned to the pocket watch balanced on his lap. At one point, he took a bite of the sandwich that was still on the table.

Eventually, he waved me off, mild disgust etched on his face.

I sat with my arms wrapped around myself, wrung out and waiting for the next order.

"Get out," he said, frowning down at the pill bottle.

"You'll give them to him?" I croaked.

"I said, get out."

I unlocked the door and walked woodenly down the steps into the bright dawn with my torn shirt hanging over one scarred shoulder.

The crew outside did their best to avoid looking in my direction. Robert slumped between two of Ben's men, head bobbing against his chest.

"What did you do?" Kahn snapped, standing silhouetted in the doorway.

"We had to choke him out a bit, sir." One of the men volunteered. "He wouldn't stop fighting us."

"What a waste," Kahn mumbled. "Bring him inside and get him dressed." He stepped out of the stagecoach to let the two men maneuver a half-senseless, moaning Robert up the steps. Before Kahn retreated inside himself, he caught my gaze, flipped the cap off the pill bottle and dumped the capsules into the mud.

"No." I lurched toward him, but a hand caught my elbow.

David Kahn ground the medicine into the muck as Ben's men descended the stagecoach steps. Then he turned his back on me, climbed inside, and closed the door.

"No." I wrenched out of my captor's grip and stumbled toward the pills, crashing to my knees, and clawing through the mud.

"Hey, now." Ben draped his jacket over my shoulders and shuffled around to squat across from me. "How about we stop. That's enough now, yeah?" His voice sounded as raw as mine.

"I can't. They're pills. Antibiotics from the market. Expensive. For Robert," I panted.

"Iris, listen to me. No one at that roadside market sells antibiotics, else I'd have stocked up myself." He grabbed my hands delicately. Bright blood splattered onto the mud, and I realized it was Ben's. Red streamed from a puncture wound on his forearm. A pair of surgical scissors jutted out of the front pocket of his ballistic vest. "Whatever that bastard told you those pills are, they're not."

I sat hard, cold water soaking through my new pants. *They aren't even antibiotics.* I hadn't even helped. I'd made things worse, like I always did. Like Kahn knew I would. Oh Sol. I hadn't even helped.

Once I started crying, I couldn't stop.

Ben crouched in the mud beside me, wrapped his arms around me and held me. He didn't say anything else. He just let me cry.

CHAPTER
TWENTY-TWO

When I could breathe again, Ben held me at arm's length and spoke to me like I was a toddler. "Look at me, now. I need you to tell me if you're hurt." Rage washed over his face before he choked it down. "If you're hurt anywhere *physically*. Broken bones. Cuts. Anything that needs tending to?"

I gaped at his bleeding arm and shook my head. "H-he didn't hurt me. Didn't do anything. He just made me scream so that Robert would think he did. I-I'm sorry about the scissors. He grabbed them before I could stop him."

Ben pulled his hand down his face and a long sigh bled out of him. He looked relieved. "Don't worry about the scissors."

"I-I left your med pack in the coach." I couldn't stop staring at his wound, the brightness of it, how Robert's back had looked like bloodless old meat in comparison.

"I'll get it later. Let's get you out of the mud, yeah?" He cupped a hand under my elbow and helped me to my feet.

His crew strung up sleeping bags to wall off the back of the cook trailer into a private area. Lawrence boiled a big pot of water. I washed and changed into my second set of clothes with a strange detachment, like I was a newcomer to my own consciousness: Iris 2.0 performing mundane tasks for the first time. Hoping everyone didn't realize that I was an imposter in my own body. One who glitched even more than the previous version. I lost the rest of the day. By the next night, it was all just a blur of watch guards taking turns sitting beside me, offering me hot tea and uncomfortable silence.

We were walking far behind the caravan again, fighting off mosquitos and squinting at the stars because the whimpers of pain from the stagecoach had grown so loud that I'd started crying until I hyperventilated.

Ben tugged at the bandage on his forearm as he led Smokey stiffly beside me. "You want to make this better for your boy, not worse."

"What is that supposed to mean?" I snapped, but the words came out brittle. My voice hadn't recovered from yesterday.

He kept his gaze pinned to Stagecoach One. "It means your master is a shrewd asshole and those pills he baited you with were placebos. You need to stop swallowing hooks every time he sets them out. It makes it worse for your boy."

"Maybe they were painkillers?"

"They weren't, Iris. I went and picked them up right after he threw them into the mud before they dissolved—in case they were something valuable. They looked like sugar pills, same as the ones our med kits have for diabetics. So, I checked all our kits and sure enough, the sugar pills were missing, and so were all the painkillers. That's likely what Kahn's been feeding Robert to keep him functional, but the med kits didn't have a large supply, and by the sounds of it, he's running out of them."

Or Robert's run out of Belladonna. The thought crept into my mind.

Ben continued, "Your master doesn't seem to have the inkling or experience to care for wounds. You want your boy to live? The first thing you have to do is calm yourself down and the next thing you have to do is take care of his infection. Quickly. I don't have antibiotics, but I've got lots of hydrogen peroxide."

"I *was* calm, Ben!" My voice cracked and I swiped at my runny nose. "I didn't do anything wrong. I did everything he asked me to."

His Adam's apple bobbed and a muscle in his jaw twitched. "Keep your boy calm then. He seems to have murderous intent of late and I can't promise I'll be there to intervene next time. Do you know what happens if we show up at Mullan without a master? It'll be the noose for all of us. They'll send a message up the line and our families will die too. I'm not sacrificing my crew for you or him, understand?"

Heat rushed to my cheeks. My joints ached and my gut twisted, but I pushed it all down and kept my next words as even as possible. "Is that what you tell Grace? Calm down. Do what you're told, and it'll all go better for you?"

"Grace isn't stupid enough to make enemies of powerful men," he spat. "And if she were, I'd tell her to do whatever she needed to do to survive."

He doesn't know, the realization hit me. *He doesn't know that his own sister disguises herself as a boy, ferries covert messages, and smuggles slaves out of the colliery right under Clowes's nose.* Ben said he found a letter under Robert's door, but he didn't know it was Grace who delivered it. *And if she hasn't told him, he's sure as hell not going to believe it coming from you.* I'd have to convince him another way.

"Is this surviving?" I clutched his arm and he flinched. "Jumping when they say jump. Eating when they say eat. Screaming when they say scream?"

Smokey bumped his head between us and nibbled my fingers gently. I let him peel my hand off Ben's arm and patted his muzzle as we walked.

"Don't touch me and don't touch my horse. He's taken people's hands off for less."

He's trying to derail you. Don't let him.

"This isn't surviving, Ben. It's dying really slowly. You know it is. Is that what you want for her?"

"Shut your mouth."

I couldn't. The words wouldn't stay in. I didn't want them to. "That's what Clowes tells her, I'll bet. Shut your mouth. Be a good girl and bend over, Grace."

Ben hauled Smokey to a stop, jammed his hand into a saddlebag, and snatched out a hunting knife. It took every stitch of strength I had left not to shrink from the malevolence in his eyes as he thrust the weapon toward me, hand trembling. "Keep talking about my sister. I'll cut out your tongue. I swear to God."

It's not you he hates. It's Clowes. I swallowed hard.

"She works in the kitchens. I kept her out of the mines. Kitchen staff has the softest jobs of all of us." Desperation leaked into Ben's words. He sounded like a little boy in search of reassurance, and I couldn't give it to him. "I've kept her safe. Since we were small," he insisted.

I edged forward until the blade bobbed in front of my nose, until I was close enough to smell Ben's sweat, and I spoke my next words carefully because everything was balancing on that blade's edge now. My future, Robert's, Grace's, Ben's. Every one of us. I was about to push us all off without a backward glance. "I slept in the locked cellar for three nights, and every single night after midnight, Clowes sent for a girl. Every. Single. Night. They came back crying—kitchen girls like Grace. And they didn't come back with cut up arms, so it wasn't Mrs. Clowes calling for them. It was her husband. You said so yourself:

powerful men use us like tools. So, if you've been telling Grace to do whatever she has to to survive, you'd better be doing it with open eyes, Ben, because you're not keeping her safe anymore than you're keeping me safe."

His face twisted and his head dropped, but the knife stayed pinned in position. Several breaths shuddered out of him, and hope sparked in my chest as layers sloughed off Ben Breyman like gaudily painted plaster.

I'd done it. I'd reached him. I was nearly sure of it until he straightened.

His eyes were cold as glacier ice, and his mouth had twisted into that awful rictus of a smile. "Get on the goddamned horse, Iris," he growled.

That was the last time we walked together behind the caravan.

WE GATHERED MORE transient travelers that night. Trickling in from roadside stands and gravel intersections, they matched our pace like birds settling into formation, drafting behind an unwilling leader. They stopped when we did, waiting every time Ben checked in at a semaphore tower.

People on bikes with spare brake cables and sprockets slung around their necks towed rickety trailers labelled with lists of town names and filled with stamped parcels and envelopes. Occasionally other travelers would flag the bikers down to toss copper into the pails wired between their handlebars before adding more correspondences to the canvas mail bags.

A man riding a lumbering bull wandered through our ranks selling loaves of poppyseed bread braided into rings and displayed hung in stacks on his ride's impressively long horns.

Four scantily clad women with deep red sunburns, cracked,

bleeding lips and blistered bare scalps rode double on a pair of white mules, handing out hand-written pamphlets. "Brave the sunlight, friends. Have you found Helios yet? Open your heart. Open your eyes," they urged anyone who was unfortunate enough to cross their path. One of them zeroed in on my scarred cheeks and pressed her mule toward me.

"Helios has touched you, sister. Emerge from the shadows and seek his face again. He misses his children, especially those he's already kissed." She handed me a pamphlet and I accepted it with an awkward nod, leaning away from her when she reached out to touch my cheek.

I waited until she was out of sight and pocketed it without reading it.

Like before, Ben's crew tolerated the motley congregation until dawn and then scattered them all, threatening to shoot anyone who came within sight of our morning camp. Vagrants roosted beyond the horizon but flocked back the next evening as soon as we started rolling.

Kahn didn't let me see Robert and Ben didn't talk to me at all, but at midnight, while Ben checked in at a tower, Lawrence beckoned me to his cook wagon.

Without any preamble, he handed me a brown glass bottle. "You'll want to give his whole back a good soak." He carried on talking like he was reciting a recipe. "It'll sting like the devil and foam up something fierce, but you don't want to go light on it."

Blinking down at the bottle, I realized it was hydrogen peroxide for Robert. "Th-thank you. I—"

"Now this is long expired, but the adhesive still has some stick to it." He pulled a packet of wound closure tape from his apron pocket and followed it up with a box of gauze pads and a roll of tape. "Don't close up any gash that looks infected. Leave them open so they can drain. Should clear him up in a week if Master Kahn lets you at him a few times a day." He nodded toward Stagecoach One. "I'd see what you can do about that, if I were you."

"What I can do about it?" I repeated dumbly, pocketing the bandages and tape.

"Knock on the door, love. Tell your master you want to serve. He's got to be sick of listening to the boy moaning by now."

The idea of approaching Kahn willingly stirred acid in my stomach and sent needles bristling through my arms and legs. *Tell your master you want to serve.* Oh Sol, nothing was further from the truth. I wouldn't be able to make Kahn believe it. I was a terrible liar and he'd see right through me. *Don't be such a fragging coward. Robert needs you!* I bit the inside of my cheek hard enough for the flare of pain to wash out every conflicting thought in me. "Do you have anything to drink? Something I can offer him?"

"Just topped off the icebox tonight and he's partial to cold mint tea. A good slave would know that." Lawrence winked to take the sting out of his words.

"One mint tea then. Lots of ice."

"Yes, ma'am." He leaned into the interior of the cook wagon, toweled off a thick green glass, and chipped several chunks off the main slab in the icebox. Crushing several sprigs of mint into the glass, he topped it off with cold tea and handed it over.

Gripping the glass and tucking the sloshing bottle of peroxide under my arm, I marched to Stagecoach One and smacked the door with my bare palm.

"Hello, sir? I was wondering if you might like a cold drink?" Static crackled between my ears as I waited for a response and got none. Taking a deep breath through my nose, I tried again. "Mr. Kahn? I made you an iced tea. I thought it might be getting stuffy in there?" Zuse, this wasn't going to work. I raised my hand again to knock a last time and the door clicked open.

David Kahn leaned out, holding a handkerchief over his

nose. "If your aim is to win me over with bribery, you'll have to offer something more substantial than tea."

Choking back hot words, I curtsied. Actually Soldamned curtsied. "Of course. Sorry, sir." I spoke through my teeth, turning from him.

"I didn't say I wouldn't take it," he said crisply.

Don't dump the drink on him. Don't. "Perhaps you'd both like some fresh air, sir. I have something to treat Robert's wounds. It would only take a moment." I didn't hand over the tea.

"Dramatics." Kahn eyed the glass. "The boy exaggerates. He's on the same dose of painkiller as he was before. Both of you show an exceeding lack of self-control, a fault I intend to remedy when we get to Mullan." The apathy in his voice was sickening. The fact that he was complaining about Robert's state when he'd been the sole cause of it astounded me. I had no idea how to respond, so I stood there gaping at him.

Kahn stood quickly, and I flinched. He descended the steps and plucked the tea from my hands. "Close your mouth and tend to the boy," he said. "See if you can do something about the smell."

"Yes, sir." I stammered and plunged up the stairs.

It smelled like the bunker room that Elaine had converted to a field hospital back home. That unsettling mix of raw meat and stale breath hit me hard. My scalp tingled and my mouth dried out as I saw Robert leaning against the far window.

Sweat pasted his hair to his forehead and ringed the underarms of his rumpled shirt. It was the same one he'd worn two days ago.

The fire in my belly snuffed out, leaving me choking on fumes. I'd been ready to fight, full of bottled rage from my short interaction with Kahn and braced to stand my ground against whatever Robert threw at me, but I hadn't been ready for this.

He looked like his father. Old and worn down. As I closed the distance between us, Robert's bloodshot eyes focused on me, his hands twitched, and he swallowed loudly. "Hey," he whispered.

His pupils are normal. No belladonna.

"Hey. Hot in here tonight." I chirped far too brightly.

"You didn't leave."

"No, I didn't." I sat beside him, clasping the hydrogen peroxide tightly enough that my fingers cramped. "Did you actually think I would?"

"No." A ghost of a smile curled his chapped lips. "You never do what you're told." A long sigh bled out of him, and he wiped moisture from his cheek. I couldn't tell if it was tears or sweat.

"Robert, Kahn didn't hurt me. I need you to know that. He didn't even touch me, just told me to scream at the top of my lungs so you'd think he did."

His teeth flashed and his gaze dropped. "You'd tell me that even if it wasn't true."

"I wouldn't lie about something like that," I said softly.

"Yeah, you would." His fingers plucked at the cuff of his sleeve. "So would I. We lie all the time, holding things back, trying to protect each other, both of us thinking we know best."

Those words felt sharp and fragile at the same time, like broken glass. I didn't know what to say, so I settled on action instead. Putting down the bottle and pulling the bandages out of my pocket, I leaned toward him and started undoing his shirt buttons. He didn't stop me.

"We weren't supposed to be like this."

"Yeah?" I fought to keep my voice even. He sounded so defeated and the only way I knew to counter that was to pretend to be strong. "What were we supposed to be like?"

"I was supposed to be capable, someone you could lean on, someone who would hold the pieces together when you felt like your world was falling apart. I wanted to take care of you, Iris, not be the one who needed rescuing."

"Bit sexist," I said flippantly, even as my chest ached. "How am I supposed to be a badass if I'm not allowed to rescue you?"

A tired laugh puffed out of him.

I latched onto the wisp of the old Robert, the way the corners of his eyes crinkled when he smiled wide and said, "Go on. Keep telling me how we're supposed to be."

His blue-gray eyes met mine. They were darker and softer than Ben's, and despite the puffy bags beneath them, they still held a warmth that gave me hope. "I'm supposed to sweep you off your feet. You're supposed to fall for me hard enough that you forget cowboys ever existed."

I snort-laughed and ignored how his hands shook as he shrugged out of his shirt.

"You teach me to hunt, and I teach you penmanship."

"Unlikely." Gently, I tugged on the bandage where it was already shedding off his shoulder.

"We fall wildly in love and when I ask you to marry me, you say yes." He was mumbling now, talking more to himself than me. "We build a house at the lake where I watch you fish. It has a big porch so we can lay on a blanket and look out at the night sky. And it's got lots of room for kids."

Kids. Zuse. My mind flew back to Radia and John, unabashedly starting a family without caring how uncertain their world was. I'd never thought about what it would be like to be pregnant. Even when Robert and I had shared a bed, and I'd been caught up in the momentum of the moment, I hadn't thought about it. *Of course, you didn't. You never think of consequences.* My hands froze for long enough for him to notice.

"Sorry. Too much?"

"No, I just . . ." I peeled back the bandage and my skin crawled at the clotted discharge and swollen red skin bordering each of the welts on Robert's back. "I-I've never thought about being a mom other than swearing that I'd be nothing like my own."

"I miss my mom, my family." His voice cracked.

I watched the hitching rise and fall of his ribs as he struggled to compose himself.

"I know they seemed like a real mess from the outside, but they were good people, good parents. They loved each other and they loved me. Things were supposed to be different for them too and Corporate just crushed the life out of them. Kahn sucked them dry. That's what he does."

"We won't let him do that to us, okay?" There I went, lying again. Tears stung my eyes, and I was glad that Robert's back was to me so he couldn't see my face.

"No, we won't." The cold malice in his voice startled me. He sounded like Ben, and I hated that.

Robert doesn't hurt people. Even if he could, he's too weak and he has no weapons in here. I took a steadying breath and clasped the brown glass bottle. "Let's go outside and get you cleaned up, okay? This is going to hurt a lot before it gets better."

"I know," he croaked. "I'm ready."

And I shivered because it didn't feel like we were talking about hydrogen peroxide anymore.

CHAPTER
TWENTY-THREE

made Robert scream twice a day for the next three nights. He spoke less each time. Every disinfectant treatment seemed to leach strength out of him he couldn't gain back. At one point, it was bad enough that I asked him if he had any of Sybil's belladonna left to ease his pain.

He brushed his fingers over the cuff of his shirt and swallowed hard. "No, I took it all," he said slowly.

Kahn left us alone, granting me access to Stagecoach One with a soft smile that I wanted to beat off his face. He enjoyed it, watching me hurt Robert, and he relished keeping him cooped up away from me the rest of the time.

Outside of the coach, Ben stopped speaking to me completely, so I turned my efforts to winning over Lawrence. Whenever his leader left for a tower check-in, I used every minute he was gone trying to sway the cook, promising him and his wife safety and refuge in our city. The man seemed receptive but remained doggedly faithful to Ben.

"What has he ever done for you, Lawrence?" I hissed while cutting up carrots into julienne strips for Mr. Kahn's salad. "I'm offering you an out. He's never been brave enough his whole life to take that leap."

"You wouldn't understand, love." He whisked together a raspberry vinaigrette. "This crew, we've dug so far down together, we've gotten used to the hole, down in the muck. And every rope ever thrown to us, it's been a snake in disguise. Besides, most of us have done things dark enough, we feel like we don't deserve a spot in the light anymore. Ben most of all."

"He doesn't get to drag you all down with him." I plucked two wooden spoons from the cutlery bin—just spoons. We were under strict orders not to let Robert get a hold of anything sharp again.

"That's how drowning works." Lawrence sniffed. "We all drag each other down."

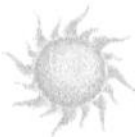

We passed an abandoned city surrounded by overgrown potato fields, fallow oats, and skeleton cherry orchards, its southern borders lapping against a lake that dwarfed ours back home.

"What do you think made people leave places like this? They had enough food, by the looks of it," I asked Lawrence. He'd taken to letting me ride beside him on the cook wagon most nights. Ben scowled about it but didn't stop it.

"What I heard? All these crops attracted wild pigs. Scores of them. They're still a big problem down here. Breed like rabbits, grow big enough to wipe out a whole season's worth of food in a few weeks, run around in gangs, ornery as all hell. A boar would gore you soon as look at you. They pushed most people right out of the area. That's what all the marauders down this way live on. Gamey old pork for breakfast, lunch, and dinner, can you imagine? Some folks say that's why they're such a wild people. You eat enough hot-blooded animals, and it starts to rub off on you."

My thoughts latched onto the young marauder girl, back at Painted Bluff, how thin and hungry and fierce she'd been. "Maybe they're just pissed that the whole world pushed them out of their homes so they could claim them as their own. We're the boars in their world." I picked at my nails.

"Where'd you hear that?" Lawrence frowned. "I can't even picture a marauder living in a proper house."

"In school. We have books written by some of the first marauder leaders. Lots of them started out as activists for people with disabilities, the poor, those with mental health issues. Everything fell apart for people like that when the world crashed. They ended up out on the streets and got lumped in with anarchists and guerilla fighters. Vicious types."

"They write books? Marauders?" Lawrence shook his head, squinting at the semaphore tower in the distance. In the dusk light, its rigging was slowly swinging from a crooked T shape to a backwards F, mimicking the mast on the south horizon that had changed symbols moments ago, passing on coded messages one word at a time.

"Some of them write books, yeah. Why?"

The cook rubbed his thumbs over the reins in his hands. "We call them the savages, out there in the wilds penning books, meanwhile I don't even know how to read tower code. None of the crew do."

I lowered my voice and pinned my gaze to Ben, far ahead of us, surrounded by a group of goat herders hassling him to buy their cheese. "Where I come from we learn new code all the time, and I'm a quick learner. We'll figure it out. I can send the tower messages when we run, Lawrence."

"Won't work. Clowes changes the code on the regular and Ben's the only one who knows when he does. Even the tower operators don't know what messages they're sending, so they can't be blackmailed into sending covert messages. They just pass along symbols without knowing what they mean."

"Clowes ever send you on trips away from the tower lines?"

"Short ones. No more than a few days with a firm deadline for when we're going to return."

"So, if something happens to Ben on a trip like this, then what? No one else can send word back to Clowes that the rest of you are still on mission? Your whole crew loses their families back home? What kind of a setup is that?" I hissed.

Lawrence turned to glance at me with calm, solemn eyes. "The kind Clowes builds." He pointed his chin at Ben. "The kind that traps a smart boy like that behind bars thicker than steel. You think he's selfish. I know you do. But he holds our fate in his hands every time we set foot on the road, and he knows it well. He ain't never thinking about himself, love. That's why you won't get him to turn, and you won't get us to either. We're all tangled up and it's too late to undo all the knots now."

As the days passed, the snow-capped mountain range to the southwest loomed larger. Robert's wounds started to heal, and the hydrogen peroxide bleached patches of white skin on my fingertips faded. Kahn kept us apart. Ben only spoke to me when required and always with that maddening false smile on his face, ever the showman. I lost hope that I could turn any of his men before we reached Mullan.

On the eighth evening of our journey, we set out on the winding road, sandwiched between rolling hills of crackling gold scrub grass littered with the broken skeletons of monstrous irrigation systems. They looked like the rusty molts of massive spiders, all hollow curled up legs, bristling with sprinkler tips.

As we passed a field full of fat snow geese, I ached for my crossbow, and for Johan's quiet company. Vagabond groups who'd spent the day sheltering under solar blankets in the ditches hastily packed hammock stands and glommed back onto our caravan like burs on a horse's hide. Watching them from the luggage trunk, I had just wondered for the umpteenth time about the necessity for all this caution when a gunshot cracked across the valley.

Screams buffeted through the convoy. Geese launched into flight and scattered, a chorus of honking and humming wings in the cold, pink-marbled sky. People curled to the ground or clotted around livestock. Horses shrieked and tossed their heads as they were swamped.

"Hold," Ben bellowed from the head of the line. "Lawrence, move your wagon up."

I pressed my back further into the trunk of the stagecoach, blood whooshing between my ears so loudly that I barely heard Robert calling my name from inside.

Lawrence yelled at the crowd to get out of his way and steered his horses to the right of Stagecoach One, his gaze pinned to an irrigation shack far out in the field. "Come on, out of the line of fire," he whispered to me, hauling me onto the bench beside him and pushing me into the footwell before yelling to Ben. "The pumphouse. It's the only cover for miles."

"I see it." Ben drew his gun and kicked at the people raking their hands over Smokey's flanks. Plowing through them, he joined his mounted crew behind the cover of the coach. "Everyone, shut up! Kit, you hit?"

The stagecoach driver answered from where he was curled into his driver's box. "I'm good. Went over my head."

Those who hadn't scattered to take cover in the ditches clasped their hands over their heads and settled into muffled whimpers and hoarse, desperate calls to each other.

Ben projected his voice like he did this for a living. I

supposed he did. "You're a bit far from the mountain pass. Lousy place for an ambush, wouldn't you say?"

An answering gunshot pinged off the side of the stagecoach prompting another round of squealing from the pronated crowd.

"Don't waste precious ammunition." Ben braced his pistol on his forearm. "I know how hard it is to come by and the coach is bulletproof. We've got nothing of value in there save a master and I've got eight well-armed men out here itching to use their weapons. Lots of innocent folks just trying to get to their destinations safely. Now, I know how hungry your lot has got to be if you're desperate enough to brave the bald ass prairies to strip a caravan. How about we make a deal that lets both of us walk out of this without killing anyone?"

There was nothing but silence from the pumphouse. A toddler started crying farther up the line, piercing wails that rose in intensity when their mother tried to shush them.

Ben's sharp eyes scanned up and down the convoy. His gaze settled on a man laying spreadeagled on his stomach in the dust, clutching the rope halters of a pair of fat cows with lanky calves in tow "We can offer you two cows. Heavy with milk with calves ready for fattening."

"No, sir!" The man's eyes goggled. "Please, they're all I've got. My whole livelihood!"

Ben lowered his voice and offered him that soft, frightening smile. "You'll be saving all our lives, sir. I'll make sure you're compensated, and you won't have to worry about the cost of feed for the rest of your journey. Now, do you want to be a hero, or do you want to die on this road?"

"I don't wanna die." The man blubbered while one of his cows snuffled his hair with her wet nose.

"Good man." Ben immediately moved his attention back to the irrigation shed. "What do you say?"

"You'll shoot us as soon as we come get them." A gravelly woman's voice with a heavy accent shouted back.

"I wouldn't waste my bullets, ma'am. You let us move on down the road and we'll leave the livestock behind. Come on and fetch them once we're clear. We've got children here and I'd like to keep things civil as possible for their sakes."

"You have any ammo? For a 7mm Rem Mag?" a deeper voice asked.

"So, you can use it against us next time we meet up? No, sir." Ben snorted. "Don't waste my time."

"How about one of them vests?"

Lawrence whistled through his teeth, smiled softly, and winked at me scrunched in the footwell. "That'll set him off," he muttered.

This isn't funny. What the hell is wrong with these people?

Ben rolled his shoulders against the weight of his ballistic vest. "How about we start shooting you up and see who runs out of ammo first? Don't turn a pretty offer into an ugly mess."

The group around us started whimpering again.

Kahn yelled from inside the stagecoach. "What is the hold up? Wrap this up and move."

Ben's false smile grew wider, bunching his cheeks unnaturally. "Yes, sir. Right away." To the marauders at the pumphouse, he yelled, "You hear that? The master here says we're done, so you can take my original offer, or we can see how many holes we can punch through those rusty tin walls before we land some shots. Your choice."

The harsh hiss of restrained arguing from the pumphouse reached us. Over the thud of my heart in my ears, I made out the words ". . . rather go home with meat than tell your children you're riddled full of holes out here in the dust." My legs cramped, knees throbbing against the splintered wood of the wagon's footwell. I couldn't stomach the flatness in Ben's eyes, so I pinned my gaze to Lawrence's boots. One of them had a sloppy leather patch over the toe cap. Black tar leaked between the ragged stitches.

"We'll take the livestock," the woman with the gravelly voice declared. "Leave them tied to the pipes in the field across the way."

"Pleasure doing business." Ben tipped his hat and nodded at one of his crew. "Jacob, see it gets done. Let's move out."

The cattle called out forlornly as the caravan moved on without them, their former handler crying unabashedly as he looked over his shoulder.

I sat up beside Lawrence and kept my neck craned until the livestock looked like miniatures in a false landscape. The five figures scuttling toward the animals looked more like ants than humans at this distance, covered in scuffed carapace armor and single-minded in their focus. They shot one of the calves where it stood.

Later, the cattle herder gawked with mild horror at the copper Ben doled into his palm. He looked like he was holding worms instead of rolls of wire. "This is only h-half of what they're worth, sir."

"They saved your life. And all of ours too. I'm sure your fellow travelers will be thankful enough to offer you their own tokens of gratitude. Did you honestly expect to travel *this* road without paying some sort of toll?"

"Do you have faith in humanity, Lawrence?" I asked the cook later that night.

He coughed and side-eyed me before saying, "That's a hell of a question for this time of night. We getting all philosophical now?"

"Do you?" I rubbed the goose bumps on my arms.

"Do I have faith?" He scoffed. "Not sure if anyone really cares what the cook thinks, love."

"Humor me. You've seen a lot more of the world than I have."

He picked his teeth for a long spell before answering, "S'pose I have faith in some of humanity. There's always been good and bad to it. I don't think that's changed much since Cain and Abel. The bad just sticks with folks for so much longer 'cause it hurts and we remember what hurts better than we remember anything else." He thumbed toward Stagecoach One. "Like your boy in there will remember his first whipping better than his first kiss, I'll bet. Doesn't mean the kiss was less important than the whipping. Doesn't mean there aren't good folks out there just 'cause the bad ones are louder. Humanity's always been a two-sided coin, hasn't it? People too. Ain't none of us entirely good or bad. I believe in that."

I ran my thumbnail along a groove in the wooden bench. "And I believe good people need to speak up or they go bad inside eventually. They become what they're surrounded by. How much longer do you want to be surrounded by masters, Lawrence?"

He chuckled, exposing several nubs of teeth. "You're a damned persistent one, I'll give you that."

His casualness fired up an irritated heat in my stomach. "How many more times do you want to set foot on the road knowing if you make one mistake out here everyone you love back home dies?"

"How many times are you going to let your master hurt the one you love, huh? If we're asking the hard questions, let's start with that one. You think I have any more control over my life than you do yours? We don't control the path we're on, Iris. We just ride the current best we can."

"Why did he give them the cows?" I blurted.

"Pardon?"

"Ben. Why did he give the marauders the cows? You all had ballistic vests. The stagecoach is bulletproof. He could have just shot them, like he threatened, and likely you all would have survived unscathed."

"Most likely, yes."

"But he spent the copper anyway."

"There were children in the caravan. He didn't want to see them shot up. Besides, there's less pigs up this way and the marauders here are starving on the regular. We come this way often. We grease their palms a bit, and our way goes easier next time."

"So that's the line then."

"I'm not sure I follow, love." Lawrence frowned.

"That's the line between Ben's good and his bad, where his humanity runs out. He doesn't like *seeing* children die or people starve. He'll act to avoid that, but so long as they're doing it hidden away in the slave quarter back home, he can turn a blind eye."

"That's not fair." His voice dropped. "He's saving who he can, love. If he could save you and your boy by trading a few cows, it'd be done. If I could save my wife from the mines easy as that, none of us would be here."

"What's your wife's name, Lawrence?" I asked.

His big jaw clenched. He shook his head and rubbed his thumbs over the reins for several long seconds before whispering. "May."

"May?" I grabbed his knee. "Oh, my Sol, I know May. I was in her tenement house. S-She's shorter than you. Warm smile. Gap in her teeth, right here?" I tapped my front teeth.

Lawrence took a deep shuddering breath and his face twisted. "Yeah, that's her. That's my May. She's always taking the new ones in and getting them on their feet. Sweet Jesus, of course Ben took you to her. He knew she'd take you under her wing." His eyes filled with tears that he blotted with the back of his wrist. "How is she? I haven't seen her in . . . Clowes only lets me send letters and May doesn't know how to read. She just sends me back pressed flowers, and I've kept every one of them."

I put my hand on his shoulder. "She's good, Lawrence. Strong. She looks after a whole house full of us, but they were starving us out when I left. Clowes's men dug up all the gardens and closed the food store. I'm not sure she'll be good for long."

"I can't do nothing about that from here." Lawrence's voice cracked.

"Yes, you can. Talk to Ben," I said. "He listens to you."

CHAPTER
TWENTY-FOUR

'd failed.

The reality of it gripped me on our last day on the road. The next time the sun rose, we'd be in Mullan, and I'd be a slave with no way to get back home to the people I loved. Vinton, Mom, and Dad wouldn't even know what had happened to me. I'd spent the whole Soldamned trip hyper-focused on convincing a crew of men who'd stuck together since childhood to change their ways, and I'd failed.

Lawrence hadn't spoken to Ben, or if he had, he'd not convinced his crew boss of anything.

David Kahn would work me to death in some fragging copper mine and no one would even know. Except Robert. I was changing his bandages inside the stagecoach when I broke down.

"Hey. Shhh." He turned around, his back only half bound, and tucked me against his chest as wretched, hitching sobs overtook me. "What's wrong?"

There wasn't any strength in his grip and no steadiness in his voice. That's what was wrong. When I'd taken his dressings off earlier, I'd tried to convince myself that his wounds weren't redder and more swollen than yesterday, but now, in his embrace, there was no denying it. Robert's skin burned with fever. His face was flushed and clammy. Despite all our efforts, despite all his pain, his infection was coming back. I was running out of hydrogen peroxide, and I hadn't saved him at all. "I'm sorry," I wailed.

"Don't. Don't let them win, Iris. We're still here." He kissed the top of my head. "I've got you."

"I waited too long. You're too sick. I-I should have just taken you. We could have run during the day. Stolen a horse."

"I was in no shape to ride a horse then. And I'm no better now." He murmured into my hair. "Ben had watch shifts set up 24/7. You can't beat yourself up."

"I can't do this. I don't have anything to fix this, Robert." My chest squeezed tight enough that I had to gulp for air. "Kahn said he wants to break you," I wheezed. "I won't be able to stop him. Not by myself."

"Breathe with me, Iris." He stroked my back. "Come on. Just breathe."

"I can't." Nausea flooded my stomach, and my heart thrashed behind my ribs.

"Yes, you can. You're the strongest person I know." He tucked my hair behind my ear. "Just be here with me. Just breathe."

But the unravelling in my head was boiling over, too hot to condense into a single moment. Pressing my ear against Robert's too-hot chest, I lost myself in the white noise of his heart, the way his shaking hands splayed over my back like I was a sand sculpture he was trying to hold together, and the tide was coming in. "I love you." The words slipped out of me, newborn and fragile.

Robert's breathing hitched. His chest stiffened, and he

exhaled shakily before kissing the top of my head again. "I love you too."

"Promise me you're not leaving me."

He shifted to grab my hand. His fingers were cold and trembling. He hooked my pinky finger with his. "Pinky swear," he croaked.

THE MOUNTAINS TOWERED AHEAD of us, cloaked in bristling pine forests and veins of crisp snow. We'd started early and the afternoon sun blinded us as Ben eased Smokey alongside the stagecoach where I slumped in the luggage trunk. "We need to talk about this next stop."

"We're talking now, are we?" I sneered. I'd been wondering why we'd broken camp hours earlier than usual to slather on sunscreen, don wide-brimmed hats, and travel in broad daylight, but I felt so cornered and helpless, I couldn't help but lash out.

"You don't have time to be petty, ma'am."

"When will I get the chance to be petty with you again, *sir*?"

He clenched his jaw and shook his head. "The next stop, it's called Paradise and it's anything but. It's a troll settlement."

For a moment, my curiosity overpowered my anger. "Troll settlement?"

"The people there control the only bridge for hundreds of kilometers, and they've made sure the river is impassable by any other means. Their council interrogates anyone who wishes to cross before deciding if they're worthy. Normally, they accept a generous donation to their church, but I'm afraid they're going to take a special interest in you. In your scars."

My fingers brushed my cheek, and a flush crept up my neck. "Why would they care about scars?"

"They're Helioans. Sun worshippers. They only conduct business during the day. That's why we're aiming to hit town with plenty of light still left. They close the bridge crossing at night. And they're always looking to recruit new acolytes from the folks who are passing through, especially those the sun's already kissed. With visible scars like yours, they'll figure you've come to join the fold."

I remembered the women with the shaved heads and the ghastly sunburns handing out pamphlets earlier in our trip. One of them had tried to touch my cheek. *Helios has touched you, sister,* she'd earnestly said. Later, I'd pulled the pamphlet out of my pocket and read it. It had been filled with senseless religious prattle. I'd read it over several times, fascinated by the outlandishness of it.

"Maybe I'd like to join the fold," I said. "I think I'd rather be a sun worshipper than a slave."

A dry laugh huffed out of Ben. He wiped sweat from his brow. "Thought you might say that. Even if I weren't bound to deliver you to Mullan, I wouldn't leave you with them. They're touched, and not by any god either. Some types just go off the rails when the world ends. The Helioans are one of them. Trust me, you're better off a slave than one of them."

"That's the thing, Ben. I don't trust you."

"Fair enough." His voice was tired as he broke eye contact and scrubbed at the stubble on his chin. "Call it friendly advice then."

"Ben Breyman's school of slavery again. I'm all ears."

He winced, a glimpse of genuine hurt before he masked over the rawness.

Guilt congealed the anger in my belly into something too heavy to digest.

"The Helioans tie their acolytes out in the sun for days. They leave them a bit of water and instructions to *gaze upon the face of*

Helios. If their high priestess feels someone isn't making their best effort to commune with their new god, she has their eyelids cut off. They die from shock or infection when their eyes shrivel up and start rotting in their skull. It's an excruciatingly long death, I'm told."

"Mother of Sol." My toes curled in my boots.

"Those that are accepted into the coterie don't fare much better. Lots of them die of heat stroke. That's considered an honor, being welcomed into the arms of Helios while in the midst of prayer. Those that don't die are sun-addled—not that any of them are right in the head. Blistered skin, eyes clouded over by cataracts, skin cancer lesions, they're all considered marks of beauty and they move you up the ranks pretty quickly. Most of the Helioan high council are half-blind and riddled with tumors. If you join the fold, Iris, they'll leave you to dry out in the sun like a raisin, and they'll ask you to thank them for it. If you survive, they'll turn you into breeding stock. You'll likely die with a child in your belly or cancer eating up your insides. I wouldn't condemn an enemy to Helioan life."

I swallowed hard. "Funny. You're just fine condemning one to slavery."

"We're not enemies, Iris." He examined me intently.

"Yes, we are. You're leaving me with a man you know is going to kill me. You aren't even lifting a finger. You honestly expect me to behave and hide my face from the people you're bribing so you can cross their bridge and follow your orders like a good little slave. And Clowes is never going to reward you for it. He's going to keep a chokehold on you until the day you die. You know what? I wouldn't condemn any enemy to *that.*" I suffocated in the heat of my own breath, nostrils stinging, teeth clamped, waiting for him to snap back so we could escalate this. I wanted to fight or kick something. I wanted to run or scream until this pressure in my chest drained out of me.

Ben rode beside me in silence, head bowed so that I could

only see blonde curls sweeping behind his ear and a vein twitching on his tanned neck. "I'm trying to help you and me both."

"No, you're trying to help you. Only you. You want something." I straightened and locked gazes with him when he raised his head. "Stop fragging bullshitting me. You haven't talked to me for days and suddenly this afternoon, we're friendly again. What is it, Ben? Just spill. Be real for once in your life."

"Grace has bad teeth," he blurted.

"What?"

"That's one of the reasons she doesn't talk. She's had a bunch of them pulled. I don't know why she got the lion's share of cavities growing up and I didn't, but after Mom and Dad died, we weren't eating proper meals or brushing our teeth." A short, sharp laugh burst out of him. "You don't never want to be raised by a big brother, let me tell you."

Vinton did fine while Mom and Dad worked themselves to death. He'd protect me a hell of a lot better than you. I wanted to say the words but swallowed them instead. It hurt to even think about my family. I certainly didn't want to talk about them.

"She's had some bad infections," Ben carried on. "Her jaw's bothering her right now. Clowes won't spare her any penicillin, so I bring some when I can. The last batch was too long ago and not strong enough. People trade the Helioans whatever they've got to cross their bridge. Not just copper. All the high-ticket items. Paradise has got a pharmacy stocked better than any other for hundreds of kilometers. Penicillin is a top seller, and they don't gouge like other towns do, but they're awfully stingy on who'll they'll trade it to. They've denied me the last two times I've been through. Your boy wasn't looking so lively this afternoon. His infection's back?"

I clamped my teeth and nodded wordlessly.

"Well then, I'd wager he could use some antibiotics desperately right about now. I'll buy it and split it with you fifty-fifty if you help me."

"Help you?" I narrowed my eyes.

"Pretend you're interested in joining the Helioans. Take every pamphlet they hand you with wide-eyed wonder. Play it up. They're not above using bait to catch a fish they think will bite. I'll give you enough copper to buy the penicillin, and they'll be more likely to sell it to a fresh face as opposed to an irritable caravan leader they've seen one too many times. And I'll stay close enough to pull you out of any situation that gets too uncomfortable."

"No."

Ben looked genuinely shocked. "No?"

"No. I won't help you." Fire curled in my belly and sharpened my words. "This isn't you saving us. This is you making yourself feel better as you abandon us. Penicillin or no, Kahn will find a way to kill us both. And you're just going to let it happen. Your sister has more balls than you ever will. At least she's actually *trying* to save people."

His cheeks flushed and his expression froze. "What exactly is Grace doing now?" he asked slowly.

I saw the opening in his armor and stabbed as deeply and viciously as I could. "She was Robert's contact. She carried his letters to me. She runs slaves out of the colliery in the false bottom coal car. It was Grace who got me out before you fragged everything up and brought me back, you coward."

His nostrils flared, and Smokey danced beneath him as he white-knuckled the reins "You're lying, she wouldn't risk us like that."

I leaned out of the luggage trunk, teeth bared. "Why in the hell would I lie to you, Ben? You've already condemned us. What would I gain?"

"Forget it." He cranked his hat down over his eyes. "Forget I asked."

"What would I gain?" I yelled after him as he kicked Smokey into a trot and left me seething.

BY THE TIME we closed on Paradise, numbness had settled back around me like cold mud, the kind that seeps in when your body is too drained to feel anymore. I knew my detachment wasn't acceptance so much as exhaustion, but I didn't care. I was tired of feeling too much. I didn't have any fight left in me. So, when Ben approached the stagecoach a second time, I didn't even try to avoid him. We both knew what my answer would be. If I had any chance of stopping this infection from killing Robert, of course I'd take it.

As Ben closed, Smokey stuck his head into the luggage trunk and I scratched under the gray horse's chin, breathing in the sweet musky scent of him.

"He doesn't let anyone do that." Ben shook his head, flabbergasted. "Anyone else and he'd take off their fingers."

"You're just trying to scare me," I murmured.

"Ask any of the crew. He's tried taking pieces out of all of them."

"Just means I'm better at winning over horses than people."

Smokey pulled his head back.

I leaned against the stagecoach wall and closed my eyes.

"Have you heard him in there at all?" Ben nodded toward the cabin.

"No." I gulped. Usually there was the murmur of Kahn speaking to Robert, filling his head with poison, but this afternoon, I'd heard nothing, and the silence was terrifying. "He's sleeping, I hope."

Ben nodded and cleared his throat. "I've been thinking over what you told me about Grace. It makes sense she wouldn't tell me. I'm Clowes's dog and she's not. She's not as tied up in it. And he doesn't think much of girls. Figures they're all as vacant-headed as his wife and her entourage.

"But Grace has always been smart as a whip. Smarter than me. And she's always had a heart that was too big. She'd do it. She'd run people out every chance she got. And she'd be clever enough to keep it on the down low, even from me. Goddamned her." His voice wobbled, and he turned his head away from me for several breaths before composing himself enough to meet my gaze with his cold blue one.

"I can't do what she does, Iris. I'm not on the low down. I'm front and center with Clowes. He keeps me at his side when I'm at his house, and he tracks me with the towers when I'm in the field. I make one wrong move, and he'll kill her and not just her. I'd be throwing my whole crew under the bus. We show up in Mullan without both of you, Kahn will message Clowes before we get back. We show up without Kahn, we're all dead. We flee and our families die. My hands are tied here, you understand? You think I want to leave you and your boy? That I wouldn't save you if I thought there was any way I could make it work? As long as Clowes and Kahn live, as long as they hold Grace and Robert against us, giving you a shot at survival is the best I can do."

"I'll do it." I croaked. "If you teach them to read code."

"What?" Ben's head raised. "Teach who?"

"I'll help you get the penicillin if you promise you'll teach your crew to read tower codes."

His sharp blue eyes narrowed. "Lawrence put you up to this?"

"He doesn't know I'm asking. They should know how to send messages without you. The only reason you haven't done it yet is because you want them to need you. You want them to be tied to you just as tightly as you're tied to them. They are, Ben, without you forcing them. They'll stay. They're loyal."

Ben ducked his head and scrunched his face to quash whatever emotion was trying to surface. "You'll never know if I do it." His words sounded strangled. "I could promise you and get what I want and then never teach them."

"You could." I wrapped my arms around myself. "You won't though."

CHAPTER
TWENTY-FIVE

Paradise looked like most other towns we passed. Cottages with stone foundations shared ratty lawns with faded ATCO trailers, RVs wrapped in canvas tarps, and yurts with tarred roofs. A wide, sluggish river hugged the west banks of the settlement, flanked on both sides by massive panel fencing topped with barbed wire. It was fronted by rows of half-buried pikes that still held up the tattered remains of the last two fools who'd attempted to climb the barrier.

Helmeted guards patrolled the east side of the bank closest to the bridge. Everyone else in Paradise was bareheaded. It was hard not to stare at the first few Helioans we passed. Many of them had lost a lot of hair. What was left of it grew through scalps riddled with scabs. The women wore bikini tops and shorts, and the men went bare chested. Their skin ranged from dark and leathery to puffy and purple. One woman was sunburned so badly she had yellow blisters on her calves ballooning to the size of eggs.

Binocular lenses, eyeglasses, and broken shards of mirrors had been glued to the walls of the buildings surrounding Main

Street so that it was impossible to traverse it without the glare of the sun blinding you in intervals. Children with cracked lips and peeling skin mobbed us as the caravan eased to a stop at the end of a growing line toward the bridge. I flinched as a young girl with green eyes and gobs of tightly curled black hair pressed a grimy pamphlet into my hand and jammed a corn husk doll with stiffly tied limbs toward my face. Its head was a faceless bundle of bunched golden sheaves.

"Only costs fifty grams, pretty lady. All proceeds to Helios Himself." The words shot out of her mouth with the rehearsed tones of a practiced saleswoman.

"No, thank you."

"Half price, then. Because He knows you." She pointed to my scarred cheeks and bobbed into a clumsy curtsy. When her lip started bleeding, she brushed it away and kept talking. That's when I noticed she had dark brown blotches of dye down both her arms. She didn't leave until Ben shooed her off.

"Why do all these kids have their arms painted like that?" I asked under my breath.

"Henna melanoma marks." He kept his eyes on his crew who were busy herding all the hangers-on who'd travelled with us away from the stagecoach and Lawrence's wagon. "If you don't have skin cancer yet, they're the next most fashionable thing."

"Zuse, there have got to be other routes south, and you go and pick this one?"

Ben shrugged. "Kootenai pass is blocked by avalanches, and the trolls at Bonners Ferry are cannibals. At least the Helioans don't try to eat the strangers passing through."

"Yeah, they're lovely," I whispered as a man with the skin on his sternum carved off in the shape of a sun leered at me and touched his own scarred cheeks.

"Helios be with you, sister. Pray with me later?" he asked.

Ben smiled and nodded at him. "She's praying with me, friend. Step off."

Uncomfortable heat flushed my face. "Never took you as the religious type."

"I can call him back if you like. Praying involves orgies here."

I coughed. "I'm good, thanks."

Ben waited until my admirer had moved along before tying Smokey to the rear of the cook wagon. "You ready? It'll be an hour at least before the council works their way through this cue. We can be to the pharmacy and back before then."

I twisted the pamphlet the girl had given me in my hands. It was the same as the one I'd been handed by her cohorts so many days ago. Full of nonsense.

And those whose faces I have touched, never will I forget them. For they will feel My radiant love again. And woe to the hands that tries to shade their eyes . . .

It just went on like that for pages and pages. I took a deep breath. "Let's go."

"You'll do fine." He smiled softly, a real smile. I didn't think I'd seen one on Ben before.

"Sure." I exhaled shakily.

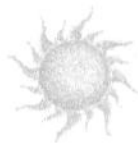

"Penicillin, one hundred capsules, please." I kept my fidgeting hands clenched in my pockets and forced myself to look the silver-haired woman behind the counter in the eyes. *She's blind,* I realized as I took in her clouded irises and the fact she didn't quite meet my gaze back. *Fantastic, Ben's using me for my scars, and we get a pharmacist who can't see.*

"That's a top shelf item, dear. Limited stock. Do you have any idea how much that much penicillin costs?" She wiped weathered hands down her white apron.

I knew exactly how much, in fact. Ben had filled my pockets with several ingots of copper the size of my fingers, each one heavier than the stone it was purified from. I'd wondered briefly as he'd handed them to me if they'd been sourced from the Mullan mine.

"Are these yours or Clowes's?" I had asked.

"Does it matter?"

"Seems like an awfully big allowance is all. What happens if you steal from him?"

"He cuts off my hands," Ben answered casually. "I don't steal from him. I get a budget for each mission, and I don't go over it."

"Then how can you afford penicillin for your sister, and clothes for me, and cows to bribe marauders with? Pretty sure those weren't budgeted items."

"I don't owe you any of my secrets, ma'am. Where I get my copper from is none of your business."

Now, it felt like those copper ingots were the only thing holding me down. My nerves crackled with static. Peeling the cold bars out of my pockets, I placed them on the counter. They clunked loudly enough to elicit a gasp from the people waiting in line behind me. "I can pay."

The blind pharmacist sucked in her cheeks before speaking slowly. "It sounds like you can, but I can't fill an order that big for a passer-through. Helios takes care of His children first."

I leaned further toward her, well aware that Ben stood around the corner outside. "I'm not passing through. I've been abducted into slavery," I whispered. "My kidnapper is standing outside right now waiting for me and he's armed. I was touched by Helios once as a child and I need your help." The pharmacist opened her mouth to interrupt me, but I blurted, "And those whose faces I have touched, never will I forget them. For they will feel My radiant love again. And woe to the hands that try to shade their eyes, or turn them away from My light, lest I burn the crops they pluck to feed them and dry up the water they cup to drink." I'd memorized the phrase from the pamphlet. "Help me, please, sister. Don't turn me away."

"Enoch?" The pharmacist tilted her head.

A skeletal man with no hair and a face puffy with water retention turned from the shelf beside me where he'd been stocking small glass vials. He stared down his nose through his glasses.

"Tell me what I'm looking at." The woman nodded toward me.

Before I could draw back, the sickly man grabbed my chin and turned my head to examine my scars. "She's seen the light, but not for a long time. Pale as a corpse."

I slapped his cold hand away. "My parents feared Helios. They didn't let me worship when I was young. But I'm not like them." So far, I hadn't lied. If I fell too deeply into deception, my face would give me away, I knew it. I was a terrible liar. The only way I could pull this off was to keep as close to the truth as possible. "I'm not asking for asylum."

"Good. Slavers are too well armed for us to rescue anyone they consider property. And I'll not be the catalyst for a gunfight at my doorstep," she said. "What do you ask for then?"

"A small kindness. I have the copper to pay. This medicine may save the one I love." My voice shook. "Consider me a sister instead of a stranger. I don't forget kindnesses. I don't imagine Helios does either."

"You don't know Helios at all then, child," she whispered more to herself than me. "Give me the rest of the copper you're holding back, and I'll fill your prescription."

I plunked the last two ingots onto the counter, and Enoch counted out the capsules into glass vials and stoppered them with corks before handing them to me.

Filing past the intense stares of those still cued, I swallowed bile and pushed through the cracked glass exit door, sucking in long breaths of outside air.

Ben grabbed me by the elbow as soon as I rounded the corner of the building. "Well?"

"I have them," I choked.

"One hundred capsules?"

I nodded.

"And you didn't ask for asylum?"

"You made it abundantly clear what would happen if I did." If I caused trouble and there was any sort of disagreement at the bridge checkpoint, the armed guards outnumbered Ben's crew two to one, and our caravan would be banned from crossing, perhaps permanently. The Paradise bridge was the only mountain pass for hundreds of kilometers. Kahn would make sure everyone involved in such an inconvenient blow to his business suffered greatly. Slaves who attempted to escape were flogged—like Robert had been on my behalf. Slaves who attempted escape twice were killed.

"Let me see them." Ben held out his hand, scanning the boardwalk as he did. This much penicillin in our pockets would likely get us robbed by anyone who'd witnessed me buying it, but Ben's ballistic vest, holstered gun, and keen eye seemed to be an effective enough deterrent for now.

I handed over one of the pill bottles and kept the other one clutched in my pocket.

Elation washed over his face, only for a moment, genuine and unrestrained. He gripped my arm hard like he needed my support just to process what he held. "Thank you, ma—Iris. Thank you. I won't forget this."

"Yes, you will." My eyes stung and my head pounded. "You'll forget both of us as soon as you turn your back on Mullan."

"I'll put in a good word with the crew boss at the mine. The boys there will look out for you as best they can, and I make regular trips down—"

"Stop." I shrugged off his arm. "What makes you think we'll last until the next time you come, Ben? Huh?"

He sobered, face dropping and lips pinching.

"There's only one way to make things better for us and we've already established that you're not risking your men for it. So just teach them the code. That was our deal. We're done."

I clenched my teeth and walked back toward main street as quickly as I could without attracting attention. Ben settled in step beside me, and blessedly kept his mouth shut as we trekked back to the waiting caravan.

It was nearly at the front of the cue when we reached it. Ben stiffened as Kit, the stagecoach driver, stood, curled his hand into the shape of an upside-down gun, and pointed at Stage-coach One.

"What is it?" I asked as he swore quietly.

"Trouble with your Master. Come on."

"Robert." *Oh Sol.* He was sick and I'd left him alone with Kahn.

CHAPTER
TWENTY-SIX

Kahn paced outside Stagecoach One as we approached.

"Robert?" I called again, stomach dropping.

"I didn't give you permission to leave. Where have you been?" Kahn frowned at me, his voice unnervingly calm.

"Problem, sir?" Ben asked.

"The boy is sickly again. Practically delirious with fever, and it's her job to change his bandages." Kahn's gaze flicked to Ben's hand on my arm. "She ran, didn't she? Fool doesn't even have the capacity to preserve her own life, nor his."

"Iris?" A thready moan sounded from within the coach.

Oh Sol, he sounds bad. My eyes filled with tears.

"She didn't run, sir." Ben let go of my elbow. "Apologies. I borrowed her. Mr. Clowes had a list of items for me to pick up from the pharmacy and the woman behind the counter there doesn't like dealing with men. I thought I could get a better deal if I used Iris to do my purchasing. But I should have asked first."

"Iris?" Robert called again.

"I'll go to him," I said.

"You will not. I'm not finished with you. And *you*," Kahn pointed to Ben, "don't cover for her. You can be sure Darwin will hear about . . ." Behind his steel-rimmed glasses, his eagle-eyes homed in on my pocketed hand. "What are you holding? Show me your hand."

I recoiled, bumping into Ben's shoulder.

Kahn plunged, clamping a hand over my wrist and digging short-clipped nails into the soft spot between the bones.

"Nothing," I whimpered. "It's nothing."

"Don't . . . hurt her." Robert wailed from the coach.

Kahn peeled the glass bottle from between my fingers and held it up to the sun. "Penicillin." His voice dropped. "My God, she's stolen penicillin."

"I didn't," I gasped.

"It's mine, sir," Ben said. "It was on the list. Clowes wanted me to buy it."

"Don't try to deceive me, boy," Kahn snapped. "Darwin may be foolish enough to trust you, but I'm not daft. This medicine is worth more copper than he'd send his wife abroad with. Did you know I reviewed the cargo manifest before we left? And your *allowance* was listed there."

Ben flinched, and Kahn shook the vial he held. "The figure was nowhere near the amount necessary to procure this. That puts you in a rather delicate spot. I do not tolerate thieves or liars, and neither does your master."

Ben held out his hands. "I'm not lying, sir. We didn't steal it. You can check at the pharmacy where we purchased it if you like, but if we want to be in Mullan by nightfall, we need to make this bridge passage now. They do not tolerate conflict here. Of any kind. If we're turned away, we can expect to spend twice as many nights as we already have retracing our steps to come down from the west. There's no other route. I can't think of anything I want to avoid more right now."

"Likewise," Kahn sneered. "Let's not delay. Mullan will come soon enough, and I'm content to have you both put on trial and hanged then."

"Don't hurt her!" Robert bellowed louder.

Ben's fingers twitched, and he bared his teeth in a terrible grin. "The cue is moving. Shall we get on our way, sir?"

"Don't let me delay you." Kahn smiled coldly back at him. "I'll be taking your gun, though, Ben, in case you're harboring any daft ideas." He nodded toward the Helioan guards. "As you said, these people likely won't tolerate a stand-off on their bridge crossing, and it looks as if they greatly outnumber your men, so give me your weapon, and tell your crew to stand down. They needn't suffer for your mistakes."

For the first time, I noticed that Lawrence, Kit, and the others stood stiffly with their hands hovering over their guns.

"Easy boys," Ben drawled, eyes hard but mouth still curled into a rictus of a smile. He unbuckled his holster, folded the straps around the gun and held it out. "Master Kahn's feeling insecure, and it's our job to make that right. If he feels better with a weapon on his person, I don't mind obliging. Plenty of guns to go around. We can go now, sir?"

"Indeed. And I'll be keeping the door locked until we reach Mullan. If you don't take me there directly, or if I suspect we're off course, I'll put the coach into lockdown mode."

Ben's smirk wavered.

Robert's moaning died down.

"Ah, your master hasn't enlightened you about his machine's lockdown option? I suppose that makes sense. It's designed to be used as a last resort in ambushes." Kahn took his time buckling the holster around his waist. "Or *mutinies*. Apparently, the audible alarm carries for miles and Darwin was good enough to tell me that—while he hasn't trained his semaphore operators to decipher the codes they're sending—they're all well-versed on the procedure should any of them hear the emergency alarm going off on his personal coach. They've been played a recording of the sound and instructed to send an SOS signal—or light a beacon fire—should they ever hear it. If the alarm goes off, day or night, it overrides any other message and triggers a red alert in both directions on the tower line."

The blood drained from Ben's face.

My heart kicked in my chest like something with hooves was hung up between my ribs and stealing all my breath.

Kahn adjusted his glasses. "If I press one button in that cabin, Mullan's ample security force comes running, and Clowes dispatches your families back home. So, let's have a civil final leg, shall we?" He climbed the steps and closed the stagecoach door while we were all still processing his words.

"Why did you give him a gun?" I wheezed. "He'll do it. He'll kill us."

"Mother of God, Ben." Lawrence sagged, "A trial? A hanging? What did you just get us into?"

Ben Breyman's cheek twitched. "Not your mess, boys. Just mine. And I'll handle it." But his words didn't hold their regular certainty.

CHAPTER
TWENTY-SEVEN

I didn't remember most of the rest of the trip. I phased out into numbness. We pressed the horses at speed and didn't stop for the next six hours. By the time we reached our destination, we'd long ago outpaced our retinue of fellow travelers, and the caravan was down to our original team of two wagons, twelve horses, and twelve people.

I never actually saw Mullan. The mountain's shadow had already swallowed the valley by the time we arrived, and a drizzle of icy rain siphoned away the last light. The old highway trail curved enough that the town itself remained out of sight.

A party stood stationed below an overpass outside of town. Tucked under the bridge, half a dozen armed men crowded around a group of thirty or so people in matching patched coveralls. There were children among them.

I pressed my ear against the stagecoach as it drew to a stop and listened hard for voices within but heard nothing.

"Lord save us," Lawrence muttered to Ben. "Don't like this. That's Tweed, isn't it? What in the blazes is a shift supervisor doing meeting us with slaves out here?"

"This little prick? Who knows." Ben took a deep breath. He

schooled his face into a jovial smile and dismounted as a thin man swimming in an oversized trench coat and an honest to Sol top hat, clacked toward us.

Fingers tingling, I slipped down from the luggage rack to stand in the rain. Lawrence saw me, but didn't stop me, just shook his head slowly.

The approaching man looked like a child caught playing dress up, the smile on his face greasy. "Ben Breyman. Nice hat."

"Michael Tweed. Wish I could say the same."

The small man's face soured. "You kept me waiting long enough."

"I believe we're right on time," Ben said. "Weren't expecting a welcome wagon this far out though."

I hunched behind the carriage wheel and shifted to the balls of my feet, dizzy with fear. *Don't panic. When the door opens, get to Robert. That's all that matters.*

Michael Tweed tugged at the wrists of his trim leather gloves. "I could have saved you all the trip if Clowes wasn't such a self-centered idiot. Master Grenfeld said I was a natural next in line for master."

"Did he now?" Water flicked off the brim of Ben's hat as he tossed his chin toward one of the armed men standing with the slaves. "I could have sworn he favored Adam over there. Sensible man. He wouldn't march a group of people out into the freezing rain for absolutely no reason."

The man Ben indicated nodded and waved.

"Where is your good master tonight?" Ben asked.

Tweed's lips peeled back over a set of unnaturally small teeth. His cheeks twitched and his dark eyes bulged, bright but empty of emotion. Sol, he looked more rodent than human. "Already left. Didn't want no part in this. Took his wife, went south, and left *me* in charge. Clowes sends another master down here who just wants to strip slaves for elsewhere, so I'm saving him some time. He don't need Mullan, whoever he is. So, I decided he doesn't get to have it. I'm civilized though. Sending him home with a parting gift. He can have all these slaves and head home right now." He tapped his temple. "You've got to think like a master, see?"

"Look at you." Ben crooned. "They tease us all with promises of promotions to master, but damned if they don't keep that circle cinched small enough to only include moneyed men, don't they, Lawrence?"

"Sure do." The cook whistled through his teeth, keeping one eye on me.

"I forget." Ben clasped his hands behind his back and cocked his head. "Do you come from money, Michael?"

The small man scoffed. "I'm smart enough to make my own fortune. That's why I'm a head supervisor while your sorry lot is leading slave trains down donkey trails."

"Yeah, you're a real firecracker." The tendons popped on Ben's wrists even as he kept his voice to an even drawl. "Maybe you'll have better luck warming up to Master Kahn here. You seem so damned eager to steal his job, couldn't even wait for us to roll into the town proper, could you? Just fixed on crossing the man before he even gets into Mullan. Well, I'd hate to delay your introduction further." Ben backed up. I shrunk behind the coach as he slapped the side of it hard enough to make it rock on its shocks. "Master Kahn, we've got a shift supervisor out here who says he can do your job better than you."

"You jackass," Tweed spat. "You'll pay fo—"

"Help!" A voice yelped from within the coach.

Everyone froze, like a program stuck in an infinite loop. A bloom of needling adrenalin shot from my core through my limbs before Robert's second call knocked us all out of statis.

"Shit. Someone help us!"

The lock tumbler clunked on the stagecoach door.

I darted toward it as Ben wrenched it open.

"I-I thought he was sleeping." Robert was deathly pale.

Sweat plastered his hair to his face. He clutched a fistful of Kahn's shirt as the man slumped on the bench across from him. "We both were. Oh Sol, I don't think he's breathing!"

"Move," Ben bellowed. "Iris, grab his feet!"

I gaped and robotically helped haul Kahn out into the rain. His face hung slack and gray, and his eyes looked like black buttons, pupils blown unnaturally wide.

Ben tore his hat off and tilted Kahn's head back. Seconds stretched painfully and then Ben yelled, "Lawrence. On his chest!"

The cook crashed to his knees in the mud and braced his interlaced hands over the unresponsive man's sternum. "What the hell happened?"

"I-I don't know. I dozed off. He did too." Robert panted from the stagecoach. "Oh, Sol. We were just sleeping. I woke up when you knocked, and he didn't."

"He's still warm," Lawrence puffed between compressions.

I reached into the stagecoach and clutched Robert's hand as he knelt in the doorway.

Michael Tweed bent over Kahn. "What's wrong with his eyes?"

"His tongue's swollen up. I'm barely getting any air in." Ben glanced up but didn't answer.

Tweed straightened, horror dawning on his face. "Has he been drugged? What did you do to him?"

"Nothing," Ben growled.

Tweed pointed a trembling finger at Kahn's face. "His eyes. Oh God, what did you do? Help!" he screeched.

That's when Ben Breyman grabbed his gun from Kahn's waist and shot Michael Tweed in the face.

CHAPTER
TWENTY-EIGHT

The man's body hit the ground before his top hat did. His legs were still bicycle kicking when Ben side-stepped around him. The crew whipped out their weapons as their counterparts under the bridge jerked their rifles into firing position. "This doesn't need to get messier." Ben projected his voice. "Adam, you listening to me?"

"Jesus Christ, Ben." Lawrence mumbled, still on his knees beside Kahn, his pistol dipping with each breath.

One of the children amongst the slaves let out a keening wail before their mother hugged them into her thigh.

A cough burst out of David Kahn. He sucked in a gurgling breath.

"Well shit, Looks like we're at a crossroads here." Ben lowered his pistol. "We just got your new master alive and breathing again, and none of you seem terribly relieved. You preferred him dead? Hell, I know for a *fact* we all prefer Michael Tweed that way. How many of your people has that prick worked to death?"

The guards under the bridge shifted uncomfortably.

"Dozens." A tall man near the back of the slave group shouted. "My uncle among them."

Ben nodded and pointed down the road toward town. "As of right now, no one else knows what happened here. It's up to you to tell whoever comes blazing up that road what caused that gunshot just now. Now, you can say we delivered an incapacitated master and killed a supervisor, but if you do Clowes will come after you just as hard as he comes for us. And then he'll send another useless waste of skin that doesn't know shit about Mullan to keep you all in line and bleed you dryer than the last rich scavenger did."

Kahn gurgled again, and Lawrence propped him onto his side. Something fell out of Kahn's shirt pocket as he did.

The vial of penicillin.

Ben spread his hands wide. "Or we can keep this in-house. Michael Tweed died because he's a senseless twit who likes to hide under bridges past sunset and we mistook him for a marauder. David Kahn made it to town as healthy as a horse, he just delegates most of his work to folks like you, Adam. Haven't you and Vernon been talking for years about breaking Mullan out of slavery and paying your workers a fair wage? Here's your chance. Whatever fit Master Kahn just suffered, it looks like it will require some recovery time. Maybe around the clock monitoring. I'm sure you can all convince him of the new order of things around here during his convalescence. All that Clowes knows about this place is what you have your tower man tell him. I'm willing to bet these fine folks with you are ready to fight for their freedom. Whole lot more of them than you, aren't there?" Ben let his skittish audience chew on those words before adding, "My crew and I are going to leave now. Adam, you can turn this into a shootout and all the extra bodies will be your fault. Or you can go back home, get your new master to a doctor, get these people out of the rain, and make the best of this. Your choice." He turned on his heel and strode back toward us.

Robert tugged my hand, pulling my gaze from the medicine he so desperately needed. The world was going fuzzy again.

"Iris. Get in the coach," he rasped.

"Put your guns away," Ben snapped to his men. And as he turned his back on me, I darted toward Kahn, snatched the vial of penicillin out of the mud, and pocketed it.

"Move out." Ben ordered, and when he turned back to me and his glassy gaze met mine, the fear in them shook me to the core.

THE INSIDE of Stagecoach One felt like a womb, soft and jostling, muffling the harshness of the outside world. Robert sat slumped on the floor, propped against one of the benches. He was too weak to climb onto the seat and too heavy for me to lift.

I knelt opposite him. "Come on. Stay with me." I yanked the cork out of the vial with my teeth. *How many do I give him? Two? Three?* I let go of his hand to shake the capsules into my palm.

My mind wouldn't stop replaying the moment when Michael Tweed's cheekbone crumbled into his eye, how the rest of his face had only registered mild surprise, like he'd been jolted by a static shock instead of a bullet.

"Take these." I pressed two capsules into his hand. "Antibiotics. Do you need water?"

He shook his head and dry-swallowed the pills.

The coach listed hard enough to send us skidding toward the door. Two tin cups juddered off the table and bounced toward us. One of them spilled its half-full contents. The other was empty. I reached to pick the closest one up.

"Don't touch it," Robert hissed, catching my wrist.

I blinked at the cup rolling back and forth on the composite planking for several breaths before understanding clicked into place. When I looked up at Robert, the anguish in his fever-bright eyes froze me.

I swallowed hard, peeling my arm out of his weak grip.

His fingers trembled as he pulled a tiny, empty vial from the torn cuff of his shirt.

"Why?"

"He was going to kill you, Iris."

CHAPTER
TWENTY-NINE

The coach jostled to a stop and the door flew open. Ben charged in, gun drawn, and voice flat. "Out." He seized the front of Robert's shirt and hauled him toward the steps.

"Stop," I yelped, clambering after them. "Ben, stop. He can't stand."

We pitched out into a sharp, cold night, mud greasy beneath our feet. Tall trees crowded an overgrown cutline. Saplings whipped against our legs and the horses surrounded us, their barrel sides slick and heaving like bellows, wide nostrils puffing gouts of condensation. The crew milled around us like ghosts in the mist.

Ben shoved Robert away from him, and he fell to his hands and knees, grimacing as it jarred his wounds.

I shouldered between them, blood buzzing between my ears as Ben paced, gripping his gun like it was the heaviest thing he'd ever held.

"You." He stared past me, wild eyes fixed on Robert. "You are going to explain to my men right now why you just tried to kill all of us."

"They're smart." He panted. "They can . . . figure it out."

"So can any asshole with half a brain in their skulls!" Ben bellowed. "Jesus Christ, you bawled for help the second you heard a knock on the door, almost like you already knew the man wasn't breathing. You could have at least closed his eyes. Tweed could tell the second he saw him that it was an overdose. If he dies, you're a murderer. If he lives, he's coming for all of us. You stole from Sibyl's stock? She sure as hell is going to notice a missing vial. Do you have any idea how much she pays for the stuff?"

"She gave it to me. For the pain. She won't tell."

"You don't know Sibyl!" Ben hissed. "She'll let it slip. You leave Fernie with enough poison on your person to drop a horse and then Kahn turns up at Mullan at the edge of death, eyes dilated big as black holes? Clowes will put two and two together."

"We're dead men walking," Lawrence mumbled.

"No, we're not." I licked my lips.

"Our families are." The cook's voice cracked. "First light of dawn tomorrow, soon as the tower operators can see well enough. All it'll take is one message up the line. Fast as lightning. They'll be dead long before we reach them."

"Not if Ben warns them first," I said.

"How in the hell is he supposed to do that?" Kit piped up from his driver's seat. "Even if we had access to birds, there isn't a pigeon out there that can pass a message faster than the towers."

"Ben doesn't need birds." I straightened, leveling a hard stare at him, galvanized by his sudden silence. "He's been sending secret messages up the towers for a long time."

He dropped his chin to his chest, shook his head, and wiped his nose.

"What's she talking about, Boss?" Lawrence frowned.

"She's talking bullshit, that's what." Kit's voice trembled.

"Ain't no way to send a message under the table using the towers. Even if you're among the handful of folks who can decipher the code, you can't send your own. It don't matter how much you bribe the operators. My old man tried. He was a codebreaker before Clowes executed him. Dispatched a few 'unofficial' correspondences down the line without logging them. Paid the codebreaker at the other end to keep them out of his books too. Poor bugger didn't realize that Clowes sends auditors to random towers to make sure *all* the logs match up. Everything is double and triple checked. You can't send a message without Clowes seeing it. Tell her, Ben."

He cleared his throat, gaze flicking back up to me, blue eyes as cold as gunmetal. "I haven't been sending any messages that Clowes doesn't see."

He's challenging me? Now, when I've got him cornered? I snorted. "He sees them, alright. He just doesn't know what he's seeing. You're not sending covert messages. You're adding to ones already going down the line."

A hint of that grim salesman's smile warped Ben Breyman's face. "You've had a long day, ma'am. I don't think you know what you're talking about."

Frag him.

"Oh, I do, Ben. I might not be worldly, or smart, but I'm observant as hell and it's amazing what people who underestimate you will let you see. I worked with your sister, remember? We washed dishes together for three days. At first, I couldn't figure out why Grace always put up her hand to scrub pots. It was one of the messiest jobs we had, and she picked it every chance she got. Then I noticed that the little window over the pot sink lined up with the semaphore tower on the church across the way. She was watching messages, and she had a little notepad and pencil in her pocket. I imagine the other kitchen staff didn't pay any mind to that. She doesn't talk. Only natural she carries something around to communicate, right, Ben?"

The smile dropped off his face, and his Adam's apple twitched.

"Guess which signals made her stop doing dishes, dry off her hands, and take out her notepad?" I waited for him to volunteer an answer and, when he clenched his jaw instead, I said, "Orange flags. I didn't know what those meant, but I *did* notice a funny thing on this trip. Nine times out of ten, when you checked in at a tower, that orange flag popped up after you left."

"Error flags." Kit frowned at me. "You were asking me about them."

"Lawrence told me your dad was a codebreaker and you were good enough to fill me in on the rest. An operator raises an error flag if they've accidentally sent a wrong symbol down the line, or if the tower receiving doesn't mirror their code properly. It means 'Ignore previous symbol. There's been a mistake,' but by then, the wrong character has already been sent up the line with the rest of the message. The error flag follows it. And the incorrect symbol gets written down, then crossed out in every logbook. They were important enough that Grace noted every single error flag she saw and wrote down the symbol sent just before it."

"Sweet Jesus," Lawrence exhaled. "You've been using the error flags to transmit messages under the table."

"And Grace knows how to decipher them," I said. "Funny how you've been raking in enough copper to assuage hungry marauders and buy expensive medicine. I imagine it's big business moving information faster than anyone else can. Merchants pay through their teeth to get advance intel on things like the price of wool rising, or which towns aren't gouging on penicillin, don't they, Ben?"

"Son of a bitch." Kit's voice shook. "You've been holding out on us?"

"Don't you dare accuse me of that, Kit Youngchief," Ben barked. "You have no idea how much I've spent greasing palms to keep us all alive on these Godforsaken runs. I'm doing this to help us all."

"Seems like you'd tell us if that's the case," one of the other men snapped back.

"How long?" another prodded.

Smokey stamped his foot and crowded closer to his rider.

"It doesn't matter how damned long!" Ben chopped a hand through the air. "None of that matters right now. When have I not treated you boys like my own flesh and blood? You tell me! When did I not put you first? We're all about to be hung for a crime he committed." He jabbed a finger at Robert. "And I'm still putting you first. I just shot a man in the head to buy us time. And suddenly you're all ready to turn on me, is that what we're doing here?"

"No, Ben." I spoke quietly. "We're asking you to make that jump you've been waiting your whole life to make. You've never had anywhere to land until now. Come home with us. Send a message up the line and tell Grace to get out."

"What makes you think we've come up with a signal for that?" he sputtered.

"Because she's your sister and you're a crew boss who prepares for every eventuality. I'll bet you and her have gone over exactly what the signal to run is, and how to contact every member of your crew's family to tell them to do the same. Kahn's incapacitated. You want to break free of Clowes, Ben? You'll get no better chance than this."

He squeezed his eyes shut and pinched the bridge of his nose. "None of you get it, do you? If it was that damned simple, don't you think I'd have gotten our people out by now? Say I send the signal to run. Every guard on the wall has pictures and names of the people we love. Clowes made damned sure his company men know them on sight. And he ordered me to tear apart that coal car you escaped in. The yard men inspect every rail car extra close now, thanks to you. Trust me, there's no way out of Fernie if Clowes doesn't want you to go."

"There is if Fernie falls," I said quietly.

"Yeah?" Ben snorted, "And just how are you planning to tip that last domino from hundreds of miles away?"

"You tell the miners that Mullan rioted and won. Kahn's not a master anymore. They hear that and they'll tear Clowes apart. They were ready to, Ben. They just need one more push."

He shook his head. "Nope. Using the error flags doesn't work like that. A message that complex would take me *days* to send. I can only send a few symbols at a time. Too many error codes all clumped together would raise suspicion. Even the words 'Mullan fell' would take too long. Sure as hell, we'd get caught if I visited a tower that many times."

"Could you send your signal to run, plus three letters?" I asked.

"What?"

"Three letters and your signal for Grace to run. Is that too many?"

"It's pushing it, but it'd get through in one message. What in the hell are you gonna send Grace in three letters that'll let her know Mullan fell?"

"Owl."

"*Owl?*" he repeated it.

"O-W-L. The bird," I said.

Lawrence straightened. "Lord, that's their symbol. The rebels at the mine. May drew me a picture. They're all wearing arm bands with owls stitched on them."

I kept my eyes on Ben. "You send that, and Grace'll know what it means. She'll get out, and she'll spread the word. Clowes will fall."

We all stood there with the moon cresting the trees overhead and the smell of wet clay and petrichor filling our noses. The horses' bridles clinked softly. Robert stared at me with something akin to wonder on his face, and Lawrence chewed his lip and squinted at his crew boss like he could sway his choice if he just looked hard enough.

A long sigh seeped out of Ben Breyman. "Alright, boys." He holstered his gun. "Let's pull the rug out from under him."

CHAPTER
THIRTY

We're going to make it. The thought had been expanding in my mind, hot, bright, and fragile as blown glass. Ben had sent our coded message. We'd ditched Stagecoach One and Lawrence's cook wagon, taken the back trails, and driven the horses hard all the way home. The strong dose of penicillin was clearing up Robert's infection, and he was healing and regaining strength as best as he could on the back of a horse. We were both new to riding. Muscle soreness and saddle sores paired with little sleep and less food had made for an excruciatingly long nine days. But all of that melted away as we closed on Painted Bluff.

It's actually happening. I'm going back. I'm going to hug my parents and Vinton, Oupa and Olivia. I hadn't allowed myself to hope this hard in a long time. The buoyancy in my chest took all the weight off my stiff legs. I sat higher in my saddle and breathed deep of sage-scented air, hungry for the tang of marshy water on the dawn wind.

But we didn't smell the lake as we approached. Instead, it was smoke. The acrid, chemical kind you get when you burn something manmade. The stench of it clung to my throat, and the bottom of my whole world dropped out beneath me when we crested a rise and saw a thick column of black blotting the sky ahead, right where our city should be.

"No," I croaked.

"Aw, shit," Kit whispered.

"It might not be home." Robert offered half-heartedly.

It was. Of course, it was.

Curls of charred debris floated on the wind, clouds of ashen paper moths clinging to our hair and smudging our clothes. One half-scorched piece settled against my chest, and I plucked it off, fingers trembling as I recognized the careful handwriting of one of our city scribes. *Oh Sol, Cache is burning.*

Robert curled over his horse and started coughing.

Ben eyed him warily and said, "Let's get upwind, yeah? Come in from the north and see what we're dealing with."

We skirted the overgrown ruins of Savona on the southeast end of the lake, crossed the river, and scrambled up the ruins of an old logging road into the clay-ribboned badlands of my childhood. A heaviness wedged behind my sternum. My hands were going numb even as I scrubbed my palms on my thighs. Nausea soaked through me thick and sour. There was no sign of our marauder allies. *The other group came back. The one we drove off.* I couldn't do this. I couldn't handle another loss. The sun was too hot. My eyes hurt, and Robert's soft assurances buzzed in my head like trapped insects. My family *had* to be safe.

It wasn't until we approached the northern border of what had been our city that I saw a pair of Blue Helmets approaching and anxiety eased its grip on my chest. I'd never been so relieved to see the Firewalls in my life. "Thank Sol," I blurted as I stopped, sliding down my horse, and finding my footing on shaky legs. When I turned, there was a gun in my face.

My mind lurched back to the night in Robert's side yard. The mud. The stench of rotten meat. Vannevar's voice in my ear and her fingers snarled up in my hair. *Not now. Oh Sol. Just breathe through it.*

Ben's crew froze around me.

"Don't," one of the Blue Helmets barked when Ben put his hand on his own weapon.

My mind snagged on small details. A thin scarf covered the man's face. His fatigues were several sizes too big, cinched around his waist and bunched around badly scuffed boots. *The Firewalls shine their boots every night.*

"Who are you?" I squeaked.

"We don't want trouble," Robert said.

The man who hadn't spoken yet snorted. His hands were gnarled and liver spotted. "Can't say I believe you. Trouble follows *her* wherever she goes." His papery voice pulled at my memory, but I couldn't place him with his face obscured and my brain misfiring. "He'll want to see her. The rest of you wait here unless you'd like to be shot." His watery eyes flicked to the hill flanking us. "Our snipers have a line on you all, so let's behave, right?"

I scanned the hilltop and saw the dull flash of another blue helmet, a man with a rifle and scope belly down in the scrub. *What if they're all dead already? Everyone I know.*

"She doesn't go alone." Robert dismounted, heedless of the guns swinging in his direction. "I'm coming."

"Fine." The older man waved his hand dismissively. "This won't take long."

And he and his partner escorted us into what used to be Painted Bluff.

The Browser's garage and the generator building were the only structures left standing. Cache was burning. Gouts of smoke and flame spewed out of its doors. Its contents had exploded onto the street. The heat on my cheeks made me wince. We picked through toppled skeletal shelves and soggy, charred paper thick on the street like layers of sloughed off skin.

Every hand-bound book, each meticulously printed volume, the largest collection of knowledge I knew of. All the texts my father had scribed for twelve hours a day, icing his hand through arthritis flare- ups. Translations of digital source materials that my brother and the other Browsers had risked their lives for daily. Everything my culture had been built on.

Destroyed.

If I wasn't being steered by Robert's strong hand at my elbow, I would have shut down completely.

Farther down the street, all five Greenhouses were smashed. They lay like beached whales, deformed by their own weight, warped ribs bright and bare in the sunlight, work benches buried beneath shattered plexiglass, ventilation fans clinging to their supports and creaking softly in the wind. Johan and Olivia's home was a blackened shell. Dead pigeons littered the ground below the loft. The long entrance stairs had been ripped away leaving the doorway I'd pinched my finger in as a girl opening into nothingness.

"Iris," Robert said, gripping my arm hard. I realized I'd stopped in the middle of main street, tottering, air whistling in and out of me like I was breathing through a straw. "I can't stay here. We've got to move." He was wheezing too. His free hand clamped his shirt over his nose and mouth.

His asthma. The smoke. Move, you idiot.

My vision tunneled as our escort led us toward the bunker. The remains of David Kahn's burned-out house had been demolished. Scorched metal walls bisected by jagged cutting torch slashes lay crumpled around the fully exposed double-door bunker entry. One of the false Firewalls fished a radio out of his pocket and spoke into it. "We've got something he'll want to see." When there wasn't an answer, the man frowned and fiddled with the crooked antennae until the radio squealed and a garbled, crackling response came.

"Good luck. He's in a mood."

A lock clunked and the doors screeched open. I clawed at Robert's arm as the ground swallowed us up and surrounded us with sickly pale LED lights, faded green paint, and the damp must of rotting apples. Scraps of clothing were strewn down the hallway, trampled sweaters, random shoes, a crushed set of dentures. *Where is everybody?* My pulse drummed behind my eyes as we approached what had been Elaine's makeshift hospital.

The older Blue Helmet knocked once on the door before shouldering it open.

"Jesus Christ, knock! How many times do I—"

The man inside stopped midsentence as his guards pressed us into the dim room.

The cots had been haphazardly stacked against one wall, tubular frames and sagging yellowed mattresses. A single wooden desk sat in the middle of the bloodstained floor. A man slumped behind it. I blinked, trying to focus on him.

Then the smell of blueberry moonshine filled my nostrils. My legs went slack.

"Well look what the cat dragged in. A little beetle."

"Nate," I choked.

CHAPTER
THIRTY-ONE

've gotta be honest. I was hoping for Kahn when I lit up a signal fire," Nate said. "You almost missed the show. It's been burning for days, and we're running out of fuel to throw on it." He leaned back, fingering the silver flask in his hand, speech soft but eyes hard. "How's it feel losing your little library of Alexandria, Iris? 'Cause I'm feeling a bit like Julius Caesar."

I couldn't speak. My tongue sat swollen and dead in my mouth.

"Betrayed. Stabbed in the back by all those I trusted." My uncle's smile was icy.

"*I* didn't betray you, Nate," I whispered. "Where are they?"

"Nate?" Robert turned to stare at me, horrified realization dawning on his face. "Your *dead* uncle?"

Nate slapped the desk hard enough to make us flinch, teeth flashing as his red-rimmed eyes focused on Robert. "You must be the boyfriend. She didn't tell you? No surprise there. I'm the black sheep of the family and we didn't leave on the best of terms, did we, Iris?"

"Where are they? What did you do?"

"What did *I* do?" Nate thundered, launching to his feet. The chair behind him toppled backward, and Robert shouldered ahead of me, ready to defend. "Naw. Nope. We're going to talk about what *you* did, Beetle."

That name. I used to love it. Now it poured off his tongue like something bitter and poisonous. "I escaped." I enunciated each word slowly. "You were holding me prisoner, ready to *sell* everyone I loved, and I escaped." He looked too thin, cheeks sunken, beard unkempt.

"And then you got into bed with self-same slavers you were so pissed about? Cozied up with Darwin Clowes and Coaltana as soon as you burned your bridges with me? Who's the hypocrite, huh?"

"What's he talking about?" Robert murmured.

"You keep him in the dark too?" Nate paced behind the desk, moonshine clutched in one white-knuckled hand, the other shoved deep in his jacket pocket, fingering something I hoped to Sol wasn't a gun. "Thought you could sweep me under a rug, and I'd just disappear?"

"You pulled my home apart," I barked, heat blotching my cheeks. "You promised to help us but instead you used me, and if I'd left you able to, you would have hunted me down. I just cleared a path big enough to get home."

"You killed her." My uncle's voice dropped to a malicious whisper. He pointed at me hard enough to make the moonshine in his flask slosh.

"What?" I froze.

"You don't even know, do you?" Nate sat heavily, never taking his iron gaze off me. "You killed her."

"I didn't kill anybody," I blurted, but a horrible cold nausea already swept through me. *You set a fire in the armory.* An old, converted root cellar behind Nate's house. *But it was locked. No one was inside.* I'd also drained the diesel tank so they wouldn't be able to start the fire pumps, and I'd drained the water tank closest to the house too. I'd left as much chaos behind me as I could to buy myself time to escape Nate's compound, but I'd done it to feed the hollow revenge in my belly too. My uncle had played me and conned my city. He'd started a civil war to bring Kahn down, and yeah, I'd wanted to knock him down a few pegs, but that was all. "I just started a fire. I never to meant to hurt anyone, Nate."

He pulled something out of his pocket and set it on the desk before him. It landed with a metallic clunk, but I couldn't make it out with his long fingers curled over it.

Oh Sol, his hand.

It was red and withered. The skin was rough, mottled and shrink wrapped over his bones. Burn scars. Severe ones.

"I never meant to hurt anyone either, Iris," Nate murmured. "Not at the start."

Robert licked his lips and put his arm in front of my chest. "We should go. We'll just leave, sir."

"Orin," Nate hollered. "Lock the door."

"Got it." The old man's muffled voice answered from outside. He'd been the one I recognized. He'd been manning the pigeon loft on the night I left Nate's.

I winced at the sound of a bolt snapping closed.

"That's the thing about starting fires, Beetle. Sometimes they get away from you." Nate slurred, taking a deep swig, and sighing loudly. "Yours did. Orin woke me up and by the time I got to the backyard, the grass was on fire. We tried to stomp it out, but the wind picked up and it got to the diesel spill. I couldn't figure out why there was fuel spilling everywhere, couldn't get the tank nozzle to shut off." He glanced down at his mangled hand, voice distant and analytical. "Got some on me and it started my sleeve on fire. I remember Orin pulling me away and hollering for water. But there was no water. You took care of that too, didn't you? It grew so fast after that. The farm-house . . ." He shook his head, voice thickening. The bitter pain in his eyes brought tears to my own. "The farmhouse was so old. It went up like a roman candle. That's when I started looking for Christie beside me. Shouting her name, but s-she wasn't outside." His face crumpled. He sucked in a wheezing breath and dropped his chin to his chest, clutching the object on the desk like it was the last thing in the world he had to hold onto.

Christie. Oh Sol, no.

"She always slept like the dead. I should have shook her awake when Orin got me. Should have dragged her out of bed then 'cause it was too late after. I didn't even think, and I couldn't get to her. I tried. The smoke was too thick and the heat . . . The fire was roaring like a jet engine." Breath left him in a rattling exhale. "I couldn't get to her."

"Nate," I gagged. "Oh, my Sol."

"Zuse," Robert breathed.

"I loved her," my uncle choked.

"I know you did." My face twisted, and my vision blurred.

"I found her the next day, under a pile of debris. Mostly bones. Her hands were burned off. They were just gone. Why would her hands be gone?"

I gagged.

"After that, half of the crops died. Just rotted. Like the whole place just gave up after she died. Christie held it all together. Always did. She was the glue."

"I'm sorry," I sobbed. I'd killed the crops. Full of heat and vengeance, I'd dropped potato blighted plants into the field's water tanks before I left.

"You will be," he answered quietly, tears running into his beard unchecked, face suddenly slack. "This whole damned city will be. Eye for an eye."

Oh Sol. He killed them. He really did it. Horror must have been plain on my face, because Nate's dead gaze rose slowly to mine, and he bared his teeth.

"I pulled in any favor anyone ever owed me. I used my good reputation, and I borrowed more than I'll *ever* be able to pay back. It cost me everything. But it got me all the weapons I needed. More than enough to scare off your hired marauders and push out that joke of a security team you rented from Fernie. And now, this is all mine." He raised both his arms and that's when I recognized the object in his hand. It was a hand grenade. Robert's eyes tracked it too, wide and afraid.

"You like it? I bought a whole case of them. Military surplus. Older than you, Beetle. The fuses get real touchy as they get older. That's what the salesman told me. Some of them work fine. Others won't detonate at all, but *some* of them . . ." He tapped the grenade on the desk and smiled coldly at it. "Some of them get unstable enough that as soon as you pull the pin, they blow up right in your face, tear you to pieces before you even feel it." He made a choking sound. "Ain't that just my whole life? People cutting me to ribbons when I least expect it. It'd be nice not to feel it." He took another long swig from his flask. "So far, half of them have been duds. Half of them have worked though. Real showstoppers. Noisy. Scary as hell. Cleared the garbage out of here real quick. I've got a good feeling about this one."

Garbage? "Our family, Nate. Your family." My voice shook.

"It was worth it to see the look on her face: Anne backing into the woods with a damned nightie and city shoes on, looking like she'd seen the devil himself. That's what I am now, yeah?"

"Where are they?" I gulped, latching onto the fact that he'd pushed them into the woods.

He shook his head, spinning the grenade on the desk like it was a bottle. "Maybe I'll tell you if you bring me Kahn."

"Kahn's more than six hundred kilometers south of here." Robert spoke quietly. "And likely dead. I poisoned him."

"Bullshit," Nate coughed out a laugh. "Scrawny carpet walker like you taking down a snake like Kahn? Bull. Shit."

"He's at a copper mine in Mullan, Idaho," I said. "The miners there are rioting. So are the ones in Fernie. If Kahn or Clowes are still alive, they won't be for long. It's over, Nate." *Come on. You can bring back some semblance of your uncle and find out where your family is.*

He whistled through his teeth. "So, we all die in our miserable castles, then. Kings of nothing. Looks like you don't need me, and I don't need you, Beetle." He straightened and bellowed "Orin. Our guests are ready to leave."

"Nate, wait."

"Iris, do me a favor," he said without looking up from the grenade on his desk. "Don't ever come back here. You set foot anywhere near *my* property again and I will cut you down. I'll shoot you and everyone you love."

CHAPTER
THIRTY-TWO

We need to go. Iris, come on. Look at me. Iris!"

I sat outside in the dirt, legs spreadeagled.

Robert was kneeling, cupping my cheeks with both hands. I blinked until his face unblurred. Ash smudged his forehead. He was covering his mouth and nose with his shirt. I didn't know where we were. The last thing I remembered was seeing smoke over our city. Memories coupled and then peeled apart in my brain, white and jolting like static electricity. *Nate's here.*

"What the hell is wrong with her?" someone growled.

Painted Bluff is gone.

"Give her a minute!" Robert snapped.

"We've given her five. Just throw her over a horse. They're going to start shooting!"

My family is missing. A man bellowed out a countdown, like I was a bogging program, and everyone ticked down the seconds until I came online.

"What happened?" I puffed.

"I'll tell you on the way." A frightened smile pinched

Robert's face and he stroked my hair. "Let me help you up. It's not safe to stay here. We have to go, okay? We have to ride."

He's talking to me like I'm breakable. I stared down at my own hands scratching at my arms. *I glitched and shut down.*

My head felt full of seed fluff as Robert hauled me to a stand, guided my foot into a stirrup, and boosted me into a saddle. He vaulted on behind me. I craned my neck to find the source of the angry counting and saw a man lying on the hillside with a gun aimed our way. His face was red from shouting.

"Seems like that went well," Lawrence said as he led my horse past at a trot. *Ben's crew. We were bringing them home. Oh Sol, there is no home.*

"I told you this was a mistake!" Kit hollered to Lawrence as our horses bolted out of the valley and away from the pillar of smoke. No one answered him.

We stopped at a clearing. Everyone swung off their horses with tensed jaws and squared shoulders.

"Stay up here, okay?" Robert whispered into my ear before dismounting.

"What the hell was that?" Ben shouted, jabbing a finger at his chest. "She said we'd be safe here. I sent my sister here because *she* said we'd be safe." He raked his fingers through his hair. "I should have sent them south."

"You didn't." Robert spoke quietly. "We can't change what happened while we were gone."

"I'm done." Kit shook his head like he smelled something bad. "I've got to find my mother. This is bullshit. I'm going back to Fernie."

"Fernie's a firebomb by now," Lawrence said.

"How do we know that?" Kit fired back. "How do we know it even fell? All she did was send one stupid word up the line."

"We've been over this already, it fell. The towers confirmed it," Ben countered.

We'd kept to the back trails, but we'd sighted semaphore

towers far on the horizon a few times. Ben had watched them through binoculars from the cover of the woods. Three days in, there'd been several messages from Fernie asking Mullan for immediate armed reinforcements, then there'd been a red alert sent up the line, all of the towers holding the same symbol for an extended period of time. Ben had frowned at that because it was only ever associated with Stagecoach One. Then the towers had all gone dead, abandoned by their operators one after the other, we assumed.

Robert spoke up. "If your people made it out of Fernie, they would have got here long before us. They had way less ground to cover. Either they got pushed out with our families, or Nate was already here when they arrived, and they've retreated to hunker down somewhere they think they'll cross us. We can still find them."

"None of us are wasting another damned second babysitting you and her," the driver shouted.

"Kit Youngchief, I don't recall making you crew boss." Ben spoke in a menacingly cold voice.

"I'm just saying what we're all thinking, Boss. We've got families of our own to save and they ain't here." The driver locked eyes with Lawrence. "Come on, you want to find May don't you?" Then to Robert, "Tell her to get off the horse."

"Kit." Lawrence sighed.

"We're riding. Who's with me?" Kit yelled.

"Open your eyes!" Ben bellowed. "We've been pushing hard for days. Lawrence can't ride anymore. His knees are swollen as hell. The horses are spent, and we're out of food. We don't need your fool mouth running off right now. We need to find shelter before the sun gets high, rustle up something to eat, get a good sleep, and plan this out. We can't go at it bullheaded."

"There's nowhere safe!" Kit sneered. "*They* don't even know where to start looking for their people and I'm not starving in the woods with a bunch of useless suits."

"I know where to look," I said and no one heard me, so I sat higher in the saddle and spoke louder. "I know where to look for my people, and I can find food."

Kahn had razed Johan's secret gardens when he'd stumbled upon them while searching for me before the first uprising, but it was a hasty pillaging by people unused to spending time in the dirt. After I'd escaped Nate's, and we'd driven out the hostile marauders and brokered a fragile peace with the ones who remained, the ruined gardens had taken a back seat to repairing the greenhouses and starting new crops closer to home. But even if Kahn had ordered all the plants pulled, there were bound to be some potatoes, carrots, and onions left behind. If I were Johan and Olivia heading a group of freshly homeless and hungry city folk, the gardens would be my first stop.

It was midmorning when we broke into the clearing that I'd hiked to countless times before. It seemed like a distant life. Had it been only a few months since I'd last visited, blissfully unaware of how my life would turn? Had it only been this morning that I thought I'd be reunited with my family? It felt like days had passed since then, not mere hours.

"This isn't food. It's a patch of weeds." Kit growled.

Robert put out a hand to steady me as I shifted to dismount.

I fought against the primal part of me that wanted to push him away and wall off from him. Days ago, in a quiet moment, we'd promised each other that we wouldn't do this anymore, keep things from each other, tackle the world alone when we needed help, push each other away when we were hurting. *We're stronger together*, Robert had said. *Something more than what we are alone, something worth protecting.*

You still didn't tell him about Nate, even then. And now, you're a murderer. Oh Sol. Blackness pulled at me, and I fought to keep from going under again. *Don't shut down again. Don't. Just take one step.*

So, I took Robert's hand when he offered it, and I let him walk the garden rows with me. Soil had been turned here recently, not more than a week ago. Footsteps peppered the soft black loam, thin soles with no tread. City shoes. Johan had brought everyone here. I'd been right. Hopefully they'd left something behind.

We pulled thick branches from the undergrowth, set up a lean-to under the shade of a large pine, and started a fire. Then we used larger boughs to turn over mounds of soil. It took twenty minutes, but we found enough carrots and potatoes to fill our stomachs. There was even a turnip—a bit wormy, but salvageable. We boiled them all. It was the first hot meal we'd had in days, and even with no seasoning, it tasted like something that could have come from Christie's kitchen, the kind of meal you remembered long after it was done. Tender new potatoes, sweet, crisp carrots, and buttery turnip. We ate so fast we burned our mouths. When tears sprang to my eyes, that's what I blamed it on, not the memory of Christie, petite, headstrong, a formidable force of one. She had seemed utterly invincible. And I'd killed her.

"You and Johan tended this all along?" Robert asked through his last mouthful, and I welcomed the soft distraction of his voice.

"And Olivia," I said. "Right under Kahn's nose."

"Does your uncle know about it?"

I nodded.

"Then we should go. He seemed pretty adamant about putting some distance between you and him, and he probably considers all this his now."

"I'm sorry." My voice shook.

"About what?"

"All of this. I never told you about Nate," I gasped. "The fire." My throat ached.

"Come here." Robert put his arm around my shoulder, pulling me close until our foreheads touched. "Don't apologize for the world putting you in a shitty situation and making you fight your way out of it."

"I killed her. I—" The words stuck in my throat. I clenched my teeth.

"Don't." Robert whispered, slipping his hand into mine.

"What?"

"Don't listen to that voice in your head that's dragging you down. It wasn't your fault that she died. Okay? And we're not finished, Iris. You're going to get us through this."

"Me?" My voice tripped into a higher register.

"Yeah, you. Know how I know?" He stroked my thumb.

I twisted my face into a smile because if I didn't, I'd start crying again. "Enlighten me."

"Because you don't give up on other people. You fight harder for them than you ever do for yourself. When someone needs help, you never let them down. You don't hold anything back. You give them every last scrap without caring if there's anything left for you. I wouldn't want to be the one standing in your way."

You're wrong. I fail everyone. All the time. I couldn't answer him. Heat pooled behind my eyes, and I stared over his shoulder to avoid his gaze. That's when I saw it. Tied to a branch behind Robert was a scrap of beige nylon stocking.

Since I was a child, Johan had gone door to door collecting old nylons from the women in Corporate. I remembered it because it creeped out my mother. "What on earth does he need ladies' stockings for anyway?" she'd whisper to Dad whenever the old gardener knocked. I found out when I became a gardener myself. Oupa cut old nylons into strips to use as plant ties because they were sturdy but soft enough not to chafe a young plant's growth. There was no reason for one to be tied to a tree though.

I stood and tugged the out-of-place fabric off its branch. Then I scanned the woods beyond. Further in, past a fallen log, I spotted another beige strip, secured at eye level. Hope bubbled up in my chest.

The man who had taught me to track had left me a trail to follow.

CHAPTER
THIRTY-THREE

e heard the motorcycles before we saw them. The horse's ears swiveled to the clatter of diesel engines picking their way up the narrow logging road ahead of us.

"That them?" Ben asked.

"Sol, I hope so," I murmured, heart high in my throat, listening to the sound that had heralded my older brother's arrival home for years.

"They'll be armed, and we don't want to startle anyone." Robert turned to Ben. "If it is them, they should see Iris and me first."

"Come on then, boys. Get the horses into the brush." Ben waved at the others.

"A surprise party," Kit grumbled loosening his gun in its holster. "My favorite."

"Stand behind your horse for cover." Robert nodded to me. "Until we're sure."

I did.

My horse tossed his head and pulled toward the ditch, and I

let him graze there, reins slick in my sweating hands as he tore out mouthfuls of grass and carefully worked it around his bit.

Robert's mare nickered softly and nosed his hand. He flinched but then pulled something from his pocket, one of Lawrence's homemade molasses chews. The mare plucked it from his palm with soft lips, and he wiped his hand down his dirty dress pants, gaze pinned to the road ahead.

If Lawrence was right, and life was just a current we did our utmost to navigate, then Robert was the best swimmer I knew. He'd gone from the sheltered life of a corporate rich boy to a civil war. He'd sold himself as a corporate hostage, wrestled stuck motorcycles down narrow paths, and survived David Kahn's cruelty. He'd ridden in the carriage normally reserved for Prime Ministers. I'm not sure he'd ever touched a horse before last week, never mind ridden one, but here he was distractedly offering one treats from his pocket while waiting to greet a band of armed motorcyclists, like he'd done it a thousand times before. He was heedless of the incongruity of his torn formal clothes paired with the set of oversized hiking boots Kit had given him when his Oxfords fell apart. And through it all, he was still Robert. Robert who loved me as I was and told me I was a badass.

He was the badass. Saving me. Every day. It was him. Always had been.

I wanted to thank him for all of it right there in the middle of the washboard gravel road with Ben's crew staring out at us from the woods, but I couldn't find a way to do it that didn't sound utterly ridiculous. My timing was never right.

Then the motorcycles popped over the rise ahead. Four of them. Sommer 462s. I stiffened behind my horse, and Robert murmured something that might have been a prayer. The first helmeted rider spotted us, raised his fist over his head, and slowed to a stop. Gravel crunched as the other riders passed the hand signal on and slowed. Sun flashed off one of the bikes as its sturdy landing gear lowered while the machine rolled to a halt. Its rider's legs were strapped against the gas tank with thick Velcro strips. Stowed behind him was a folded wheelchair. He drew a pistol but didn't aim it.

"Vinton," I breathed. *Oh Sol, it was him.* I dropped the reins. "Vinton!"

He froze.

I ducked around my horse and tumbled toward him, nearly rolling my ankle in a pothole.

He peeled his helmet off, his hair a spiked mess. "Iris?"

"Vinton!"

"Iris." He lowered his gun and dropped his helmet. It smacked onto the road and rolled away. "How? Zuse, come here."

I flew past Mark and crashed into my brother.

He locked his arms around me hard enough to press the breath out of me. "Come here. Oh, my Sol. How . . ." His words pinched off, and I only realized he was crying when his shoulders shuddered. "You were supposed to be on the train, Soldamnit," he croaked. "You were coming home with us. They said you were in the next car. I never would have left. We thought you were—" He stiffened, and I felt him shift, raising his gun.

"We've got company," Mark barked.

"Tell me this isn't a trap." My brother hissed in my ear, still holding me clamped against his chest while he aimed his handgun over my shoulder, toward the woods.

I clasped his arm. "Don't shoot. It's Ben. His crew. They're with us. They saved us."

"Who the hell is Ben?" Vinton growled.

"The cowboy?" Mark asked.

I nodded. "They didn't want to alarm you."

Robert waved Ben, Lawrence, Kit, and the others out of the

woods. They led their horses onto the road with their weapons holstered.

"Why in Sol's name were they hiding like they meant to ambush us?"

"Nate took the city. We didn't know if he got the bikes too."

"All but these four. We were out on a run." My brother pressed me away from him, slipping his pistol back into its holster, wiping his eyes, and then punching me in the shoulder. "Zuse, I can't believe it's you."

"Hey, Iris." Mark popped off his helmet, grinning.

"Hey, Mark."

The two other Browsers flipped up their visors and waved. John and Radia—her pregnant belly just starting to show. I waved back.

Robert led both of our horses to Ben before walking directly up to Vinton and holding out his hand.

"Well, if it isn't Pretty Boy." My brother's sharp eyes took in his torn clothes and the whip scar peeking over the collar of his shirt. "I'd punch you in the face, but it looks like you've run through a meat grinder since we last talked."

"Let me heal up first, yeah?" Robert grinned crookedly. He didn't put his hand down.

Vinton caved and pulled him into a rough handshake. "I think I like him better all scuffed up," he said to me.

"Camp isn't far." Mark addressed Ben and his crew, "And there's some people there who'd like to see you sooner rather than later, I'll wager."

The crew froze.

Ben gripped Smokey's reins hard enough to whiten his knuckles. His next words were hoarse, quiet, and steeped in fragile hope. "A girl with black hair. Eight others with her?"

"That's them." Mark smiled softly. "Grace Breyman and company. She's pissed that you're late."

"I'm not late," Ben choked. His face dropped, weary and

unwinding, like an actor on a dim stage exhaling after the final curtain call. Then he ducked his head and cried.

CHAPTER
THIRTY-FOUR

As we navigated through a dusty forest trail, I glimpsed marauder scouts with machine guns nodding at us as we passed. All at once, a mob of children started trotting alongside the motorcycles and the horses.

A girl with charcoal stripes painted down her face and a macrame sash slung over her T-shirt shouted and waved to me. "Mîciwin?" Her face was plumper now, but I still recognized her from our first harrowing meeting at the lake, when that sash had been a gun strap for the semi-automatic weapon she'd wielded.

Vinton parked his bike in a clearing carpeted with pinecones and his Browsers pulled up beside him. The kids swarmed Mark and tugged at his pockets as he dismounted.

"Picikwâs?" they asked.

"No. No picikwâs. Next run, I promise." He turned to me and shrugged. "I bring 'em back dried apples when we go to Golden. The kids are crazy for them." He nodded to the sprawling crowd of mismatched tents, drying racks, and clothes lines strewn before us. I recognized the faces of some of the people greeting us, the marauders we'd formed a fragile alliance with before I'd left for Fernie. "We only had the clothes on our backs when your uncle pushed us out. No food. No shelter. Nothing. And they took us in, no questions asked."

I nodded, but I was only half listening. Inside, I was bracing for my reunion with my parents. It was bound to be over-whelming—anything involving my mother was. I rallied myself for the too tight hugs from my father and the awkward silence that would follow. I rehearsed what I would say in response to the aggressive rapid-fire questions from my mom, how I'd main-tain eye contact with her no matter how stern her face looked, how I wouldn't cringe as she raked her hands through my hair with an air of ever-constant disappointment.

But the meeting was nothing I expected it to be.

I didn't even recognize Mom when she approached me white-faced with her long hair loose and tangled over her shoul-ders. She was wearing gardening coveralls that were torn at the knees and boots wrapped in duct tape, and she broke down completely as soon as we touched, her touch feather-light and trembling. She kept saying my name over and over again like she couldn't believe I was real. I couldn't make out anything else through her sobs. She cried into my shoulder until my shirt was soggy and Dad gently pulled her away.

"Oh, Sweetheart," he puffed as he crushed me in a hug. He'd grown a beard, like Nate's, and it looked so incongruent on his face, aging him, and making him look more severe. I flinched as it scratched my cheek. "We thought we'd lost you." He took a shuddering breath and held me away from him. "I'd watch every city in the world burn if it meant I could still hold onto you, you know that right? You know how much we love you?" His eyes were swimming with pain, like he was talking to a ghost.

"I love you too, Dad," I said, but all I could think of was the awful agony in Nate's eyes as he told me about Christie.

"Robert!" Paul Lycos's sharp voice cut through me and

although Dad's hug hampered my view, I saw Robert fall into his father's arms.

"Son? Oh Sol, you're here. I thought you left me. I'm sorry," he babbled. "I'm so sorry."

"Dad, it's okay." Robert gasped as his father squeezed him too hard. "Careful, my back. It's hurt."

"What happened?" His face twisted and his mad gaze pinned to me. "What did she do?"

I winced and turned away from them.

Johan and Olivia deftly stepped in. They gave me short, quick hugs and kisses before waving me toward the cookfire. "Come and see us once you've eaten and settled in," Olivia whispered. "Don't think you can get away with one measly hug."

All around us, Ben's crew reunited with their families. Kit fell into his mother's arms and grinned through his tears. Lawrence hobbled toward May. Her face crumpled as she put his arm over her shoulder and chided him for riding hard enough to aggravate his knees. Ben clutched his sister Grace like the girl would dissolve if he ever let her go.

We ate rabbit stew. We recounted our stories as best as we could as many times as we could until Vinton and Mark started bustling people away from our fire. Olivia tacked a fresh tarp onto my parents' tent and Mom made me up a bed. Robert fell asleep on my shoulder until his dad woke from a fitful sleep, screaming his son's name.

Oliva and Johan kept me company, until my mentor's head started nodding and his granddaughter helped him to his tent. In the end, it was Vinton and I left slumped around a dying fire.

"How's it been, really?" I asked.

"Shitty." He scrubbed a hand through his dirty hair. "We lost some folks right off the bat. Don't know if they just scattered or got killed. Johan and Olivia have still been trying to teach our people to hunt out here. You can imagine how that's going. The marauders have been bagging most of the kills. But we've got seventy people, plus their twenty or so. Then there's the miners Clowes sent. About a dozen of them stayed after Nate drove out the armed goons Fernie sent them with. That's a hell of a lot of mouths to feed and no copper to pay for it. There's been some lean days."

"Luckily, John and Radia's run out west went better than ours in Fernie. The biodiesel plant agreed to send a bulk shipment to us in exchange for one of their motorcycles and some proprietary documents on battery manufacturing. All that fuel was still heading to Painted Bluff after Nate flushed us out. Thanks for the heads-up that he was still alive and bat shit insane, by the way."

My cheeks burned. "I'm sorry. It hurt to see what he turned into, and I wasn't . . ." I blinked into the coals. "I wasn't okay when I got back. The longer I didn't tell you and Mom and Dad about him, the harder it was to bring it up."

"Well, we sure as shit weren't about to giftwrap him a shipment of diesel after he punted us. We had enough fuel to make a run to Golden, so Mark and I made a deal with the boys at the Petro-Can station there. You remember Amos?"

I nodded. I remembered him and his co-worker aiming a shotgun at us when we rolled up to his pumps on the first night we'd set out from our city. That seemed ages ago now.

"We intercepted the shipment and offloaded it into his bulk tanks at the gas station. Offered him a deal at the same rate the plant sells it to him direct. He didn't have enough copper on hand to pay us, but Golden is a trading hub, so he had plenty of bulk dry goods for us, and he's got a line on some guns and ammo. We're picking them up next week. Hell, he's even lined up a few more crossbows for us to look at. You should come. Radia's coming. She's due for a checkup at the docs."

I cringed at the thought of leaving home when I'd just found it again. "If you sold the diesel, how are you fueling the bikes for all these runs?"

"We only sold Amos three quarters of it. He sent our share in bulk totes up the rails to the old train yard in Kamloops. Did you know Coaltana was building a new railway through there?"

I shook my head.

"I had no idea it was there until last week. It's too far north to see it from the highway and it's weird. It swings north of the main line and heads toward Painted Bluff, but just stops in the middle of the forest. Real handy for us though. It's not far. We stashed the totes in a shed in the yard. Hid them well, so it's easy to get to them and there's enough fuel to last us a bit."

"So now what?" I leaned over to brush a spark from the fire off his thigh. There were several pinholes in his pants already from previous sparks that had gone unnoticed, burns he hadn't felt. "We camping for the rest of our lives?"

"You just brought us nine more people with guns. We outnumber Nate's people, and by next week, we'll have more weapons than him too. We take Painted Bluff back, that's what's next."

I swallowed hard. "There's nothing left there, Vinton. He burned it all. Just copper in the ground. Is it worth losing more lives over?"

My brother fixed me with a hard stare. "Where are we going to go, Iris? Take a good look at this place." He waved a finger at the tents surrounding us. "Chocked full of people who are damned sick of being pushed out of their homes. No established gardens. No trade routes. Can't set up proper infrastructure in time. The marauders have insulated tents, but not nearly enough to go around. Not enough wood stoves, either. We won't survive the winter out here. And Nate is sitting pretty with a skeleton crew in an empty bunker that'll hold all of us. There's no choice here. We go home or we freeze to death."

It was all too big to grasp. Another fight for our lives. More blood. More deaths. I was too exhausted to consider it right now, and it must have shown on my face because my brother smiled wryly and softened his next words.

"Besides, you don't want to live with me if I have to sleep on a leaky air mattress for the rest of my damned life."

I smiled back at him. "I thought you were invincible."

"Damn straight." He poked a finger at the hole in his pants and then stared at the coals for a long time before asking, "You love him?"

I didn't need to ask who he was talking about. "I do." I admitted.

"He knows you love him?"

"Yeah."

My brother cracked his neck and then nodded slowly. "Good. He's good for you."

"Don't punch him in the face."

"No promises. Don't have ugly little carpet walker babies with him."

I snorted. "No promises."

I went to bed after that. A sleeping bag had been spread over a pallet of pine boughs tucked against a tent that looked like it had been salvaged out of the trash. My parents had retired there earlier, Dad leading Mom away from the fire as she sniffled like an overtired child. I'd never seen her like that, so frazzled, so utterly out of her element.

I'd just settled into the thick flannel sleeping bag when she called my name softly through the canvas wall between us.

"Iris?"

Oh Sol, she's still awake. "What?" I shivered in the cold damp.

"Are you alone?"

I rolled my eyes. *She's on the edge right now. Don't push.* "Yes," I said.

The tent was silent for a long time, except for my father's faint snoring. I almost thought my mother had drifted off to sleep until she spoke again, so quietly I nearly didn't hear her. "I'm sorry."

I frowned. "Sorry about what?"

She coughed. "I always tried to stuff you into a box. I wanted you to fit in so badly. I thought it was the only way you would make it. I never stopped to consider how wrong the damned box was. I got so caught up in hardening you to survive, I never let you thrive."

"I'm not a plant, Mom."

"Soldamnit, I'm trying to apologize. Would you let me finish?"

I'd never heard fire in Anne's tone before. She'd always polished every word so carefully. There'd been hardness and authority in her voice, but never unfiltered emotion. This reminded me of Christie. I wondered who had she been covering with Corporate mannerisms all these years? What kind of woman was Mom before she and Dad joined a cult when the world ended? I'd never imagined her as anything other than uptight and inhuman. "Sorry." I took a deep breath through my nose. "Continue."

"You're not a child anymore, I know that. I do. You're capable out here, more than your father or me. More than Vinton. You've grown into a young woman that we're so proud of. We never told you that enough. *I* never told you enough. I'm proud of you, Iris. I love you. You don't have to prove anything."

"I love you too, Mom," I choked.

The shape of a hand pressed against the crinkled tent wall, and I reached out and pressed my palm to my mother's.

LATER STILL, Robert slipped into my bed. I'd been freezing, but he was warm and smelled like pine sap and wood smoke. I shifted the sleeping bag to cover him. His lips found mine in the dark. I breathed him in as his tongue slipped past my teeth, hot and hungry. Rain tapped the tarp overhead muffling the sound of us undressing in the dark. I ran my hand down his ribs, mindful of the bandages on his back. Goosebumps raised on his skin, and he groaned softly as we settled against each other naked and shivering.

I tasted his mouth, kissed his neck. My heartbeat thudded in my ears as I wrapped a leg around him. This was no delicate exploration, we were waves crashing into each other, birds of prey tangling midair, flames catching hold of something dry. And my body knew his in the dark, the hollow above his collarbone, the hardness of his biceps, the soft line of hair that ran from his lower stomach to his groin.

Most of the time, my world felt like too much. Too bright. People breathing sounded too loud. Touch felt abrasive. Intrusive.

This wasn't like that at all.

I drank Robert in and was still thirsty. He lay stretched against the whole length of me, but I needed to be closer. I deepened our kisses until his stubble scratched my lips, but it wasn't enough. I wanted more.

Rain poured down, rattling off the tarp, drowning out the world around us as we clutched each other in the dark.

He grabbed my thigh and pressed against me, all heat and hardness. "Iris," he whispered as I pulled him on top of me. "You sure?"

I'd never been so sure of anything in my life.

CHAPTER
THIRTY-FIVE

Three days later, we joined Vinton, Mark, John, and Radia on their run to Golden. Johan had asked if I could go with them to inspect the crossbows that were on offer. And I'd said yes. Only he and I knew the weapons well enough to recognize the difference between normal wear and an irreparable bow, and he'd assured me that travelling via motorcycle was not his cup of tea.

Robert said he'd accompany us to see if the doctor in Golden had anything that might help with his asthma. But he was coming for me. Radia could have asked on his behalf at her prenatal checkup, but we didn't want to be apart. Besides, Browsers rode in pairs, and it seemed we'd been honorably accepted into Vinton and Mark's team, so no one questioned him on it.

Long before dawn, I dressed as much as I could in my sleeping bag. My fingers were stiff, but I managed to finger-comb my hair and re-braid it before joining the others around a small cookfire with a tripod and kettle hanging over it. We gulped down scalding tea and jammed packets of flatbread stuffed with potatoes into our pockets while the Browsers went over their pre-use checks.

Johan called me over to his tent and pulled out his crossbow, a well-maintained Vortex recurve, bigger than my bow had been. "I noticed you're without yours."

My cheeks reddened. He'd had two bows. He'd trusted me with one of them, and Ben had taken it when we'd surrendered our weapons at the wall outside of Fernie. Sol knew where it was now. "It was taken from me," I said.

"I'm not scolding you, Iris. Take it." His voice was the same as it had always been, soft but firm.

"I can't. You need it here for hunting."

He shook his head. "Someone dry fired it yesterday."

I flinched. Firing a crossbow without a bolt was far from harmless. The concentrated energy that normally fired an arrow hit the string and arms undiluted. "Damage?" I asked.

"Look." He pressed the bow toward me.

I turned it in my hands, stomach sinking as my thumb caught on a hairline crack in one of the composite arms. We didn't have the parts to replace it. "Oh, Oupa, I'm sorry." I gulped.

"It was bound to happen sometime." He smiled. "Take it with you. Perhaps the dealer sells parts. Besides, you look positively terrifying with a crossbow. No one needs to know it's inoperable, and I couldn't leave it in better hands."

That sounded too final. I grabbed his cold fingers in mine and held on for far too long. "I'll have it fixed and back to you before you know it. Promise."

"*You* come back. That's all that matters." He patted my arm and then nodded toward the Browsers. They were nearly ready to roll.

Vinton and I hugged our parents.

"I wish I was going and not you." Mom's voice quavered.

"Driven a motorcycle or fired a crossbow lately?" Vinton

asked, softening his jab with a wink. "Don't worry. It's a milk run."

Robert's dad lost it when he realized his son was leaving again.

Two of the former Blue Helmets had to physically restrain Paul Lycos as he howled and screamed obscenities. "Don't you take him from me! He's mine. Don't leave me, Robert. Not again. I swear to Sol if you turn your back on me right now, you are not my son. You are nothing to me, you hear? Don't go! Don't leave!" His face purpled, and spittle gathered at the corners of his mouth.

Robert ignored the noise like his father was a toddler throwing a tantrum. He nodded stiffly when John waved him toward his bike. His face looked blank as he put on his helmet, but I saw how tightly he gripped his fists. Pretending at calmness. Wrapping up all his raw parts in scar tissue, protecting himself the only way he knew how.

"It's her!" Paul screeched, lunging toward me, towing the two men with him. "Don't let him go with her. Don't you take my son!"

One of the men restrained Paul before he reached me. The man's screeches muffled to strangled grunts.

A flush crept up my face. My nostrils stung and humiliation gripped me in its squeezing jaws.

Mark touched my elbow and guided me toward his motorcycle. The sidecar was gone. "I think that's our cue to ride." He offered me a helmet.

I jammed the headgear on, flipped down the face shield, and snugged the crossbow strap tight over my shoulder.

"Nope," Mark chided gently. "Nothing hard on your back. This isn't like the sidecar. If we crash, you'll slide, and that'll cut you up or stab you. Here." He held out his hand. "It'll fit in the saddlebag." After he'd secured the crossbow, he patted the seat and I settled onto it, wriggling back to give him room to climb on. Condensation clouded my lens and the diesel motor purred percussively beneath me. I braced my feet on the pegs and wrapped my arms around Mark's torso. He felt unnaturally broad compared to Robert.

"Ready?" He raised the kickstand and clicked the bike into gear.

"Yeah," I answered, and my helmet clacked into his as our Sommer 462 shuddered out into the night along with my brother's and his crew.

It was a black and jarring ride full of bouncing headlamps and flashing brake lights. Several times we stopped to move freshly fallen logs blocking the path. We took turns shedding our jackets and running the pocket chainsaws in pairs to buck the larger trees into movable chunks. Sawdust shavings stuck to our sweaty skin and slivers poked through our shirts.

Dawn bleached the horizon as we descended from the trailhead path, crossed over a double set of railway tracks, and eased onto the wider pavement of Tranquille Road. This far east, the lake was narrowing to our right and the rails flanked our left. By the time we reached Kamloops, it would be the Thompson River. A band of mist obscured the dark waters and a shelf of sage-carpeted hills rose to our left. The road followed the railway and was in fair enough shape to bring the bikes up to speed while still avoiding potholes. It felt like flying after the teeth-clacking crawl through the dense woods.

Radia whooped as she passed us. John followed her with Robert clinging on.

Mark held back, bringing up the rear, watching Vinton ahead of him as he always did.

Cold wind roared past. I tucked further into Mark as it licked at my neck and tugged at my braids. He curled over his machine, leaning into the turns, slaloming around heaves and dips in the fissured pavement in a synchronized dance with my brother ahead of him. The sky blazed, limning the clouds with ripe tones of pink and orange. If the sky remained overcast, we'd travel right through the day. If the sun burned off the clouds, we'd stop and seek cover in the shade.

In moments like these, I understood what pulled Vinton, Mark, and their compatriots out onto the road with nothing but two humming tires between them and the blurred pavement beneath. It seemed like the whole world was opening up, unfurling grandiose beauty with every bend we rounded. It felt like we were the first people to ever see it like this. Four metal satellites streaking through a breathtaking alien landscape.

Something cracked past my right ear like a whip.

Red splatted against my face shield. For a split second, I thought we'd struck a really big bug, but then Mark's motorcycle wobbled violently. It accelerated, fishtailed, and clipped Vinton's machine ahead of us. The wheels whipped out from under us.

My right side slammed into the pavement, battering breath from my lungs. My helmet ricocheted off the road. Through my blood-smeared face shield, I saw Mark kick the motorcycle away from us as it shuddered on its side, skipping like a stone, carving up chunks of loose black-top. I couldn't breathe.

He grabbed my arm and yanked me toward him, pinning me against his side as we slid.

Someone screamed.

Brake lights flashed, and in their glow, I saw Vinton's overturned motorcycle, skidding down the road backwards. The landing gear caught a pothole and the bike catapulted into a roll. My brother's head bounced off the pavement, and one of his legs flew free of its straps before the machine settled on its other side and ground to a stop in the dust.

Cracks and thumps cut through the stunned silence. Louder than the roar of my blood between my ears.

Gunshots. Someone's shooting at us.

CHAPTER
THIRTY-SIX

Y ou hit?" Mark screamed. He raked my bloody face shield up. "Iris?" Clutching a fistful of my jacket, he hauled me toward the ditch.

The zipper cut into my neck, and I slapped at his fist feebly, but he didn't stop until we'd tumbled off the road into a steep channel.

My ribs felt like they were on fire. The rest of me felt too numb.

Mark flopped back against the incline, clutching his right shoulder. Blood dribbled between his fingers and dripped off his wrist.

I gaped at him.

He took two breaths through his teeth before roaring "Vinton?"

The pop of pistols answered the snap of the gun strafing us. "He's down! Not moving." Radia's voice sounded muffled and far away.

She's down the road. Around the bend. She must have found cover. Oh, Sol, Robert.

"Shit. Shit. Shit." Mark's right arm hung limp. He let go of it to fumble with the holster at his hip.

I couldn't stop staring at the hole in his jacket just below his collarbone.

"Here." He shoved his pistol into my hand. It was smeared with red. Jabbing a finger at the rear of the frame, he said, "Safety is there. Shoot toward the hill." He pointed down the road, past the intersection we'd turned from. "Now."

Before I could protest, he launched onto the road.

"Wait! Zuse." I transferred the gun to my left hand, pinned my elbow against the awful pain in my ribs and rolled, firing blindly in the direction he'd indicated.

The returning gunfire ebbed and then increased.

"They want the bikes!" Mark shouted. "Get home. Bring reinforcements."

"We're not leaving you," Radia said.

John hollered from even further away. "Radia. There's more than one shooter! I can't fragging see them! Get out of there."

I kept squeezing the trigger until the gun clicked.

"Iris!" Robert roared.

"Frag! Do not—Idiot! Stay on the Goddamned bike. You're no good to her shot," John snapped.

"Go!" Mark bellowed. "Fragging GO!"

The sound of tires skidding and diesel engines upshifting rapidly sawed through the frigid morning air.

Oh Sol, they left.

Mark crashed into the ditch, his whole body curling around the limp form of my brother.

"Vinton?" Pins and needles swept over me. An image from my childhood swallowed me whole: him pitching over the rails at the tunnel, limbs slack as he tumbled down the shale ravine toward the lake.

"Eyes on the road," Mark snapped. "Do *not* let them get closer!"

"I th-think the gun's empty." My voice echoed in my head. The helmet felt suffocating, like sweaty hands clamped over my ears. Everything smelled like burned gunpowder.

"Soldamnit. Keep pointing it! No—here." Cradling Vinton's head between his knees, he reached down and snagged my brother's gun. "Take it. Don't shoot unless they do."

Whimpering, I set the weapon I'd been holding in the dirt, wiped the blood off my palm, and reached for the pistol Mark offered. Every breath hurt more than the last. When I craned my neck to peer over the road and scan the hillside, dirt exploded beside me. I hunched. "They've got us pinned."

Vinton groaned.

"Hey, I'm here." Mark's voice dropped, instantly calm and warm. "I've got you. Stay still."

"Mark?" he croaked, hands flailing.

"Shhh. It's okay. Try not to move."

"Where's Iris?"

Hot tears flooded my eyes at my name on his lips.

"She's here too. Just relax for a second. You crashed. Let's just breathe, yeah?"

"Why are we in a ditch?" He reached a shaking hand out and Mark shifted to clasp it in his.

"Snipers. Tell me where it hurts."

"You're bleeding on me," he murmured, dazedly wiping red splotches from his neck and then frowning at his smeared fingers. His eyes widened. "Shit. You're bleeding."

"Don't sit up." Mark leaned into Vinton's chest.

"You're hurt. Shot?" My brother's voice sharpened.

Mark grunted. "They just winged me. I'm going to check you over. You hit your head and blacked—"

"Frag you. Let me up. Life-threatening bleeds trumps anything else."

"It's not life-threatening."

"*I'm* going to be life-threatening if you don't let me up. I swear to Sol, Mark, I'll punch you in the teeth until I break my hand. Get off."

"He's speaking in full sentences." I puffed. "That's good." Dizziness settled over me, thick and tingling.

"You're not helping." Mark shook his head and sagged back, snapping at Vinton. "Keep low. I didn't save you just to watch you get your head blown off."

My brother levered up onto his elbows easing off his helmet and frowning down at the cracked lens and deep gouges down one side. "Med kits and solar blankets?"

"Still on the bikes." Mark tugged his jacket zipper down with one bloodied hand.

I swallowed, turning my attention back to the road, cocking my head, and listening for voices or footsteps.

"Oh Sol, your foot." Mark's voice quavered enough that I glanced back.

They were blinking down at Vinton's legs. His left foot was twisted outward at an unnatural angle, the heel of his boot cocked upward.

Nausea tugged at me as I remembered his ruined legs after the fall.

Mark swallowed hard, all the color draining from his face. "That looks bad."

Vinton scrubbed his chin and smiled faintly. "Well, hell. Do you think I'll ever walk again, Doc?"

"Shut up."

"Take your shirt off. We need it for bandages."

After Vinton staunched Mark's bleeding and wrapped his shoulder, he helped him back into his jacket. "You good, Iris?" he asked, slapping Mark away as he ran a hand over his skull and checked both his pupils.

"My ribs hurt."

"What kind of gentleman are you?" My brother frowned at Mark. "You didn't even check the lady first, Zuse."

I gripped the gun tighter so my hands wouldn't shake. The first round of adrenalin was draining out of me, and pain was sinking its teeth in. "Check his leg first," I panted. "It needs to be splinted."

"Splinted with what?" My brother spread his arms wide, glancing down the grassy ditch in both directions. "There's nothing here."

"His other leg," Mark said. "I'll need help tying them together."

Vinton shook his head. "Zuse, you two. I can't even feel it."

"Doesn't mean it's not causing damage. Sol knows you won't do what you're told and keep it immobilized. Look, it's spasming already."

My brother frowned down at his twisted, twitching foot with mild disgust. "Fine. Give me the gun." He rolled onto his stomach before we could stop him. "I don't want some bastard sneaking up on us while you're both playing nurse."

I handed over the weapon and clawed off my helmet.

Vinton lay on his belly at the edge of the ditch while we used his shirt to make several long strips of fabric. Mark felt for protruding bones through my brother's ripped riding leathers, and when he was satisfied that there were no open fractures, we secured his legs together snuggly, unthreading the laces from his boots and using them to lash his feet together as best we could. We left the injured one in the awful, twisted position and then elevated both his legs.

"Best we can do until we get a hold of a traction splint." Mark sighed.

I didn't know what that was.

Sweating, both of us reclined against the incline with the sky red and fierce above us.

My ribs felt like hot metal pokers.

"They broken?" Vinton asked.

"Maybe."

"Unzip and lift your shirt."

"I'm fine," I said.

"I'm checking to make sure you're not bleeding internally you null."

Mark turned away as my brother inspected my side. "No big bruises or lumps yet. Just keep stabilizing."

I'd forgotten how much first aid training the Browsers all had, how casual they were about the fact that their designation required it.

A tense silence settled over us. The ditch filled with the sounds of our shaking breaths and flies buzzing.

When I couldn't stand it anymore, I whispered, "You think they're still up there?"

"Hand me my helmet," Vinton beckoned to Mark. When he complied, my brother braced on one elbow and thrust the head-gear upward.

An immediate crack sounded, and the helmet hurtled out of his grip and rolled down the incline.

"Yup," Mark said.

"Hey!" Vinton bellowed. "Maybe we can make a deal here? Grab one of the bikes for scrap and leave the other one for us, yeah? Truce?"

Wind puffed up from the river, and the sun crested the horizon, orange, engorged, and flecked with spots. Nobody answered.

Vinton settled onto his stomach, handgun aimed obstinately up the hill. "You sent John and Radia on?"

Mark nodded. "Yeah, we were getting hammered."

"Good."

I can't do this. The thought stabbed at me. I couldn't lay exposed in the wilds with a wounded brother and the sun burning into me. I felt like a petrified nine-year-old girl again. "Why aren't they coming down to take the bikes?" My voice shook.

Mark tried to shrug and grimaced. "They will. They know we're hurt. They'll let us bleed out a bit, bake under the sun a bit, give us some time to drop our guard before they attack. No use risking injury with a fire fight when they can just wait until we're too weak to be a threat."

"Marauders?"

"Ballsy, whoever they are." Vinton grunted. "Radia and John will circle back to camp and bring the cowboy and his crew. I imagine a bunch more armed men on horses should sway things in our favor a bit, especially if they come at these assholes from behind. All we've got to do is wait for them. Settle in, roomies. I'll take first shift."

MARK SLEPT with his helmet on to pillow his head and protect him from the sun. The tinted face shield was flipped down. I could tell he still breathed by the faint puff of fog expanding and condensing inside the lens. Flies clotted around him, drawn by the scent of blood and every now and then, he twitched in his sleep. High overhead, the sun hung pale and ruthless. The hill was quiet, and the soft warble of ducks squabbling on the lake shore floated up to us.

Vinton had taken guard duty for a second time.

I was settled gingerly onto my uninjured side. My arm ached from pressing against my ribs. So long as I didn't breathe too deeply, the throbbing was manageable. I'd draped my jacket over my head and my cheek was sticking to my bare arm. I was supposed to be resting but couldn't. My mind wouldn't shut off.

He hasn't moved in a while. My brother was always shifting. Not fidgeting, not like I did. No, this type of movement had been drilled into him ever since he broke his back. If Vinton didn't mindfully change his position every so often, he got bedsores. A year after his fall, he got one on his backside so deep it took three months to heal. He couldn't put any pressure on it, couldn't sit up at all, not for *three* months. It had driven Vinton crazy being bed-bound like that, and every time I'd seen Mom or Dad changing the dressing on the awful, gangrenous-looking hole, guilt ate me alive all over again. *My fault.*

And here we were again, baking in a ditch, my brother and his boyfriend broken, their bikes dead on the road, because I'd burned down Nate's house, killed Christie, and driven him to evict everyone I knew and burn my city down. *You never learn. Never change. Even now, you're feeling sorry for yourself, and you're supposed to be looking after him.* I sucked in several shallow breaths through my nostrils before clearing my sore throat. "Talk to me."

"You're supposed to be sleeping," he groaned without looking back.

"You aren't. You have a concussion."

"I wasn't. I have a headache. You're not helping."

Tears pricked my eyes. My brother had a way of needling me until I was nothing but sore spots. "I'm sorry." I whimpered. Sol, I sounded pathetic.

Vinton did turn then, jaw twitching and eyes fierce. "Don't." He thrust a gloved finger at me. "Don't do that."

"I *am* sorry."

"I said stop," he snapped.

"You never let me apologize." I'd tried. So many times after the accident, I'd tried and every single time, Vinton had brushed me off and changed the subject.

"Zuse, you've apologized a million times, Iris," he hissed. "How many is it going to take? When's it gonna be enough, huh? You keep looking at me like I'm half the person I could have been. When's that going to stop?"

"I don't look at you like that."

"Yes, you do, like I'm wasted potential." He shook his head

and faced the road.

Heat made my head swim. "Because I took so much from you," I blurted.

"Bullshit!" He whipped back around. "*You* took from me? Broke my back with your bare hands, did you? Put shoes with no grip on my feet that morning? Forced me to be a nosy prick and follow you into that tunnel? You've got such a Sol complex, Iris! Everything that happens around you, doesn't happen *because* of you, Zuse."

"Some things do. Your whole life changed."

"Did it ever occur to you that it changed for the better?" he rasped. "That I *like* my life? I never worked for anything before the accident. I was a useless little twit. Everything just landed in my lap, but I've worked my ass off to be better. I met Mark, and he loves me as I am. Life happens, Iris. Shit happens. And not because you're being punished for screwing up, it just happens. You deal with whatever gets dished out to you. You swallow it and you move on. I'll never walk again. So what? My bike hit the road hard enough that I'll probably never ride again either, and you know what? I'll survive it. I'll do better than that. Because you only get one chance at life and I'm not going to spend mine raking myself over the coals pining for what might have been. I'm going to enjoy what is. You need to start doing the same. I didn't follow you onto the tracks because you made me. We didn't come on this run because you forced us. We came because you're worth standing up for. You've got a good heart. You bring people together. All sorts. Because you do the right thing. People follow that, Iris."

My face twisted and my breath hitched, triggering a stab of agony through my chest. I let my jacket fall over my face in hopes that my brother wouldn't see my tears.

"Sorry I made you cry," he mumbled.

"No," I wheezed when I could breathe again. "Sometimes you need an asshole."

CHAPTER
THIRTY-SEVEN

was the one holding the gun when the low thrum of a diesel engine and the clatter of metal wheels on rails closed in from the west.

"Vinton," I whispered, tapping his elbow with my boot. He was cradled in Mark's good arm, his jacket open, his bare chest rising and falling evenly. I'd readjusted the coat multiple times, but my brother kept peeling it open in his sleep, and his skin was reddening with sunburn. "Someone's coming down the tracks."

They both started awake, clutching each other. Vinton reached for his empty holster.

The sound of the approaching motor throttled back to an idle and brakes squealed. Voices yelled down from the hillside.

"Shit," Vinton whispered. "Looks like their reinforcements got here first. Give me the gun."

I froze, clutching the weapon hard enough that my fingers ached. I barely processed my brother's words because I had homed in on the conversation drifting toward us, accompanied by scuffing, cautious footsteps.

"Watch yourself. They're still in the ditch. Figured you'd like to flush them out yourself."

"How many?" A voice I'd locked in my heart since I was a little girl asked.

Nate. My lungs froze. Of course, it was Nate. Who else would come up the rails from the west?

"Iris. Give me the gun," Vinton hissed.

Out on the road, someone I didn't recognize answered Nate. "Four bikes total. Six people. We pegged two machines and the others got away. Headed east."

"When?" Nate's voice rasped.

"First thing this morning. We came and got you right away."

"I told you I wanted the motorcycles *recovered*, not totaled."

"Not our fault they laid them down so hard. We just winged—"

Boots scuffed to a stop, maybe thirty paces up the road.

Vinton grabbed my leg, mouthed my name, and held out his hand, eyes pinned to the weapon. But I couldn't hand it over, couldn't fathom shooting at my uncle even after all that had happened.

"Jesus Christ, is that a crossbow?" Nate's voice was high and shaking "And a wheelchair. Did you *shoot* them?"

"Y-you ordered us to KOS anyone who trespassed—"

"What?"

"Y-yesterday. You said anyone on your turf, kill on site."

"I was drunk out of my tree! That's my niece and nephew. My family!" Nate roared. "Put your guns down. Now. All of you. You hear me? Lay them down."

"But—"

"NOW. On the road!" His booming voice echoed off the hillside. "Iris?"

I recoiled at the sound of my name. A set of boots crunched toward us determinedly. Long strides. Quick pace.

"Vinton? Iris, honey, answer me. It's Nate."

Shoot him, my brother mouthed, face pale and eyes hard.

"I messed up, Beetle. *Really* messed up, but I'm gonna fix it now, you hear? I've got a nurse with me. You remember Alice's daughter, Janice?"

I remembered Alice. The older woman gone with Nate to help a crew clear the mudslide blocking our munition delivery to Painted Bluff. Marauders had shot her in the head, and my uncle had come home with her blood all over his jacket. I shuddered.

"Listen," Nate said. "I brought a bunch of med supplies. We just wanted the bikes. I've got some trigger-happy idiots out here, but everything's under control now. We put our guns down. I'm going to come help you now. Don't shoot me, okay?"

I thought of all the animals I'd ever hunted, the ones who had heard me coming. They'd known I was closing in and lost their chance of escape but had still frozen until it was too late. That's what it felt like as my uncle's footsteps closed on my brother, Mark, and I, exhausted, injured, and huddled in a ditch. I didn't want fear to be the feeling Nate instinctively triggered in me. But it was.

"Janice, get over here! Bring your bag." Nate's voice muffled as he yelled back over his shoulder. An eternity passed before a lighter set of footsteps quick-walked in our direction. "Janice isn't armed. She's just going to come down there and help you, okay? Now, we can see a blood trail leading right into the ditch. They tell me you've been in a stand-off all morning. Let's take some big breaths and get out of this sun without anyone else getting hurt, yeah? Truce?"

He was twisting things again, making us out as the dangerous ones, wounded renegades who were liable to lash out unprovoked at an innocent bystander. I wasn't stupid, but I was tired, hurting, and desperate to get Vinton and Mark medical help. Nate's resonant voice, that earnest tone he used when he wanted things to go his way, still pulled at me like it always had.

I found myself responding, even though the word made me feel sick to my stomach. "Truce."

"Zuse, Iris!" Vinton rolled onto his back, his face twisted in disgust. "He's playing you."

"He already had us cornered." I thumbed the safety back on, clutched the gun to my chest, and sat up, grimacing at the fresh knife of pain the movement sent through me.

"Aw, shit. Aw, Jesus." Nate towered over us, broad hat and waxed canvas trench coat making him look like one of the severe gunslingers on the covers of Johan's old western books. "Bring the stretcher and get over here. Both of you. Come look at what you did to these kids."

A woman in jeans with a ballcap and a blonde ponytail eased into the ditch, her eyes pinned to Vinton's leg. She slid a large backpack off her shoulder. "Hey, my name's Janice. I'm gonna ask you a few questions and then we're getting out of here, okay? You were all wearing helmets when you crashed? Anyone hit their head hard enough they lost responsiveness?"

"He did." I pointed at my brother.

"Shut up, Iris," he growled.

"How long?" She pulled a pencil and notepad from her bag, before kneeling next to Vinton and peering into his eyes.

"Not more than a minute."

"Numbness in your arms or legs?"

My brother sneered. "Only for the last seven years."

"You must be Vinton," she answered unphased.

"Oh, my uncle talks about me, does he? I thought Iris was his one and only." He locked gazes with Nate, his smile cold.

"Anyone else experiencing numbness, tingling, or loss of movement?" The woman glanced at Mark and me.

"If we're doing triage, Janice. How about we start with the gunshot wound?" My brother pointed at Mark's shoulder.

"How about you tell me if you've ever had autonomic dysreflexia after an injury?"

"No. T12, L1 burst fracture. Not complete. If my blood pressure's rising, it's because no one is looking at the damned gunshot wound!" He snatched her notepad and held it out of her reach. "ABC's are good. No head, neck, or spine—nothing new anyway." He pointed at Mark. "High velocity gunshot wound. Broken collarbone. Clean exit wound." His finger swung to me. "Bruised or cracked ribs, no paradoxical movement or chest penetration." Then he pointed at himself. "Tibia fibula fracture. Concussion. Can we get out of this ditch now and get his wound cleaned up?"

We did.

Nate helped me up while his people loaded Vinton into a stretcher. I recognized Orin amongst them. When my uncle tried to ease the pistol out of my hand, I yanked it back.

"Come on, Beetle." His blue eyes met mine, raw and tired, but sober. "I think there's been enough accidental shootings today. I don't have it in me to see anyone else I know gunned down, alright?" He grabbed the gun's barrel and I let go of the handle. I don't know why I let go.

They led us back to their rig on the tracks. It was a wooden box car with slats missing down the sides. A diesel motor from a truck had been bolted to the front of it along with a cab and two seats. Another driver's cab was scabbed onto the rear. Two men with rifles—probably the ones who'd shot us—sat placidly in the rear cab.

After Nate's people loaded us into the dark, dusty interior, Janice settled us on blankets and started pulling bags of ice out of a portable cooler, and the others laid down a ramp and fetched our motorcycles from the road. Rows of rifles hung in racks on the walls and below them, crates of ammunition, and several large metal clamps—I couldn't fathom what those were for.

They were able to roll Mark's machine up the ramps, and Vinton's folding chair, but the front tire on my brother's motorcycle had warped enough that it wouldn't turn. It took four men to wrestle it through the doorway.

My brother flinched when they dumped it unceremoniously onto the train car floor. Timbers reverberated under our backsides. Vinton stared at his discarded motorcycle, ribboned in harsh strips of sunlight. Its handlebars were twisted, crash bars crumpled and scraped raw. One of the stabilizers had torn right off and its actuator was warped and bent beyond repair. There were no spares. It was irreplaceable.

My stomach dropped at the sight of it.

He'd been right. My brother was done riding as he knew it.

"Do you know what this is, Iris?" He spoke in a low voice, gaze still rivetted to his ruined machine, even as Nate's men swung closed a divider panel between us. They locked themselves and the bikes on the rear-end of the car with the sliding door, the guns, and all the ammunition, caging us in the bare front end of the unit. "This is a cattle car. Never in the history of the world has something good happened after people got stuffed into a cattle car."

"She's in here with us." I thumbed to Janice.

"Must have pissed off Nate." Mark spoke up as the nurse peeled back the bloody wad of fabric at his shoulder.

She pursed her lips.

"Aw, you did, didn't you?" Vinton snorted.

"This is going to hurt," she said and then she irrigated Mark's wound with a spray bottle of saline solution.

Mark screamed.

Vinton held him.

Nate and Orin settled into the front cab outside. Doors slammed, the little diesel engine rattled to life, and the train car lurched ahead—to the east, not the west.

We're not going back to Painted Bluff. Why are we going east?

"Sol help us," Vinton murmured.

CHAPTER
THIRTY-EIGHT

We kept stopping periodically on the rails. Nate's people would go out onto the tracks to clear branches from the rails. They used long lever bars to release the clamps hidden underneath—the same clamps as the ones in the rear of our cattle car. Once we rolled past, the workers reinstalled the devices behind us. That's how we made it to the railyard in Kamloops, in fits and starts.

The yard itself was a burned-out wasteland. Black, crumpled shells of buildings sagged around its edges, and rails twisted apart like broken zippers. Craters peppered the right of way, and soggy chunks of drywall clotted in the hollows like leaf litter. A nearby semaphore tower listed heavily, its communication gear torn off.

I hadn't seen this on our trip down to Fernie. The highway hadn't run close enough. It looked like a warzone, like Painted Bluff, only the destruction wasn't so fresh. It was older, softened by time and erosion.

A single line had been cobbled together through the chaos. New rails rested on freshly leveled soil.

Why is Coaltana rebuilding this line if the main one is fine? The question vied for attention in my mind, but I was too loopy to hang onto it.

Janice had secured Mark's arm in a tube sling and given us enough heavy-duty painkillers that he was out cold in my brother's arms. Vinton hadn't taken any meds, but he was sleeping too. I leaned my forehead against one of the rough lumber rails, just to stay upright. Our nurse was reorganizing her med bag for the third time. A half-melted bag of ice rested against my ribs. They barely hurt anymore, but I felt dizzy and detached from myself. Through the slats, I saw Nate walking the single, newly constructed line with Orin.

It looked out of place amidst the burned-up buildings and craters and rusty, serpentine twists of blown apart rails. Nate pointed to a spot on the rails.

"Here's good. Bring two, just in case. It's a heavy beast." He waved at one of his men in the cattle car. The guy hoisted two of the large clamps from the rear storage area and brought them over to Nate. Orin and the man slid the jaws of the clamp onto the rail and inserted a bar into the lever sleeve on its side. They heaved downward and it clicked loudly, apparently locked into place. They did the same for the next one, installing it a few feet further down the rail.

When they were done, my uncle came and stood outside the cattle car, peering up at me. *How surreal to be looking down on someone so tall.* I knew I should be more worried about our situation, but everything kept slipping away from me. Nate fished in his deep coat pockets, producing a hand-rolled joint and a box of matches. "How you feeling?" he asked, pinching the twisted paper between his lips, striking the match, and cupping his hands close to his face.

I couldn't stop staring at the tight, ropey skin wrapping his burned fingers. "You don't smoke."

"I did before Christie." He took several short inhales,

coaxing the flame to life before exhaling twin trickles of smoke from his nose.

"It'll kill you."

He coughed, a wry smile pulling up one corner of his mouth. "This stuff? Doubtful. Besides, can't say I'm much interested in life at the moment, Beetle."

I remembered the canteen in my lap. Janice had given it to me. I liked Janice. Unscrewing the cap with hands that felt like mittens, I took several swallows of warm, stale water before pointing at the clamps on the rails. "What are those?"

Nate took a long drag and held his breath before exhaling. The pungent smell of marijuana smoke filled my nostrils. "Derailer clamps," he said. "My rail runners use them if a competitor isn't smart about respecting their territorial borders. All the railroads used to use them on their sidings as a last resort safety measure to derail any runaway cars before they hit the mainline."

"You expecting company?" My stomach sank as I asked.

He pinched his lips and didn't answer.

"What are we doing here, Nate?" I tried again.

"You're leaving. I'm giving Janice to you as a parting gift. I meant what I said about staying off my land and I'm being more than fair here. You can go back to wherever it is your folks are holed-up with a nurse and extra medical supplies, everything you and your brother need to heal up."

He's lying. Why would he give us a nurse unless she pissed him off enough to get banished along with us. And he wouldn't have brought us east.

"We wouldn't need to heal up if you didn't shoot us," I said. It was easier to stare him down from this height, with wooden planks between us and medication dulling the horrible itch I usually got if I looked someone in the eye for too long.

"I didn't mean for you to get hurt, honey. It's eating me up inside, alright? It was a misunderstanding."

"Misunderstanding?" I gaped. Someone behind me snorted, the only other person awake on this side of the partition. Janice. "Maybe you shouldn't tell people to kill us on sight if you don't want us hurt."

He dropped his gaze and scrubbed at his beard. "I, uh, I say things I don't mean when I'm drunk."

The nurse checked circulation below the traction splint she'd strapped onto Vinton's injured leg before sighing. "Maybe you shouldn't be drunk most of the time then, Nate."

That's why he's pissed at her. Why she's in here with us. She gives him shit when he's an idiot. It probably reminds him of Christie, and he'd hate that.

"You don't have to worry about that anymore, do you, Janice? 'Cause you're not part of the team anymore. All you gotta worry about now is staying the hell off my lake," Nate said.

"Claiming the whole lake now, are you?" She scoffed.

"Not sure I signed up for world domination." Orin huffed dropping the lever bar into the driver's cab.

My uncle's face went dead. His gaze shifted slowly to the old man. "Seems like I keep letting you all down. Maybe you'd like to lead instead? Make all the hard decisions with no sleep, with no notice?"

"Didn't sign up for that neither."

"Then how about you both keep your mouths shut." Nate took another long toke. "What were you and your brother heading east for, Iris?"

Suddenly, I knew what he was doing, taking advantage of me when I was tired and half-baked on medication, my brain too relaxed and my tongue too loose. "We're going to make sure Darwin Clowes is dead." I lied.

"Right. Just like how your boy killed David Kahn. I have a hard time wrapping my head around that. How about you tell me what this is actually all about?"

"You're starving us, so we were going to get food. How about *you* tell me what this is actually about? Who's coming? Who are you derailing?" I didn't want to kill Nate. Didn't want him dead. I had to bring him back, the old Nate, the one who wasn't irreparably damaged by his sister's ignorance, Kahn's cruelty, and Christie's death.

"You're friends with Darwin Clowes's people?" Nate flicked ashes at his feet. "My scouts said there were cowboys with you when you came running home. Ben Breyman? Clowes's little lackey?"

I watched an ember smoldering in the dry grass. Of course, Nate would know who Ben was. They'd both travelled extensively. Both had a network of connections that were bound to cross lines at some point. Nate had been Kahn's hand in the world—until Kahn had tried to kill him—and Ben had been Clowes's.

"Ben doesn't belong to him anymore," I chose my words carefully. "He helped us set off the riots in Fernie. We all hate Clowes. He made us slaves."

"Sure seems like you're running back to him pretty quick for someone who hates him. Right after you came to see me too. Seems like something he'd do." He flexed his unscarred hand and restrained rage colored his next words. "Send my own niece back to me to see how many people I had left, how many guns."

"We're not spies," I spat.

"Do you know what happened here?" He spread his arms and took a step back, circling with the joint spreading a halo of smoke around him. "Do you know what I did? This isn't the first time Clowes has tried to get his claws into my business."

I blinked at the charred buildings, folded like crumpled houses of cards, the deep pockmarks blistering the terrain around us, creosote-stained ties splintered and jutting out of the ground, rails draped crookedly across it all like cooked spaghetti.

My lungs felt sluggish. "You did this?" I remembered

Christie showing me Nate's library, the staggering realization that my sweet, bearish uncle had crippled an entire refinery when they got too competitive. *Oh Sol.* He'd made sure we relied on him entirely for supplies. "Nothing comes from the east," I murmured.

"*Nothing* comes from the east," he repeated. "Clowes and Kahn were real chummy before the world ended. Kahn entrusted him with a whole damned mine, but the sneaky bastard was always sending scouts up the rails to see how he could weasel into your city. Always ready to pull the rug out from under his old golfing buddy. You all had no idea, not even Kahn, but I had my rail runners. I saw him spidering toward you, building a tower line all the way up to Kamloops. Running that damned locomotive like he was something out of *Murder on the Orient Express*. He would have swallowed you all right up. Ousted Kahn. You'd have been a coal slave years ago. I gave him the benefit of the doubt until he started building a rail line north of the lake, trying to come in the back door. Persistent bugger. My boys kept installing clamps on the line, but he kept creeping that locomotive up the rails and having his crews remove the derailers before they hit them." He shrugged "Couldn't let it stand then. Had to protect you all."

"What did you do?"

"I had a bunch of dynamite set aside for clearing rails after avalanches. Never did feel particularly comfortable storing that kind of firepower in the armory behind the house—a good thing too, or you'd have blown us all to bits. So, I brought it here in the middle of the night. Detonated some far enough from the worker's bunkhouses that it just blew in their windows. Soon as they fled, we used the rest to take out the rails and their supply yard. You should have heard it. The way it thundered down the valley." He grinned, eyes flashing. "I think Clowes heard it all the way down in Fernie."

I shivered.

"You all heard it in the city too. Next delivery drop I told Kahn it was an avalanche. Big one. Took out the rails, bridges, roads, everything on the east end of the lake. He never even came to look. Too far outside his precious borders, the narrow-minded prick. So long as he could keep sucking you all dry, he was in his element. So long as food and fuel kept showing up, he didn't care which direction it came from." He dropped the nub of the joint and twisted it under his boot, turning to squint at the new rail line slicing through the carnage. "But look at this. The second Kahn goes belly up, Clowes is crawling all over the place again, recruiting my own family against me. Parasite."

Nate's people had been arguing with him. They didn't want to fight, and they wouldn't stand without him. I needed him to back down and let us in. "Clowes is in Fernie. Under siege or dead in the riots. And Kahn is a prisoner in the south—if he's alive. We're not with them," I said.

"I wish I could be sure of that, Beetle. But snakes are hard to kill. Soon as you told me about Kahn, I knew in my gut he'd be coming back for what was his. So, I posted scouts further out. Here. On the highway. Down Clowes's precious tower line to Fernie. That's when we found out he'd reinstalled this northern line. So, we installed derailer clamps all down it and the main-line both. Hid them under branches and debris. Posted some snipers to keep an eye on things. That's when we saw your crew heading east, toward your supposed enemy—"

"Listen to me." I shifted. The bag of ice slid to the floor. "We were going to Golden—"

"Then, explain to me why," Nate interrupted, "there's a loco-motive steaming north right now to meet you? We spotted that too and there's only one person 'round these parts with a train like that, Beetle."

My face dropped. *A locomotive? A train. Clowes. Oh, Sol. He got out of Fernie, and he's coming for Ben and Grace. For Painted Bluff.* Fear iced up my belly. "We don't know anything about a train," I croaked. "We're not with him. We're not like him. Neither are you. You don't have to hurt people to get what you want. You don't have to take everything just because that's what they did to you. Or it never ends."

"Oh, it's ending, Iris. One way or another, it's ending." He put his hand in his jacket pocket and cocked his head. "Orin, you hearing this? How many does that sound like?"

"More than two, that's for sure," the old man grumbled.

And then I heard them too. The drumbeat of compact diesel engines. Sommer 462s. Heading this way fast.

CHAPTER
THIRTY-NINE

Despite Janice's protests, I pulled myself to a wobbly stand and pressed against the front corner of the cattle car, peering through the space between the slats. Nate walked to the back end of the car outside and slapped the side. "Look alive, ladies and gents. Let's do this without wasting my ammunition, yeah?"

Vinton and Mark startled awake at the noise.

Janice's voice was tight when she spoke to them. "We're not sure who all is coming. Stay down unless you want to get shot again. So long as we stay behind the engine block, we should have some cover."

On the other side of the divider, five of Nate's people grabbed rifles off the rack and leaped back out of the car.

"What's happening?" Mark groaned, but I couldn't answer him. Every thought in my head distilled down to one word.

Robert.

The motorcycles rolled into the east end of the yard, driving single file up the track. Three machines and four riders. Nate and his armed entourage met them as they stopped. I didn't recognize the front driver, but their passenger was unmistakable.

I'd know him anywhere, the way he stood, his easy stride. *Robert. Oh Sol. They caught him. He didn't make it home.* I sagged against the wooden slats as John parked his bike, and both he and Robert removed their helmets and put their hands over their heads at gunpoint.

Nate's men herded them toward us.

"Iris, oh thank Sol!" Robert blurted as he came up the ramp. He stepped around the bikes and rushed the divider, reaching through the bars.

"Hi." I gulped, my cold hand trembling in his warm grip.

"You're hurt." He frowned.

"Move." One of Nate's men shouldered Robert aside and pulled a key from his pocket to unlock the padlock on the partition gate.

"Don't hug me." I held my hands out as it swung open.

"You *are* hurt. Where?"

"Just ribs."

He stroked my cheeks, kissed me, and then stood there, pressing his forehead to mine and breathing shakily. "I thought I lost you," he whispered. "I looked back, and you were on the ground sliding. The guns. I tried to come back but John grabbed me. I thought you'd been—"

"I know." I gulped. "I'm fine."

"Who's she?" John pointed toward Janice.

"Janice." Mark slurred with a grin. "She gave us painkillers."

"Good ones, by the looks of it." John looked the nurse up and down.

"She's his new best friend," Vinton frowned. "I was hoping you'd be our heroes. Come in guns blazing for the big rescue."

John leaned in close to my brother, held his stare, and offered him the barest nod before saying loudly, "Sorry to disappoint."

Radia made it then. Nate's scouts didn't catch her. Ben and his crew are coming.

The partition gate closed and locked. While Nate's riders updated their boss outside, John settled in to do the same.

"We tried to lose them, but they caught us skirting back west," he said and then whispered only for our ears. "Just us, thank Christ." He shook his head. "I don't get it. Why the hell take the trouble of rounding us all up instead of killing us where we stood, and just taking the bikes?"

"Nate's not like that." I swallowed, mind winding up like an engine gathering speed.

"Soldamnit, Iris. Stop idolizing him," my brother snapped. "He left us all in the woods and is waiting for winter to come kill us!"

"No, that's not what I meant." Connections were clicking in my brain, each one vaporizing the fog of medication and replacing it with fear as sharp as ozone. "Nate holds onto things. And if there's any way to use them to his advantage later, he does. That's why we're here and not just the bikes. He knows Darwin Clowes. He knows how big a bounty a master like that would put on Ben's head, Grace's head. Ours too. Nate wanted to sell all of us at Painted Bluff to Coaltana before. He's still selling us now."

"He was going to sell the whole city?" Robert frowned.

"Would have been nice to have had that bit of intel earlier," Vinton retorted.

"Stop it." Mark slapped him lightly.

I kept talking. I had to get this out before it fell apart in my head. "He'll give us back to Clowes. Especially if he's afraid of him coming for land he's claimed as his own. The bunker. The copper. It's all Nate has left."

"Great. So, we're a peace offering then. A fragging gift basket he's sending to Fernie to make an alliance and save his own ass?" John cracked his head against the sidewall and frowned.

"How does that even work if Clowes is dead and Fernie is on fire?"

"Clowes isn't dead, and he's not in Fernie," Vinton croaked. "Nate said his scouts pegged his train coming this way. Must be close. That's why he's dragged us all out here."

"Zuse. This'll be a right shit show." John lowered his voice, a grim smile on his lips. "Let's hope our company comes before his does."

"Nate!" Janice yelled loud enough that we all jumped. "I've got something you'll want to hear."

"Shit." Vinton glared at her and then John.

John winced, realizing his slip. "Narc," he snarled and made to lunge toward the nurse, but she pulled a handgun out of her med bag and aimed it coolly at him.

"I'm all ears, Janice." Nate strode toward us, a soft, terrible smile on his face.

"Let me out of the cage first."

"Ask nice. You insulted me earlier."

"Please let me out of the cage before I use up your precious ammunition."

Nate let her out.

When she told him we had reinforcements coming, he swore loudly and his whole team backed away, skittishly.

"Goddamnit, I knew it! They're surrounding us." For several breaths he cursed and paced with his hands clasped behind his head. "You." He stopped midstride to stab a finger at one of the motorcyclists. "Go up the line, see how close that train is. Nicholas, go west and see if you can't pick off some cowboys. The rest of you, carry as much ammo as you can, spread out and find some cover. The bastards are coming at us from all sides, and I want as many angles as we can get."

The riders trotted toward the parked motorcycles.

"We're shooting first now?" Orin intercepted Nate, bristling.

"You said we'd negotiate if it came to this. That's why we're stopping the train."

"Negotiate? Did you hear Janice? They're surrounding us. Open your eyes."

"My eyes are open. I'm not the one hellbent on revenge. We're not soldiers, Nate. We can just leave. We don't have to be here for them to derail. Let's just go home before any of them get here. It's not too late to stop this."

"I AM stopping this!" Nate roared.

"How the hell are any of us supposed to trust you if you keep talking out of both sides of your mouth?" Orin yelled back. "You promised us somewhere safe to live. That's all any of the rest of us wanted. You want a crew to follow you after this? Don't ask us to shoot up a bunch of people. Negotiate a deal."

Everyone around them froze.

"We talking mutiny now?" Nate asked.

"No," Orin answered. "We're talking *talking*. Negotiating. You used to be good at it, Nate. And this has gone too far."

"I *negotiated* away every damned thing I had to get us here!" Nate pressed into the old man's personal space, towering over him. "I can't *ever* pay back the favors I owe. You understand? We lose the city. We lose *everything*. Now, I'll talk as pretty as you please to the circling predators. I'll sing like a jay bird, if you like. But when that doesn't work, and I give the signal to shoot, you better damn well do your part."

"What signal would that be?" Orin drawled. "Been getting so many mixed messages from you lately, *boss,* they're getting hard to parse."

"I'll make it a nice obvious one for you," Nate snapped before turning his back on him and bellowing, "What the hell are we all waiting for?"

The riders fired up their motorcycles and skidded out of the yard in opposite directions. The rest of the crew clambered into the rear of the cattle car, snatching up ammunition boxes before sprinting back out toward the ruined buildings lining the yard.

That's when we heard the yelling. The rider who'd just gone east accelerated back toward us, dust billowing behind him as he waved his arm and bawled over the clatter of his engine. "Train's here! Already here! Coming up the line right now."

"Son of a bitch!" Nate's shoulders dropped as the rider hopped the tracks to pass the parked motorcycle, bouncing over the uneven terrain. He aimed his machine up the cattle car ramp and filled the interior with a low throaty growl and the tang of diesel exhaust before cutting the engine and jamming the kick-stand down.

"MOVE!" Nate roared. "All of you, get to cover, NOW!"

"Shit. Shit. Shit." The rider in the rear compartment lunged off his bike, flipped open an ammunition box, and grabbed several clips with clumsy hands.

I couldn't stop staring at Nate. His people darted into collapsed outbuildings, barking brief instructions to each other while my uncle straightened to his full height. He didn't reach for a gun or seek cover. Instead, he strode past the parked Sommer 462, taking his hat off and setting it on top of the first derailer clamp. Then he scuffed to a stop ahead of it, straddling the second clamp and standing there quietly with his hands in the pockets of his canvas jacket. There was a stoicism in his stance that terrified me more than anything else yet.

I knew that resignation. That dreadful surrender of walking a dark path you never meant to take and feeling like you had to do it alone because you'd fragged the whole world up enough to cut everyone else off from you. We were the same that way. Scrabbling so hard to survive alone, and tearing everyone around us to pieces instead.

Let him know he's not alone, my heart cried.

"Sasquatch!" I shouted through the cracks in the boards and my ribs seized with enough pain to make white spots scatter across my vision. I clamped my teeth and leaned into Robert's solid support. Nate turned around slowly, like a sleepwalker. "Shoot first," I said.

"What?"

"Shoot first and we'll stand with you. All of Painted Bluff. Take out Clowes and I promise you, everyone else on that train will scatter. I've been there. I've been a slave in his mines. He doesn't have a grip on anything. It was all Kahn. Fernie's fallen and Kahn's not here to save him. Clowes's men don't respect him. Take him out, and they'll run. And if they don't, I'll fight them with you. Just let us out. We're family. We love you. I-I love you."

A faint smile touched my uncle's lips.

The sound of a steam locomotive chuffing toward us thumped like a heartbeat in my head.

"Sasquatch. That name." Nate chuckled softly. "You know, I always wanted to be as big as you built me in your head, Beetle, when you were little."

"You are," I croaked, agony swimming in my chest. "You still can be."

He cleared his throat. "I'm sorry, Beatle. I mean that. You're going to be just fine. I always knew it." And then he turned away.

Just turned away.

No. No. Shit. You didn't reach him. I sagged against Robert, sick and dizzy.

CHAPTER
FORTY

The drumming of pistons and a towering column of steam announced the locomotive long before it rounded the bend into the east end of the train yard. It whumped through the still afternoon air like an enormous prairie grouse staking out its territory with loud, indignant wingbeats.

Then the black engine rounded the bend, panting gouts of hot mist, the weight of it creaking and rumbling toward us. We all fell silent at its powerful approach.

Nate stood unflinching, framed by gunmetal steel and billowing white as the locomotive's tender and two rail cars snaked into view.

A reedy whistle sounded, cutting high above our heads in wobbling tones. Voices shouted, choked out by the monster of iron and smoke heaving toward us. Wheels seized and squealed. Cars jerked. Chains clanked, and the train groaned to a stop several meters away from Nate and the motorcycles behind him. Steam vented from its sides in a long, frustrated hiss.

"Clear the rails." The engineer barked from her porthole

window behind the massive, ticking boiler. "We have an armed escort."

"I can see that." Nate whistled. "Fancy one too."

The two box car doors were open. Half a dozen men leaned out each side. They wore scuffed dress shirts and wrinkled trousers. Some of them still wore ties. They all held polished rifles and pistols that looked more like mantlepiece decorations than weapons of war. Clowes's middle managers. He must have scraped every faithful lackey out of Fernie when he fled.

"Move, or we'll move you ourselves." The engineer yelled, reaching over her head and yanking on the pull for the whistle. A hollow, impatient squeal pierced the air.

"What's the hurry?" Nate hollered back when it was done. "I've got a gift for your Commander in Chief. How about we start things out with a civilized introduction?"

"He ain't coming out for an ambush."

My uncle took his hands out of his pockets and showed his palms. "You folks are the only ones pointing any guns right now. I'd say you're holding the upper hand. Listen, next time, let me know you're coming, and we can have a nice little business lunch together. Maybe a round of golf."

"Last chance." The engineer shrugged and pulled a lever. The locomotive's pistons loaded. It let out a deep chuff, and its wheels creaked forward.

"I don't think your boss would appreciate you destroying a Sommer 462. German engineering and all. I'll bet these are some of the last of their kind in the world. Would he like a few of his own?"

"Move." The train huffed closer swallowing Nate in its shadow.

He scuffed back a few steps, and bellowed, "I have a derailer on the line, assholes!"

"Stop!" A voice from the first box car ordered. "What did he just say?"

"I said, I have a derailer on the line, and I have your lost slaves. Come down like a man and let's make a deal, Darwin."

He's selling us. He's actually going to do it.

I struggled to hear over the ringing in my head. Robert gripped my elbow sharply, and I realized I was sliding down to the floor.

"I've got you," he whispered. "Iris, listen to me. I'm right here, no matter what."

I wanted to crawl into his arms and cry. I wanted to shut out the world and lose myself in his comfort. I wanted him as far away as possible, somewhere safe without whip scars on his back.

The train stopped again. A ramp scraped down one of the box cars, but it wasn't Clowes who stepped out.

My heart stuttered.

Nate's hands twitched into fists.

Robert swore softly.

It was David Kahn.

I couldn't reconcile the image of him spilling out of Stagecoach One and lying limp in the mud with the man who stalked toward my uncle now. Kahn's gray hair was as severely combed as ever, steel glasses framing his eagle eyes. He'd lost his suit jacket, and his dress shirt—though still buttoned snugly at the neck and cuffs—had blood splattered down one sleeve. He held an ornate silver revolver in one hand and a lever bar in the other.

I couldn't breathe. Could barely make out what the man was saying.

"Nathaniel Wray." Kahn spoke my uncle's name slowly, tapping the lever bar on the tracks as he walked. "Not deceased. Imagine my surprise."

"Heard you were supposed to be dead too. But look at you." Nate cocked his head at the gun. "Isn't that pretty. Don't think I've ever seen you with a weapon in your hands before."

"Needs must." Kahn glanced down at the gun disdainfully. "It belonged to Clowes."

"Does it even shoot?"

A ghost of a smile crossed Kahn's face at the jab. "Well enough. Just yesterday, I shot Darwin in the head with it and took his train."

Bile rose in my throat. He'd said it like he'd simply unplugged a computer or slapped a mosquito. My mind went back to Michael Tweed and the horrible hole in his face.

"Now I'm insulted." Nate rocked on his heels. "You shot him *personally*? Yet, I had to make do with one of your Blue Helmet's botching the job."

"That's the problem with outsourcing instead of severing business ties oneself." Kahn hefted the lever bar in his hand. "Convenient, but not consistently reliable. I've since learned from my mistakes."

"God, I hope so, because outsourcing Coaltana to a cockroach like Darwin was one hell of a mistake. He was about as useful as tits on a bull. I heard Fernie isn't faring so well. That he spent all your hard-earned copper on bolo ties, imported tobacco, and interior decorating. Heard you had troubles in Mullan too. Long way south, and you made it back in one piece? Not bad for a carpet walker." Nate's tone was casual, like he was talking to a neighbor across his lawn, not his nemesis.

"I have my means." Kahn turned to the derailer clamp in front of Nate, studying it in that maddeningly impassive manner of his. "I slipped out of Mullan and sent a red alert up the tower line. It's one of the few things Clowes did right, that system. Remarkably efficient. He sent relay riders down to fetch me and when Fernie fell after that, he sent word down the line to have me meet him at his rail hub instead of in town. Saved me rolling into a riot. But it did not negate his past failures, and I've lost my patience for incompetence." His cold gaze flicked back up to Nate. "*And* outsourcing. I'm here to take back what's mine." He dropped the lever bar and it bounced with a clang onto the rails between the two men. "You'll remove that clamp now so we can be on our way."

"Yeah, there's been some . . . restructuring since you've been gone." Nate's voice hardened. "I'm the new CEO. And I'm a bit sensitive about folks charging up my lines looking to take *my* city by force. You understand, I'm sure."

"I don't believe you have the fortitude or the fire power to stand in my way, Mr. Wray."

Nate sneered. "I was your *buyer*, David. I've got lines all the way to the coast. Across oceans. If I want fire power, I get it. You should thank me for that, really. Without me, you would have lost your city long ago. I extended your stay. Gave you years that weren't yours to have. Look around. I blew this whole yard to hell back when Clowes overstepped his bounds."

Kahn's facial expression didn't change, but the silver revolver twitched in his hand. "I'm not sure I know what you're talking about."

"Of course, you don't. You figured Clowes thought the sun shone out your ass. Thought you could control him, and he wouldn't cross you because he was stupid. But he did. He built those towers and this rail line right under your nose, chatting you up with a shit-eating grin on his fat face, all while trying to take you up your ass end. He had a whole crew camped here, building a supply hub right up against your borders. Took a bit of explosives, but I convinced them they should go home and not come back. And I made sure they stayed away too. Wasn't until Clowes figured I was dead and you were deposed that the cockroach came back." He indicated the clamp between his feet. "Pity, I'm out of dynamite. It's a better show. But I've got dozens of these installed on every line leading to Painted Bluff, and they do the trick just fine. You'll never get this hulking thing up to speed, and every time you stop to clear the track, my people will be there to pick you off from the hills."

"You're lying." Kahn's brow creased. "Remove the clamp."

"I'm just looking out for you again, David. Same as always. I always kept the wolves off your back."

"Cleared off the competition is more like."

"I protected you, kept you fed and pampered, and you repaid me by sending out a hit man." He shrugged. "So, I took your city, and I burned it to ashes. I figure that makes us square, David."

"I do not." Kahn cocked the hammer on his revolver.

"Be reasonable." Nate spread his hands wide. "I know you want a piece of the copper pie, and you've got ties to refiners that I don't. So, let's negotiate. One businessman to another."

No. My heart felt like it was ready to explode out of my chest. *Nate. No.*

"Hell, I'm feeling neighborly," he continued. "You get off my property right now, clean yourself up, line me up a copper refiner with some decent experience, and I'll give you ten percent of all my profits."

"Quite bold of you to assume you're in any position to negotiate when I'm the one holding the gun." Kahn's words were clipped.

"Bold of you to think you're the only one out here holding a gun." Nate nodded toward the abandoned sheds. "I've got folks lined up on you right now who'll be happy to put a bunch of holes in you if you shoot me. There's nowhere to go but back the way you came."

Kahn's cheek twitched. "Forty percent."

Nate snorted. "Not a damned chance. Twenty, and I'll give you everyone in that rail car as a slave."

The lone motorcyclist in the rear compartment swore loudly and started pacing.

No. I wasn't going to be Kahn's slave, and I'd never let the bastard touch Robert again. *Frag that. Do something. Anything.*

"He's lying," I barked, and the instant pain in my ribs took my breath away, but I had the man's attention.

Kahn squinted over my uncle's shoulder, eyes hungry and hotter than I'd ever seen them.

"Ben is coming to ambush you," I gasped. "All his men. Horses. Guns. Our whole camp. Enough to cut you all down. Nate's not going to cut you a deal. He's just buying time until they get here so he can kill you all."

At the sound of my voice, something monstrous swept over Kahn's face. His cheeks flushed and his nostrils flared. He bared his teeth like a wild dog before regaining his composure. "Your niece?" he choked to Nate.

"Mother of Sol, Iris." Robert's broken whisper sounded in my ear. "Why'd you do that?"

I stared at Nate with my cheek squashed against the rough planking, and my legs folded under me all wrong. I couldn't take my eyes off him. *Don't Nate. Don't. Don't. Don't sell me.* But deep down. I knew he'd do it, before he even spoke.

"Oh, I've got her. All tied up with a bow. And I've got her boy too. He told me he poisoned you. That true?"

"Twenty percent and I want her *now*," Kahn growled.

This is it. He's going to kill me in front of Robert.

"Deal." My uncle held out his big hand.

Robert's grip tightened on me. His breathing came too fast.

No. All my air swept out of me. *No no no.*

Kahn stepped over the dropped lever bar and clasped Nate's hand.

My uncle tightened his grip, yanked him in close, and wrapped an arm around his neck cutting off his startled cry. For a moment, it looked like the two men were hugging.

Kahn's eyes bulged. He tried to raise his gun, but it was pinned between them.

Nate reached his hand into his pocket, withdrew something spherical, and brought it to his mouth.

A gurgling cry burst out of Kahn. He shot Nate in the thigh.

My uncle bellowed but clung on, spitting a metal pin from between his teeth. Blood spurted from his leg in startling gouts.

"Shoot him. Shoot—" the rest of Kahn's shrill cry cut off.

A grenade thudded to the ground between their scuffing feet.

Robert inhaled sharply, yanking me sideways and rolling on top of me.

The pain hit me so hard, I couldn't see, but I could still hear.

Kahn's gun went off twice more.

Then the grenade exploded.

CHAPTER
FORTY-ONE

Metal shards pinged off the diesel engine and hammered into the planking. Wood splinters rained into my hair. My ears rang. Gunfire erupted all around us, and the train emitted a long whistle that didn't stop.

"Nate?" I wheezed.

"Don't look. Stay down." Robert was still on top of me. It sounded like the whole world was shooting at us. Wood planks shattered. Stray bullets whined overhead.

"You're hurting me."

He shifted and I curled onto my uninjured side. A thick silence ballooned in my skull, pinching the noise in my ears to muted shrieks, scrapes, and pops.

"Get behind the engine," Vinton yelled, but he sounded miles away.

Mark shouted, "Let us out!"

"I don't have the key!" The motorcyclist in the rear compartment shrieked, cowering between the bikes.

"Then shoot the damned lock!" Vinton snapped as bullets buzzed overhead.

Adrenaline boiled over in me, and I twisted away from Robert, pressing against the nearest gap in the front wall.

Outside, black smoke was still clearing. Where Nate and David Kahn had been standing, two bodies lay splayed. A starburst pattern of gore and debris haloed them. They looked more like limbless effigies than humans, bloodied and charred stand-ins for the men who'd been there moments ago. They didn't look like anything that had ever been alive.

Movement caught my eye. Someone from the train crew scrabbled up the rails, dove for the lever bar, and jammed it into the first derailer clamp. He yarded it upward until it clicked. Then he kicked it off the rails. I fixated on the gore smearing his sleeve and how he stumbled over one of the bodies to reach the second clamp.

Canvas jacket and jeans. That's Nate. That's my uncle. On the tracks.

The second clamp rattled off just as someone shot the crewman in the back. He crumpled onto the tracks between Nate's and Kahn's corpses.

And then the train ran over them all.

It swallowed them up under its dark belly and kept coming.

"No," I whimpered.

"What the hell are they doing?" Mark swore. "Why are they coming forward?"

The motorcycle toppled as the train struck it next. It bounced off the cattle sweep and rolled down the incline as the engine advanced, whistle still blaring.

"Shit," John craned his neck, squinting. "It's the cowboys. They've flanked them from behind."

Sure enough, through the cloud of steam, I saw silhouettes of horse riders galloping in from the west. Ben and his crew. But not just them, I realized as they closed. The marauders rode with them too, banners waving, faces painted. Anyone who could double on a horse had come.

"They're blocked in." Mark gulped. "They're making a run for Painted Bluff. We're lighter. They'll knock us off the rails."

"Shoot the lock!" Vinton begged.

The motorcyclist stood up and lunged toward the divider, pistol drawn.

Robert pulled me away from the front wall and out of his line of fire just in time to see a bullet pass cleanly through the rider's helmet. Just above where his ear would be, a shard of fiberglass flew off leaving a small hole in the white foam beneath. He twitched. His gun fired and a chunk of wood between my feet splintered. Then he collapsed.

I snagged my knees up toward my chin. Robert swore and held me tighter.

"Shit." John breathed hard. "Brace. Brace. It's hitting us."

The train whistle screamed right on top of us. The cattle car kicked hard on impact, metal crunching, timbers shattering. My head snapped back into Robert's chest, and the dead man flopped against the divider, his handgun skidding under the bars toward me. I tried to swipe it closer with one foot, but the whole rail car juddered just then, front end tilting into the air. The gun skittered back. Ammunition crates skated across planks. We slipped toward the divider, clinging to each other, heels scraping floorboards. With a deep moan, the cattle car twisted and tipped. The motorcycle still propped on its kick-stand teetered before smashing onto its side into the other two.

"Hold on!" Mark yelled.

The world tilted sideways. We crashed into the sidewall. Someone's elbow clobbered my side. That's the last thing I remembered.

MY HEAD ROARED. Vibrations sang through every bone in my body. The screech of metal on metal and a rumbling that sounded like an avalanche nested deep in my chest. Dust and the smell of hot oil filled my nose and mouth every time I tried to inhale.

"Iris! Iris, wake up." Robert held my chin, shaking me.

I opened my eyes and tried to focus on his face above me. Blood trickled down his forehead.

"There!" John yelled. "The hinges sheared off."

A pile of people squirmed all around me in the haze. The cattle car shuddered violently as the engine plowed it down the rails on its side. John lay on his back, kicking at a broken hinge in the partition wall. "Shit. I can't get it to open wide enough."

"Wait. We don't have to." Vinton bellowed. "I think . . . I think we're slowing down."

He was right. Brakes squealed and steam vented. It took a long time for the train to ease to a halt.

A single gunshot rang out as it did.

"Next weasel-faced company man who sticks their head out that door loses it." Ben Breyman roared. Tears pricked my eyes at the sound of his voice. Horses snorted and blew around us. "Levi Atchison, we grew up together, but if you touch that throttle again, so help me God, I'll set a bullet ricocheting in that cab that'll cut you to pieces where you stand. You're outgunned. Your boss is dead. Sit your asses down and throw your weapons out here if you don't want to join him."

A shadow crossed the slats of our overturned car. Kit Youngchief cupped his hands and pressed his face to one of the gaps. "Cavalry's here and ain't you all a mess. How many injured?"

"Haven't kept a tally," Vinton snapped back. "Get us out of here."

"Lawrence, grab me that metal bar and let's pry these boards off," Kit shouted over his shoulder.

Radia skidded to her knees outside. "John?"

"I'm here," he said.

"Oh, thank Sol," she sobbed. "You fragging scared me."

"You're not supposed to scare someone in her condition," Mark said.

Their voices were too loud. The harsh sunlight and the agony at my ribs made my pulse pinch behind my eyes. Robert held my trembling hands in his and whispered, "Hang on. Almost out, Iris. We're almost out."

I was folding into myself, smaller and smaller, too compact for pain or panic or grief. Lawrence's rich voice droned above me as he and Kit rolled me onto a blanket, carrying me out of the overturned cattle car. A makeshift solar shade crinkled over us. Robert sat on one side of me and Vinton on the other.

Orin, Janice, and the rest of my uncle's people spilled from the sheds in the rail yard far behind us with their hands up. Then the old man spoke with Ben. They shook hands.

I couldn't stop my mind from replaying Nate's deadly handshake, how quickly he'd pulled Kahn against him like it was a dance he'd rehearsed thousands of times, how he'd kept his arm clamped around Kahn's neck even when the man shot his leg. The blood. The shrillness in Kahn's voice as he saw the grenade.

I covered my ears.

More people were laid on blankets beside us. All the wounded in a row. Janice pulled dressings out of her med bag and started yelling orders. Her words felt like staples in my head.

Ben lined up what was left of Coaltana's company men with their hands against a box car. His crew patted them down before turning them over to the marauders who gave them water bottles and led them east.

I couldn't look east. East was where Nate's shredded body was. I'd never see his bright eyes again or hear that booming voice. He'd never wrap me in another bear hug. Everything that he was, was gone.

Just. Gone.

I whimpered.

"I'm here, Iris." Robert stroked my back. It felt like thistles brushing my skin, but I couldn't find the words to tell him to stop. "Tell me what you need," he said. "I'm here."

Everything else fuzzed out except his voice. I hung onto it. I hung onto him until there was nothing else.

SIX MONTHS LATER

peeled my mittens off with my teeth and sat on the log in
the dark. Where I'd once planted a pail of snap pea seeds in
the scrap of wilderness behind my parent's old house, a
hand-made cross jutted out of the snow. I hadn't known where
Nate wanted to be buried; beside Christie, I imagined. But Orin
told me that my uncle had buried the woman he loved alone,
somewhere in the woods behind the farmhouse. None of them
knew exactly where.

I could have looked. I could have gone there, to my uncle's
compound, and searched for Christie's grave, but I didn't think I
could face her or handle seeing the remains of the place I'd
burned. And I was still selfish. Nate had circled my life in such
an eccentric orbit. He'd never been consistently close. I wanted
him close now. In the blanched glow of the moonlight, I smiled
down at the imprint of slim shoes in the snow. The dried flower
arrangement propped against the cross was tidy and new. Mom
had been here today.

I liked to come at night. When I woke up sweating, gripped
by nightmares of grenades tearing apart everyone I loved,
Vannevar shooting me in the face, or Robert flayed by a whip as

I desperately tried to reach him, I came here. And I talked to Nate. I'd tell him about what was eating at my mind, how the wide-open future seemed nearly as terrifying as my locked-down past. Sometimes, I swore I heard his boisterous laugh and his laid-back voice answering back: *When in doubt, keep it simple, Beetle.* I felt closest to him out here, where he'd first planted that seed of curiosity for me.

When I could breathe again, I trudged back home. Green and red aurora warped and whipped over the miner's new modular housing units. The roofs were draped in thick snow. We'd made it through the worst of winter, but cold weather clung on well into spring, and we'd just endured another snowstorm.

Painted Bluff had ballooned to twice the size it had been before it burned. We'd all laid down our arms the day Nate died. Orin and his URLs, our people, the marauders, the miners, Ben's crew and his family, we'd all made peace and returned to the ruined city ready to build something together.

We shoveled debris from the streets. Elaine, May, and Janice set up a med bay in the bunker. After a few weeks, they downsized and converted most of it into a school. Now, the walls down there were plastered with posters of chunky rainbows with dripping paint and faded elegant pages of bird books. Mom and Dad were among those who volunteered to teach. There were plenty of young children in the miner's families that Painted Bluff drew in, and none of them would slave underground or be groomed for corporate life. They would write. They would draw. They'd garden.

Vinton's Browsers and Ben's crew often made supply runs together. Levi the train engineer had stayed on, so they even took the steam locomotive on one run, bringing back diesel totes, temporary shelters, aluminum tubing, and rolls of thick polyethylene plastic to restore the greenhouses.

Johan and Olivia hunted with new crossbows. In those early

days, I couldn't draw a bow or help with construction until my ribs healed, so I gardened and fished instead.

The marauder girl— her name was Danis—still called me Girl with the Boat.

I walked past the fruits of my labors now. Vast steppe gardens crawled up the hillside beyond the glowing greenhouses and rebuilt pigeon loft. On main street, the rafters of the new library stretched into the night, and the hum of the generators thrummed like a giant beehive.

Lights were on in the Browser's garage. They'd salvaged what they could from the damaged machines and had six operable motorcycles. One of them belonged to Vinton. Mark had torn apart the old sidecar and used it to fabricate a narrow cargo platform and permanent stabilizer for my brother's new ride. The setup wasn't as elegant as Vinton's old motorcycle, nor was it an ideal set up for narrow trails, but it kept him in the driver's seat, and besides, the Browsers no longer needed to scour the countryside for new knowledge. They mostly rode to Golden and back. *A milk run.* Vinton especially enjoyed riding the highway to Kamloops to hassle Ben as he headed up the crews working to expand our tower lines to the east.

Ben Breyman insisted he was going to teach my brother to ride a horse, a notion Vinton snorted at. "I'm serious. There are custom saddles. Roads are falling apart, and you can't ride a rust bucket forever," the cowboy had insisted, frowning at my brother's immaculately maintained machine.

"It doesn't shed, shit, or bite." Vinton had fired back. "And it always goes where I tell it to. I don't need forever. I'll ride it as long as I'm able, thanks."

Ben tipped his hat and grinned. "I'll be here when you finally see reason."

I smiled at the memory, briefly considering stopping into the garage, but I'd been running a class on how to set snares all day, and I didn't have it in me to strike up another conversation, even if it was with my brother or his husband. Instead, I took a deep breath and carried on. Diesel, crisp snow, and woodsmoke filled my nose. The smells of my childhood.

Further out of town, away from the tracks and closer to the lake shore, the frame of a single-story house with a wide front porch glowed in the fiery night sky. It wasn't finished yet, but Robert would be there anyway. He worked on it under solar shades during the day, and he often came back here on nights when he couldn't sleep.

I trudged through white drifts in the narrow side yard and found him on the deck. He had cleared off all the snow and was sitting on the stairs, blanket covering the baby carrier at his chest.

"Night owl." I sat beside him.

John and Radia's baby, Katerina, peered at me from under multiple layers, red-cheeked, eyes large and dark, like the little dolls that had lined the walls in Arlene and Marty's house.

"Her too." Robert absently rubbed the baby's back. Her parents were in Golden, sourcing out a milk goat to supplement Radia's supply. They usually left Katerina with Johan, but his arthritis was acting up, and Robert had offered to take the baby. He was a natural with her, something that amused and terrified me at the same time.

"Are you supposed to have her out in the cold like this?" I tucked the blanket tighter around them both.

"She's not cold. I just shoveled the deck. We're both baking." He flashed me a grin in the dark. "Besides, this is the only way I know how to impress girls, take them out to look at the sky at night."

"Is it working?" I turned to take in the polished, windswept ice, the black pines fringed with frost, and the cloudless night sky draped with bands of flickering neon light, like Sol was painting with watercolors.

"Oh, it will. Sometimes it takes a bit to win them over."

I leaned my head against his shoulder. "Nightmares?"

"Nah. Just my back." He had nerve damage from his scars.

"So, you shoveled snow?" I asked tartly, straightening to glare at him.

He smiled. "So, I shoveled snow."

I shifted to gently massage the spot between his shoulder blades that always tightened up when he was in pain. His breathing hitched but eventually evened out. Then his head tipped back, and he blinked up at the sky. Reds and greens reflected in his pale eyes.

"Hard day?" Paul Lycos was in med bay again. He'd grown more erratic. Janice had diagnosed him with Dementia a few months ago.

Robert took off his gloves and folded my hand into his. "He didn't recognize me."

I kissed his knuckles. "I'm sorry."

"I'm not." He sighed, and the fog of his breath crystallized above our heads. "It's easier on the days he doesn't recognize me. Does that make me a bad person?"

"No." I tucked my head against his shoulder. "You're the best person I know."

We sat in silence for a while, light wavering around us, eerie green pillars toppling and rematerializing in the sky, the baby's quick breaths fluttering in between us. Robert stroked the back of my hand with his thumb. A crisp breeze raised the snow on the lake into coiling plumes. The airy whistle of geese wings and a few forlorn honks sliced across the cold sky overhead, and I looked up to see a V of Canadian Geese gliding over us.

"Robert?" I whispered.

"Hmmm?"

"Tell me how we're supposed to be."

"We're supposed to be like this, Iris." He leaned over and kissed me softly. "We're supposed to be just like this."

JOIN THE CURSED DRAGON SHIP NEWSLETTER

Want more just like this one? Sign up for our newsletter so you don't miss out on the adventure. You'll get:

- A free book for signing up
- Advanced notice of new releases
- First word of books on sale
- Opportunities for free books
- Most up-to-date information on author appearances.

We're busy and know you are too. We won't send more than one newsletter a month.

Register below.

ACKNOWLEDGMENTS

A huge thank you, as always, to Kelly Colby and L.R. Bridgwater, our fantastic editors. Without you this book would have been a mess of ideas with far too many commas in all the wrong places. To Cursed Dragon Ship Publishing for championing us and our work. To our critique partners, especially Jennifer Lane and Al Hess for giving this book direction when it was far from shiny. And a huge thank you to Kit O'Kane and family for taking the time to help us with Cree translations. *Madness of People* wouldn't be out in the world without the kindness and grace of folks like all of you!

ABOUT SHELLY CAMPBELL

At a young age, Shelly Campbell wanted to be an air show pilot or a pirate, possibly a dragon and definitely a writer and artist. She's piloted a Cessna 172 through spins and stalls and sailed up the east coast on a tall ship barque—mostly without projectile vomiting. In the end, Shelly found writing fantasy and drawing dragons to be so much easier on the stomach. Shelly's grimdark fantasy novels *Under the Lesser Moon* and *Voice of the Banished* were published by Mythos and Ink. She also has a quiet horror novel, *Gulf*, with Silver Shamrock publishing, and has co-authored *Making Myths and Magic* with Allison Alexander. It's a field guide to writing sci-fi and fantasy published by Mythos and Ink.

ABOUT MEGAN KING

Megan King has been a singer, dancer, artist, and most recently, an author, where she fills her time turning weird dreams into story ideas. She supports her arts habit by working as an optician. In her spare time, she listens to Canadian alt rock music pretty constantly and spends time with her family, which includes two dogs and a very large cat.

MISSED BOOK ONE? GET IT NOW.

One mind different from the rest must save her community from itself.